Sheikh's
CONVENIENT
MARRIAGE

D0620629

Sheikh's
COLLECTION

May 2017

June 2017

July 2017

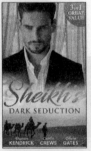

August 2017

September 2017

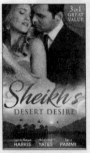

October 2017

Sheikh's
CONVENIENT
MARRIAGE

Sharon
KENDRICK

Kate
HEWITT

Tara
PAMMI

MILLS
BOON
&

HarperCollins
PUBLISHERS
Since 1817

Published in Great Britain 2017
By Mills & Boon, an imprint of HarperCollins*Publishers*
1 London Bridge Street, London, SE1 9GF

SHEIKH'S CONVENIENT MARRIAGE © 2017 Harlequin Books S.A.

Shamed in the Sands © 2014 Sharon Kendrick
Commanded by the Sheikh © 2014 Kate Hewitt
The Last Prince of Dahaar © 2014 Tara Pammi

ISBN: 978-0-263-93109-9

09-0717

Our policy is to use papers that are natural, renewable and recyclable products and made from wood grown in sustainable forests.
The logging and manufacturing processes conform to the legal environmental regulations of the country of origin.

Printed and bound in Spain
by CPI, Barcelona

SHAMED IN
THE SANDS

SHARON KENDRICK

For Olly Wicken,
whose imagination and expertise
helped bring Gabe to life.
Thank you.

Sharon Kendrick once won a national writing competition by describing her ideal date: being flown to an exotic island by a gorgeous and powerful man. Little did she realise that she'd just wandered into her dream job! Today she writes for Mills & Boon, featuring often stubborn but always to die for heroes and the women who bring them to their knees. She believes that the best books are those you never want to end. Just like life…

CHAPTER ONE

GABE STEEL WAS naked when he heard the sound of knocking.

He picked up a towel and scowled. He wanted peace. No, he *needed* peace. He'd come to this strange city for all kinds of reasons—but none of them included being disturbed when he had just stepped out of the shower.

He thought about the harsh light of spring he'd left behind in England. The way it could still make his heart clench with pain at this time of year. He thought how guilt never really left you, no matter how deeply you tried to bury it. If you scratched beneath the surface you could always bring up stuff you didn't want. Which was why he didn't scratch. Ever.

But sometimes you couldn't escape it, no matter how hard you tried. Hadn't one of the staff sent someone up earlier, asking if he would like any special arrangements made for his birthday? He'd wondered how the hell they had known it was his birthday—until he realised that they had seen his passport when he'd checked in yesterday.

He stood still and listened. The knocking had stopped and everything was quiet again. He started to slide the towel over one hair-roughened thigh when the sound resumed, more urgently this time.

At any other time and in any other place, he would have ignored the unwanted summons and carried on with what he was doing. But Gabe recognised that these were not normal circumstances. This job was a first. He'd never been the guest of a member of a royal family before. Correction. The *head* of a royal family. He'd never worked for a sultan before—a man who ruled over one of the world's wealthiest countries and who had already lavished on Gabe a breathtaking amount of hospitality. And maybe that was what was beginning to irritate him most of all—because he didn't like to be beholden to anyone, no matter how exalted their position.

Uttering a muttered curse beneath his breath, Gabe wrapped the towel around his hips and crossed a room so vast that back home the walk might almost have qualified as a workout. He'd stayed in some amazing places in his time, and his own place in London was pretty mouth-watering. But he had to acknowledge that this penthouse suite in Qurhah's finest hotel took luxury to a whole new level.

The knocking continued. A low drumming sound he found impossible to ignore—and its persistence made his impatience increase. He pulled open the door to find a woman standing there. Or rather, a woman who was doing her best not to look like a woman.

Tall and slim, her body was completely covered and her features were in shadow. She was carrying a briefcase and wearing a trench coat over a pair of jeans, with a fedora hat pulled down low over her face. Her appearance was so androgynous that she could almost have been mistaken for a man. But Gabe could smell a woman's scent in a pitch-black room, even when she wasn't wearing perfume. He could accurately assess the hip-width of a pair of panties from nothing more than a cursory glance. Where the opposite sex was concerned, he was an expert—even if his expertise went no further than the physical.

Because he didn't do *emotional*. He didn't need a woman to unpick his mind at the end of a stressful day, or cry on his shoulder in the mistaken belief that it might make his heart melt. And he certainly didn't want some unknown female turning up today, when his heart was dark and his schedule full.

'Where's the fire?' he demanded.

'Please.' Her voice was low and urgent and very faintly accented. 'Can I come in?'

His lips gave the faintest curve of contempt. 'I think you must have the wrong room, sweetheart,' he said and started to shut the door.

'Please,' she repeated—only this time he could hear panic underpinning her words. 'Men are trying to find me.'

It was a stark appeal and it stopped Gabe in his tracks. It wasn't the kind of thing he heard in the slick, controlled world he called his life. It took him back to a time and a place where threat was a constant. Where fear was never very far away.

He stared down at her face and he could see the wide gleam of alarm in eyes shadowed by the fedora.

'Please,' she said again.

He hesitated for no longer than a heartbeat before something kicked in. Some unwanted protective urge over which he seemed powerless. And he didn't do powerless.

'Come in,' he said abruptly. He caught the drift of her spicy perfume as she hurried past, and the fragrance seemed to cling to his skin as he closed the door and turned to face her. 'So what's the story?'

She was shaking her head and turning to look at the door as if she was petrified somebody was going to burst in behind her.

'Not now,' she said in that soft accent, which was making his senses start to prickle into life. 'There's no time. I'll tell you everything you need to know But only when it's safe. They mustn't find me here. They mustn't.'

She was looking at the far side of the vast room, where the open bedroom door revealed the unmade bed, on which he'd been taking a catnap before his shower. He saw her quickly turn her head away.

'Where can you hide me?' she questioned.

Gabe's eyes narrowed. He thought her attitude was arrogant—almost imperious—considering the way she'd burst in on him like this. He was the one doing *her* a favour—and a little gratitude wouldn't have gone amiss. But maybe now was not the time to give her a lecture on the etiquette of gate-crashing—not when she was looking so jittery.

He thought about where he used to hide whenever the bailiffs bashed on the door. The one room which always seemed safer than any other.

'Go through into the bathroom,' he said, flicking his fingers in the direction of the en-suite. 'Crawl underneath the tub and stay there until I tell you otherwise. And your explanation had better be good enough to warrant this unwanted intrusion into my time.'

But she didn't appear to be listening. She was already moving towards the bathroom with an unconscious sway of her slender bottom before she was lost to view.

And somehow she had managed to transfer her anxiety to Gabe and his body began to react accordingly. He could feel adrenalin coursing through his bloodstream and the sudden pounding of his heart. He wondered whether he should put on some clothes and then realised there was no time, because he could hear the heavy approach of footsteps in the corridor outside.

The rap on the door was loud and he opened it to find two men outside, their eyes as dark and pinched as raisins. Loose suits did little to conceal their burly strength, and Gabe could detect the telltale bulges of gun holsters packed against each of their bodies.

The taller of the two let his gaze flicker to Gabe's still-damp torso and then to the small towel which was knotted at his hip. 'We are sorry to disturb you, Mr Steel.'

'No problem,' said Gabe pleasantly, registering that they knew his name, just as everyone else in the hotel seemed to. And that their accents sounded like a pronounced version of the one used by the mystery woman currently cowering in his bathroom. 'What can I do for you?'

The man's accent was thick. 'We are looking for a woman.'

'Aren't we all?' questioned Gabe conspiratorially, with a silken stab at humour. But neither man took the bait and neither did they respond to the joke. Their faces remained unsmiling as they stared at him.

'Have you seen her?'

'Depends what she looks like,' said Gabe.

'Tall. Early twenties. Dark hair,' said the smaller of the two men. 'A very…striking woman.'

Gabe gestured towards the tiny towel at his hips and rubbed his hands over his upper arms, miming a chill which wasn't quite fictitious, since the icy kick of the air-conditioning was giving him goose-bumps. 'As you can see—I've been taking a shower. And I can assure you that nobody was keeping me company at the time—more's the pity.' He glanced over his shoulder towards the room before turning back to them, his forced smile hinting at a growing irritation. 'Of course, you're perfectly at liberty to look for yourselves, but I'd appreciate it if you could do it swiftly. I still have to get dressed and shaved—and I'm due to dine with the Sultan in a couple of hours.'

It worked. The mere mention of the Sultan's name produced the reaction he'd hoped for. Gabe thought it almost comical as he watched both men take a step back in perfect unison.

'Of course. Forgive us for interrupting you. We will take up no more of your time, Mr Steel. Thank you for your help.'

'My pleasure,' said Gabe, and closed the door softly behind them.

His footsteps across the carpet were equally soft, and when he opened the bathroom door, the woman was just slithering out from under the bathtub like some kind of sexy serpent. He felt the instant rush of heat to his groin as she scrambled to her feet and began brushing her hands over her body.

The fedora had fallen off and as she raised her face and he got a proper look at her for the first time he felt awareness icing his skin. Because suddenly he was looking at the most arresting woman he had ever seen. His mouth dried with lust. She looked like a fantasy come to life. Like a character from the *Arabian Nights* who had wandered into his hotel bathroom by mistake.

Her olive skin was luminous and her dark-fringed eyes were a bright shade of blue. A ponytail of black hair hung almost to her waist—hair so shiny that it looked as if she might have spent the morning polishing it. Despite the silky trench coat, he could see that her breasts were neat and her legs so long that she would have been at home on any international catwalk.

Her face remained impassive as he looked her over, as if she was no stranger to submission. Only the faintest flush of pink in her cheeks gave any indication that she might be finding his attention unsettling. But what did she expect? If you burst into a strange man's bedroom and demanded refuge, then surely the normal rules of conduct flew right out of the window.

'They've gone,' he said shortly.

'So I heard.' She hesitated. 'Thank you.'

He noticed the way her gaze kept flickering towards his bare torso and then away again. As if she knew she shouldn't stare at him but couldn't help herself. He gave a grim kind of smile. It wasn't the first time he had encountered such a problem.

'I think you owe me an explanation,' he said. 'Don't you?'

'Sure.' She bent to pick up her briefcase, and as she

straightened up she did that not-quite-looking thing at his chest again. 'Just not…not in here.'

Was the intimacy of the setting too much for her? he wondered. Was she aware that beneath the tiny towel his body was beginning to respond to her in a way which might make itself embarrassingly obvious if he wasn't careful? He could feel the hot pump of arousal at his groin and suddenly he felt curiously vulnerable.

'Go through there,' he said abruptly. 'While I get dressed.'

The stir of his erection had subsided by the time he'd pulled on some jeans and a T-shirt and walked through to the sitting room to see her standing with her back to him. She was staring out of the panoramic windows which overlooked the city of Simdahab, where golden minarets and towers gleamed in the rich light of the late afternoon sun. But Gabe barely noticed the magnificent view—his attention remained captivated by the mystery stranger.

She had removed her trench coat and had slung it over the back of one of the sofas—was she planning on staying?—and suddenly there were no more concealing folds to hide her from his eyes. His gaze travelled to where denim clung to the high curves of her bottom, to where her dark ponytail hung down her back like a dark stream of satin.

She must have sensed that he was in the room because she turned round—the ponytail swinging in slow motion—and from this angle he thought the view was even better. She looked at him with those clear blue eyes, and suddenly all he could see was temptation.

He wondered if she had been sent to him by the

Sultan—a delicious package for him to open and enjoy at his leisure. Another lavish gift, just like the others which had been arriving at his hotel suite all morning. It was said that, despite his relative youth, the Sultan was an old-fashioned man and this might be a very old-fashioned gesture on his part. Mightn't the powerful potentate have decided to sweeten up Gabe with a woman? A submissive and beautiful woman who would cater to his every whim…

'Who are you?' he questioned coolly. 'A hooker?'

Her face showed no reaction to his crude question, but it seemed to take for ever before she spoke.

'No, I'm not a hooker. My name is Leila,' she said, and now her blue eyes were watchful.

'Pretty name, but I'm still no wiser.'

'Mr Steel—'

Gabe shook his head in faint disbelief. 'How come everyone in this city knows my name?'

The woman smiled—her lips softening into cushioned and rosy curves. And even though he had never paid for sex in his life, in that moment he almost wished she *were* a hooker. What would he get her to do first? he wondered. Unzip him and take him in her delicious mouth, and suck him until he came? Or lower those narrow hips and bounce around on him until he cried out with pleasure?

'People know who you are because you are the guest of the Sultan,' she was saying. 'Your name is Gabe Steel and you are an advertising genius who has come to Qurhah to improve our global image.'

'That's a very flattering summary,' offered Gabe drily. 'But I'm afraid that unsolicited flattery doesn't really do it for me and it still doesn't explain why you're here. Why you burst into my hotel room uninvited and hid in my bathroom...*Leila.*'

For a moment there was silence.

Leila's heart pounded against her ribcage as she heard the blatant challenge in his voice, which countered the silky way he emphasised her name. Her mind was in a muddle and her senses felt raw and exposed. She had taken a risk and she needed to follow it through, but it was proving more difficult than she'd anticipated. Everything so far was going according to plan but suddenly she was filled with a powerful rush of nerves. She wondered how she could have been so stupid. How she could have failed to take into account Gabe Steel himself and the effect he would have on her.

She looked into his grey eyes. Strange, quicksilver eyes, which seemed to pierce her skin and see straight through to the bones beneath. She tried to find the right words to put her case to him, but everything she'd been planning to say flew clean out of her mind.

She wasn't used to being alone with strange men and she certainly wasn't used to being in a hotel room with a foreigner. Especially one who looked like this.

He was gorgeous.

Unbelievably gorgeous.

She'd read up about him on the internet, of course. She'd made it her business to do so once she'd discovered that her brother was going to employ him. She'd found out all the external things about Gabe Steel. She knew he owned Zeitgeist—one of the world's biggest advertising agencies. That he'd been a millionaire by the age of twenty-four and had made it into multi-millions by the time he reached thirty. At thirty-five, he remained unmarried—though not for the lack of women trying to get a wedding ring on their finger. Or at least, not according to reports from the rather more downmarket sources.

She'd seen images of him, too. Crystal-clear images, which she'd gazed at with something approaching wonder as they'd flashed up onto her computer screen. Because Gabe Steel seemed to have it all—certainly in the physical sense. His golden-dark hair gave him the appearance of an ancient god, and his muscular body would have rivalled that of any Olympian athlete.

She'd seen photos of him collecting awards, dressed in an immaculate tuxedo. There had been a snatched shot of him—paparazzi, she assumed—wearing faded jeans and an open shirt as he straddled a huge motorbike, minus a helmet. On one level she had known that he was the type of man who would take your breath away when you met him for real. And she hadn't been wrong.

She just hadn't expected him to be so…charismatic.

Leila was used to powerful men. She had grown up surrounded by them. All her life, she'd been bossed around and told to show respect towards them. Told that men knew best. She gave a wry smile because she had witnessed how cruel and cold they could be. She'd seen them treat women as if they didn't matter. As if their opinions were simply to be tolerated rather than taken seriously. Which was one of the reasons why, deep down, she didn't actually *like* the opposite sex.

Oh, she deferred to them, as she had been taught, because that was the hand which fate had dealt her.

To be born a princess into a fiercely male-dominated society didn't leave you with much choice other than to defer. There hadn't been a single major decision in her life which had been hers and hers alone. Her schooling had been decided without any consultation; her friends had been carefully picked. She had learnt to smile and accept—because she had also learnt that resistance was futile. People knew what was 'best' for her—and she had no alternative but to accept their judgement.

Materially, of course, she had been spoiled. When you were the only sister of one of the richest men in the world, that was inevitable. Diamonds and pearls, rubies and emeralds lay heaped in jewellery boxes in her bedroom at the palace. Her late mother's tiaras lay locked behind glass for Leila to wear whenever the mood took her.

But Leila knew that all the riches in the world couldn't make you feel good about yourself. Expensive jewels didn't compensate for the limitations of your lifestyle, nor protect you from a future you viewed with apprehension.

Within the confines of her palace home she usually dressed in traditional robes and veils, but today she was looking defiantly Western. She had never worn *quite* such figure-hugging jeans before and it was only by covering them up with her raincoat that she would have dared. She was aware of the way the thick seam of material rubbed between her legs. The way that the silky shirt felt oddly decadent as it brushed against her breasts. She felt *liberated* in these clothes, and while it was a good feeling, it was a little scary too—

especially as Gabe Steel was looking at her in a way which was curiously…*distracting*.

But her clothes were as irrelevant as his reaction to them. She had worn them in order to look modern and for no other reason. The most important thing to remember was that this man held the key to a different kind of future. And she was going to make him turn that key—whether he wanted to or not.

Fighting another wave of anxiety, she opened the briefcase she'd been holding and pulled out a clutch of carefully chosen contents.

'I'd like you to have a look at these,' she said.

He raised his eyebrows. 'What are they?'

She walked over towards a beautiful table and spread out the pictures on the gleaming inlaid surface. 'Have a look for yourself.'

He walked over to stand beside her, his dark shadow falling over her. She could detect the tang of lime and soap combined with the much more potent scent of masculinity. She remembered him wearing nothing but that tiny white towel and suddenly her mouth grew as dry as dust.

'Photographs,' he observed.

Leila licked her lips. 'That's right.'

She watched him study them and prayed he would like them because she had been taking photos for as long as she could remember. It had been her passion and escape—the one thing at which she'd shown real flair. But perhaps her position as princess meant that she was ideally placed to take photos, for her essentially lonely role meant that she was always on the outside looking in.

Ever since she'd been given her very first camera,

Leila had captured the images which surrounded her. The palace gardens and the beautiful horses which her brother kept in his stables had given way to candid shots of the servants and portraits of their children.

But most of the photos she'd brought to show Gabe Steel were of the desert. Stark images of a landscape she doubted he would have seen anywhere else and, since few people had been given access to the sacred and secret sites of Qurhah, they were also unique. And she suspected that a man like Gabe Steel would have seen enough in his privileged life to value something which was unique.

He was studying one in particular and she watched as his eyes narrowed in appreciation.

'Who took these?' he questioned, raising his head at last and capturing her in that cool grey gaze. 'You?'

She nodded. 'Yes.'

There was a pause. 'You're good,' he said slowly. 'Very good.'

His praise felt like a caress. Like the most wonderful compliment she had ever received. Leila glowed with a fierce kind of pride. 'Thank you.'

'Where is this place?'

'It's in the desert, close to the Sultan's summer palace. An area of outstanding natural beauty known as the Mekathasinian Sands,' she said, aware that his unsettling gaze was now drifting over her rather than the photo he was holding. He was close enough for her to be able to touch him, and she found herself wanting to do just that. She wanted to tangle her fingers in the thick, molten gold of his hair and then run them down over that hard, lean body. *And how crazy was that?*

With an effort, she tried to focus her attention on the photo and not on the symmetry of his chiselled features.

'I took this after one of the rare downpours of rain and subsequent flooding, which occur maybe once in twenty years, if you're lucky.' She smiled. 'They call it the desert miracle. Flower seeds lie dormant in the sands for decades and when the floods recede, they suddenly germinate—and flower. So that millions of blooms provide a carpet of colour which is truly magical—though it only lasts a couple of weeks.'

'It's an extraordinary picture. I've never seen anything like it.'

She could hear the sense of wonder in his voice and she felt another swell of pride. But suddenly, her work didn't seem as important as his unsettling proximity. She should have been daunted by that and she couldn't work out why she wasn't. She was alone in a hotel room with the playboy Gabe Steel and all she was aware of was a growing sense of excitement.

With an effort, she forced her attention back to the photo. 'If…if you look closely, you can see the palace in the distance.'

'Where?'

'Right over there.' The urge to touch him was overwhelming. It was the strongest impulse she'd ever felt, and suddenly Leila found herself unable to resist it. Leaning forward so that her arm brushed almost imperceptibly against his, she pointed out the glimmering golden palace. She felt his body stiffen as she made that barely there contact. She thought she could hear his breath catch in his throat. Was his heart hammering as hers was hammering? Was he too filled with an inexplicable sense of breathless wonder?

But he had stepped away from her, and his cool eyes were still curious. 'Why did you bring these photos here today, Leila? And more importantly, why were those men pursuing you?'

She hesitated. The truth was on her lips but she didn't dare say it. Because once he knew—he would change. People always did. He would stop treating her like an ordinary woman and start eyeing her warily—as if she were a strange creature he had never encountered before. And she was enjoying herself far too much to want him to do that.

So why not tell him part of the truth? The only part which was really important.

'I want to work for you,' she said boldly. 'I want to help you with your campaign.'

He raised his eyebrows in arrogant query. 'I don't recall advertising for any new staff,' he said drily.

'I realise that—but can't you see that it would make perfect sense?' Leaning forward, Leila injected real passion into her voice. 'I know Qurhah in a way you never can, because I grew up here and the desert is in my blood. I can point you in the direction of the best locations to show the world that our country is a particular kind of paradise. I've done plenty of research on what a campaign like yours would involve and I know there's room on this project for someone like me.'

She stared at him hopefully.

There was silence for a moment and then he gave a short laugh. 'You think I'd hire some unknown for a major and very lucrative campaign, just on the strength of a pretty face?'

Leila felt the sharp stab of injustice. 'But surely my "pretty face" has nothing to do with the quality of my work?'

'You don't think so?' He shot her a sardonic look. 'Well, I hate to disillusion you, sweetheart—but without the raven hair and killer figure I'd have kicked you out of here just as soon as those goons had gone.'

Leila tried to keep the sulk from her voice, because this was not what was supposed to happen. *She couldn't let it happen.* She narrowed her eyes in a way which would have made her servants grow wary if they had seen her. 'So you won't even consider me?'

'I won't consider anything until you satisfy my curiosity, and I am growing bored by your evasion. I'm still waiting for you to tell me who those men were.'

'My bodyguards,' she said reluctantly.

'Your *bodyguards*?'

She had surprised him now. She could see it in his face. She wondered how he would react if she told him the whole truth. That she had been born to be guarded. That people were always watching her. Stifling her. Making it impossible for her to breathe.

'I'm rich,' she said, by way of an explanation. 'In fact, I'm very rich.'

His grey eyes were speculative. 'So you don't *need* the work?'

'What kind of a question is that?' she questioned heatedly. 'I *want* to work! There's a difference, you know. I thought a man like you would appreciate that.'

Gabe acknowledged the reprimand in her voice. Yes, he knew there was a difference—it was just one which had never applied to him because he had always needed to work. There had been no wealth or legacy for him. No cushion waiting to bolster him if ever he fell. He had known only hunger and poverty. He had known what it was like to live beneath the radar and have your life subsumed by fear. He had needed to work for reasons of survival and for the peace of mind which always seemed determined to elude him. Even now.

'Oh, I appreciate it all right,' he agreed slowly.

'So you'll think about it? About hiring me?'

He looked down into her beautiful eyes and felt his heart twist with something like regret. He saw hope written in their azure depths—just as he saw all kinds of passionate possibilities written in her sensual lips. What would happen if he kissed this beautiful little rich girl who had marched into his hotel suite with such a sense of entitlement? Would she taste as good as she looked? He could feel the savage ache at his groin as he realised how badly he *wanted* to kiss her and for a moment temptation washed over him again.

But his innate cool professionalism reasserted itself and, regretfully, he shook his head. 'I'm sorry. I don't work that way. I run my organisation on rather more formal lines. If you really want to work for me, then I suggest you apply to my London office in the usual way. But I suspect that you've blown your chances anyway.' His eyes sent out a mocking challenge. 'You see, a long time ago I made a decision never to mix business with pleasure.'

She was staring at him, her nose wrinkling as if she was perplexed by his words. 'I don't understand.'

'Don't you?' He gave an unconvincing replica of a smile. 'Are you trying to tell me you haven't noticed the chemistry between us?'

'I—'

'Look, just take your photos and go,' he interrupted roughly. 'Before I do something I might live to regret.'

Leila heard his impatient words and some deep-rooted instinct urged her to heed them. To make her escape back to the palace while she still could and forget all about this crazy rebellion. Forget the fairy-tale ending of a legitimate job with the hotshot English tycoon. Forget the film-script scenario and get real. She needed to accept her life the way it was and accept that she couldn't just break out and change her entire existence.

But her thoughts were being confused by the powerful signals her body was sending out. She could feel the honeyed rush of heat between her thighs, where the thick seam of her jeans was rubbing against the most secret place of her body. She wanted to wrap her arms around her chest to try to quell the terrible aching in her breasts, yet she knew that would only draw attention to them.

Leila had read plenty of books and seen most of the current crop of films which had got past the palace censors. She might have been sheltered, but she wasn't stupid. This was sexual attraction she was experiencing for the first time and she knew it was *wrong*. Yet even as she silently urged herself to get out before she made even more of a fool of herself, those rebellious thoughts came back to plague her.

She thought about how her brother behaved. How

her own father had behaved. She'd heard the rumours about their sexual conquests often enough. She knew that men often acted on the kind of attraction she was experiencing right now, if the circumstances were right. People sometimes got intimate after nothing more than a short acquaintanceship, and nobody thought the worst of them for doing so. Because physical love wasn't a *crime*, was it?

Was it?

'What might you regret?' she asked, but she knew the answer to her question as soon as the words had left her lips. Because you wouldn't need to be experienced to realise why Gabe Steel's face had darkened like that. Or why he was staring at her with a hot, hard look which was making her feel weak.

'Does your mother know you're out?' he questioned roughly.

She shook her head. 'I don't have a mother. Or a father.' She kept her voice light, the way she'd learned to do. 'I'm just an orphan girl.'

His eyes narrowed. Darkened. He winced, as if she'd said something which had caused *him* pain.

'I'm sorry,' he said softly and reached out to brush the tip of his thumb over her lips. 'So sorry.'

The weirdest thing was that Leila wasn't sure if he was talking to her, or talking to himself. But suddenly she didn't care because it was happening—just like in all the films she'd seen. He was reaching out and pulling her into his arms and she could feel the heat of his body as he moulded it against her. He framed her face with the palms of his hands and now his mouth was coming down towards hers. He seemed to be moving

in slow motion, and Leila felt weak with excitement
as her lips parted eagerly to meet his.

Because for the first time in her life, a man was
going to kiss her.

CHAPTER TWO

GABE FELT THE thunder of his heart as their mouths made that first contact. The warmth of her flesh collided with his and her skin smelt of flowers and spice. Desire flooded through him like fire but his hot lust was tempered by the cool voice of reason.

This was insane.

Insane.

He thought about the way she'd burst into his suite and the surly-faced bodyguards who might return at any time. It was obvious she shouldn't be here—and he was in danger of jeopardising a deal. A very important deal. He was here on business and due to dine at the Sultan's palace in a little under two hours. There wasn't time to make love to her properly—no matter how gloriously accessible she appeared to be.

So for God's sake, get rid of her!

But the moment he chose to push her away was the moment she chose to wind her arms around his neck and to move her body against his and to whisper something breathless in a language he didn't understand. The breath died in his throat as heat pooled in his groin and he was helpless to do anything other than deepen the kiss. He could feel the mound of her pubic bone pressing against his growing arousal—making his erection exquisitely hard and almost painful. Her tiny breasts were flattening themselves against his chest and, for the first time all day, his body felt warm instead of filled with the cold and aching memories of the past.

Tearing his mouth away, he stared down into her face, trying to ignore the provocative trembling of her lips. 'That was a mistake,' he said unsteadily. 'And I think you'd better get out of here before I make another one.'

'But what if I want you to?' she questioned breathlessly. 'What then?'

He felt another fierce stab of arousal as she looked at him. Her eyes were wide. Wide and bright. Shining as brightly as the aquamarine studs at her ears. He could feel his senses warring with his moral compass. *Send her away before it's too late.* But he couldn't stop looking at her or wanting her. Her lips were soft and gleaming. They looked as if they had been specially constructed to accommodate his erection and to suck him dry.

He thought about the dull pain nailed deep into his heart and how her soft body could alleviate it—even for an hour. Because sex could obliterate pain, couldn't it? He could feel his resolve slipping away from him, like sand through his fingers, and wondered if there was a man on earth who could have resisted what was being offered to him now.

'I'm giving you one last chance to get out of here,' he said unevenly. 'And I'd advise you to take it and go.'

'But I don't want to go anywhere,' she whispered. 'I want to stay right here.'

'Then I make no apologies for doing this,' he said. 'Which I have been wanting to do ever since you first walked in.'

He started to unbutton her shirt, exposing the silken flesh beneath, and another fierce jerk of desire shot through him. She was perfect, he thought. Just perfect. Her olive skin was dark against a brassiere so white that it looked as if she'd put it on new that morning. He drifted his fingertips over the gentle swell of her breast. 'So what have you got to say about that, *Leila*?'

Beneath the tantalising touch of his fingers, Leila grew weaker still. Where were the nerves she should be feeling? And why did it feel so natural? As if she had been waiting all her life for Gabe Steel to touch her like this?

'I think it's gorgeous,' she said, praying he wouldn't stop.

'I want to kiss your breasts,' he vowed unsteadily. 'Each beautiful breast which is peaking towards me, just waiting to be kissed.'

A pulse was hammering at his temple and Leila jerked with pleasure as he lowered his mouth to one tightening nipple. His dark blond head contrasted against the snowy silk of her bra, and she could feel the fabric growing moist as he sucked her. She squirmed in time to each provocative lick of his tongue, as helpless then as she could ever remember feeling. And suddenly she understood what all the fuss was about. Why sex was so powerful. Why people did such crazy things to get it.

'G-Gabe,' she gasped, the word stumbling over itself in disbelieving pleasure.

He lifted his head to stare at her, and suddenly his grey eyes were not so cold. They seemed bright with pewter fire.

'I think we're going to have to skip the next few stages,' he said. 'In fact, if I don't get you horizontal in the next couple of minutes, I think I'm going to go out of my mind.'

He caught hold of her fingers and led her straight into the bedroom she'd seen earlier—the bed still in rumpled disarray.

Now slightly disorientated, Leila looked around in faint bewilderment because she had never seen a room in such a state before. In her ordered and enclosed world, a servant would have attended to it while she'd been in the shower—making the bed all neat and pristine again and tidying away her discarded clothes.

She had never been lowered down onto untidy sheets which were still rich with the scent of the man who had slept in them. Nor towered over by someone whose mouth was tight as he continued to undress her. She stared up at him but he wasn't staring back. He was too busy removing her trainers and then unzipping her jeans as if he'd removed countless pairs of women's jeans in his life.

He probably had.

Of *course* he had.

Leila remembered what she'd read about him on the internet. Fragments of information about all the beautiful models and actresses he'd dated came drifting back. Women infinitely more experienced than she was.

She felt the cold shiver of insecurity reminding her to face facts and not be swept away by fantasy. She knew what men were like. How they were guided by the heat in their loins or the weight of their own ambition. She knew that they viewed women simply as possessions or as adornments—or as vessels to carry children.

She must not forget that.

This might feel as if she were living out a scene from a film, but it wasn't a film. This was real life and Gabe Steel wasn't suddenly going to turn into some fantasy hero and fall madly in love with her.

She didn't believe in that kind of love.

Her head fell back against the pillow as she felt the slide of his fingertips brushing over her thigh and suddenly it was difficult to think about anything, other than how good it felt.

He tugged the jeans down over her knees and she could hear the soft rustle as they fell to the floor.

'Nice knickers,' he murmured before deftly removing her bra and shirt.

Leila blushed at his words, telling herself this was normal. This was *natural*. 'Thanks,' she said, as if men complimented her on her choice of underwear every day of the week.

He tugged off his T-shirt and stood up to unbutton his jeans, and Leila was mesmerised as he peeled them off. Her heart began to pound with excitement as his body was revealed to her, for she had only ever seen a horse from the royal stables in such a state of arousal before.

Yet he seemed proud and unashamed of his nakedness as he walked across the room and retrieved something from his suitcase. Leila saw the glint of foil and the reality of what she was about to do suddenly hit her.

Because that was a condom; she was certain of it. She might never have encountered one before, but what else could it be?

She felt the icy clamp of sweat on her forehead as reality suddenly broke into her erotic thoughts. Did all women feel this sudden sense of panic the first time? The fear that she might disappoint him?

He was putting the item on the table beside the bed, and while she knew that she should be grateful to him for being pragmatic, it destroyed the mood a little. Why was real life so messy? she wondered bitterly. In films, you never saw any of *this*. Couples seemed to find themselves in bed together almost by magic and then the scene cut to them giggling as they ran down a street, usually in Paris. Not that she and Gabe Steel would be running anywhere here in Simdahab—at least not without the Sultan's guards giving chase. And if he didn't come back here and kiss her soon, she was going to get cold feet.

But almost as if he'd read her mind, he came back and lay down beside her. His body was warm, but his face was sombre as he traced a thoughtful line around her lips.

'Suddenly so serious,' he said, his grey eyes narrowing. 'As if you've started having regrets. Have you, Leila? Because we can stop this right now if that's what you want.'

Leila closed her eyes as she felt the brush of his finger over her lips. And wouldn't that be best? To put her clothes back on and get out of here as quickly as possible. She would feel embarrassed, and he might be angry with her for having led him on, but no real harm would have been done. She could slip away and act as if nothing had happened—because nothing had.

But then she thought about what awaited her back at the palace. She thought about all the inevitable restrictions and rules which had governed her life so far. All the things she wasn't allowed to do and never would be able to do *just because she was a woman and a princess*. She thought about the royal prince her brother would probably arrange for her to one day marry. The watchful eyes of both nations as they waited for her to produce an heir, before her husband thankfully sought refuge in the pleasures of his harem, just as her own father had done.

And suddenly she thought why *shouldn't* she experience this—as millions of other women had done? The way that men did *almost every day of their lives. Why shouldn't she have this one brief interlude of pleasure before she took up the duties which lay ahead of her?*

She wrapped her arms around his neck. 'Kiss me,' she whispered. 'Kiss me. Please.'

He smiled as his mouth came down to cover hers, and suddenly it *did* feel like a fairy tale. As if her senses had been fine-tuned. As if she were capable of anything. *Anything.*

'Oh,' she said, her eyes fluttering to a close as he drifted his mouth to her neck to kiss it over and over. 'Oh.'

Now his lips had found her breast and she could feel a thousand tiny sparks of pleasure as his tongue flicked against her puckered skin. She splayed her hands over his chest, where his heart pounded so

strongly. She felt the coarse whorls of hair which grew
there and she tugged at them—as playfully as a puppy
with a new toy. His groan of delight filled her with
confidence and she let her fingers drift downwards to
explore the muscular flat of his belly and another helpless groan made her feel invincible. As if she could
do anything or be anyone.

Anyone but herself.

He kissed her until she thought she would go out
of her mind with longing. Until her heart was full of
him. And suddenly, she wanted more. She could feel
the restless movements of her body, orchestrated by a
desire which seemed outside her understanding. Her
fingers were kneading at his broad shoulders and she
could hear him give a low laugh—as if her hunger
pleased him. She could feel him tense as he began to
nudge her legs apart with one insistent knee.

Her breath caught in her throat as he slid his hand
between her thighs, and she cried out as he touched
her where no man had ever touched her before.

'God, you're wet,' he groaned.

'Am I?' she questioned almost shyly.

'Mmm,' he affirmed as his finger began to strum
against her, moving against her heated flesh in a light
and silken rhythm.

Against his shoulder, Leila closed her eyes and
felt as if she might melt beneath his touch. It felt gorgeous. He felt gorgeous. Gorgeous Gabe Steel who
had stopped touching her and was now tearing at the
little packet of foil he'd left beside the bed.

His face was formidable as he moved over her
again and suddenly it was happening, almost without warning. He was lifting up her hips and making

one deep, long thrust inside her, and she was crying out—only this time her cry sounded different, because the pain was very real. She felt him grow still and her heart plummeted as she saw the new expression on his face. The intense pleasure had changed into an expression of disbelief as he stared down at her.

'No,' he said, shaking his head. 'No.'

'What?' she gasped, because he was deep inside her and now that her body had adjusted to accommodate him, it felt amazing.

'You're a virgin?'

She sensed that he was about to pull out of her, but she had come this far and she couldn't bear him to stop. Some deep instinct was governing her now, and she prevented his withdrawal by the simply expedient of tightening her body around him. She saw his eyes grow at first angry and then smoky as tentatively she moved her hips upwards so that he was deeper still.

'So what if I am?' she whispered. 'Somebody's got to be the first and that somebody happens to be you. Please, Gabe. I want to experience pleasure the way that other women do. I want you to show me how. I know you can show me how.'

Gabe shook his head as he felt her slick heat yielding to his helpless thrust. The potent combination of her innocence and tightness and the erotic words she was whispering was making him harder than he could ever remember feeling before. But she was a virgin, he reminded himself. *Unbelievably, she was a virgin.* She had come to his room—this complete stranger—and given herself to him without any kind of ceremony. What kind of woman did that? He felt perplexed and resentful at having been lured into a situation which wasn't what it seemed.

So call a halt to it right now.

He swallowed. 'This is—'

'Heaven,' she said, her voice an irresistible murmur. 'You know it is. Don't stop, Gabe. Please don't stop.'

Her heartfelt plea was his final undoing. His anger evaporated and Gabe gave a groan of submission. Why fight it when she didn't want him to stop and… oh, God, neither did he? Pushing himself up on his elbows, he stared down at her beautiful face as he began to move inside her.

Her eyes were closed and he was glad about that. He didn't want to have to *look* at her; he just wanted to feel. He pushed deeper into her moist heat and groaned again, because she felt so good. She felt unbelievable. Was this why men spoke wonderingly about virgins, because they were so tight? Or because it gave a man a sense of power to know that he was the first?

But in the midst of all his macho triumph, he fought another wave of helplessness which was unfamiliar to him. Gone was the slick and seasoned Gabe who could last all night. He felt like a teenager who wanted instantly to explode inside her. But he mustn't. This had to be nothing less than amazing, because it was her first time. He *had* to take it slowly.

Yet it wasn't easy. He found himself stunned by the intense pleasure which was radiating through every pore of his body and not just because she was so tight. He realised how liberating it was not to have any emotional expectations hovering over him like a dark cloud. This really *was* sex without strings. Sex without the fear that she would fall in love with him and want more than he was ever prepared to give.

His thumb on her clitoris, he tilted her back against the pillows, listening to the rising volume of her cries. He watched as she began to move inexorably towards orgasm. Suddenly, she opened her eyes, and he met a clear flash of startled blue. As if she couldn't quite believe what was happening to her.

'Gabe?' she whispered, her accented voice unsteady.

'Relax.' He gave another deep thrust. 'Just. Let. Go.'

He saw her lips frame something which was destined never to be said as her eyelashes flew down to shutter out the blue. And then her body started to quiver helplessly around him and her back began to arch. He heard the words she said as she convulsed around him, although she spoke them in a language he didn't understand. He kissed away the muffled little cries which followed and tried to ignore her fingernails, which were now digging painfully into his back. He waited until her body was almost still before he let go himself, spilling out his seed in great wrenching bursts he never wanted to end.

For a moment he felt so dazed that it was almost as if he'd been drugged. Today, of all days—his body was warm and pulsing with life, instead of feeling empty and cold or deliberately anaesthetised. From between slitted eyes, he surveyed her. Her glossy black hair was tumbling down over her breasts and her perfect olive skin was flushed.

He lifted his hand to her cheek and felt her shiver beneath that light touch. 'Who are you?' he questioned, but she leaned over him and kissed his lips into silence.

'Shh,' she said, and her voice was very gentle. 'You look weary. Go to sleep, Gabe. Just go to sleep.'

CHAPTER THREE

'HAVE YOU BEEN listening to a word I've been saying, Leila?'

Leila gave a start as her brother's impatient question cut through the confusion of her thoughts. In the air-conditioned cool of the palace, she wondered if the hectic colour had faded from her cheeks and for once she gave thanks to the veil which concealed them from the Sultan. But there were other signs, too. She knew that. The mirror had told her so when she'd looked in it a short while ago.

Had the telltale glitter disappeared from her eyes? She prayed it had. Because if her clever and dictatorial brother Murat ever guessed how she had spent that particular afternoon...

If he had any idea that she had given her virginity to a man who had been a stranger to her.

She shivered.

He would kill her.

'Of course I was listening,' she defended.

His black eyes narrowed. 'So I was saying...what?'

Leila swallowed as she searched around in the fog of her memory for something to remind her. 'Something about the banquet you're holding tonight.'

'Very good, Leila.' He nodded. 'It seems you were paying attention, after all. A banquet in honour of my English guest, Gabe Steel.'

The sudden tremble of her knees at the mention of his name made Leila glad that she was sitting down. 'Gabe Steel?' she echoed and his name tasted nearly as sweet on her lips as his kisses had done.

Murat gave an impatient click of his tongue. 'He is coming here tonight. You *knew* that, Leila.'

Leila forced a smile, acknowledging the power of the human mind to deny something which made you feel uncomfortable. It was the same as going for a ride in the desert—you knew that in the sand lurked snakes and scorpions, but if you thought about them for too long you'd never get on a horse again.

Of course she had known that Gabe was coming here tonight but—as with all the Sultan's formal banquets—she hadn't been invited. If she had, then there would have been no need to have gone to the advertising executive's room in secret to make her doomed job application. And then to have acted like some kind of...

Briefly, she closed her eyes. She mustn't think about him. She mustn't.

Yet try as she might, it was impossible to stem the flashbacks which plagued her, as if someone were playing a forbidden and erotic movie inside her head on an endless loop. She couldn't seem to stop remembering the way he'd made love to her and the way he had made her feel.

She knew that what she had done today had been wrong. It had flown in the face of everything she had been brought up to believe in. In Qurhah, women who were 'good' saved themselves until marriage. Especially royal princesses. There was simply no other option and up until today she had never questioned it. Yet she had seized the opportunity to let the powerful tycoon take her to his bed without a second thought. She had wanted him with a hunger which had taken her by surprise, and he had wanted her just as much, it seemed. For the first time in her life, she had behaved in a way which was truly liberated.

She remembered the gleam of his dark golden hair against the white of the pillow after he'd made that strange low cry and shuddered deep inside her. The way he had fallen asleep almost immediately— a sleep so deep that for a moment she'd had to check he was still breathing. He hadn't even stirred when she'd slipped from the bed—her body still warm and aching and her skin suffused with a soft, warm glow.

Silently, she had crept around the hotel suite— gathering up her discarded clothes, which she'd put on in the bathroom with trembling fingers, terrified that he would hear. And she hadn't wanted him to hear. She had known that her only option was to slip away before he awoke because she couldn't face saying goodbye, Not when she was feeling in such a volatile emotional state and she wanted nothing more than to snuggle into his warm embrace and kiss those sensual lips of his again.

Because that was simply not on the cards. There was no future for them. She knew that. Not now and not ever—and she sensed that in her vulnerable postorgasm state she might have been tempted to overlook that simple fact.

She sucked in a deep breath, telling herself that

what was done was done and she wasn't going to feel ashamed about something she had enjoyed so much. Not when for the first time in her life she had behaved like a free-thinking woman instead of a puppet whose strings were constantly being pulled by her powerful brother, the Sultan.

But she could also see now that her thinking had been skewed. She had been foolishly naive to approach the Englishman in the first place. Had she really imagined that Gabe Steel—no matter how powerful he was in his own country—could persuade her brother to let her work with him? Did she really think she could go from pampered princess to Westerner's aide in one easy transition?

She could feel Murat's eyes on her and knew he was waiting for some kind of response. He might be her brother, but he was first and foremost the Sultan—and, as such, the world always revolved around Murat.

'There is no need for me to express my hope that your banquet will be successful, Murat,' she said formally. 'For that is a given.'

There was a pause as he inclined his head, silently acknowledging her praise.

'I thought you might wish to attend,' he said.

For the second time, Leila was glad she was sitting down. She narrowed her eyes, thinking she must have misheard him. 'The banquet?'

The Sultan shrugged his shoulders. 'Why not?'

'Why not?' She laughed. 'Is that a serious question? Because it's "business" and these affairs are traditionally men only.'

Murat gave a little shake of his shoulders and Leila thought he seemed a little *unsettled* tonight. Which wasn't like her brother at all. Maybe the cancellation of his arranged marriage had affected him more than it had appeared to do at the time.

'Then perhaps it is time that Qurhah embraced the untraditional for a change,' he said.

Leila stared at him in growing disbelief. 'What on earth has brought all this on?'

Murat glowered. 'Does there have to be a reason for everything? You have harangued me for many years for a more inclusive role in state affairs, Leila—'

'And you always ignore everything I say!'

'And now that I am actually proposing a break in tradition,' he continued implacably, 'I am being subjected to some sort of inquisition!'

Leila didn't answer because her heart had grown disconcertingly light. She tried to ignore the flutter in her stomach and the rush of blood to her cheeks, but she couldn't ignore the glorious words which were circling round and round in her mind. She had been invited to the banquet! She was going to see Gabe again!

Her heart pounded. How would it feel to face him again at a formal palace dinner? And how would he react to seeing her in the last place he would ever expect to see her?

She felt the sudden rush of nerves and sternly she told herself not to get carried away. It didn't matter how he reacted because that was irrelevant. Yes, he had been the kind of lover that every woman dreamt of, but Gabe was just a man. And she knew about men. She knew about the pain and heartbreak they caused women. The muffled sound of her mother's tears had characterised her childhood and she reminded herself not to weave any foolish dreams about Gabe Steel.

'You are very quiet, Leila,' observed the Sultan softly. 'I had imagined you would be delighted to meet my Western guest.'

Leila gave a cautious smile. 'Forgive me for my somewhat muted response,' she said. 'For I was a little taken off-guard by your unexpected generosity. Naturally, I shall be delighted to meet Mr Steel.'

'Good. And you will wear the veil, of course. I like the thought of our Western visitor observing the quiet decorum of the traditional Qurhahian woman.' Murat frowned. 'Though I hope you're not coming down with a fever, Leila—for your complexion has suddenly grown very flushed.'

Gabe barely registered the gleaming golden gates which had opened to allow his bulletproof car through. Just as he had failed to register the colourful and bustling streets of Simdahab on his way to the palace. The journey through the city had been slower than he had anticipated—mainly, he suspected, because the car was so heavily armoured. He guessed that was one of the drawbacks to being a fabulously powerful sultan—that the risk of assassination was never far from the surface.

Yet instead of focusing on the task ahead or reflecting on the cultural differences between the two countries, as he usually would have done, he had spent the entire journey thinking about the woman it was probably safer to forget.

Leila.

When he'd woken from a deep sleep in that sex-rumpled bed, he had known a moment of complete and utter peace—before disjointed memories had come flooding back. For a moment he'd thought that he must have dreamt the whole bizarre incident. And then he had seen the faint red spots of blood on the sheet—not knowing if it had sprung from her broken hymen or when her fingernails had clawed deep into the flesh of his shoulders at the moment of orgasm.

He stared out of the car window at the vast splendour of the palace gardens, but this faint feeling of disorientation would not leave him.

He had always been successful with women—and not just because of his hard body and what the press had once described as his 'fallen angel' looks. He had quickly learnt how best to handle the opposite sex, because he could see that it was in his best interests to do so. To take what he wanted without giving any false hope. He'd learnt that guaranteeing pleasure was the most effective way of having someone overlook your shortcomings—the main one being his aversion to emotion. He knew that he couldn't give love—but he could certainly give great orgasms.

He'd seen it all and done it all—or so he'd thought—though he'd avoided any situation involving cameras or threesomes. But he had never had a beautiful, virginal stranger turning up at his hotel room and allowing him to seduce her within minutes of meeting.

He felt his heart miss a beat as he recalled the way she had made him feel. That initial hard thrust against her tight hymen. Who *was* she? And why had she chosen to give her innocence to a man she didn't know?

He thought about the photographs she'd shown him. Nobody could deny that she was talented. Did she think that her sexual generosity would guarantee her the offer of a job? Yet if that was the case, then surely she would have left him her card—or some number scribbled down on a sheet of hotel notepaper, so that he could contact her again. But she hadn't. There had been nothing to mark the fact that she'd been there. Only her very feminine fragrance lingering with the unmistakeable scent of sex when he'd woken to find an empty space beside him and silence in the adjoining suite of rooms.

Gabe shook his head as the limousine drew to a halt and a robed servant opened the door for him. He must put her out of his mind and concentrate on the evening ahead. It didn't matter who his mystery virgin was. It had happened and it was over. He could shut the door on it, just as he did with every other aspect of his past. He was here at the palace to meet formally with the Sultan and none of the other stuff mattered.

Buttoning up the jacket of his suit, he stepped out onto the honey-coloured gravel of the forecourt and in the distance he could see a long line of similar limousines already parked. The turreted palace gleamed red-gold in the light of the setting sun, like something out of an upmarket Disney film. Gabe wondered how long it had taken to build this impressive citadel—an unmistakeable symbol of beauty and power, set in an oasis of formal and surprisingly green gardens.

The evening air was thick with the scent of roses and soft with the sound of running water from the stream which traversed the palace grounds. In the distance, he could see soaring mountain peaks topped with snow and, closer, the circular and steady flight of what looked like a bird of prey.

That was what he should be thinking about, he reminded himself grimly. Not a woman who had made him feel slightly...

He frowned.

Used?

Had she?

'Gabe! Here you are at last. May I welcome you to my home?'

An accented voice broke into his thoughts. Gabe turned to find the Sultan standing on the steps to greet him. A tall and imposing figure, he was framed by the dramatic arches of the palace entrance behind him. His robes and headdress were pure white and the starkness of his appearance was broken only by the luminosity of his olive skin. For a moment, a distant memory floated across Gabe's mind before it disappeared again, like a butterfly on a summer's day.

Gabe smiled. 'Your Most Imperial Highness,' he said. 'I am most honoured to be invited to your palace.'

'The honour is all mine,' said the Sultan, stepping forward to shake him warmly by the hand. 'How was London when you left?'

'Rainy,' said Gabe.

'Of course it was.' The two men exchanged a wry look.

Gabe had first met the Sultan at the marriage of one of his own employees. At the time, Sara Williams had been working as a 'creative' at his advertising agency before she'd ruffled a few feathers by bringing her rather complicated love-life into the office.

During that rather surreal wedding day in the nearby country of Dhi'ban, the Sultan had told Gabe that he knew of his formidable reputation and asked if he would help bring Qurhah into the twenty-first century by helping change its image. Initially, Gabe had been reluctant to accept such a potentially tricky commission, but it had provided a challenge, in a life where fresh challenges were rare.

And he had timed it to coincide with an anniversary which always filled him with guilt and regret.

'You are comfortable at your hotel?' asked the Sultan.

For a moment, Gabe felt erotic recall trickle down his spine. 'It's perfect,' he said. 'One of the most beautiful buildings I've ever stayed in.'

'Thank you. But you will find our royal palace more beautiful still.' The Sultan made a sweeping gesture with his hand. 'Now come inside and let me show you a little Qurhahian hospitality.'

Gabe followed the monarch through the long corridors of the palace, made cool by the soft breeze which floated in from the central courtyard. Past bowing ranks of servants, they walked—overlooked by portraits of hawk-faced kings from ages gone by, all of whom bore a striking resemblance to his host.

It was more than a little dazzling but the room which they entered defied all expectation. Tall and as impressive as a cathedral, the high-ceilinged chamber was vaulted with the soft gleam of gold and the glitter of precious gems. People stood chatting and sipping their drinks, but the moment the Sultan entered everyone grew silent and bowed their heads in homage.

What must it be like to have that kind of power over people? wondered Gabe as he was introduced first to the Sultan's emissary and then to a whole stream of officials—all of them men. Some of them—mainly the older generation—were clearly suspicious of a foreigner who had been brought in to tamper with the image of a country which had always fiercely prided itself on its national identity. But Gabe knew that change inevitably brought with it pain, and so he listened patiently to some of the reservations which were being voiced before the bell rang for dinner.

He accompanied Sultan into a vast dining room, where lavishly laid tables were decorated with fragrant roses coloured deep crimson. Inexplicably, he found his eyes flickering towards their dark petals and wondering why the sight of them unsettled him so. Like the blood on his sheets, he thought suddenly—and a whisper of apprehension iced his skin.

'I have seated you next to the Ambassador of Maraban, who is one of the most influential men in the region,' said the Sultan. 'With my sister on the other side. Her English is excellent and she is eager to meet with you, for she meets few Westerners. Ah, here she comes now. Leila!'

But Gabe didn't need to hear his host say her name to know the woman's identity. He knew that from the moment she entered the banqueting hall. Even though her body was swathed in flowing silk and even though a matching veil of palest silver was covering half her face, there could be no mistaking her. No amount of camouflage could disguise that sexy sway of her body—or maybe it was because in some primeval and physical way, he still felt connected to her.

He could still smell her on his skin.

He could still taste her in his mouth.

He could still remember the exact moment when

he had broken through her tightness and claimed her for his own.

Why the hell had she kept her identity hidden from him?

The Sultan was saying something, and Gabe had to force himself to listen and to pray that the sudden clamour of his senses would settle.

'Leila.' The hawk-faced leader smiled. 'This is Gabe Steel—the advertising genius from London of whom you have heard me speak. Gabe, I'd like you to meet Princess Leila Scheherazade of Qurhah—my only sister.'

For a moment Gabe was so angry he could barely get a word out in response, but he quickly asserted the self-possession which was second nature to him. He had worked all his life in an industry which traded on illusion and knew only too well how to wear which-ever mask the occasion demanded. And so he produced the slightly deferential smile he knew was expected of him on meeting the royal princess. He even inclined his head towards her, before catching a peep of a crystal-encrusted sandal which was poking out from beneath the folds of her gown. And the sight of those beautiful toes sent a surge of anger and lust shooting through him.

'I am honoured to meet you, Your Royal Highness,' he said, but as he straightened up he saw the sudden colour which flushed over the upper part of her face. He saw the brief flicker of distress which flared in the depths of her blue eyes. And that distress pleased him. His mouth hardened. It pleased him very much.

'The pleasure is also mine, Mr Steel,' she said softly.

'Leila, please show our guest to his place.' The

Sultan clapped his hands loudly, and once again the room grew silent. 'And let us all be seated.'

Silently, Gabe followed Leila across the dining room and took his place beside her. In the murmured moments as two hundred guests sat down, he seized the opportunity to move his head close to hers. 'So. Are you going to give me some kind of explanation?'

'Not now,' she said calmly.

'I want some sort of explanation, Your Royal *Highness*.'

'Not now,' she repeated, and then she lifted her fingers and began to remove her veil.

And despite the anger still simmering away inside him, Gabe held his breath as her features were slowly revealed to him. Because in a world where nudity was as ubiquitous as the cell phone, this was the most erotic striptease he had ever witnessed.

First he saw the curve of her chin and, above that, those sensual lips, which looked so startlingly pink against her luminous skin. He remembered how those lips had felt beneath the hard crush of his own and he felt himself harden instantly. He tried to tell himself that her nose was too strong and aquiline for conventional beauty and that there were women far more lovely than her. But he was lying—because in that moment she looked like the most exquisite creature he had ever seen.

And she had deceived him. She had lied to him as women always lied.

Taking a long draught of wine in an effort to steady his nerves, somehow he hung on to his temper for as long as it took to charm the ambassador during the first course, which he had no desire to eat.

He wondered if it was rude to completely ignore Leila, but he didn't care—because he still didn't trust himself to speak to her again. It wouldn't look good if he exploded with anger at the exalted banqueting table of the Sultan, would it? Yet he found his gaze drawn inexorably to the way her fingers toyed with the heavy golden cutlery as she pushed food around her plate.

The ambassador had turned away to talk to the person on his left and Gabe took the opportunity to lean towards her, his voice shaking with suppressed rage. 'So is there some kind of power game going on that I should know about, Leila?' he said. 'Some political intrigue which will slowly be revealed to me as the evening progresses?'

Her heavy golden fork clattered to her plate and he saw the apprehension on her face as she turned to face him.

'There's no intrigue,' she answered, her voice as low as his.

'No? Then why all the mystery? Why not just tell your brother that we've already met. Unless he doesn't know, of course.'

'I—'

'Maybe he has no idea that his sister came to my hotel today,' he continued remorselessly. 'And let me—'

'Please.' Her interruption sounded anguished. 'We can't talk here.'

'Then where do you suggest?' he questioned. 'Same time, same place tomorrow? Maybe you'd already planned to return for a repeat performance, wearing a different kind of disguise. Maybe the mas-

querade aspect turns you on. I don't know.' His eyes
bored into her. 'Had you?'

'Mr Steel—'

'It's Gabe,' he said with icy pleasantry. 'You remember how to say my name, don't you, Leila?'

Briefly, Leila closed her eyes. She certainly did.
And she hadn't just *said* it, had she? She'd gasped it
as he had entered her. She had whispered it as he'd
moved deep inside her. She had shuddered it out in a
long, keening moan as her orgasm had taken hold of
her and almost torn her apart with pleasure.

And now all those amazing memories were being
swept away by the angry wash from his eyes.

She wished she could spirit herself away. That she
could excuse herself by saying she felt sick—which
was actually true, because right at that moment she
did feel sick.

But Murat would never forgive her if she interrupted the banquet—why, it might even alert his suspicions if he suspected that she found the Englishman's
presence uncomfortable. He might begin to ask himself why. And surely the man beside her—*the man
who had made such incredible love to her*—couldn't
keep up this simmering hostility for the entire meal?

'Look, I can understand why you're angry,' she
said, trying to keep her tone conciliatory.

'Can you?' His pewter eyes glittered out a hostile
light. 'And why might that be? Because you failed to
reveal your true identity to me?'

'I wasn't—'

'Or because it's only just occurred to you that you
might have compromised my working relationship
with your brother?' His voice was soft but his words

were deadly. 'Because no man likes to discover that his sister has behaved like a whore.'

He leaned back in his chair to study her, as if they were having a perfectly amicable discussion, and Leila thought how looks could deceive. The casual observer would never have noticed that the polite smile on his lips was completely at odds with the angry glitter in his grey eyes.

'I was behaving as other women sometimes behave,' she protested. 'Spontaneously.'

'But most women aren't being pursued by bodyguards at the time,' he continued. His voice lowered, and she could hear the angry edge to his words. 'What would have happened if they had burst in and found us in bed together?'

Leila tried desperately to block the image from her mind. 'I don't know.'

'Oh, I think you've got a pretty good idea. What would have happened, Leila?'

She swallowed, knowing that he was far too intelligent to be fobbed off with a vague answer. 'You would have been arrested,' she admitted reluctantly.

'I would have been arrested,' he repeated grimly and nodded his head. 'Destroying my reputation and losing my freedom in the process. Maybe even my head?'

'We are not that barbaric!' she protested, but her words did not carry the ring of conviction.

'It's funny really,' he continued, 'because for the first time in my life I'm feeling like some kind of stud. Wham and bam—but not much in the way of thank you, ma'am.'

'No!' she said. 'It wasn't like that.'

'Really? Then what was it? Love at first sight?'

Leila picked up her goblet of black cherry juice and drank a mouthful, more as a stalling mechanism than because she was thirsty. His words were making her realise just how impulsive she had been and how disastrous it would have been if they'd been caught. But they *hadn't* been caught, had they? Maybe luck—or fate—had been on their side.

And the truth of it was that her heart had leapt with a delicious kind of joy when she'd seen him again tonight, in his charcoal suit and a silver tie the colour of a river fish. She had stared at the richness of his hair and longed to run her fingers through it. Her eyes had drifted hungrily over his hard features and, despite everything she'd vowed not to do, she had wanted to kiss him. She had started concocting unrealistic little fantasies about him, and that was crazy. Just because he had proved to be an exquisite lover, didn't mean that she should fall into that age-old female trap of imagining that he had a heart.

Because no man had a heart, she reminded herself bitterly.

'Love?' She met the challenge in his eyes. 'Why, do you always have to be in love before you can have sex?'

'Me? No. Most emphatically I do not. But women often do, especially when it's their first time. But then I guess most women aren't just spoiled little princesses who see what they want and go out and take it—and to hell with the consequences.'

Leila didn't react to the *spoiled-little-princess* insult. She knew people thought it, though no one had ever actually come out and said it to her face before.

She knew what people thought about families like hers and how they automatically slotted her into a gilded box marked 'pampered'. But what they saw wasn't always the true picture. Unimaginable wealth didn't protect you from the normal everyday stuff. Glittering palace walls didn't work some kind of magic on the people who lived within them. Prick her skin and she would bleed, just like the next woman.

'It was an unconventional introduction, I admit,' she said. 'To bring my work to your hotel room unannounced like that and ask you for a job.'

'Please don't be disingenuous, Leila. That's not what I'm talking about and you know it.' He sounded impatient now. 'Which guide to interview technique did you study before you started removing your clothes and climbing all over me? *The 1960s Guide to Sexual Behaviour*? Or *A Hundred Ways To Make The Casting Couch Work For You*?'

'You didn't seem so averse to the idea at the time!'

'Funny that,' he mused. 'A beautiful woman comes up to my suite, turns her big blue eyes on me and starts coming on to me. She brushes my arm so lightly that I wonder if I'd imagined it, though my senses tell me I hadn't. Then she pirouettes around so that there can be no mistaking the tight cut of her jeans or the cling of her blouse as she shows off her amazing body. She gazes into my eyes as if I am the answer to all her prayers.' *And for one brief moment hadn't he felt as if he could be?*

There was a pause as Leila forced herself to scoop some jewel-coloured rice onto her fork—terrified that someone might notice that she hadn't eaten a thing and start asking themselves why. Had she done everything which Gabe had accused her of? Had she behaved like some kind of *siren*? She lifted her head to look at him. 'You could have stopped me,' she said.

Gabe stilled as he met the challenge sparking from her blue eyes. Because hadn't he been thinking the same thing ever since it had happened? He could have stopped her. He *should* have stopped her. He should have waited until her bodyguards had gone and then told her to get out of his room as quickly as possible. He could have dampened down his desire, using the formidable self-control which had carried him through situations far more taxing than one of sexual frustration. He could have told her that he didn't have a type, but that if he did—she wouldn't be it.

He didn't like women who were *obvious*. Who had persistent exes or *brothers who were sultans*. He had an antenna for women who were trouble and it had never failed him before. He resisted the tricky ones. The neurotic and needy ones.

But something had gone wrong this time.

Because he hadn't resisted Leila, had he? He had broken his own rules and taken her to bed without knowing a single damned thing about her. And he still couldn't work out why. He shook his head slightly. It had been something indefinable. Something in those wide blue eyes which had drawn him in. He had felt like a man whose throat was parched. Who had been shown a pool of water and invited to drink from it. He had felt almost...

His eyes narrowed.

Almost *helpless*.

And that was never going to happen.

Not twice in a lifetime.

'I could have stopped you,' he agreed slowly.

'So why didn't you?'

He didn't answer straight away because it was important to get this right. He wanted to send out a message to her. A very clear message she could not fail to understand. That it had meant nothing to him. That it would be a mistake to fall for him. That he caused women pain. Deep pain.

'Sometimes sex is like an itch,' he said deliberately. 'And you just can't help yourself from scratching it.'

Her face didn't register any of the kind of emotions he might have expected. No indignation or hurt. He suspected that hers was a world where feelings as well as faces were hidden. But he saw her eyes harden, very briefly. As if he had simply confirmed something she had already known.

'I'm sure that the romantic poets need have nothing to fear from your observations,' she said sarcastically.

He picked up his goblet of wine, twirling the long golden stem between his fingers. 'Just so long as we understand each other.'

She leaned forward, and he caught a drift of some faint scent. It made him think of meadow flowers being crushed underfoot. He found it...*distracting*.

'Oh, I get the message loud and clear,' she said. 'So forgive me if I ignore you as much as possible for the rest of the meal. I think we've said everything there is to say to each other, don't you?'

CHAPTER FOUR

LEILA GRIPPED THE side of the washbasin as terror sliced through her like the cold blade of a sword. She wanted to scream. Or to throw back her head and howl like an animal. But she didn't dare. Because her fear of discovery was almost as great as the dark suspicion which had been growing inside her for days.

She stayed perfectly still and listened, her heart thudding painfully in her chest. Had anyone heard her? Had one of the many unseen servants been close enough to the bathroom to catch the sound of her shuddered retching?

She closed her eyes.

Please no.

But when she opened them again, she knew that she could no longer keep pretending. She couldn't keep hoping and praying that this wasn't happening, because it was.

It had started with a missed period. One day late. Two days late—then a full week. Her nerves had been shot. Her heart seemed to have been permanently racing with horror and fear. She was *never* late—her monthly cycle was as reliable as the morning sunrise. And the awful thing was that she'd had to *pretend* that it had arrived. She'd forced herself to wince and to clutch at the lower part of her stomach as if in discomfort, desperate not to alert the suspicions of her female servants. Because in that enclosed, watched world of the palace, nothing went unnoticed—not even the princess's most intimate secrets.

She had told herself that it was just a glitch. That it must be her body behaving in an unusual way because it had been introduced to sex. Then she had tried not thinking about it at all. When that hadn't worked, she'd made silent pleas to Mother Nature, promising that she would be good for the rest of her life, if only she wasn't carrying Gabe Steel's baby.

But her pleas went unanswered. The horror was real. The bare and simple fact wasn't going away, simply because she wanted it to.

She was pregnant.

Her one brief experiment with sex—her one futile attempt to behave with the freedom of a man—had left her with a consequence which was never going to leave her. Pregnant by a man who never wanted to see her again.

She was ruined.

With trembling fingers, she tidied her mussed hair, knowing she couldn't let her standards slip. She had to maintain the regal facade expected of her, because if anyone ever *guessed*...

She thought about the meagre options which lay open to her and each of them filled her with foreboding. She thought what would happen if her brother found out, and a shudder ran down her spine. She gripped the washbasin, and the cold porcelain felt like

ice beneath her clammy fingers. Murat must not find
out—at least, not yet.

She was going to have to tell Gabe.

But Gabe had gone back to England and there were
no plans for her to see him again. He had spent a further fortnight working here in Qurhah without their
paths ever crossing. Why would they? He had made
it clear that he wanted to forget what had happened
and she had convinced herself she felt the same way.
She'd found herself reflecting how strange it was that
two people who'd been so intimate could afterwards
act like strangers.

Even the farewell dinner given in honour of the
English tycoon had yielded no moments of closeness.
She and Gabe had barely exchanged any words at all,
bar a few stilted ones of greeting. During the meal
she'd read nothing but cool contempt in his pewter
eyes. And that had hurt. She had experienced for the
first time the pain of rejection, made worse by the
dull ache of longing.

Her mind working overtime, Leila shut the bathroom door behind her and walked slowly back to her
private living quarters. Gabe Steel might not be her
first port of call in normal circumstances, but right
now he was the only person she could turn to.

She had to tell him.

But how?

She looked out over the palace rose gardens where
the bright orange bloom which had been named after
her in the days following her birth was now in glorious display.

If she phoned him, who wasn't to say that some
interfering palace busybody might not be listening

in to her call? And phoning him would still leave her here, pregnant and alone and vulnerable to the Sultan's rage if he found out.

But if she left it much longer it was inevitable he would find out anyway.

A sudden knock at the door disturbed her, and her troubled thoughts became magnified when one of her servants informed her that the Sultan wished to see her with immediate effect.

Leila's mouth was dry with fear as she walked silently along the marble corridors towards Murat's own magnificent section of the royal palace. Had he guessed? Was he summoning her to tell her that she had brought shame on the royal house, and that she was to be banished to some isolated region of their vast country to bring up her illegitimate child in solitude?

But when she was ushered into his private sitting room, Murat's demeanour was unusually solicitous, his black eyes narrowed with something almost approaching *concern*.

He began by asking whether she was well.

'Yes, I am very well,' she lied, praying that her horror at this particular question would not show on her face. 'Why...why do you ask?'

Murat shrugged. 'Just that you seem to have been almost invisible lately. You don't seem to have been yourself at all. Is something wrong, Leila?'

He'd *noticed*!

Despite her wild flare of fear, Leila knew that she must not react. She must not give her clever brother any inkling that she was concealing a desperate secret. With a resourcefulness she wasn't aware she possessed—though maybe desperation was in itself an inspiration—Leila shrugged. 'I have been feeling a little discontented of late.'

His eyes narrowed. 'In what way?'

She licked her lips. 'I feel as if I have seen nothing of the world, or of life itself. All I know is Qurhah.'

'That is because you are a princess of Qurhah,' Murat growled. 'And your place is here.'

'I know that,' said Leila, thinking that he made her sound like an ancient piece of furniture which had never been moved from its allocated place on the rug. 'But you travel. You get to visit other countries. And I...I have seen nothing of the world, other than the surrounding lands of the desert region.'

The Sultan's black eyes narrowed. 'And?'

She forced herself to say the words, to make him think that she had accepted the future which had been planned for her. A future which could now never happen, because what prospective royal husband would wish to take a bride who carried another man's child?

'I know that my place is here, Murat,' she said quietly. 'But before I immerse myself in the life which has been mapped out for me—could I not have an overseas trip?'

Beneath his silken headdress, Murat's dark brows knitted together. 'What kind of trip?' he echoed.

Leila could hardly believe she'd got this far and knew she mustn't blow it now. She thought about the tiny, forbidden life growing inside her and she drew in a deep breath. 'You know that Princess Sara has a place in London?'

'So I gather,' said Murat carelessly.

Leila watched her brother's reaction closely, but if

he was hurt to hear the name of the woman he'd once been betrothed to, he didn't show it.

'She often writes to me and tells me all about the fabulous shopping in the city,' Leila continued. 'Many times she has asked me to visit her there. Couldn't I do that, Murat—just for a few days? You know how much I love shopping!'

There was silence for a moment. Had she made her request sound suitably fluffy? If she'd told her brother that she wanted to go and see a photographic exhibition which was being launched, he would never have approved. He was one of those men who believed that shopping kept women subdued. Lavish them with enough *stuff* and it kept them satisfied.

'I suppose that a few days could be arranged,' he said eventually.

Leila gave a little squeal of joy—showing her brother the gratitude she knew would be expected of her—but it was with a heavy heart that she packed for her forthcoming trip. She thought about the terrifying secret she carried. About how humiliating it was to have to seek out a man who did not want her, to tell him something he would be appalled to hear.

Arrangements were made between the palace and Princess Sara, who Leila had known since she'd been a child. Sara had once been promised to Murat himself but was now married to Suleiman, and they had homes all around the world.

With a retinue of bodyguards and servants, Leila flew by private jet to England where they took over the entire top floor of the Granchester Hotel in central London. She was one step closer to Gabe. One step closer to sharing her news—and didn't they say that a problem shared was a problem halved?

But then she remembered his cold face as she'd sat beside him at the banquet. She forced herself to recall the fact that he had never wanted to see her again. There was to be no fairy-tale ending with this man, she reminded herself sombrely. She looked out of the penthouse windows of her hotel suite, across a beautiful park alive with flowers—and a terrible feeling of isolation came over her.

She could see couples openly walking together—their arms looped around each other as they kissed. A young child chased a dog and, behind him, a woman wheeled a pram. Everyone seemed part of the world which lay before her eyes—all except her. And Leila couldn't remember ever feeling quite so alone as she did right then.

Knowing she couldn't keep putting off the dreaded moment much longer, she picked up the hotel phone and dialled Gabe's office, her heart pounding with apprehension. She had to go through two different people before his voice came on the line, and when it did—he sounded distant.

Wary.

Terror gripped her as she realised she was about to drop a live grenade into his perfect life.

'Leila?'

'Yes, it's me. How…how are you, Gabe?'

'I am well.' There was a pause. 'This is a surprise.'

'I imagine it is.' She drew in a deep breath. 'Look, I need to see you.'

'I thought we'd agreed that wasn't such a good idea.

And anyway, I'm back in England now and I'm not planning to return to Qurhah for a while.'

Leila stared out of the window. The child which had been chasing the dog had fallen over and a woman—presumably the child's mother—was picking him up and comforting him. She realised how hopelessly ill-prepared she was to become a mother and her heart clenched. 'I'm in England too,' she said. 'In fact, I'm in London.'

She could hear so much more in that second pause. She imagined his mind working overtime as he tried to figure out what the hell she was doing in England and why she was calling him. And if he asked her outright—would she have the guts to tell him on the phone?

'What are you doing in London?'

For a moment, she didn't answer. He asked the question so casually. Did he think, with the arrogance which seemed to be second nature to all alpha males, that her desire for him was so great that she was prepared to trample over her pride in order to seek him out? Didn't he have a *clue* what she might be about to say? That their rash act of passion might have yielded this very result? 'That's what I'd like to talk to you about.'

'Where are you staying?' he asked. 'I'll come over.'

Her gaze drifted down to the traffic which was clogging the park road, knowing it would be much easier if he came here than having to negotiate her way round this strange new city. But if Gabe wanted nothing to do with this new life…then might that not complicate matters further? Why implicate him to her retinue as the father of her baby, unless he was willing to accept that role?'

'I'm at the Granchester. But I don't want you to come here. It's too...public.' She gripped the phone more tightly. 'Can I come to your place?'

At the other end of the line, Gabe listened to her hesitant words, and his eyes narrowed. It was a presumptuous question and one he would usually have deflected. Invitations to his home were rare and *he* was the one who did the inviting. His apartment was his refuge. His sanctuary. It was where he went to escape. If ever he spent the night with someone, he preferred somewhere which provided him with a clearly marked exit route. Where *he* could be the one doing the leaving.

But Leila was different. Her royal status set her apart from other women. It made people break rules for her. Unwillingly, he felt the quickened beat of desire as he remembered her blue eyes and the silky texture of her olive skin. His mouth dried as he recalled her hot, tight body. He leaned back in his chair and stared at the ceiling. Why the hell hadn't she told him who she really was at the time?

'This is all very mysterious,' he said. 'Do you want to tell me what it's all about?'

'I'd rather do it in person.'

Oh, would you, my presumptuous princess? With a flicker of irritation, Gabe waved an impatient hand at Alice, his newly promoted assistant, who had just stuck her head around his office door. 'Very well. I'll send a car for you at seven.'

'No,' answered Leila flatly. 'That won't be possible.'

'Excuse me?'

'My bodyguards will not permit me to visit a man's apartment. It must be done in total secrecy. Will you be there tonight—at two a.m.?'

'Two a.m.?' His deep voice reverberated with incredulity. 'Are you out of your mind? Some of us have work to go to in the morning.'

'I'm afraid that the cover of darkness is the only solution to ensure I won't be seen, and I can't afford to be seen,' she said, a note of determination entering her voice. 'It will be best if you send the car for me then. But I need to know if you'll…if you'll be alone?'

'Yes, I'll be alone,' said Gabe coldly—and gave her the address.

Leila's heart was racing as she replaced the phone, but she couldn't shake off her feeling of apprehension—and hurt—as he cut the connection without even the politeness of a formal goodbye. Was he always this cool towards the women he'd slept with—as if he couldn't wait to put as much distance between them as possible? And how the hell was he going to react when she told him?

She told her retinue that she intended to rest for the remainder of the evening and instructed them to order themselves food from room service. Then she phoned Sara, cutting through the princess's delighted exclamations by telling her that she needed a favour.

'What kind of a favour?' asked Sara.

'Just that if my brother calls and asks if we're having a good time together, you tell him yes.'

'I think it's unlikely that your brother will call me himself,' said Sara drily. 'Is there something going on, Leila? And does that something have to do with a man?'

'How did you guess?'

'Because with most of my girlfriends, it's usually a man,' answered Sara with a wry tone. 'Don't suppose it's anyone I know?'

Leila hesitated. In a way she was wary of saying anything, but part of her wanted to blurt it out. 'Actually, you do. You used to work for him and he came to your wedding.'

There was a long silence. 'I hope you don't mean Gabe Steel?' said Sara, her voice low and disbelieving.

'That's exactly who I mean.' Leila could feel a skitter of panic washing over her skin. 'Why, what's the matter with him?'

'There's nothing the *matter* with him—that's the trouble. Just about every woman in London is or has been in love with him at some point. He's gorgeous, but he's a heartbreaker, Leila—and my advice is to stay away from him.'

It's too late for that now.

'I can't,' said Leila slowly. 'Will you cover for me, Sara?'

Sara's sigh came heaving down the phone. 'Okay, I'll cover for you—just so long as you promise me you won't do anything stupid.'

I already have, thought Leila, but she injected a breezy note into her voice.

'I promise,' she said as she put the phone down.

She could hear the sound of the room-service trolleys being trundled along the corridor towards the rooms of her retinue. Praying that their attention would be occupied by the novelty of eating Western food and that they would eat too much of it, she settled down to wait.

Shortly before ten, she allowed her servants into the room to turn down the bed and generally fuss around while she did a lot of exaggerated yawning.

The next few hours seemed to tick by with agonising slowness but Leila was too strung out to be sleepy, despite her long flight. Just before two o'clock she dressed and slipped on her raincoat and peered outside her room to find the corridor empty. With a surreptitiousness which was becoming second nature, she took the lift down into the empty foyer and walked straight outside to where Gabe's car was waiting.

Her heart was hammering as the plush vehicle whisked her through the darkened streets of London, before coming to a halt outside a looming tower of gleaming glass which overlooked the wide and glittering band of the river Thames.

And there was Gabe, waiting for her.

The pale moonlight illuminated his features, which were unsmiling and tense. As the vehicle drew to a halt she could see that he was wearing faded jeans and a sweater which hugged his honed torso and powerful arms. He looked shockingly sexy in a rock-star kind of way and that only added to Leila's feelings of discomfiture. As he bent to open the car door his eyes looked as forbidding as a frozen lake which had just been classified as unsafe.

Her mouth felt dry. Her legs were unsteady as his narrowed gaze raked over her. How was she going to go through with this?

'Hello, Leila,' he said, almost pleasantly—and she realised he was doing it again, just as he'd done on the night of the banquet. His civilised words were sending out one message while his eyes glittered out something completely different.

'Shall we go inside?'

Glass doors slid silently open to let them inside the apartment block. She was aware of a vast foyer with a jungle of elaborate plants. A man sitting reading by lamplight at a desk seemed to show surprise when he saw her walking in beside the tycoon with the dark golden hair. Or maybe she was imagining that bit.

But she certainly wasn't imagining Gabe's detached manner as they rode in one of the glass elevators towards the top of the tall building. She might as well have been travelling with a statue for all the notice he took of her, but unfortunately she wasn't similarly immune.

She tried to look somewhere—anywhere—but he filled her line of vision in his sexy, off-duty clothes. Her gaze stayed fixed determinedly on his chest for she didn't dare lift it to his face. She tried to concentrate on the steady rise and fall of his breathing instead of giving in to the darkly erotic thoughts which were crowding into her mind. He didn't want her—he couldn't have made that more clear. Yet all she could think about was the way his hands had slid round her waist when he'd still been deep inside her, the spasms dying away as he'd pumped out the last of his seed.

His seed.

The elevator stopped, the doors opened and Leila stepped out—straight into a room which momentarily took her breath away. An entire wall consisted of windows which commanded a breathtaking view of the night-time city, where stars twinkled and skyscrapers gleamed. The floors were polished and the furniture was minimalist and sleek. It was nothing like the ancient palace she called home and she felt as if she had walked into a strange new world.

For a moment she just stood and stared out of the windows. She could see the illuminated dome of St Paul's Cathedral and moonlight glittering on the river Thames. There was the sharp outline of the Shard and the pleasing circle of the London Eye. For years she had longed to come here, but never like this—because now she was seeing the famous city through the distorted lens of fear.

'Can I get you a drink?' he asked.

Leila allowed herself a moment of fantasy that this was a normal date between two people who had been lovers. How would that work? Would he open champagne and let her drink some before taking the glass from her hand and kissing her? Was that how he usually operated? Probably not at two in the morning when his night was being disturbed by a woman he was indifferent to...

For a moment she wondered what she might have done in this situation if she'd been a normal, Western woman—with all the freedoms that those women seemed to take for granted. There would have been no need for her to behave like this. Moving around under cover of darkness. Having to throw herself on the mercy of someone who didn't want her...

'No, I don't want a drink, thanks,' she said. 'That's not why I'm here.'

'Then why don't you sit down,' he suggested, 'and tell me why you are?'

She sank onto a leather sofa which was more comfortable than it looked. 'Look, there's no easy way to say this—and I know it's going to come as a shock, but I think I'm pregnant.'

For a moment Gabe didn't say a word. He couldn't. It was a long time since he had felt fear, but he felt it now. It was there in the hard beat of his heart and the icy prickle of his skin. And along with fear came anger. The sense that something was happening to him which was outside his control—and hadn't he vowed a long time ago never to let that happen to him again?

Yet on some instinctive and fundamental level, her words were not as shocking as she had suggested. Because hadn't he already guessed what she was going to say? Why else would she have pursued him like this across thousands of miles? She was a desert princess and surely someone like her wouldn't normally seek out a man who'd shown her nothing but coldness, no matter how much she had enjoyed the sex.

But none of his thoughts showed in his face. He had been a survivor for too long to react to her dramatic words—at least, not straight away. He had spent his life perfecting this cool and impenetrable mask and now was not the time to let it slip. He studied her shadowed eyes and seized on the words which offered most hope. The only hope.

'You only *think* you're pregnant?'

She nodded. 'Yes, but I'm pretty sure. I've been sick and my…'

Her words tailed off, as if she couldn't quite bring herself to say the next bit, but Gabe was in no mood to help her out—and certainly in no mood to tiptoe around her sensibilities. Because this was the woman who had disguised herself. Who had burst into his suite and come on to him without bothering to tell him who she was. She might have been a virgin but she certainly hadn't acted like one—and he was damned if he was going to let her play the shy and sensitive card now. Not when she was threatening to disrupt the ordered calm of his life. Disrupt it? She was threatening to blow it apart.

He felt a sudden flare of rage. 'Your what?' he prompted icily.

'My period is late!' she burst out, her cheeks suddenly turning red.

'But you haven't done a pregnancy test?'

'Funnily enough, no.' She bit her lip. 'It's not exactly easy for me to slip into a chemist back home to buy myself a kit. Somebody might recognise me.'

He wanted to say, *You should have thought of that before you let me strip you naked and lead you to my bed.* But he was culpable too, wasn't he? He had deflected the advances of women before and it had never been a problem. So why hadn't he sent this one on her way? Why hadn't he read any of the glaring clues which had warned him she was trouble? Had the subterfuge of her disguise and the fact that she was being pursued by bodyguards turned him on? Brought colourful fantasy into a life which was usually so cool and ordered?

'I used a condom,' he bit out.

Like a snake gathering strength before striking again, she drew her shoulders back and glared at him with angry blue eyes. 'Are you seriously suggesting that somebody other than you could be the father, Gabe?'

He remembered the way her trembling hand had circled his erection until he had been forced to push it away, afraid he might come before he was inside her. Had she inflicted some microscopic tear in the condom with those long fingernails of hers? *And had that been deliberate?*

But he pushed those thoughts away, because nothing was certain. And a man could drive himself insane if he started thinking that way.

'I'm not suggesting anything, because at the moment all we have is a hypothetical situation,' he said. 'And we're not doing anything until we have facts. There could be a million reasons why your period is late and I'm not going to waste time thinking about some nightmare scenario which might never happen.'

Nightmare scenario.

Leila flinched as his words cut into her like the nicks of a dozen tiny blades. That was all this was to him. *Remember that. Hold that thought in your mind and never forget it. A nightmare scenario.*

Had she thought that he would make everything all right? That he would sweep her into his arms as men sometimes did in films and stroke her hair, before telling her that she had no need to worry and he would take care of everything?

Maybe she had. Maybe part of her had still bought into that helpless feminine fantasy, despite everything she knew about men and the way they treated women.

'Perhaps you could go and buy a pregnancy test for me,' she suggested, staring out at the dark sky, which was punctured by tiny stars. 'Since I find the thought of braving the London shops a little too much to contemplate at the moment.'

Something small and trembling in her voice made Gabe's eyes narrow in unwilling comprehension. He wasn't used to picturing himself inside the skin of a woman—except in the most erotic sense—but he did so now. He tried to imagine this pampered princess transplanted to a foreign country, bringing with her this terrible secret. How must it feel to give such momentous news to a man who did not want to receive it?

'We're not having some do-it-yourself session,' he said flatly. 'I will make an appointment for you to see someone in Harley Street tomorrow.'

Her eyes were suddenly wide and frightened.

'But somebody might tip off the press if I am seen going to the doctor's. And my brother mustn't find out. At least, not in that way.'

'Haven't you ever heard of the Hippocratic oath?' he questioned impatiently. 'And patient confidentiality?'

Leila almost laughed. She thought that, for a man of the world, he was being remarkably naive. Or maybe he just didn't realise that royal blood always made the stakes impossibly high. It made the onlooking world act like vultures. Didn't he realise that professional codes of conduct could fall by the wayside, when a royal scoop like this offered an unimaginably high purse?

'I'll take your word for it,' she said.

Gabe watched as she reached for her handbag. She was wearing that same damned raincoat, which reminded him uncomfortably of their erotic encounter in Qurhah. For one tempting moment he entertained the thought of having sex with her again. It had been the most amazing sex of his life and he still couldn't work out why.

Because he had been the first?

Or because her touch had felt like fire on a day when his heart had been as cold as ice?

He remembered the way her long legs had parted eagerly beneath the quest of his hungry fingers. The way she had moaned when he had touched her. He could almost feel the eager warmth of her breath on his shoulder as he'd entered her, as no man had done before. Vividly, he recalled the sensation of tightness and the spots of blood on his sheets afterwards. He closed his eyes as he remembered seeing them spattered there like some kind of trophy. It had felt *primitive*, and he didn't do primitive. He did cool and calculated and reasoned because that was the only way he'd been able to survive.

Pain gnawed at his heart as he tried to regain his equilibrium, but still his body was filled with desire. Wasn't it also primitive—and natural—for a man to want to be deep inside a woman when she'd just told him she might be carrying his child?

His mouth tightened. If he pulled her into his arms and started to kiss her, she would not resist. No woman ever did. He imagined himself reacquainting himself with her scented flesh, because wouldn't that help him make some kind of sense of this bizarre situation?

'Leila,' he said, but she had stood up very quickly and was brushing her hand dismissively over the sleeve of her raincoat, in a gesture which seemed more symbolic than necessary.

'I must get back before anyone realises I've gone,' she said.

She walked across to the other side of the room, and Gabe felt the bubble of his erotic fantasy burst as she fixed him with a cool look. For a moment it almost seemed as if she had just rejected his advances—even though he hadn't actually *made* any.

'Phone me at my hotel and tell me where to meet you tomorrow,' she said. 'I will have to use Sara as a decoy again, but I'm sure I can manage it.'

'I'm sure you can,' he said with the grim air of a man whose whole world was about to change, whether he wanted it to or not.

CHAPTER FIVE

'So,' SAID LEILA slowly. The word was tiny and meant nothing at all, but one of them had to say *something*. Something to shatter the tense, taut silence which had descended on them the moment they'd left the consulting room. Something to make Gabe move again instead of sitting there frozen, staring out of the windscreen as if he had just seen some kind of ghost.

He had brought the car to a halt in a wide, tree-lined street, and Leila was glad he'd driven away from the Harley Street clinic which had just delivered the news she had already known.

He hadn't said a thing—not a thing—but she'd noticed the way his hands had tightened around the steering wheel, and the ashen hue which had drained his face of all colour.

She was pregnant.

Very newly pregnant—but pregnant all the same.

A new life growing was beneath a heart now racing as she waited—though she wasn't really sure what she was waiting for.

She remembered Gabe's barely perceptible intake of breath as the expensively dressed consultant had delivered the results of the test. The doctor had looked at them with the benign and faintly indulgent smile he obviously reserved for this kind of situation. Probably imagining they were yet another rich young couple eager to hear what he had to say. Had he noticed the lack of a wedding ring on her finger? Did anyone actually care about that kind of thing these days? She swallowed. They certainly did in Qurhah.

She wondered if the medic had been perceptive enough to read the body language which existed between the prospective parents. Or rather, the lack of it. She and Gabe had sat upright on adjoining antique chairs facing the medic's desk, their shoulders tense. Close, yet completely distant—like two strangers who had been put into a room to hear the most intimate of information.

But that was all they were really, wasn't it?

Two strangers who had created a life out of a moment of passion.

She turned in the low sports car to glance at Gabe. She didn't know what to do. What to say or how to cope. She wanted something to make it better, but she realised that nothing could. Something unplanned and ill-advised had resulted in both their lives being changed—*and neither of them wanted this*.

The sunlight illuminated his chiselled features, casting deep shadows beneath the high slash of his cheekbones. But still he hadn't moved. His profile was utterly motionless, as if it had been carved from a piece of golden dark marble.

She knew she couldn't keep sitting there like some sort of obedient chattel, waiting for his thoughts on what had happened. She wasn't in Qurhah now. No longer did she have to play the role of subservient female. She had always longed for equality—and this was what it was supposed to be about. Taking control of her own destiny. Learning to express her own feelings instead of waiting for guidance and approval from a man.

Knotting her fingers together in a tight fist, she knew something else, too. That she didn't want this icy-eyed Englishman to feel that she had trapped him. What kind of a man was he who could sit there like a statue in the face of such news? Didn't he feel *any-thing*? 'Whatever happens, I'm not going to ask you for anything,' she said. 'You must understand that.'

Gabe didn't answer straight away—and not just because her accented words sounded as disjointed as if she had been speaking them in her native tongue. He had learnt when to be silent and when to speak. Once—a long time ago—he had given in to the temptation of hot-headedness. But never again. It had been the most brutal lesson and one he had never forgotten. And then, when he'd started out in advertising and was clawing his way up the slippery slope towards success, he had learnt that you should never respond until you were certain you had the right answer.

Except that this time, he couldn't see that there *was* a right answer. Only a swirling selection of options—and none of them were good. The facts were unassailable. A woman with a baby and a man who did not wish to become a father.

Who should never become a father.

He felt a dark dread begin to creep over his heart as he wondered whether history always repeated itself. Whether humans were driven by some biological imperative over which they had no control. Driven to make the same mistakes over and over again.

'Not here,' he said, his voice tight with restraint. 'I don't intend discussing something as important as this in the front seat of a car. Do up your seat belt and let's go.'

But he could see that her hands were trembling as she struggled to perform the simple action. He leaned forward to help her, and her proximity left him momentarily disorientated. The warmth radiating from her body seemed to have intensified the spicy scent of her perfume. The sunlight was bouncing off the ebony gloss of her hair and her lips looked so unbelievably kissable that he was left with the dull ache of longing inside him.

And wanting her would only complicate things. It would cloud his mind and his judgement at a time when he needed to think clearly.

Clipping in the seat belt, he quickly moved away from the temptation she presented and started up the engine.

For a while they were silent as they stop-started through the busy streets, where outside the world carried on as normal. While inside...

He shot her a glance and saw that her face looked as white as chalk and he found himself unexpectedly shocked at the sight of her physical frailty. 'Have you eaten?' he demanded.

She shook her head. 'I'm not hungry.'

'You should be. You haven't had any lunch.' And neither had he. The morning had passed in a dazed kind of blur ever since he'd met Leila at the Harley

Street clinic, where she had been dropped off by Sara, a princess who had once worked for him.

He was still remembering the look on his assistant's face this morning when he'd told her to clear his diary for the rest of the day. Surprise didn't even come close to it. He could just imagine the gossip reverberating around the building as people started second-guessing why Gabe Steel had done the unimaginable and taken an unscheduled day off work.

And when they knew? When they discovered that the man who was famous for never committing was to become a father? What then?

'You need to eat,' he said implacably.

'I don't want anything,' she said. 'I feel sick. I've felt sick for over a month.'

'Is that intended to make me feel guilty, Leila? Because you'd better know that I won't accept all the blame.' He sent out a warning toot on his horn, and the cyclist who had shot out from a side road responded with a rude gesture. 'If you hadn't come on to me in a weak moment, then we wouldn't have found ourselves in this intolerable situation.'

Wondering briefly what the weak moment had been, Leila leaned her head back against the seat as the cool venom of his words washed over her. Yet, she couldn't really condemn him for speaking the truth, could she? It *was* intolerable—and there wasn't a thing that was going to make it better. A wave of panic hit her and the now-familiar refrain echoed around in her head.

She was ruined.

Ruined.

Outside the car window, London passed by but she

barely noticed the brand-new city which should have
excited her. She felt like an invisible speck of dust
being blown along and she didn't know where she
was going to end up. She was with a man who did not
want her but was forced to be with her, because she
carried his child within her belly.

'Where are you taking me?' she asked.

'To my apartment.'

She shook her head. 'I can't be seen at your apartment. My brother might find out.'

'Your brother is going to have to find out sooner
or later—and this isn't about him or his reaction to
what's happening. Not any more. This is about you.'
And me, he thought reluctantly. *Me*.

Without another word he drove to his apartment
and parked in the underground garage before they
took the elevator to his apartment. The rooms seemed
both strange yet familiar and Leila felt disorientated
as she walked inside. As if she was a different person
from the one who had arrived here in the early hours
of this morning.

But she was.

Yesterday nothing had been certain and there had
still been an element of hope in her heart, no matter how misplaced. But with the doctor's diagnosis,
that hope had gone and nothing would ever be the
same. Never again would she simply be Leila, the
princess sister of the Sultan. Soon she would be Leila,
the mother of an illegitimate child—a baby fathered
by the tycoon Gabe Steel.

The man who had never wanted to see her again.

She tried to imagine her brother's fury when she
found out but it was hard to picture the full extent of

his predictable rage. Would he strip her of her title? Banish her from the only land and home she had ever known? And if he did—what then? She tried to imagine supporting herself and a tiny baby. How would she manage that when she'd never even *held* a baby?

She was so preoccupied with the tumult of her thoughts that it took her a few minutes to realise that Gabe had left her alone in his stark sitting room. He returned a little while later with his suit jacket removed and the sleeves of his shirt rolled up. She noticed his powerful forearms with their smattering of dark golden hair and remembered the way he had slid them around her naked waist. And wasn't that a wildly inappropriate thing to remember at a time like this?

'I've made us something to eat,' he said. 'Come through to the dining room.'

His words made Leila's sense of disorientation increase because she came from a culture where men didn't cook. Where they had nothing to do with the preparation of food—unless you counted hunting it down in the desert and then killing it.

She told herself that he wasn't listening to what she'd said—and she'd said she wasn't hungry. But it seemed rude to sit here on her own while he ate and so she followed him into the dining room.

This was not a comfortable room either. He was clearly a fan of minimalism, and the furniture looked like something you might find in the pages of an architectural magazine. Tea and sandwiches sat on a table constructed from dull metal, around which was a circle of hard, matching chairs. The table sat beneath the harsh glare of the skylight, which made Leila think she was about to be interrogated.

And maybe that wasn't such a bad idea. She certainly had a few questions she needed to put to the man now pushing a plate of food towards her.

She held up the palm of her hand. 'I don't—'

'Just try,' he interrupted. 'Is that too much to ask, Leila?'

The hard timbre of his voice had softened into something which sounded almost gentle and the way he said her name suddenly made her feel horribly vulnerable. Or maybe she was imagining that. Maybe she was looking for crumbs of comfort when all he was doing was being practical. She realised that she felt weak and that if she didn't look after herself she would get weaker still. And she couldn't afford to do that.

So she ate most of the sandwich and drank a cup of jasmine tea before pushing away her plate. Leaning back against the hard iron chair, she crossed her arms defensively over her chest and studied him.

She drew in a deep breath. 'You can rest assured that I don't expect anything from you, Gabe. You've made your feelings absolutely plain. That afternoon was a mistake—we both know that. We were never intended to be together and this…this *baby* doesn't have to change that. I want you to know that you're free to walk away. And that I can manage on my own—'

'What are you planning to do?' The question fired from his mouth like a blistering fusillade of shots. 'To get rid of it?'

The accusation appalled her almost as much as the thought that he should think her capable of such an action, and Leila glared at him. *He doesn't know you*, she realised bitterly. *He doesn't even* like *you*.

'How dare you make a suggestion like that?' she

said, unable to keep the anger from her voice. 'I'm not ready to be a mother. I'm not sure I ever wanted to *be* a mother, but it seems that fate has decided otherwise. And I will accept that fate,' she added fiercely. 'I will have this baby and I will look after him—or her. And nothing and no one will stop me.'

Some of the tension had left him, but his mouth was still unsmiling as his gaze raked over her face. 'And just how are you planning to go about that?' he demanded. 'You who are a protected and pampered princess who can't move around freely unless under cover of darkness. What are you going to tell your brother? And how are you intending to support your-self when the child comes?'

She wished there were some place to look other than at his eyes, because they were distracting her. They were reminding her of how soft and luminous they'd been when he had held her in his arms. They were making her long for things she could never have. Things like love and warmth and closeness. A man to cradle her and tell her that everything was going to be all right.

But she didn't dare shift her gaze away from his, because wouldn't that be a sign of a weakness? A weakness she dared not show. Not to him. Not to her brother. Not to anyone. Because from here on in she must be strong.

Strong.

'I have jewellery I can sell,' she said.

His smile was faint. 'Of course you do.'

She heard the sardonic note in his voice. Another *rich princess* reference, she thought bitterly. 'Things my mother left me,' she added.

'And how do you propose getting your hands on this jewellery?' he questioned. 'Are you planning to take a trip to Qurhah and smuggle it out of the safe? Or perhaps you're thinking of asking your brother to mail it to you?'

'I could probably…I might be able to get one of my servants to get it to me,' she said unconvincingly. 'It would be risky, of course, but I'm sure it could be doable.'

Gabe gave a short laugh. Of all the women who could have ended up carrying his baby, it had to be her. A spoiled little rich girl who just snapped her beautiful fingers and suddenly money appeared. Did she really think it was going to be that easy?

His customary cool composure momentarily deserting him, he leaned across the table towards her. 'Do you really think your brother will be amenable to you taking funds out of the country to support an illegitimate baby?'

Her face seemed to crumple at the word, and Gabe felt a brief twist of regret that he had spoken to her so harshly. But she needed to confront the truth—no matter how unpalatable she found it.

'You have to face facts, Leila,' he said. 'And you're not going to find this easy. At some point you're going to have to tell your brother what's happened.' He saw the way her eyelids slid down to conceal the sudden brightness of her eyes, the thick lashes forming two ebony arcs which feathered against her skin. 'Have you thought about what his reaction might be?'

'I have thought of little else!'

'So what are you planning to tell him?'

The lashes fluttered open and the look in her eyes

was defiant, though the faint tremble of her lips less so. 'Oh, I won't mention your name, if that's what you're worried about.'

'I am not frightened of your brother, Leila. And neither am I denying what happened—no matter how much I might now regret it.' His mouth hardened. 'I'm asking what you are intending to tell Murat.'

She didn't answer for a moment and when she did, her voice was heavy. 'I guess I'm going to have to tell him the truth.'

'Or your unique version of the truth?' he questioned wryly. 'Won't the Sultan think that his sister's innocence has been compromised by a man with enough experience to have known better? It might suit your purpose—and his—to convince him that you were taken advantage of by an Englishman with something of a reputation where the opposite sex is concerned. Mightn't it be more acceptable for him to think of you as a victim rather than a predator?'

'I'm no victim, Gabe!' she flared back. 'And I'm no predator either, no matter how much it suits *you* to think that. I certainly didn't plan to seduce you—I was a virgin, for heaven's sake! I just…just gave into the "chemistry" you were talking about. And you certainly didn't seem to be objecting at the time.'

'No, you're right. I didn't put up much in the way of a fight.' His face tightened—as if her words were taking him some place he didn't want to go. 'But your brother is going to wonder when and where this great love affair of ours took place.'

She flushed. 'Obviously, he doesn't know that I came to your hotel room.'

'Actually, you came *in* my hotel room,' he reminded

her sardonically. 'Don't forget that part of the story, Leila—because it's probably the best part of all.'

Her flush deepened as his words brought back memories of the way it had been that day. The way he had kissed her and told her she was beautiful. In those few brief and glorious moments, she'd thought she'd found her heart's desire. For a short while she had felt as perfect as it was possible to feel.

But those feelings were in the past and they had been nothing but fantasy. All that was left was the brittle reality of the present—so why torture herself by remembering something which had been so fleeting?

'That's irrelevant,' she said. 'And I'm not scared of my brother.' But then some of her bravado left her. Tiredly, she lifted up her hands and buried her face in them as the warm darkness enveloped her like a welcoming cloak.

'Leila?' His voice was suddenly soft. 'Are you *crying*?'

'No, I am *not*!' she said fiercely, but she kept her face hidden all the same.

'Then look at me,' he commanded.

Rebellion flared inside her. She didn't *want* to look at him because, although there were no tears, she was afraid of what he might be able to read in her eyes. She didn't want to expose her sense of deflation and defeat. The liberated woman she'd yearned to be seemed to have slipped away into the shadows and was nowhere to be seen. And she had no one to blame but herself. She had gone to a *known playboy's* bedroom and let him kiss her. Why had she thought that having sex with a total stranger was somehow *empowering*?

'I have a solution,' he said.

His words broke into her thoughts. She lowered her hands but her head remained bent—as if she had found something uniquely fascinating to look at on the dark denim of her jeans. 'You have a magic wand with the power to turn back time, do you?'

'Unfortunately, I'm clean out of magic wands, so it looks like I'll just have to marry you instead.'

At this, her head jerked up, her gaze meeting his in disbelief. 'What?'

'You heard. And you're clever enough to realise it's the only option. I have no choice, other than to make you my wife—because I can see it would be intolerably cruel to let a woman like you face this on your own.' His eyes glittered like ice. 'Because you are not on your own. I share equal responsibility for what has happened, although you are a princess while I am…'

His face grew taut and Leila saw the sudden flare of pain which had darkened his grey eyes.

'You're what?' she prompted breathlessly.

For a moment he said nothing. A sudden darkness passed over his face, but just as quickly it was gone. The billionaire tycoon was back in control.

'It doesn't matter. For obvious reasons, this child cannot be born illegitimate. You will not need to hide your head in shame, Leila. I didn't ever want to be a husband.' His cool eyes flashed silver. 'Or a father. But as you say—fate seems to have decided otherwise. And I will accept that fate. We will be married as soon as possible.'

It should have been the dream solution but to Leila it felt like no such thing. She didn't want to marry a man who looked as if he were destined for a trip to the gallows, or to live with the realisation that she had trapped him into a life he didn't want. She couldn't imagine ever bonding with this icy *stranger*.

'I won't do it,' she said stubbornly. 'I won't tie myself to a man who doesn't want me. And you can't make me marry you.'

'You think not?' The smile he gave did not meet his eyes. 'You'd be surprised what I can do if I set my mind to it—but I'm hoping that we can come to some kind of *amicable* agreement. These are the only terms I am offering and I'd advise you to accept them. Because you're not really in any position to object. Your brother will disown you if you don't and I doubt whether you have a clue how to look after yourself. Not in a strange city without your servants and bodyguards to accede to your every whim. You cannot subject a baby to a life like that and I won't allow you to, because this is my baby too. You will marry me, Leila, because there is no alternative.'

CHAPTER SIX

LEILA STARED INTO the full-length mirror at someone who looked just like her. Who moved just like her. A woman who was startlingly familiar yet who seemed like a total stranger.

She was eight weeks pregnant by a man who didn't love her and today was her wedding day.

She glanced around the luxury hotel room to which she would never return. Her suitcases had already been collected by Gabe's driver and taken to his riverside apartment, which was to be her new home after she became his wife. She thought about the bare rooms and the minimalist decor which awaited her. She thought about the harsh, clear light which flooded in from the river. As if such a soulless place as that could ever be described as home!

He had asked her to be his bride, yet he had made her feel as if she was an unwanted piece of baggage he had been forced to carry. She had eventually—and reluctantly—agreed with him that marriage seemed to be the only sensible solution, when his phone had begun to ring. *And he had answered it!* He had left her sitting there as if she'd been invisible while he had conducted a long and boring business call right in front of her. It had not been a good omen—or an encouraging sign about the way he treated women.

Inside she had been seething, but what could she do? She could hardly storm out onto the unknown streets of London—or rush back to the safety of Qurhah, where nobody would want a princess who had brought shame onto her family name. She had felt trapped—and her heart had sunk like a heavy stone which had been dropped into a river. Was she destined to feel trapped for the rest of her days, no matter where in the world she lived?

Her reflected image stared back at her and she regarded it almost objectively. Her bridal dress of cobalt-blue was sleek and concealing and the hotel hairdresser had woven crimson roses into her black hair. She had refused to wear white on principle. It hadn't seemed appropriate in the circumstances. Much too romantic a gesture for such an occasion as this—because what was romantic about an expectant bride being taken reluctantly by a man who had no desire to be married to her?

Yet didn't some stupid part of her wish that it could all be different? Didn't she wish she were floating along on a happy pink cloud, the way brides were *supposed* to do? Maybe all those books and films she'd devoured during her lonely life at the palace had left their mark on her after all. She had no illusions about men or marriage, but that didn't stop her from wanting the dream—like some teenager who still believed that anything was possible.

But at least this was to be a quiet wedding. And a quick wedding—which had presented more of a problem.

The three-week wait required by English law had not been practical for a couple in their situation. As a desert princess, she could not live with Gabe and she had no desire to spend weeks in limbo at the Granchester Hotel, no matter how luxurious her suite there. Short of flying to Vegas, the only alternative was to get married in the Qurhahian Embassy in London—for which she needed her brother's permission. And she hadn't wanted to ask him, because she hadn't wanted to tell him why she needed to marry the Englishman in such a rush.

Yet she'd known she was going to have to break the news to Murat some time, hadn't she? She'd known she was going to have to tell him she was having Gabe's baby—so how could he refuse to grant her use of the embassy? She knew—and he knew—that the niece or nephew of the Sultan could not be born outside wedlock.

It had been the most difficult conversation of her life—not helped by the fact that it had been conducted by telephone. Her nervous stammering had been halted by Gabe taking the phone from her and quietly telling the Sultan that he intended to marry her. She wasn't sure what Murat actually said in response because Gabe had just stood there and listened to what sounded like an angry tirade thundering down the line.

But the Englishman had stood his ground and, after calmly reasserting his determination to take her as his bride, had handed the phone back to Leila.

Beneath Gabe's grey gaze, she had explained to Murat that while she would prefer to do this with his blessing, she was perfectly prepared to do it without.

Such a wait would, of course, mean living with a man who was not her husband.

The Sultan had sounded shocked—as much by her attitude as by her words—for she was aware that few people ever openly defied him. But unexpectedly, his voice had softened and for a moment he had sounded just like the Murat she'd thought no longer existed. The one she'd seen all those years ago, after their mother had died. When for once he had let down his guard and Leila had sobbed in his arms until there were no tears left to cry. And afterwards she'd noticed his own damp cheeks and seen the grief which had ravaged his dark face.

That was the only time in her life she had seen her brother showing emotion until now, when he asked her a question which came out of nowhere.

'And do you love him, Leila?' he had asked her quietly. 'This man Gabe Steel.'

Leila had closed her eyes and walked to the far end of the room, knowing that a lie was the only acceptable answer. A lie would make Murat leave them alone. A lie would confer an odd kind of blessing on this strange marriage.

'Yes,' she had answered in a low voice, glad that Gabe was not within earshot. 'Yes, I love him.'

And that had been that. Blessing conferred. They were given permission to use the embassy although Murat told her he would not be attending the nuptials himself.

In fact, the ceremony was to have only two witnesses—Sara and her husband, Suleiman, who had also known Leila since she had been a child. A relatively informal lunch following the ceremony was to be their only celebration. Time had been too tight to arrange anything else, although Gabe told her that a bigger party for his colleagues and friends could be arranged later, if she was so inclined.

Was she? She didn't know any of his colleagues or friends. She knew hardly anything about him—and in truth he seemed to want it to stay that way. It was as if the man she was marrying was an undiscovered country—one which she had suddenly found herself inhabiting without use of a compass. She was used to men who told women little—or nothing—but this was different. She was having his baby, for heaven's sake—and surely that gave her some sort of *right* to know.

On the eve of their wedding, they had been eating an early dinner in the Granchester's award-winning rooftop restaurant when she'd plucked up enough courage to ask him a few questions.

'You haven't mentioned your parents, Gabe.'

His expression had been as cold as snow. 'That's because they're dead. I'm an orphan, Leila—just like you.'

The cool finality in his tone had been intimidating but she wasn't going to give up that easily. She had put down her glass of fizzy water and looked him squarely in the eyes.

'What about brother or sisters?'

'Sadly, there's none. Just me.' The smile which had followed this statement had been mocking. 'Tell me, did you bring your camera to England with you?'

The change of subject had been so abrupt that Leila had blinked at him in confusion. 'No. I left Qurhah in such a hurry that my camera was the last thing on my mind.'

'Pity. I thought it might have given you something to do.'

'I'm going to buy myself a new one,' she said defensively.

'Good.'

It was only afterwards that she realised he had very effectively managed to halt her line in questioning, with the adroitness of a man who was a master of concealment.

But now was not the moment to dwell on all the things which were missing from their relationship, because Sara had arrived to accompany her to the embassy for the wedding and Leila knew she must push her troubled thoughts aside. She must pin a bright smile to her lips and be prepared to play the part expected of her. Because if Sara guessed at her deep misgivings about the marriage, then mightn't she try to talk her out of it?

They embraced warmly and Sara's smile was soft as she pulled away and studied her. 'You look utterly exquisite, Leila,' she said. 'I hope Gabe knows what a lucky man he is.'

Somehow, Leila produced an answering smile. Lucky? She knew Sara had guessed the truth—that she was newly pregnant with Gabe's baby. But Sara wasn't aware that the thought of having a baby didn't scare her nearly as much as the fact that she was marrying a man who seemed determined to remain a stranger to her. She thought of his shuttered manner. The way he had batted back her questions as if she had no right to ask them. How could she possibly cope with living with such a man?

Yet as she made a final adjustment to her flowered headdress she felt a little stab of determination. Couldn't she break through the emotional barriers which Gabe Steel had erected around his heart? She had come this far—too far—to be dismissed as if what she wanted didn't matter. Because it *did* matter. *She* mattered. And no matter how impossible it seemed, she knew what was top of her wish-list. She wanted Gabe to be close to her and their baby. She'd had enough of families who lived their lives in separate little boxes—she'd done that all her life. Sometimes what you wanted didn't just *happen*—you had to reach out and grab it for yourself. And grab it she would.

'Let's hope he does,' she said with a smile as she picked up her bouquet.

But her new-found determination couldn't quite dampen down her flutter of nerves as the car took her and Sara to Grosvenor Square, where Gabe was standing on the steps waiting for her.

She thought how formidably gorgeous he looked as he came forward to greet her. Toweringly tall in a charcoal suit which contrasted with the dark gold of his hair, he seemed all power and strength. She told herself she wouldn't have been human if her body hadn't begun to tremble with excitement in response to him.

But he was only standing there because he had no choice.

Because she was carrying his baby.

That was all.

'Hello, Leila,' he said.

Her apprehension diminished a little as she saw the momentary darkening of his quicksilver eyes. 'Hello, Gabe,' she answered.

'You look…incredible.'

The compliment took her off-guard and so did the way he said it. Her fingers fluttered upwards to check the positioning of the crimson flowers in her hair. 'Do I?'

Gabe read the uncertainty in her eyes and knew that he could blot it out with a kiss. But he didn't want to kiss her. Not now and not in public. Not with all these damned embassy officials hovering around, giving him those narrow-eyed looks of suspicion, as they'd been doing ever since he'd arrived. He wondered if they resented their beautiful princess marrying a man from outside their own culture. Or whether they guessed this was a marriage born of necessity, rather than of love.

Love.

He hoped his exquisite bride wasn't entertaining any fantasies about love—and maybe he needed to spell that out for her. To start as he meant to go on. With the truth. To tell her that he was incapable of love. That he had ice for a heart and a dark hole for a soul. That he broke women's hearts without meaning to.

His mouth hardened.

Would he break hers, too?

CHAPTER SEVEN

THE MARRIAGE CEREMONY was conducted in both Qurhahian and English, and Gabe reflected more than once that the royal connection might have intimidated many men. But he was not easily intimidated and essentially it was the same as any other wedding he'd ever been to. He and Leila obediently repeated words which had been written by someone else. He slid a gleaming ring onto her finger and they signed a register, although his new wife's signature was embellished with a royal crest stamped into a deep blob of scarlet wax.

She put the pen down and rose gracefully from the seat, but as he took her hand in his he could feel her trembling and he found his fingers tightening around hers to give her an encouraging squeeze.

'You are now man and wife,' said the official, his robed figure outlined against the indigo and golden hues of the Qurhahian flag.

Sara and Suleiman smilingly offered their congratulations as soft sounds of Qurhahian *Takht* music began to play. Servants appeared as if by clockwork, bearing trays of the national drink—a bittersweet combination of pomegranate juice mixed with zest of lime. After this they were all led into a formal dining room, where a wedding breakfast awaited them, served on a table festooned with crimson roses and golden goblets studded with rubies.

Leila found herself feeling disorientated as she sat down opposite Suleiman and began to pick at the familiar Qurhahian food which was presented to her. The enormity of all that had happened to her should have been enough to occupy her thoughts during the meal. But all she could think about was the powerful presence of her new husband and to wonder what kind of future lay ahead.

Who *was* Gabe Steel? she wondered as she stabbed at a sliver of mango with her fork. She listened to him talking to Sara about the world of advertising and then slipping effortlessly into a conversation about oil prices with Suleiman. He was playing his part perfectly, she thought. Nobody would ever have guessed that this was a man who had effectively been shotgunned into marriage.

He must have sensed her watching him, for he suddenly reached out his hand and laid it on top of hers, and Leila couldn't prevent an involuntary shiver of pleasure in response. It had been weeks since he'd touched her, and she revelled in the feeling of his warm flesh against hers—but the gesture felt more dutiful than meaningful. She couldn't stop noticing the way Suleiman and Sara were with each other. The way they hung off the other's every word and finished each other's sentences. She felt a tug of wistfulness in her heart. Their marriage was so obviously a love-match and it seemed to mock the emptiness of the relationship she shared with Gabe.

She turned to find his cool grey gaze on hers.

'Enjoying yourself?' he said.

She wondered what he would say if she told him the truth. That she felt blindsided with bewilderment about the future and fearful of being married to a man who gave nothing away.

But Leila was a princess who had been taught never to show her feelings in public. She could play her part as well as he was playing his. She could make her reply just as non-committal as the cool question he'd asked.

'It's been a very interesting day,' she conceded.

Unexpectedly, he gave a low laugh—as if her un-emotional response had pleased him. He bent his lips to her ear. 'I think we might leave soon, don't you?'

'I think that might be acceptable,' she said, swallowing in an effort to shift the sudden dryness in her throat.

'I think so too,' he agreed. 'So let's say goodbye to our guests and go.'

The unmistakeable intent which edged his words made Leila's heart race with excitement. But hot on that flare of anticipation came apprehension, because the sex they'd shared that afternoon in Qurhah now seemed like a distant dream.

What would it be like to make love with him again after everything that had happened? What if this time it was a disappointment—what then? Because she suspected that a man as experienced as Gabe would not tolerate a wife who didn't excite him. Wasn't that why men in the desert kept harems—to ensure that their sexual appetites were always gratified? Wasn't it said in Qurhah that no one woman could ever satisfy a man?

Her heart was pounding erratically as he led her outside to his waiting car. Leila slid inside and the quicksilver gleam of his eyes was brighter than her new platinum wedding ring as he joined her on the back seat. Suddenly, she imagined what her life might have been like if Gabe had refused to marry her, as he could so easily have done. She imagined her brother's fury and her country's sense of shame and she felt a stab of gratitude towards the Englishman with the hard body and the dark golden hair.

'Thank you,' she said quietly.

'For what?'

'Oh, you know.' She kept her voice light. 'For saving me from a life of certain ruin—that sort of thing.'

He gave a short laugh. 'I did it because I had to. No other reason. Don't start thinking of me as some benign saviour with nothing but noble intentions in his heart. Because that man does not exist. I'm a cold-hearted bastard, Leila—or so your sex have been telling me all my adult life. And since that is unlikely to change, it's better that I put you straight right from the start. The truth might hurt, but sometimes it's a kinder pain than telling lies. Do you understand?'

'Sure,' said Leila, her voice studiedly cool as her fingers dug into the wedding bouquet which she would have liked to squash against his cold and impassive face. Couldn't the truth have waited for another day? Couldn't he have allowed her one day of fantasy before the harshness of reality hit them? But men only did that kind of mushy stuff in films. Never in real life.

'But understand something else,' he added softly.

'That my lack of emotion does not affect my desire for you. I have thought of nothing else but you and although I badly want to kiss you, you'll have to wait a little while longer. Because while I'm fairly confident the press haven't got hold of this story, I can't guarantee that the paparazzi aren't lying in wait outside my apartment. And we don't want them picturing you getting out of the car looking completely ravaged, do we, my beautiful blue-eyed princess?'

'We certainly don't,' said Leila, still reeling from his cold character assessment—followed by those contrasting heated words of desire.

But there were no paparazzi outside the apartment—just the porter who'd been sitting behind the desk the first time she'd been here and who now smiled as they walked into the foyer.

'Congratulations, Mr Steel,' the man said, with the tone of someone who realised that normal deference could be relaxed on such a day. 'Aren't you going to carry the lady over the threshold?'

Gabe gave a ghost of a smile as he stared down into Leila's eyes. 'My wife doesn't like heights,' he said. 'Do you, darling?'

'Oh, I absolutely loathe them,' she said without a flicker of reaction.

But irrationally, she felt a stab of disappointment as they rode upstairs in the elevator. Despite what he'd said in the car, it wouldn't have hurt him to play the part of adoring groom in front of the porter, would it? They said that men fantasised about sex—well, didn't he realise that women did the same thing about weddings, no matter how foolish that might be?

'Why are you frowning?' he questioned as the door of his apartment swung silently shut behind them.

'You wouldn't understand.'

Tilting her chin with his finger, he put her eyes on a collision course with his. 'Try me.'

She tried all right. She tried to ignore the sizzle of her skin as he touched her, but it was impossible. Even that featherlight brush of his finger on her chin was distracting. Everything about him was distracting. Yet his grey eyes were curious—as if he was genuinely interested in her reasons. And wasn't that as good a start as any to this bizarre marriage?

So start by telling him what it is you want. He has just advocated the use of truth, so tell him. Tell him the truth. She held his gaze. 'If you must know, I quite liked the idea of being carried over the threshold.'

Dark eyebrows arched. 'I thought you might find it hypocritical under the circumstances.'

'Maybe it is.' She shrugged. 'It's just that I've never been carried anywhere before—well, presumably I was, as a baby. But not as an adult and never by a man. And this might be the only stab at it I get.'

'Oh, I see,' he said. He took the bouquet from her hand and placed it on a nearby table. 'Would carrying you to bed compensate for my shocking omission as a bridegroom?'

She met the glitter of his eyes and excitement began to whisper over her skin. He was flirting with her, she realised. And maybe she ought to flirt right back. 'I don't know,' she said doubtfully. 'We could try it out and see.'

He gave a flicker of a smile as he bent and slid one arm under her knees, picking her up with an ease

which didn't surprise her. Leila might have been tall
for a woman but Gabe made her feel tiny. He made
her feel all soft and yearning. He made her feel things
she had no right to feel. Her arms fastened themselves
around his neck as he carried her along a long, curving corridor into his bedroom.

She'd only been in here once before to unpack her
clothes and find a home for her shoes. But then, as
now—she had been slightly overwhelmed by the es-
sential *masculinity* of the room. A vast bed was the
centrepiece—and everything else seemed to be concealed. Wardrobes and drawers were tucked away out
of sight, and she could see why. Any kind of clutter
would have detracted from the floor-to-ceiling windows which commanded such a spectacular view over
the river.

She tried to imagine bringing a baby into this stark
environment and felt curiously exposed as he set her
down on her gleaming wedding shoes.

'Won't we…be seen?' she questioned, her gaze
darting over his shoulder as he began to unfasten her
dress.

'The windows are made specially so that people
can't see in from the outside,' he murmured. 'Like car
windows. So there's no need to worry.'

But Leila had plenty to worry about. The first time
they'd done this, there had been no time to think. This
time around and she'd done nothing *but* think. How
many women had stood where she had stood? Women
who were far more experienced than she was. Who
would have known where to touch him and how to
please him.

His fingers had loosened some of the fastenings,

and the dress slid down to her waist, leaving her torso bare. She felt *exposed*. And vulnerable. He bent his head to kiss her shoulder, but she couldn't help stiffening as he traced the tip of his tongue along the arrowing bone.

He drew his head away from her and frowned. 'What's wrong?'

'I don't know. This feels so...' Awkwardly, her words trailed off. She could pretend that nothing was wrong but she remembered what he'd said in the car. That the truth could hurt, but lies could hurt even more. And if she kept piling on layer after layer of fake stuff, her life would be reduced to one big falsehood. In a marriage such as theirs—wasn't the truth the only way to safeguard her sanity? 'So cold-blooded,' she said.

'You're nervous?'

'I guess so.'

'You weren't nervous last time.'

'I know.' She licked her lips. 'But last time felt different.'

'How?'

'Because we weren't thinking or analysing. There was no big agenda. No frightening future yawning ahead of us. It just...happened. Almost like it was meant to happen.'

For a moment she wondered if she'd said too much. Whether that final sentence had sounded like the hopeless yearning of an impressionable young woman. The truth was all very well, but she didn't want to come over as *needy*.

He stroked his hand down over her cheek and moved it round to her neck. His grey eyes narrowed and then suddenly he dug his fingers into her hair and brought his mouth down on hers in a crushing kiss.

It was the kiss which changed everything. The kiss which ignited the fire. All the pent-up emotion she'd kept inside for weeks was now set free. And suddenly it didn't matter that Gabe had warned her about having ice for a heart because, for now at least, he was all heat and flame and maybe that was enough to melt him.

She clung to him as his mouth explored hers, and he began to pull the pins from her hair. Silken strands spilled down around her shoulders, one after another. She could feel them tickling her back as they fell. Cool air was washing over her skin as he unclipped her bra and her breasts sprang free.

He stopped kissing her and stood for a moment, just observing her. And then, very deliberately, he reached out and cupped a breast in the palm of his hand, his eyes not leaving her face as he rotated his thumb against the nipple.

'Gabe,' she said indistinctly.

'What?' The thumb was replaced by the brush of his lips as he bent his head to the super-sensitive nub, and Leila closed her eyes as pleasure washed over her. Her senses felt raw and alive—as if he'd just rehabilitated them from a long sleep. She reached towards his shirt buttons, but the effort of undoing even one seemed too arduous when his hand was skimming so possessively over her waist and touching the bare skin there.

With a low laugh which sounded close to a growl, he freed the last fastenings of her dress and let it slide to the ground.

Stepping out from the circle of concertinaed silk, she looked up at his dark face, and something about his expression made her heart miss a beat. All her doubts and fears were suddenly replaced by something infinitely more dangerous. Something which had happened the last time she'd been in this situation. Because wasn't there something about Gabe Steel which called out to her on a level she didn't really understand? Something which made her feel powerful and vulnerable all at the same time.

He was a cool English billionaire who could have just thrown her to the wolves. Who could have rejected his child and made her face the consequences on her own. But he had done no such thing. He had been prepared to shoulder the heavy burden of responsibility she had placed upon his shoulders. Gabe Steel was not a bad man, she decided. He might be a very elusive and secretive one—but he was capable of compassion. And wasn't she now better placed than any other female on the planet to discover more about a person who had captivated her from the start? Couldn't she do that?

Her torpor suddenly left her as she reached towards his shirt and began to slide the buttons from their confinement. Her confidence grew as she felt his body grow tense. She could hear nothing but the laboured sound of his breathing as she opened up his shirt and feasted her eyes on the perfection of the golden skin beneath.

Bending her head, she flickered her tongue at his tight, salty nipple and she felt a sharp thrill as she heard him groan. She had never undressed a man before—but how difficult could it be? She tugged the charcoal jacket from his shoulders and let it fall on top of her discarded wedding dress. The shirt followed— so that now he was completely bare-chested, like those men she'd seen fighting for coins in one of the provincial market squares outside Simdahab.

Undoing the top button of his trousers, she was momentarily daunted by the hardness beneath the fine cloth, which made unzipping him awkward. But his fingers covered hers, and he guided her hand down over the rocky ridge, and Leila's heartbeat soared, because that shared movement felt so gloriously intimate.

With growing confidence, she dealt with his socks and shoes—and he returned the favour by easing her out of her panties and stockings.

Before long, they were both completely naked, standing face to face next to the bed. His hands were splayed over her bottom and her breasts were brushing against his chest. She could feel his erection nudging her belly and the answering wetness of her sex as she wrapped her arms around his neck.

'Are you sure we can't be seen?' she whispered.

'Why, is that your secret fantasy?' he questioned, pushing her down onto the soft mattress. 'People watching and seeing what a *naughty* princess you can be?'

Leila said nothing as his mouth moved to her neck and he moved his hand between her legs. She closed her eyes and tried to concentrate on the stroking movement of his fingers. But even intense pleasure could not completely obliterate the sudden troubled skitter of her thoughts. Was this what playboy lov-

ers enjoyed most, she wondered—to share fantasies?
Didn't he realise that she was still too much of a novice to have any real fantasies?

His eyes were dark as he moved over her, but
she could see the sudden tautness of his mouth. She
wondered if he was wishing that this were just un-
complicated sex. That he was not tied to her for the
foreseeable future, and that there was not a baby on
the way.

'Is something *wrong*?' she whispered.

'Wrong?' he echoed unsteadily. 'Are you out of
your mind? I'm just savouring every delicious moment. Because for the first time in my life I don't
have to worry about contraception. I'll be able to feel
my bare skin inside you—and it's a very liberating
feeling.'

His description sounded more mechanical than af-
fectionate but Leila told herself to be grateful for his
honesty. At least he wasn't coating his words with
false sentiment and filling her with false hopes. And
why spoil this moment by wishing for the impossible,
instead of enjoying every incredible second?

Tipping her head back, she revelled in the sensation of what he was doing to her.

The way his lips were moving over hers.

The way his fingers played so distractingly over
her skin, setting up flickers of reaction wherever they
alighted.

The way he…

'Oh, Gabe,' she breathed as she felt him brushing
intimately against her.

Slowly, he eased himself inside her, the almost-entry of his moist tip followed by one long, silken thrust. For a moment he stilled and allowed her body to adjust to him.

'I'm not hurting you?' he questioned.

Hurting her? That was the last thing he was doing. She was aware that he fitted her as perfectly as the last piece of a jigsaw puzzle which had just been slotted into place. She had never felt as complete as she did in that moment, and wouldn't the cool Gabe Steel be horrified if he knew she was thinking that way?

'No,' she breathed, shaking her head. 'You're not hurting me.'

'And does it feel—different?'

She met the smoky question in his eyes. 'Different?'

'Because of the baby?'

Would it terrify him if she told him that yes, it did? That it felt unbelievably profound to have his flesh inside her, while their combined flesh grew deep in her belly. Much too profound for comfort. She pressed her lips against the dark rasp of his jaw.

'I don't really have enough experience for comparison,' she whispered.

He tilted her face upwards so that all she could see was the gleam of his silver gaze. 'That sounds like a blatant invitation to provide you with a little more.'

'D-does it?'

'Mmm. So I think I'd better do just that, don't you?'

She gasped as he began a slow, sweet rhythm inside her. Her fingertips slid greedily over the silken skin which cloaked his moving muscles. Eagerly, she began to explore the contours of his body—the power of his rock-hard legs and the taut globes of his buttocks.

She felt part of him.

All of him.

She felt in that moment as if anything was possible.

'Gabe,' she moaned, her body beginning to tense.

His mouth grazed hers. 'Tell me.'

'I c-can't.'

'Tell me,' he urged again.

'Oh. *Oh!*'

Gabe felt her buck beneath him in helpless rapture. His mouth came down hard on hers as her back arched, his fingers tightening over her narrow hips. He became aware of the softness of her belly as he pressed against her and then he let go—spilling his seed into her with each long and exquisite thrust.

For a while he was aware of nothing other than the fading spasms deep within his body and a sense of emptiness and of torpor. Automatically, he rolled away onto the other side of the bed where he lay on top of the rumpled sheet and sucked mouthfuls of air back into his lungs. His eyelids felt as if they'd been weighted with lead. He wanted to sleep. To sleep for a hundred years. To hold on to a sensation which felt peculiarly close to contentment.

But old habits died hard and he fought the feeling and the warm place which was beckoning to him, automatically replacing it with ice-cold logic. All he was experiencing was the stupefying effect of hormones as his body gathered up its resources to make love to her again. It was sex, that was all. Surprisingly good sex—but nothing more than that. How could it ever be more than that?

Meeting her bright blue gaze, he flickered her a non-commital smile.

'What a perfect way to begin a honeymoon,' he drawled.

CHAPTER EIGHT

It was a honeymoon of sorts.

Leila supposed that some people might even have considered it a successful honeymoon. With time and money at his disposal, Gabe set about showing her a London she'd only ever seen in films or books—and the famous city came to life before her eyes.

They visited Buckingham Palace and the famous Tower where two young princes had once been imprisoned. They took a ride on a double-decker bus, which thrilled Leila since she'd never been on public transport before. They went to galleries and museums and saw some of the long-running West End shows.

He showed her a 'secret' London too—a side to the city known only to the people who lived in it. Restaurants with flower-filled courtyards which were tucked away behind industrial grey streets and intimate concert halls where he took her to hear exquisite classical music.

And when they weren't sightseeing they were having sex. Lots of it. Inventive, imaginative and mind-blowing sex, which left her gasping and breathless with pleasure every time. She told herself she was lucky—and when she was kissing her gorgeous new husband, she *felt* lucky.

But while she couldn't fault the packed schedule Gabe had arranged for her, sometimes it felt as if she were spending time with a tour guide. Sometimes he was so…*distant*. So…*forbidding*. She would ask him questions designed to understand him better. And he would find a million ways not to answer them. He would change the subject and ask her about growing up in Qurhah. And although he seemed genuinely interested in her life as a princess, sometimes he made her feel as if she was a brand new project he was determined to get right.

He remained as enigmatic as he'd done right from the very beginning. She had married a man who kept his thoughts and feelings concealed and inevitably, that made anxiety start to bubble away beneath the glossy surface of her new life.

It was only during sex that she ever felt on the brink of a closeness which constantly eluded her. When he was making love he sometimes looked down at her, his face raw with passion and his eyes flaring with pewter fire. She wanted him to tell her what it was that kept him so firmly locked away from her. She wanted to look within his heart and see what secrets it revealed. But as soon as his orgasm racked his powerful body, she could sense him distancing himself again.

Oh, he would hold her tightly and bury his lips against her damp skin and tell her that she was amazing. Once he even told her that she was the best lover he'd ever had. But to Leila, his words seemed empty and she was scared to believe them. As if he was saying them because he knew he ought to say them, rather than because he meant them.

She would lie there hugging her still-trembling body while he went off to take a shower, forcing herself to remember that she was only here because of the life growing inside her. A life so new that sometimes it didn't seem as if it were real...

One morning they were lying amid a tumble of sex-scented sheets after a long and satisfying night of lovemaking, when she rolled onto her stomach and looked at him.

'You know, you've never even told me how you made your fortune.'

He stretched out his lean, tanned body and yawned. 'It's a dull story.'

'Every story has a point of interest.'

He looked at her. 'Why do you ask so many questions, Leila? You're always digging, aren't you?'

She met his cool gaze. 'Maybe I wouldn't keep asking if you actually tried answering some of them for a change.'

She could see the wariness in his eyes, but for once she refused to be silenced or seduced into changing the subject. Even if their marriage wasn't 'real' in the way that Sara and Suleiman's was—didn't her position as his wife give her some kind of right to know? To find out whether, beneath that cool facade, Gabe Steel had a few vulnerabilities of his own?

'So tell me,' she murmured and dropped a kiss on his bare shoulder. 'Go on.'

Gabe sighed as he felt her soft lips brushing against his skin. He had never planned to marry her. He hadn't wanted to marry her. Reluctantly, he had taken what he considered to be the best course of action in circumstances which could have ruined her. He had done the right thing by her. Yet instead of showing her gratitude by melting quietly into the background and making herself as unobtrusive as possible, she had proved a major form of distraction in ways he had never anticipated.

From the moment she opened her eyes in the morning to the moment those long black lashes fluttered to a close at night, she mesmerised him in all kinds of ways.

The way she rose naked from the rumpled sheets—a tall, striking Venus with caramel skin and endless legs. The reverse-heart swing of her naked bottom as she wiggled it out of the room. The way she slanted him that blue-eyed look, which instantly had his blood boiling with lust.

But he knew that women often mistook a man's lust for love; and that lust always faded. In the normal scheme of things, that wouldn't matter, but with Leila it did. He couldn't afford to let her fall in love with him and have the all too predictable angry outcome when she realised it wasn't ever going to be reciprocated. He didn't want to hurt her. He didn't want her to start thinking that he could feel things, like other men did. She was the mother of his child and she wasn't going anywhere. He might not have wanted to become a father, but he was going to make damned sure that this baby was an enduring part of his life. Which he guessed was why he found himself saying, 'What exactly do you want to know?'

'Tell me how you first got into advertising,' she said. 'Surely that's not too difficult.'

'Look it up on the internet,' he said.

'I already have.' She remembered how she'd checked him out before that fateful meeting in Simdahab. 'And although there's lots of stuff about you winning awards and riding motorbikes and being pictured with some of the world's most beautiful women—there's not much in the way of background. Almost as if somebody had been controlling how much information was getting out there.' She stroked her finger down his cheek. 'Is that down to you, Gabe?'

'Of course it is.' His response was economical. 'I'm sure your brother controls information about himself all the time.'

'Ah, but my brother is a sultan who rules an empire and has a lot of enemies. What's your excuse?'

She saw the flicker of irritation which crossed his face—a slightly more exaggerated irritation than the look she'd seen yesterday when he'd discovered a dirty coffee cup sitting on the side of his pristine bathtub and acted as if it were an unexploded bomb.

'My excuse is that I try to remain as private as possible,' he said. 'But I can see that you're not going to let up until you're satisfied. Where shall I begin?'

'Were you born rich?'

'Quite the opposite. Dirt poor, as they say—though I doubt whether someone like you has any comprehension of what that really means.'

His accusation rankled almost as much as his attitude, and Leila couldn't hide her hurt. 'You think because I was born in a palace that I'm stupid? That I have no idea what the vast majority of the world is like? I'm surprised at you, Gabe—leaping to stereotypical judgements like that.'

'Ah, but I'm an advertising man,' he said, a smile curving the edges of his mouth. 'And that's what we do.'

'I think I can work out what *dirt poor* means. I'm just interested to know how you went from that to...' the sweeping gesture of her hand encompassed the vast dimensions of the dining room, with its expensive view of the river '...well, *this*.'

'Fate. Luck. Timing.' He shrugged. 'A mixture of all three.'

'Which as usual tells me precisely nothing.'

He levered himself up against the pillows, his gaze briefly resting on the hard outline of her nipples. He felt the automatic hardening of his groin, wondering if that sudden flare of colour over her cheeks meant that she'd noticed it, too.

'I left school early,' he said. 'I was sixteen, with no qualifications to speak of, so I moved to London and got a job in a big hotel. I started in the kitchens—' He fixed her with a mocking look as he saw her eyes widen. 'Does it shock my princess to realise that her husband was once a kitchen hand?'

'What shocks this particular princess is your unbelievable arrogance,' she said quietly, 'but I'm enjoying the story so much that I'm prepared to overlook it. Do continue.'

She saw another brief flicker of sexual excitement in his eyes, but quickly she dragged the cotton sheet up to cover her breasts. She didn't want him seducing her into silence with his kisses.

'I didn't stay in the kitchens very long,' he said. 'I gravitated to the bar where the buzz was better and the tips were good. A big crowd of guys from a nearby advertising agency used to come in for drinks every Friday night—and they used to fascinate me.'

She stared at him. 'Because?'

For a moment, Gabe didn't answer because it was a long time since he'd thought about those days and those men. He remembered the ease with which they'd slipped credit cards from the pockets of their bespoke suits. He remembered their artful haircuts and the year-round tans which spoke of winter sun—at a time in his life when he'd never even had a foreign holiday.

'I wanted to be like them,' he said, in as candid an admission as he'd ever made to anyone. 'It seemed more like fun than work—and I felt I was owed a little fun. They would sit around and brainstorm and angst if they were short of creative ideas. They didn't really notice me hanging around and listening. They used to talk as if I wasn't there.' And hadn't it been that invisibility which had spurred him on—even more than his determination to break free from the poverty and heartbreak which had ended his childhood so abruptly? The sense that they had treated him like a nothing and he'd wanted to be someone.

'They had a deadline looming and a slogan for a shampoo ad which still hadn't been written,' he continued. 'I made a suggestion—and I remember that they looked at me as if I'd just fallen to earth. Some teenage boy with cheap shoes telling them what they should write. But it was a good suggestion. Actually, it was a brilliant suggestion—and they made me a cash offer to use it. The TV campaign went ahead using my splash line, the product flew off the shelves and they offered me a job.'

He remembered how surprised they'd been when he

had coolly negotiated the terms of his contract, instead of snatching at their offer, which was what they'd clearly expected. They'd told him that his youth and his inexperience gave him no room for negotiation, but still he hadn't given way. He had recognised that he had a talent and that much was non-negotiable. It had been his first and most important lesson in bargaining—to acknowledge his own self-worth. And they had signed, as he had known all along they would do.

'Then what happened?'

Gabe shrugged as her soft words floated into his head and tangled themselves up with his memories. He had often wondered about the particular mix of ingredients which had combined to make him such a spectacular success, yet the reasons were quite simple.

He was good with words and good with clients. A childhood spent honing the art of subterfuge had served him well in the business he had chosen. His rise to the top had been made with almost seamless ease. His prediction that digital technology was the way forward had proved unerringly correct. He had formed his own small company and before long a much bigger agency had wanted to buy his expertise. He had expanded and prospered. He'd discovered that wealth begot wealth. And that being rich changed nothing. That you were still the same person underneath, with the same dark and heavy heart.

'I just happened to be in the right place at the right time,' he said dismissively, because thoughts of the past inevitably brought with them pain. And he tried not to do pain. Didn't he sometimes feel that he'd bitten off his allotted quota of the stuff, all in one large and unpalatable chunk? He gave her a long, cool look.

'So if the interrogation is over, Leila, you might like to think about what you want to do today.'

Leila stiffened, her enjoyment of his story stifled by the sudden closure in his voice. Was this what all men did with women? she wondered as she swung her legs over the side of the bed and grabbed a tiny T-shirt and a pair of panties. Tell them just enough to keep them satisfied, but nothing more than that? Keep them at arm's length unless they were making love to them?

But she *knew* all this, didn't she? None of these facts should have surprised her. She'd seen the way her father had treated her mother. She'd seen how quickly women became expendable once their initial allure had worn off. So why the hell was she grasping at rainbows which didn't exist?

She tugged on the T-shirt and pulled on her panties before walking towards the window, suddenly unenthusiastic about the day ahead.

'Why don't you surprise me?' she said flatly. 'Since you're the man with all the ideas.'

She didn't hear the footfall of his bare feet straight away. She didn't even realise he was following her until his shadow fell over her and she turned round to meet the tight mask of his face. She could see the smoulder of sexual hunger in his eyes, but she could see the dark flicker of something else, too.

'What kind of surprise do you want, Leila?'

She could feel the beat of sexual tension as it thrummed in the air around them. He was angry with her for probing, she realised—and his anger was manifesting itself in hot waves of sexual desire. She told herself that she should walk away from him and that might make him realise that sometimes he treated her more like an object than a person. But she couldn't walk away. She didn't want to. And didn't they both want exactly the same thing? The only thing in which they were truly compatible...

She met the smoulder of his gaze and let the tip of her tongue slide along her bottom lip. 'If I tell you then it won't be a surprise, will it?'

'My, how quickly you've learnt to flirt,' he observed softly, his eyes following the movement hypnotically. 'My little Qurhahian virgin hasn't retained much of her innocence, has she?'

'I sincerely hope not,' she returned, 'because a wife who lacks sexual adventure will quickly lose her allure. The women of the harem learn that to their peril.'

Her assertion seemed to surprise him, for his eyes narrowed in response. His gaze drifted down to where the tiny T-shirt strained over her aching nipples.

'You are dressed for sex,' he said huskily.

She tilted her chin. 'I'm hardly dressed at all.'

'Precisely.'

He took a step towards her and backed her into the sitting room towards the L-shaped sofa which dominated one side of the room, and Leila felt excited by the dark look on his face, which made him appear almost *savage*.

She could feel the leather of the sofa sticking to her bare thighs as he pushed her down on it, and her heart began to hammer in anticipation.

'Gabe?' she said, because now he was kneeling on the ground in front of her and pulling her panties all the way down.

But he didn't answer. He was too busy parting her

knees and moving his head between them and, although this was not the first time he had done this, it had never felt quite so intense before.

'Gabe,' she said again, more breathlessly this time as his tongue began to slide its way up towards the molten ache between her legs.

'Shut up,' he said roughly.

But his harsh words were not matched by the exquisite lightness of his touch, and she couldn't help the gasp of pleasure which was torn from her lips. Her eyelids fluttered to a close as she felt the silkiness of his hair brushing against her thighs. Her lips dried as the tip of his tongue flickered against her heated flesh and she groaned.

She felt helpless beneath him—and for a moment the feeling was so intense that she felt a sudden jolt of fear. She tried to wriggle away but he wouldn't let her. He was imprisoning her hips with the grasp of his hands while he worked some kind of sweet torture with his tongue. And surely if she wanted him to stop, she shouldn't be urging him on by uttering his name. Nor clutching at his shoulders with greedy and frantic hands.

She could feel her orgasm building and then suddenly it happened violently, almost without warning. Her fingers dug into his hair as she began to buck beneath him and just when it should have been over, it wasn't over at all.

Because Gabe was climbing on top of her and straddling her—entering her with one hard, slick stroke which seemed to impale her. Gabe was moving inside her, and she was crying out his name again and tears were trickling down her cheeks—and what on earth was *that* all about? She wiped them away before he could see them.

Automatically, she clung to him as he shuddered inside her, his golden-dark head coming to rest on her shoulder and his ragged breath warm against her skin. She found herself thinking that one of life's paradoxes was that intense pleasure always made you aware of your own capacity for intense pain. And wasn't that what had scared her? The certainty that pain was lurking just around the corner and she wasn't sure why.

She closed her eyes and it seemed a long while before he spoke, and when he did his words were muffled against her neck.

'I suppose you're now going to demand some sort of apology.'

She turned her head to face him. She saw his thick lashes flutter open and caught a glimpse of the darkness which still lingered in his eyes. 'I'm not sure that making a woman moan with pleasure warrants an apology,' she said.

His face tightened as he withdrew from her and rolled onto his back, staring up at the ceiling and the dancing light which was reflected back from the river outside. He gave a heavy sigh. 'Maybe it does if that pleasure comes from anger. Or if sex becomes a demonstration of power, rather than desire.'

She didn't need to ask what had made him angry because she knew. Her questions had irritated a man who liked to keep his past hidden. A man who recoiled from real intimacy in the same way that people snatched their hands away from the lick of a flame and she still didn't know why.

Maybe she should just accept that she was wasting her time. Leila's hand crept to her still-flat stomach. Shouldn't she be thinking about her baby's needs and the practicalities of her current life, rather than trying to get close to a man who was determined not to let her?

But something made her reach out her hand and to lay it softly over the thud of his heart. 'Well, whatever your motivation was, we both enjoyed it—unless I'm very much mistaken.'

At this he turned his head, and his grey eyes were thoughtful as he studied her. 'Sometimes you surprise me, Leila.'

'Do I?'

'More frequently than I would ever have anticipated.' He stroked his hand over the curve of her hips. 'You know, we ought to think what you're going to do next week.'

'Next week?' She drew her head back and looked at him. 'Why—what's happening next week?'

'I'm going back to work. Remember?' He kissed the curve of her jaw. 'Honeymoons don't last for ever and I do have to work to pay the bills, you know.'

Suddenly she felt unsettled. Displaced. 'And in the meantime, I'm going to be here on my own all day,' she said slowly.

His grey eyes were suddenly watchful. 'Not necessarily. I can speak to some of my directors, if you like. Introduce you to their wives so you can get to know them. Some of them work outside the home, but plenty of them are around during the day—some with young children.'

Her heart suddenly heavy, Leila nodded. She didn't want to seem ungrateful and, yes, it would be good to meet women whose company she might soon welcome once her own baby arrived.

But Gabe's words made her feel like an irrelevance. As if she had no real identity of her own. Someone's daughter. Someone's sister and, now, someone's wife.

Well, she *did* exist as a relevant person in her own right and maybe she needed to show Gabe that—as well as to prove it to herself. Back in Qurhah, she had yearned for both personal and professional freedom and surely this was her golden opportunity to grab them.

'I don't want to just kill time while I wait for the baby to be born,' she said. 'I want a job.'

His eyes narrowed. 'A job?'

'Oh, come on, Gabe. Don't look so shocked. Wasn't that what I wanted the first time I ever met you?' She lifted her hand and touched the dark-gold of his hair. 'You thought my photos were good when I first showed them to you. You told me so—and I'd like to think you meant it. Wouldn't your company have work for someone with talent?'

'No,' he said.

Flat refusal was something Leila was used to, but it was no less infuriating when it was delivered so emphatically by her husband. She felt the hot rush of rebellion in her veins. 'I'm not asking you to pull any strings for me,' she said fiercely. 'Just show my work to someone in your company—anonymously, of course—and let them be the judge.'

'No,' he said again.

'You can't keep saying no!'

'I can say any damned thing I please. You're asking *me* for a job, Leila—remember? And I'm telling you that you can't have one. That's the way it works when you're an employer.'

She stared at him mulishly and thought that, at times, Gabe's attitude could be as severe as her brother's. 'Why not?' she demanded. 'I'd like to know exactly what it is you're objecting to. The accusations of nepotism, which won't stand up if I get the job on my own merits? Or is it something else—something you're not telling me?'

Gabe got off the sofa and began to walk towards the bedroom, shaking his head as if denying her question consideration. She thought that he was going to leave the room without answering when he suddenly turned back and it was only then that she realised that he was completely naked. And completely aroused. Again.

'It's your proximity I'm having a problem with,' he declared heatedly, wondering how she managed to get under his skin time and time again. 'I'll have to be with you the whole damned time, won't I? In the car. In the canteen—'

'Standing by the water cooler?' Her mouth twitched. 'Or does some minion bring you water on a silver tray in a crystal glass?'

'We're talking about my life—not yours, princess!' he iced back. 'And how can someone judge your work when you don't have it? You haven't even brought your portfolio with you, have you? You left it in Qurhah.'

'Yes, I did. But I have all the images on a USB stick,' she said sweetly. 'So that won't be a problem.'

Gabe made a stifled sound of fury as he walked away towards the bathroom, wishing for the first time ever that he had a door to slam. But he had chosen the apartment because there *were* no doors. Because one room flowed straight into the next, each characterised by a disproportionate amount of light and space. He had chosen it because it was the antithesis of the places he'd inhabited during his childhood—and now the very determined Princess Leila Scheherazade was making him want to lock himself away. She was invading his space even more than she had already done. And there didn't seem to be a damned thing he could do to stop it.

He would have someone show her portfolio to Alastair McDavid—at Zeitgeist's in-house photographic studio. And he would just have to hope that Alastair found her work *good*—if not quite good enough.

He turned on the shower and his mouth hardened as the punishing jets of icy water began to rain down on him. Because something told him that his hopes were futile and that Leila would soon have her exquisite foot in yet another door.

CHAPTER NINE

THE PANORAMIC VIEW outside his penthouse office gave him a moment's respite before Gabe refocused his gaze on the woman who was sitting at the other side of his desk.

Of course his hopes had been futile. And *of course* Leila got the job she'd secretly been lusting after. Leaning back in his swivel chair, he looked into the excited sparkle of his wife's blue eyes. Though maybe that was an understatement. She hadn't just 'got' the job, she had walked it—completely winning over Alastair McDavid, who had described her photos as 'breathtaking' and had suggested to Gabe that they employ her as soon as possible.

Gabe drummed his fingertips on the polished surface of his desk and attempted to speak to her in the same tone he would use to any other employee. But it wasn't easy. The trouble was that he'd never wanted to kiss another employee before. Or to lock the door and remove her clothes as quickly as possible. The X-rated fantasies which were running through his mind were very distracting, and his mouth felt as dry as city pavement in the summer. 'At work, I am your boss,' he said coolly. 'Not your husband or your lover. And I don't want you ever to forget that.'

'I won't.'

'While you are here, you will have nothing to do with the Qurhah campaign.'

'But—'

'No buts, Leila. I'm telling you no—and I mean it. It will only complicate matters. People working on the account might feel inhibited dealing with you—a woman who just happens to be a princess of the principality. Their creativity could be inhibited and that is something I won't tolerate.' He subjected her to a steady look, glad of the large and inhibiting space between them. 'Is that clear?'

'If you say so.'

'I do say so. And—barring some sort of emergency—you will not come to my office again unless you are invited to do so. While you are here at Zeitgeist, you will receive no deferential treatment—not from me, nor from anyone else. You are simply one of the four hundred people I employ. Got that?'

'I think I'm getting the general idea, Gabe.'

Gabe couldn't fail to notice the sardonic note in her voice, just as he couldn't fail to notice the small smile of triumph she was trying to bite back, having got her way as he had guessed all along she would. And maybe he should just try to be more accepting about the way things had turned out. Alastair McDavid was no fool—and he'd said that Leila had an extraordinarily good eye and that her photos were pretty near perfect. Her talent was in no doubt—and, since her work had been submitted anonymously, nobody could accuse him of nepotism.

But Gabe was feeling uncomfortable on all kinds of levels. For the first time ever his personal life had entered the workplace and he didn't like it. He didn't like it one bit. Despite years of occasional temptation and countless invitations, he'd never dated an employee or a client before. He had seen for himself the dangers inherent in that. There had never been some hapless female sobbing her eyes out in the women's washroom because of something *he'd* done. He'd never been subjected to awkward silences when he walked into boardroom meetings, or one of the Zeitgeist dining rooms.

The less people knew about him, the better, and he had worked hard to keep it that way. He was never anything less than professional with his workforce, even though he joined in with 'dress-down Friday' every week and drank champagne in the basement bar next door whenever a new deal was signed. People called him Gabe and, although he was friendly with everyone from the janitor to the company directors, he maintained that crucial personal distance.

But Leila was different.

She looked different.

She sounded different.

She was distracting—not just to him but to any other man with a pulse, it seemed. He had driven her to work this morning—her first morning—and witnessed the almost comical reaction of one of his directors. The man had been so busy staring at her that he had almost driven his car straight into a wall.

Her endless legs had been encased in denim as she'd climbed out of Gabe's low sports car, with one thick, ebony plait dangling down over one shoulder.

In her blue shirt and jeans, she was dressed no differently from any of his other employees, yet she had an indefinable head-turning quality which marked her out from everyone else. Was that because she'd been brought up as a princess? Because she had royal blood from an ancient dynasty pulsing through her veins, which gave her an innate and almost haughty bearing? When he looked at her, didn't he feel a thrill of something like pride to think that such a woman as this was carrying his child? Hadn't he lain there in bed last night just watching her while she slept, thinking how tender she could be, and didn't he sometimes find himself wanting to kiss her for absolutely no reason?

Yet he knew those kinds of thoughts were fraught with danger. They tempted him into blotting out the bitter truth. They ran the risk of allowing himself to believe that he was capable of the same emotions as other men. And he was not.

He frowned, still having difficulty getting his head round the fact that she was sitting in *his* office as if she had every right to be there. 'Anything you want to ask *me*?' he questioned, picking up a pencil and drawing an explosion of small stars on the 'ideas' notepad he always kept open on his desk.

'Do people know I'm pregnant?'

He looked up and narrowed his eyes. 'Why would they?'

'Of course. Why would they?' she repeated, and he thought he heard a trace of indignation in her voice. 'Heaven forbid that you might have told somebody.'

'You think that this is something I should boast about, Leila? That an obviously unplanned pregnancy has resulted in an old-fashioned shotgun marriage?

It hasn't exactly sent my reputation shooting up into the stratosphere.' He gave a dry laugh. 'Up until now, I'd always done a fairly good job of exhibiting forethought and control.'

Pushing back her chair, she stood up, her face suddenly paling beneath the glow of her olive skin. 'You b-bastard,' she whispered. 'You complete and utter bastard.

He'd never heard her use a profanity before. And he'd never seen a look of such unbridled rage on her face before. In an instant he was also on his feet. 'That didn't come out the way it was supposed to.'

'And how was it *supposed to* come out?' She bit her lip. 'You mean you didn't intend to make me sound like some desperate woman determined to get her hooks into you?'

'I was just pointing out that usually I don't mix my personal life with my business life,' he said, raking his fingers through his hair in frustration.

'I think you've made that abundantly clear,' said Leila. 'So if you've finished with your unique take on character assassination cunningly designed as a pep talk, perhaps I could go and start work?'

For once Gabe felt wrong-footed. He saw the hurt look on her face and the stupid thing was that he wanted to kiss her. He wanted to break every one of his own rules and pull her into his arms. He wanted to lose himself in her, the way he always lost himself whenever they made love. But he fought the feeling, telling himself that emotional dependence was a luxury he couldn't afford. He knew that. He knew there were some things in life you could never rely on and that was one of them.

But guilt nagged at him as he saw the stony expression on her face as she turned and walked towards the door. 'Leila?'

She turned around. 'What?'

'I shouldn't have said that.'

Her smile was wry. 'But you did say it, Gabe. That's the trouble. You did.'

Shutting his office door behind her, Leila was still simmering as she walked into the adjoining office to find Alice waiting for her and with an effort she forced herself to calm down. Because what she was *not* going to do was crumble. She could be strong—she knew that. And she needed to be strong—because she was starting to realise that she couldn't rely on Gabe to be there for her.

Oh, he might have put a ring on her finger and made her his wife, but she couldn't quite rid herself of the nagging doubt that this marriage would endure—baby or not.

Pushing her troubled thoughts away, she smiled at Alice. 'Gabe says you're to show me around the Zeitgeist building,' she said. 'Though judging by the size of it, I think I might need a compass to find my way around the place.'

Alice laughed. 'Oh, you'll soon get used to it. Come on, I'll show you the canteen first—that's probably the most important bit. And after that, I'll take you down to the photographic studios.'

Leila quickly learnt that paid employment had all kinds of advantages, the main one being that it didn't give you much opportunity to mope around yearning for what you didn't have.

Overnight, her first real job had begun and, although she was fulfilling a lifetime ambition just by *having* a job, she found it a bit of a shock. She'd grown up in a culture which encompassed both opulence and denial, but she had never set foot in the workplace before. She was unprepared for the sheer exhaustion of being on her feet all day and for being woken by the alarm clock every morning. Quickly, she discovered that dressing at leisure was very different from having to be ready to start work in the studio at eight-thirty. Her lazy honeymoon mornings of slow lovemaking were replaced by frantic clockwatching as she rushed for the shower and grappled with her long hair.

'You don't have to do this, you know,' said Gabe one morning as they sat at some red lights with Leila hastily applying a sweep of mascara to her long lashes.

'What? Wear make-up?'

'Very funny. I'm talking about putting yourself through this ridiculous—'

'Ridiculous what?' she interrupted calmly. 'Attempt to prove that I'm just like everyone else and that I need some sense of purpose in my life? Shock! Horror! Woman goes out to work and wears make-up!'

'What does the doctor say about it?' he growled.

'She's very pleased with my progress,' Leila answered, sliding her mascara back into her handbag. 'And it may surprise you to know that the majority of women work right up until thirty-six weeks.'

She sat back and stared out of the car window, watching the slow progress of the early-morning traffic. Gabe's car was attracting glances, the way it always did. She guessed that, when viewed from the outside, her life looked like the ultimate success story.

As if she 'had it all'. The great job. The gorgeous man. Even a little baby on the way.

From the inside, of course—it was nothing like that. Sometimes she felt as if her marriage was as illusory as the many successful advertising campaigns which Gabe's company had produced. Those ones which depicted the perfect family everyone lusted after with the artfully messy table with Mum and Dad and two children sitting around it, giggling.

Yet everyone at Zeitgeist knew that the model father in the advert was probably gay and that the model mum's supposedly natural beauty was enhanced by hair extensions and breast implants.

No, nothing was ever as it seemed.

Nothing.

Gabe was still Gabe. Compelling, charismatic but ultimately as distant as a lone island viewed from the shoreline. And she realised that was the way he liked it. The way he wanted to keep it. They weren't growing closer, she realised. If anything, they were drifting further apart.

One evening, they arrived back at the apartment after an early dinner out and Gabe went straight to their bedroom to change. Minutes later he reappeared in jeans and a T-shirt, with his face looking like thunder.

'What the hell has been going on?' he demanded. 'Have we been burgled?'

Leila walked over to where he stood, looking at the room behind him with a sinking heart. He had left early for a meeting this morning and somehow she'd slept through the alarm and had woken up really late. Which meant that she had left home in a rush, and it showed—particularly as today was the cleaner's day off.

Automatically, she moved forward and started to pick up some of the discarded clothes which lay like confetti all over the floor. A pair of knickers were lying on his laptop. 'I overslept,' she said, hastily grabbing them from the shiny surface. 'Sorry.'

Her words did nothing to wipe the dark expression from his face, for tonight he seemed to be on some kind of mission to get at her. 'But it isn't just when you oversleep, is it, Leila?' he demanded. 'It's every damned day. I keep finding used coffee cups around the place and apple cores which you forget to throw away. Did nobody ever teach you to tidy up after yourself, or were there always servants scurrying around to pick up after you?'

Leila flinched at the cold accusation ringing from his voice, but how could she possibly justify her general untidiness when his words were true?

'I did have servants, yes.'

'Well, you don't have servants now, and I value my privacy far too much to want any staff moving in—not even when the baby's born. So if we're to carry on living like this, then you're really going to have to learn to start being more tidy.'

The words leapt out at her like sparks from a spitting fire.

If we're to carry on living like this.

Biting her lip, she turned away, but Gabe caught hold of her arm and pulled her against him.

'I'm sorry.'

'It doesn't matter.'

'It does. That came out too harshly. Sometimes I

just…snap,' he said, his head lowering as he made to brush his lips over hers.

But Leila pushed him away. He thought that making love could cure everything—and usually it did. It was always easy to let him kiss her, because his kisses were so amazing that she always succumbed to them immediately. And when she was in his arms he didn't feel quite so remote. When he was deep inside her body, she could allow herself to pretend that everything was just perfect. Yet surely that was like just papering over a widening crack in the wall, instead of addressing the real problem beneath.

Sometimes she felt as if she was being a coward. A coward who was too scared to come out and ask him whether he wanted her out of his life. Too scared that he might say yes.

She went into the bathroom and showered, and when she emerged in a cotton dress which was beginning to feel snug against her expanding waist, it was to find him sipping at a cup of espresso.

He looked up as she entered the room, and suddenly his grey eyes were cool and assessing.

'I have a deal coming up which means that I need to go to the States,' he said. 'Will you be okay here on your own?'

'Of course,' she said brightly, but, coming in the wake of their recent spat, his words sounded ominous.

She walked over to the fridge and poured herself a glass of fizzy water, exaggeratedly wiping the few spilt drops from the work surface before going to perch on one of the bar stools.

'How long will you be gone?' she asked.

'Only a few days.'

Gabe saw the tremble of her lips, which she couldn't quite disguise, and suddenly the coffee in his mouth seemed to taste sour. Yet he knew exactly what he was doing. He was insightful enough to know that he was pushing her away, but astute enough to know that he could offer her no other option. Because the thought of getting close to her was making him *feel* stuff. And that was something he didn't do.

He put down his coffee cup with more force than he intended.

If only it could be different.

His mouth hardened as he stared into the bright blue of her eyes.

It could never be different.

That night they lay on opposite sides of the bed, the heavy silence indicating that neither was asleep, though neither of them spoke. His sleep was fractured, his disturbing dreams forgotten on waking— leaving him with a heavy headache which he couldn't seem to shift.

He was just sliding his cell phone into his jacket pocket when he walked into the sitting room to find Leila looking at his passport, which he'd left lying on the table.

'That's a very sombre photo,' she commented.

'You aren't supposed to smile in passport photos.'

Leila found herself thinking that he wouldn't have much of a problem with that. That unless the situation demanded it, his natural demeanour was unsmiling. Those chiselled cheekbones and cold eyes lent themselves perfectly to an implacable facade.

She glanced down at his birth date and her heart

gave a funny little twist as she glanced back up at him. 'Will you phone me?'

'Of course.' He took the passport from her and brushed his mouth over hers in a brief farewell kiss. 'And I'll be back on Sunday. Keep safe.'

But after he'd gone, all the energy seemed to drain from her. Leila sat down on the sofa and stared into space, her heart thumping like someone who had just run up an entire flight of stairs without stopping. The date on his passport was March fifteenth—the Ides of March. She knew that date. Of course she did. Wasn't it etched firmly in her mind as heralding the biggest change in her life?

She shook her head, telling herself not to be so stupid. It was a coincidence. Of course it was.

Over the next few days, she was grateful to be able to lose herself in the distraction of work—glad that its busy structure gave her little time to dwell on the uncomfortable thoughts which were building like storm clouds in her mind. Alastair McDavid announced that Zeitgeist had just landed a big contract to advertise a nationwide chain of luxury hotels and spas. And since spa clientele consisted mainly of women, it was in everyone's interest to use a female photographer.

'And we'd like to use you, Leila,' he told her with a smile.

Leila was determined not to let him down and the excitement of planning her first solo assignment was almost enough to quell the disquiet which was still niggling away inside her. Almost, but not quite.

Sunday arrived and Gabe texted to say that he was just about to catch his plane. She wished she was in a position to collect him from the airport, but she still hadn't learnt to drive. She had allowed her husband and his chauffeur to ferry her everywhere. It had been all too easy to lean on Gabe—and if she wasn't careful that could get to be a lasting habit.

Because for the first time she was beginning to acknowledge the very real fear that this marriage seemed destined to fail.

She remembered his cold rebuke about her general untidiness, yet she hadn't even factored in what the presence of a tiny baby was going to do to Gabe Steel's ordered existence. What if he hated having a screaming infant in his slick, urban apartment? Wouldn't he get irritated if she went off sex, as she'd been told that new mothers sometimes did?

Her distraction grew as she showered and washed her hair, then picked out a long tunic dress in palest blue silk, which she'd brought with her from Qurhah. She didn't question why she had chosen to wear that particular tunic on that particular day. All she knew was that it covered her body from neck to ankle and she wondered if she was seeking comfort in the familiar.

She pinned her hair into a simple up do and made tea while she tried not to feel as if she was waiting. But she *was* waiting. Waiting for some sort of answer to a question she wasn't sure she wanted to ask.

What was it that they said in Qurhah? That if you disturbed a nest of vipers, then you should expect to get bitten.

She heard the click of the front door opening and the sound of Gabe closing it again. He didn't call her name, but his footsteps echoed on the polished wooden floor as they approached, and her heart began to race as he walked into the room.

For a moment he stood very still and then he came over and kissed her, but she pulled away.

'How's Leila?' he questioned, his eyes narrowing as they stared into her face.

'I'm fine,' she said brightly. 'Shall I make some coffee?'

'I had some on the plane. Any more coffee and I'll be wired for a week.' He glanced down at the stack of unopened mail which was waiting for him before looking up again. 'So what's been happening while I've been away?'

'My...scan went well,' she said carefully, her fingers beginning to pleat at the filmy blue fabric of her tunic. 'And I have some good news. Alastair wants me to do the assignment for the new spa contract.'

'Good.'

She looked up from her fretful pleating and suddenly her throat felt so dry that she could barely get the words out. 'And March fifteenth is your birthday.'

He gave a short laugh. 'Interesting that you should tell me in an almost accusatory manner something I've known all my life.'

She told herself not to be intimidated by the coldness in his voice, nor to freeze beneath the challenge icing from his pewter eyes. 'That's the day we had... sex in Simdahab.'

'And?' His dark eyebrows elevated into two sardonic arcs. 'Aren't I allowed to have sex on my birthday?'

She shook her head. She was still a relative novice when it came to lovemaking, but she was intuitive enough to know that something about him that afternoon had been different. Something she hadn't seen since. There had been something *wild* about his behaviour that day. Something seeking and restless. She chose her words carefully. 'You gave me the distinct impression that having spontaneous sex with someone you'd only just met wasn't your usual style.'

'Maybe you were just too irresistible.'

'Is that true?'

Gabe met the steady stare of her bright blue eyes and, inwardly, he cursed. If she was a casual girlfriend, he would have told her it was none of her business, and then to get out and leave him alone. But Leila was his wife. He couldn't tell her to get out. *And the truth was that he didn't want to.*

He met her eyes. 'No, it's not true,' he said quietly. 'I seduced you that day because I was in Qurhah, a place where it's almost impossible to buy whisky, which is my usual choice of drink on my birthday.' There was a pause. 'And in the absence of the oblivion brought about by alcohol, I opted instead for sex.'

CHAPTER TEN

LEILA STARED INTO eyes as flat as an icy sea as Gabe's words hit her. Her fingernails were digging into the palms of her hands but she barely noticed the physical discomfort—not when this terrible pain was lancing through her heart and making it almost impossible for her to breathe. 'You used me?' she questioned at last. 'Because you couldn't get a drink?'

His laugh was bitter. 'There's no need to be quite so melodramatic about it. People have sex for all kinds of reasons, Leila. Sometimes it's because lust just gets the better of them and sometimes because it makes them forget.' He threw his passport down on the table and looked at her. 'I didn't use you any more than you used me that day. I wanted oblivion and you wanted to experiment. Am I right?'

Leila squirmed beneath the challenge of his gaze because his words were uncomfortably close to the bone. How could she deny his accusation when it was true? She *had* wanted to experiment, yes—but she'd had her reasons. What would he say if she told him that he had seemed to represent everything a man should be? Everything that she'd ever dreamed of.

That for the first time in her life, she'd actually *believed* all those romantic films she'd been hooked on.

Yet, in a way, maybe that had been seeking her own kind of oblivion. She had found pleasure with a devastatingly handsome and sexy man—and for a few brief moments she had forgotten the prison of her palace life. But she hadn't really known him as *Gabe*, had she?

She still didn't.

'What were you seeking to obliterate?' she asked carefully.

'It isn't relevant.'

'Oh, I think it is.' She sucked in a breath and held his gaze as she let it out again. 'Look, I get it,' she said. 'I get that you're a very private man who doesn't want to talk about emotions.'

'So don't ask me.'

She shook her head as she ignored the cold clamp of his words. 'But I *have* to ask you—don't you see? I know all the psychology books say that yesterday is gone. But I don't want to go on like this—not knowing stuff. I'm having your baby, Gabe. Don't you think that gives me the right to know something about your past, as well as the occasional speculation about what our future might hold?'

With an angry shake of his head, Gabe walked over to the window to stare out at one of the most expensive views in the world. It was ironic, he thought. You could buy yourself somewhere high in the sky, which was far away from the madding crowd. But no matter how much you spent or how much you tried to control your life—you could never keep the world completely at bay. You could only try. He could feel the hard beat of his heart as he turned round to face her.

'It isn't relevant,' he said again.

'It *is*,' she argued. 'We can't just keep burying our heads in the sand and pretending this isn't happening, because it is. We're going to have a baby, Gabe. A baby which needs to be cared for. Not just cared for. Loved,' she said, her voice faltering a little.

'Don't look to me for love, Leila,' he said tonelessly. 'I thought I'd made that clear from the beginning.'

'Oh, you did. You made it very clear, and I wouldn't dream of expecting you to love *me*,' she said. 'But surely our baby has the right to expect it. If you can't show our baby love—and believe me when I tell you I'm not judging you if that's the case—then don't I at least have the right to know why?'

For a moment there was silence while Gabe looked at the set of her shoulders and the steady blue gaze which didn't falter beneath his own deliberately forbidding stare. He knew what she wanted. What women always wanted. To find out why he didn't show emotion or even feel it. It was something he'd come up against time and time again—and women were the most tenacious of creatures. Countless numbers had tried—and failed—to work him out. Powerful women, rich women, successful women—they all wanted the one thing which eluded them. They saw his cold heart as a challenge; his emotional isolation as something they wished to triumph over.

Yet Leila's question had not been tinged with ambition—rather with the simple desire to understand. She was the mother of their baby and maybe what she said was true. Maybe she *did* have the right to know what had made him the person he was. But wasn't he scared to let her close? Scared of what might happen if he did?

He surveyed her from between half-shuttered eyes. 'What do you want me to tell you?'

Leila was so surprised at his sudden change of heart that it took a moment before she could speak, and all the time her head was telling her to go easy. Not to scare him off with a fierce interrogation.

'Oh, I don't know,' she said softly. 'All the usual things. Like, where you were born. I don't even know that.'

For a moment, there was silence. It reminded her of the moment before the start of a play, when the whole theatre was quiet and prepared for revelation. And then he began to speak.

'I was born in the south of France. But we moved back to England when I was a baby—to a place called Brighton.'

'Yes, Brighton. I've heard of it.' Leila nodded and began reciting, as if she were reading from a geographical textbook. 'It's a seaside town on the south coast. Is it very beautiful—this Brighton?'

In spite of everything, Gabe gave a glimmer of a smile. At times she seemed so foreign and so *naive* but of course, in many ways, she was. Maybe she thought he came from a background like hers and telling her that he had been born on the French Riviera would only feed into that fantasy.

The truth, he reminded himself. She needed to know the truth.

'Anywhere by the sea has the potential to be beautiful,' he said. 'But, like any town, there are rough parts—and those were the places we lived. Not that we stayed anywhere very long.'

'We?'

'My mother and me.'

'Your father wasn't around?'

Gabe could taste the sudden bitterness in his mouth. He wanted to stop this unwanted interrogation right now, but he realised that these questions were never going to go away unless he answered them.

And wasn't it time he told *someone*?

'No, my father wasn't around,' he said. 'He and my mother split up before I was born. Things ended badly and she brought me back to England, but she had no family of her own and no money. When she met my father, she'd been working as a waitress—and that was all she was qualified to do.'

'So, was your father French?' questioned Leila, thinking that he didn't look French.

He shook his head. 'No. He was Russian.'

Slowly, she nodded, because that made sense. Much more sense. The high, chiselled cheekbones, which made his face look so autocratic and proud. The icy grey eyes. The hair, which looked like dark, molten gold. 'So what kind of childhood did you have?' she asked quietly.

He shrugged, as if it didn't matter. 'It was largely characterised by subterfuge. My mother was always afraid that my father would try to find me and so we were always on the move. Always living just below the radar. Our life was spent running. And hiding.'

If he thought about it, he could still remember the constant sensation of fear. Of looking over his shoulder. Of being told never to give anything away to any stranger he might meet. He had quickly learnt how to appear impenetrable to those he met.

And hadn't the surveillance and masquerade skills he'd acquired stood him in good stead for his future career? He had discovered that the world of advertising was the world of illusion. That what you saw was never quite what you got. The masks he had perfected to keep his identity hidden had been invaluable in his role as a powerful executive. They were what had provided him with his chameleon-like reputation. As careers went, his background had been a perfect fit.

'My mother took what jobs she could,' he said. 'But it was difficult to juggle poorly paid work around childcare and I pretty much brought myself up. I soon learnt to look after myself. To rewire dodgy electrics and to shop for cheap food when the supermarkets were about to close.'

Leila blinked in surprise, because the image he painted was about as far away from the sophisticated billionaire she'd married as it was possible to imagine. But she still thought there was something he wasn't telling her. Some dark secret which was lurking just out of sight. *I need to know this for my baby*, she thought fiercely. *For* our *baby*.

'And?'

His mouth hardened. She saw the flash of something bleak in the depths of his eyes before it was gone again.

'I used to feel indignant that my father had never bothered to look us up. I wondered why he didn't seem to care how his son was doing—or why he'd never once offered to help out financially. It became something of an obsession with me. I used to ask my mother what he was like, but she never wanted to talk about him. And the more she refused to tell me, the more frustrating I found it.'

His words tailed off, and for a moment he said nothing. Leila held her breath but didn't speak, not wanting to break his concentration.

'As I grew older, I became more determined to find out something about him,' he continued. 'I didn't necessarily want to be with him—I just wanted to *know*.'

'Of course you did,' she said.

Their eyes met, and Gabe suddenly got a painful flash of insight. Maybe he'd wanted to know for exactly the same reasons that Leila wanted to know about *him*. Maybe everybody had a fundamental desire to learn about their roots. Or the roots of the child they carried...

'But my mother was scared,' he said. 'I can see that now. She was scared that I would run to a man she feared. That I would choose him over her.' He gave a bitter laugh. 'Of course, I only discovered this afterwards.'

'Afterwards?' she echoed as some grim ending glinted as darkly as thick blotting paper held over the beam of a flashlight.

He nodded, and the way he swallowed made Leila think of barbed wire; of something jagged and sharp lodging in his throat and making his words sound painful and distorted.

'It was the eve of my sixteenth birthday,' he said. 'We were living in this tiny hole of place. It was small and dark and I started wondering what kind of life my father had. Whether he was wealthy. Or whether he was reduced to eating food which was past its sell-by date and shivering like us, because it was the coldest spring in nearly thirty years. So I asked my mother the same question I'd been asking ever since I could remember. Did she have any idea where he was or what he did? And as always, she told me no.'

'And you believed her?' questioned Leila tentatively.

He shrugged. 'I didn't know what to believe, but I was on the brink of adulthood and I couldn't tolerate being fobbed off with evasive answers any more. I told her that the best birthday present she could give me would be to tell me the truth. That either she provided me with some simple facts about my parentage—or I would go and seek my father out myself. And that she should be under no illusion that I would find him. I was probably *harsher* than I should have been, but I had the arrogance of youth and the certainty that what I was doing was right.'

There was complete silence, and Leila's heart pounded painfully as she looked at him, for she had never seen an expression on a man's face like that before. Not even when her brother had returned from that terrible battle with insurgents in Port D'Leo and his two most senior commanders had been slain in front of him. There was a helplessness and a hopelessness glinting in Gabe's eyes which was almost unbearable to observe.

'She said she would tell me the next day, on my birthday. But...'

His words tailed off and Leila knew he didn't want to tell her any more, but she needed to know. *And he needed to say it.* 'But what?'

'I think she meant to tell me,' he said. 'But I also

think she was terrified of the repercussions. Afraid that she might lose me.' His mouth twisted. 'But when I got back from school the next day, she couldn't tell me anything at all because she was dead.'

Leila's heart lurched as she stared at him in alarm, not quite believing what he'd just said. *'Dead?'*

For a long moment, there was silence. 'At first I thought she was just sleeping. I remember thinking that I'd never seen her looking quite so peaceful. And then I saw...I saw the empty pill bottle on the floor.'

Leila's throat constricted as she struggled to say something, imagining the sight which must have greeted the young boy as he arrived home from school. She stared at him in utter disbelief. 'She... *killed herself*?'

'Yes,' he said flatly.

Leila felt a terrible sadness wrap itself around her heart. She had wanted to understand more about Gabe Steel and now she did—but she had never imagined this bleak bitterness at the very heart of his life. She could hardly begin to imagine what it must have been like for him. So that was why he had locked it all away, out of sight. That was why he kept himself apart—why he deliberately put distance between himself and other people.

She was stunned by what he had told her. Yet out of his terrible secret came a sudden growing sense of understanding. No longer did it surprise her that he didn't want to trust or depend on women—because hadn't the most important woman in his life left him?

And lied to him.

'Did you blame yourself?' she asked quietly.

'What do you think?' he bit out, his icy facade now completely shattered.

She saw emotion breaking through—real, raw emotion—and it was so rare that instinctively she went to him and he didn't push her away. He let her hold him. She wrapped her arms around him and hugged him tightly and she could feel his heart beating hard against her breast. Pressing her lips against his ear, she whispered, 'You mustn't blame yourself, Gabe.'

'No?' He pushed her away, like somebody who had learned never to trust words of comfort. 'If I hadn't been so persistent…if I hadn't been so damned stubborn—then my mother wouldn't have felt driven to commit such a desperate act. If I hadn't been so determined to find out about my *father*, she need never have died. She could have lived a contented old age and been cushioned by the wealth I was to acquire, but which she never got to see.'

For a moment Leila didn't answer, wondering if she dared even try. Because how could someone like her possibly empathise with Gabe's rootless childhood and its tragic termination? How could she begin to understand the depths of grief he must have experienced when he was barely out of boyhood? That experience had formed him and, emotionally, it had warped him.

Up until that moment, Leila had often thought herself hard done by. Her parents' marriage had been awful—everyone at court had known that. Her father had spent most of his time with his harem, while her mother had sat at home heartbroken—too distracted to focus on her only daughter. As if to compensate for that, Leila had been pampered and protected by her royal status but she had felt trapped by it too. She had been isolated and lost during a childhood almost as lonely as Gabe's.

But his circumstances had been different. He had been left completely on his own. He had lived with his guilt for so long that it had become part of him. 'Your mother must have been desperate to have taken such a drastic action,' she said quietly.

His voice was sardonic. 'I imagine she must have been.'

She stumbled on. 'And she wouldn't want you to carry on blaming yourself.'

'If you say so, Leila.'

She swallowed, because one final piece of the jigsaw was missing. 'And did you ever find your father? Did you track him down?'

There was a heartbeat of a pause before his mouth hardened. 'No.'

'Gabe—'

'No.' He shook his head. 'That's enough. No more questions, Leila. And no more platitudes either. Aren't you satisfied now?'

His eyes were blazing, and she wondered if she'd gone too far. If she'd pushed him to a point where he was likely to break. She wondered if he was going to walk out. To put distance between them, so that when they came face to face again he could pretend that this conversation had never happened.

But he didn't do any of that. Instead, he pulled her back into his arms. He stared down at her for a long moment before bending his head to kiss her— the fiercest kiss she could ever have imagined. She knew what he was doing. He was channelling his hurt and his anger and his pain into sex, because that was what he did. That was how he coped with the heavy burden he carried.

Leila clung to him, kissing him back with all the passion she was capable of, because she wanted him just as much. But she wanted so much more than just sex. She ached to give him succour and comfort. She wanted to show him that she was here for him and that she would always be here for him if only he would let her. She would warm his cold and damaged heart with the power of her love. Yes, love. She loved this cold, stubborn husband of hers, no matter how much he tried to withdraw from her.

'Gabe,' she whispered. 'My darling, darling Gabe.'

The breath he let out in response was ragged and that vulnerable sound only added to her determination to show him gentleness. Her hand flew up to the side of his face and, softly, she caressed his jaw. Did her touch soothe him? Was that why his eyelids fluttered to a close, as if he was unspeakably weary? She touched those too, her fingertips whispering tenderly over the lids, the way she had done all that time ago in Simdahab.

Beneath the tiptoeing of her fingers, his powerful body shuddered—shaking like a mighty tree which had been buffeted by a major storm. He opened his eyes and looked at her but there was no ice in his grey eyes now. Only heat and fire.

He picked her up and carried her over to the sofa, and she'd barely made contact with the soft leather before he was impatiently rucking up her filmy blue dress and sliding down her panties. His hand was shaking as he struggled with his own zip, tugging down his trousers with a frustrated little moan.

She was wet and ready for him and there were few preliminaries. But Leila didn't want them; she just wanted Gabe inside her. His fingers parted her slick, moist folds and she gasped as he entered her, closing her eyes as he filled her.

'Gabe,' she said indistinctly, but he didn't answer as he began to move.

It was fast and deep and elemental. It seemed to be about need as much as desire, and Leila found herself responding to him on every level. Whatever he demanded of her, she matched—but she had never kissed him quite as fervently as she did right then.

Afterwards, she collapsed against the heap of the battered cushions, her heart beating erratically as she made shallow little gasps for breath. She turned to look at him, but he had fallen into a deep sleep.

For a while she lay there, just watching the steady rise and fall of his chest. She thought about what he had told her and she flinched with pain as she took her mind back to his terrible story. He had known such darkness and bleakness, but that period of his life was over. He had taken all the secrets from his heart and revealed them to her—and she must not fail him now.

Because Gabe needed to be loved; properly loved. And she could do that. She could definitely do that. She would care for him deeply, but carefully—for fear that this bruised and damaged man might turn away from the full force of her emotions.

She must love him because he needed to be loved and not because she demanded something in return. She might wish for that, but it was not hers to demand.

She snuggled closer, feeling the jut of his hip against her belly. She ran her lips over the roughness of his jaw and then kissed the lobe of his ear as she wrapped her arms tightly around his waist.

'I will love you, Gabe Steel,' she whispered.

But Gabe only stirred restlessly in his sleep.

CHAPTER ELEVEN

THE DISTANT RUMBLE of thunder echoed Leila's troubled thoughts.

Had she thought it would be easy? That Gabe's icy heart would melt simply because he'd revealed all the bitter secrets he'd carried around with him for so long? That he'd instantly morph into the caring, sharing man she longed for him to be?

Maybe she had.

She glanced out of the window. Outside, the tame English skies were brewing what looked like the fiercest storm she had witnessed since she'd been here. Angry grey clouds billowed up behind St Paul's Cathedral and the river was the colour of dark slate.

She had tried to reassure herself with the knowledge that, on the surface, things in their marriage were good. Better than before. She kept telling herself that, as if to accentuate the positive. Gabe was teaching her card games and how to cook eggs, and she was learning to be tidier. He massaged her shoulders at the end of a working day and they'd started going for country walks on the weekend. Her pregnancy was progressing well and she had passed the crucial twelve weeks without incident. Her doctor had told her that she was blooming—and physically she had never felt better.

Her job, too, was more fulfilling than she could ever have anticipated. At first, Leila had suspected that most of the staff at Zeitgeist had been wary of the boss's wife being given a plum role as a photographer, but none of that wariness had lasted. According to Alastair, her outlook was fresh; her approach original—and she got along well with people.

Her photos for the spa campaign had confounded expectation—the expectation being that it was impossible to get an interesting shot of a woman wrapped in a towel.

But somehow Leila had pulled it off. Maybe it was the angle she had used, or the fact that her background had equipped her to understand that a woman didn't have to show lots of flesh in order to look alluring.

'And anyway,' she had said to Gabe as they were driving home from work one evening, 'these spas are trying to appeal to a female audience, not a male one. Which means that we don't always have to portray women with the not-so-subtle subtext that they're constantly thinking about sex.'

'Unlike you, you mean?' he had offered drily.

She had smiled.

Yes, on the surface things were very good.

So why did she feel as if something was missing— as if there was still a great gaping hole in her life which she couldn't fill? Was it because after that awful disclosure about his mother, Gabe had never really let down his guard again? Or because her expectations of a relationship were far more demanding than she'd realised? That she had been lying to herself about not wanting his love in return, when it was pretty obvious that deep down she craved it.

There were moments which gave her hope—when she felt as if they were poised on the brink of a new understanding. When she felt as close to him as it was possible to feel and her heart was filled with joy. Like the other day, when they had been lying in bed, she'd been wrapped in his arms and he'd been kissing the top of her head and the air had felt full of lazy contentment.

But then she'd realised that for the first time she could feel the distinct swell of her belly, even though she was horizontal at the time.

With an excited little squeal, she'd caught hold of his hand and moved it to her stomach. 'Gabe. Feel,' she'd whispered. 'Go on. Feel.'

She knew her husband well enough to realise that he would never give away his true feelings by doing something as obvious as snatching his hand away from her skin, as if he'd just been burned. But she felt his whole body tense as he made the most cursory of explorations, before disentangling himself from her embrace and telling her that he had to make an international call.

So what was going on beneath the surface of that cold and enigmatic face? Leila gave a sigh. She didn't know. You could show a man love, but love only went so far. Love couldn't penetrate brick walls if people were determined to erect them around their hearts. Love could only help heal a person if that person would allow themselves to be healed.

Gabe made her feel as if she'd wrested every secret from him and that he found any more attempts at soul-searching a bore. Maybe she just had to accept that this was as good as it got. That the real intimacy she longed for simply wasn't going to happen.

But that didn't mean she was going to stop loving him.

She turned away from the thundery skyline to where he was lying sprawled out on the leather sofa, and her heart gave a little twist.

She could never stop loving him.

'Gabe?'

'Mmm?'

'I was wondering if we could give a party?'

He looked up and frowned. 'What kind of party?'

'Oh, you know—something revolutionary. Invite some people along, give them food and drink, maybe play a little music. That sort of thing.'

'Very funny.' Stretching his arms above his head, he gave a lazy yawn. 'What exactly did you have in mind?'

She drew in a deep breath. 'Well, we've never really had a wedding party, have we? I mean, we had that lunch with Sara and Suleiman, but that was all. And I've become quite friendly with Alice and a few of the others from work, so I'd quite like to invite them. And then there's my brother. I'd quite like to see him.' She wriggled her shoulders. 'I'd just like a bit of a celebration before the baby comes. Some kind of acknowledgement that the wedding actually happened.'

He didn't answer straight away.

'As long as it's not here,' he said eventually. 'But if you want to hire a hotel or a restaurant, then that's fine by me.'

'Oh, Gabe,' she said, and walked back across the

room to hug him and when she stopped hugging him she could see that he was actually *smiling*.

Leila threw herself into a frenzy of organisation. She booked the award-winning wedding room at the Granchester Hotel and hired a party planner who came highly recommended by Alice.

The party's colour scheme of gold and indigo was chosen to reflect the colours of the Qurhahian flag and the cuisine was intended to offer delicacies from both cultures. A group of barber-shop singers had been booked for a cabaret spot at ten and dozens of fragrant crimson roses were on order.

Responses soon came flooding in. Everyone at Zeitgeist who'd been invited said yes. Sara and Suleiman were going to be there and also Sara's brother. Even Murat accepted his invitation, much to Leila's pleasure and surprise. It seemed that everybody wanted to attend the wedding celebration of a desert princess and a man known for never giving parties. Leila bought a new dress for the occasion—a gorgeous shimmery thing with threads of silver running through a grey silky material, which reminded her of the mercurial hue of Gabe's eyes.

She took off the day before the party but Gabe was tied up with wall-to-wall meetings all morning.

He was frowning as he kissed her goodbye. 'I'll meet you for lunch,' he said. 'And for goodness' sake—calm down, Leila. You're wearing yourself out with this damned party.'

Something in his tone had made her tilt her head back to look at him. 'You do *want* this party, don't you?'

For a moment there was silence and his smile was

faintly rueful as he shook his head. 'I never said I wanted it, did I? I agreed to it because it makes you happy.'

She stared at the door as it closed behind him.

Wanting to make her happy was a step forward, she guessed—even if it made her feel a bit like a child who needed to be placated with a new toy. Like a spoilt little princess who'd stamped her foot and demanded a party. The same spoilt princess who had finally remembered to throw away her apple cores and to remember that there wasn't a squad of servants poised to tidy up after her.

In an effort to subdue her sudden feeling of restlessness, she decided to try a little displacement therapy. Walking over to the concealed wardrobe, she pulled out her new skyscraper grey heels, which were jostling for room with the rest of her shoes. She really was going to have to ask Gabe to give her more cupboard space, since she had far more clothes than he did. Or maybe she should just do the sensible thing and acquire some for herself.

She practised walking around the bedroom in her new shoes and decided that they didn't hurt a bit. Then she jigged around a little and decided they would be fine to dance in. And in spite of all her reservations, she felt a soaring sense of excitement to think that she might get to dance with her husband for the first time ever.

Pulling open one of the wardrobe doors which Gabe rarely used, she was relieved to find it almost empty. She could shift some of her clothes in here. She took off her shoes and bent down to place them neatly on the rack at the bottom, when she noticed the corner of a drawer protruding, spoiling the otherwise perfect symmetry of the wardrobe's sleek interior.

She wondered what drew her eyes to the manila colour of an envelope inside, but it was enough to make her hesitate. Was that why she didn't immediately push the drawer shut, but slowly open it as curiosity got the better of her?

She didn't know why her heart was beating so fast, only that it was. And she didn't know why her husband should have wedged an envelope in some random drawer when he kept all his paperwork in the bureau in his study next door. Fingers trembling, she flipped open the top of the envelope because she could see that inside there were photos. Photos of a man. A stranger, yet…

Her heart missed a beat as she pulled out another photo. This time there were two men and one she recognised instantly because it was Gabe. But of course she recognised the other man too, because his features were unmistakeable.

High, slashed cheekbones. Piercing pewter eyes and dark golden hair. She swallowed. Two men standing outside what looked like a Parisian café. One of them her husband and the other very obviously his father.

But Gabe had never met his father! He'd told her that. She remembered the way his mouth had tightened and the bitter look which had darkened his eyes as he'd said it.

The envelope slipping from her fingers, Leila slid to her knees. He *had* met his father. There was photographic evidence of it right in front of her eyes. He had told her that this marriage would be based on truth, but it seemed that it was based on nothing but a tissue of lies.

Lies.

She felt the acrid taste of bile rising up in her throat and in that moment she felt utter defeat, wondering how she could have been so blind. So *stupid*. They didn't have love, no matter how much she wanted it—and now it seemed that they didn't even have trust either.

But she had ignored all the signs. She had blithely done what women were so good at doing. She had refused to listen to all the things he'd told her, because it hadn't suited her to listen. He'd told her that he didn't do love but she had thought—arrogantly, it seemed now—that she might just be able to change his mind.

And in that showy-off way, she had decided to throw a party which he clearly had no appetite for—*he'd even told her that, too*. She was planning to dress up in her new, shimmery party frock and her slightly too-high grey shoes and to explode into the flower-decked wedding room of the Granchester and make as if it were all okay. As if she were just like every other bride—happy and contented and expecting a baby. But she wasn't, was she?

Maybe she could have been that bride. Maybe she could have settled for sex and affection and companionship, without the magic ingredient of love. She knew that plenty of people were happy enough with that kind of arrangement. But not lies. Because lies were addictive, weren't they? You told one and you might as well tell a million.

The walls felt as if they were closing in on her, even

though they were made of glass. But claustrophobia was all in the mind, wasn't it? Just like trust.

She scrabbled around and found a sweater and pulled it on, because suddenly she was shivering. Shivering as if she'd caught a violent bout of flu. She grabbed her handbag and took the elevator downstairs and the porter she'd seen on her wedding day was there.

She rarely saw him these days, because usually she was rushing past with Gabe, or because they took the elevator straight down to the underground car park. It was as much as she could do to flash him a smile, but something on her face must have alarmed him for he rose to his feet, a look of concern on his face.

'Everything all right, Mrs Steel?'

The unfamiliar use of her married name startled her but, with an effort, Leila pinned a smile to her face. 'I'm fine. I just want some fresh air.'

'Are you sure? Looks like rain,' he said doubtfully.

Yes. And it felt like rain, too. Inside her heart, it felt as if the storm had already broken.

She started walking; she didn't know where. Somewhere. Anywhere. She didn't really pay attention to the route she was taking. She wasn't used to the streets of London, but she didn't care. A reckless gloom came over her. Maybe it was best that she got used to these streets now, so that when she was living on her own she would have a better idea of the geography of the city.

The rain began to fall. Slowly at first and then harder and more relentlessly, but Leila barely felt it, even though after a few minutes she was soaked right through. During the gaps between the loud thunderclaps above her, she could hear her phone vibrating in her handbag, but she ignored it.

She walked and walked until the riverbank became unfamiliar and the houses and shops less glitzy and much closer together. She saw people with angry dogs straining at their leashes. She saw youths huddled in shop doorways sheltering from the rain, dragging cigarette smoke deep into their lungs.

She didn't know how long she'd been walking when she found a café. Her wet hair hung in stringy rat's tails as she sat dripping in a steamy corner and ordered a mug of strong tea. Her phone began to ring and, uninterestedly, she pulled it out. She saw that it was Alice and that she had four missed calls—three of them from Gabe.

She pressed the answer button. 'Hello.'

'Leila, is that you?' Alice sounded frantic.

'Yep. It's me.'

'Are you okay? Gabe's been going out of his mind with worry. He says he hasn't been able to get hold of you.'

Leila stared at the steam which rose from her mug like smoke from a bonfire. 'I'm fine,' she said tiredly. 'I just needed some fresh air.'

'Leila.' Alice's voice now dipped to soft and cautious. 'Where *are* you?'

'It doesn't matter.'

'It does. You sound…strange. Let me send a car for you.'

'No.'

'Then at least tell me where you are,' pleaded Alice. 'Just to put my mind at rest.'

Wearily, Leila looked down at the laminated menu

and gave the name of the café. She would leave before Alice had a chance to send anyone, which was clearly what she had in mind. But her feet were aching and she was cold. Like, really cold. As if somebody had taken her bones and turned them into ice. So she just sat there as the minutes ticked away and the chatter of the other customers seemed to be taking place in a parallel universe.

She felt hungry, too. Hungry in a way which was unfamiliar to her and she knew that this was the baby speaking to her. Finding herself unable to ignore the unfamiliar cravings of her body, she ordered a white bread sandwich stuffed with thick slices of cheese and smothered in a sharp and pungent brown chutney.

She fell on it with an instinctive greed which seemed beyond her control and that was how Gabe found her. He walked into the humble café, his face sombre and his dark golden hair so wet that it looked almost black. Raindrops were running down over the high slash of his cheekbones and for one crazy moment it looked almost as if he were crying.

But Gabe didn't do tears, she reminded herself. Gabe didn't do emotions because he didn't *feel*. Gabe's hurt and pain had made him immune from the stuff which afflicted normal human hearts, like hers.

He walked straight over to her and leant over the table. Holding on to the back of a chair, he seemed to be having difficulty controlling his breathing and it was a moment before he could ice out his incredulous question.

'What the hell do you think you're doing, Leila?'

'What does it look like I'm doing? I'm eating a cheese and pickle sandwich.' She finished chewing a mouthful which now tasted like sawdust and stared at him. 'Anyway, I thought you were in meetings.'

'I cancelled them when I didn't hear from you. I've been going out of my mind with worry.'

'So Alice said.'

'So Alice said,' he repeated, and then his eyes narrowed. 'Don't you *care*?'

At this, she put the rest of the sandwich down on the plate but her hands were still trembling as she met the accusation in his eyes.

'Don't I *care*?' She gave a short laugh. 'I did. I cared very much. But I realise now how incredibly stupid I've been. I mean, how could I possibly think that ours was a marriage worth saving? You told me that our relationship was to be based on truth and you lied. A loveless marriage I could just about live with, but not lies, Gabe. Not lies.'

And with that, she pushed back her chair and ran out of the café.

CHAPTER TWELVE

THE COOL RAIN hit Leila's face as she met the fresh air, but Gabe was hot on her heels. She ran straight past the chauffeur-driven car which was obviously his, but he caught up with her before she'd reached the end of the street.

His hands on her elbows, he hauled her round to face him and held on to her tightly, even though she tried to struggle out of his grip.

'You can't run away,' he said grimly.

'I can do anything I like. And I want to be as far away from you as possible. So go away and leave me alone.'

'I'm not going anywhere without you and I'm not having this discussion in the middle of the street in the pouring rain.'

'Terrified it will ruin your ice-cool image?' she mocked.

'Terrified that you'll catch a cold—especially in your present condition,' he said. 'You're pregnant, Leila. Remember?'

'*Oh!*' She gave a howl of frustrated rage as she struggled again. 'As if I could ever forget!'

But he was levering her gently towards the waiting

car, and the chauffeur had leapt out to open the door. Gabe was easing her onto the back seat and Leila was appalled at how relieved she felt as warmth and luxury wrapped themselves round her body like a soft and comforting mantle.

That's just the external stuff, she reminded herself bitterly. *Money just makes things more comfortable. It doesn't change anything. It doesn't make the hurt and betrayal go away.*

She turned to face him as he slid onto the seat beside her. 'I'm not going back to your apartment!'

'We don't have to do that,' he said evenly. 'Where would you like to go instead?'

And wasn't that the saddest thing of all—that she couldn't think of anywhere? The place she most wanted to be was in his heart, and there was no place for her there.

'I don't care,' she said.

'Then let's just drive around for a while, shall we? And you can tell me what's wrong.'

'What's wrong? *What's wrong?*' She hated the way he was talking to her as if she were aged a hundred and had forgotten where she lived. It was as much as she could do not to bang her fists frustratedly against his chest. And sudden all her hurt and pain and disappointment came bubbling out. 'I'll tell you what's wrong! You told me that our marriage was to be based on truth. You told me you couldn't promise me love, but you could promise me that. And I believed you.' Tears sprang from her eyes and began to trickle down her cheeks. 'I believed you even though I wanted the impossible from you. I wanted your love, but I was prepared to settle for the truth.'

'Leila—'

'And then this morning.' Angrily, she shook away the hand which he'd placed on her arm. 'This morning I found some photos stuffed away in a drawer in the wardrobe.'

He went very still. 'So you've been spying on me, have you?'

'Don't you dare try to turn this on me! I was actually looking for a bigger home for my shoe collection—but that's not the point! The point is that I found photos of you with a man who was clearly your father. A man you told me you'd never met. You lied to me, Gabe. You *lied to me.*'

There was silence in the car, punctuated only by the muffled sound of her sobs and, reluctantly, she took the handkerchief he withdrew from his pocket and buried her nose in it.

'Yes, I lied to you,' he said heavily. 'I lied to you because…'

His voice faded away and it was so unlike Gabe to hesitate that Leila lifted her nose from the handkerchief to look at him. Her vision was blurred through her tears but she saw enough to startle her, for his eyes looked like two empty holes in a face so ravaged with emotion that for a moment he didn't look like Gabe at all.

'Because, what?'

He shook his head and turned to her as the words began to spill from his lips, as if he'd been bottling them up for a long time. 'What if you were a man and you met a woman who just blew you away, in a way you didn't recognise at the time—because it had never happened to you before? Maybe you were determined not to recognise it because it was something you didn't believe in. Something which, deep down, you feared.'

Leila sniffed. 'None of that makes sense.'

'Hear me out.' He sucked in a deep breath. 'So you walk away from this woman, telling yourself that you've made the best and the only decision you could possibly make. But you're not sure. In fact, you're starting to realise that you've just done the dumbest thing imaginable, when she turns up at your home in London. And you look at her and realise what an idiot you've been. You realise that here you have a chance for happiness right in front of your eyes, but you're scared. And then...'

His voice tailed off and she saw his features harden. 'Then?'

'Then she tells you she's pregnant and you're even more scared. Because this is a double-edged sword. On the one hand, it means you can be together legitimately without having to delve too deeply into your own emotions. Yet on the other...'

'Gabe!' Her anger forgotten now, she leaned forward—wondering what on earth could have put such a haunted expression on his face. 'Will you please stop talking in riddles? The fact is that you lied about seeing your father and nothing can change that.'

'No. Nothing can change that. But what if I told you there was a reason why my mother kept his identity from me?' He raked his fingers back through his plastered hair and his fingertips came away wet. For a moment he just stared at them, as if he might find some kind of answer gleaming back at him from that damp, cold skin.

'After she died, I felt angry and bitter—and guilty

too. But I went to London and I started working and, as I told you, success came pretty quickly.'

'Yes,' she said quietly. 'You told me.'

'I embraced my new role as a successful business-man but sometimes—not often—I would think about my father. I couldn't eradicate the curiosity which still niggled away at me. I didn't know if he was dead or alive. I wanted to confront him. I wanted to know why he'd abdicated all his responsibilities towards me. I wanted to tell him that a woman had died sooner than reveal his identity.' He clenched his fist, as if he wanted to hit something. Or someone. 'I guess I was looking for someone to blame for her death. Some-one who wasn't me.'

'Go on,' she said.

'I was rich by this point. Rich enough to find any-one I wanted and it didn't take long to track my fa-ther down in Marseilles, which is where he'd moved to when he'd left Provence. And suddenly I under-stood my mother's behaviour. I understood why she'd wanted to protect me from him. Why she'd feared his influence on me...'

His words tailed off as if he couldn't bear to say them but Leila leaned forward, her wet hair falling over her shoulders as she peered into his face. 'What, Gabe? *What?*'

'Which particular title shall I give him? Gangster or hoodlum?' he questioned bitterly. 'Because he an-swered to both. He was an underworld figure, Leila. A powerful and ruthless individual. I discovered that he had killed. Yes, killed. I discovered this when we met in Paris and not long afterwards he was gunned down in some gangland shootout himself. That photo was taken by one of his associates and it's the only one of us together. Time after time I went to burn it, but something always stopped me and I still don't know what that something is.'

'Oh, Gabe,' she whispered, her voice distorted with shock and pain. 'Why the hell didn't you tell me?'

'Because I *couldn't*. Don't you see, Leila?' His eyes were blazing as his voice cracked with emotion. 'His blood is my blood. And it's our baby's blood too. How could I knowingly pass on a legacy like that to you? How could I possibly tell the sister of the Sultan about her baby's forebears? Not just a grandmother who had committed suicide, but a grandfather who was a murderer. How could I subject you to a life of fear that those tainted genes will have been passed down to the next generation?' There was silence for a moment as his eyes burned into hers. 'I'm damaged, darling. Badly damaged. Now do you understand?'

Leila nodded. Yes, she understood. She understood this powerful man's pride and fear, but also about his deep desire to protect. And Gabe had been trying to protect her. From hurt and pain and worry. He had been trying to protect their baby too—from the heartache and fear that evil might be inherited, like blue eyes or the ability to draw.

He wanted to reach out to her, but he didn't know how.

She looked into his haunted face and her heart went out to him, but she knew that this was her golden opportunity and that she must not shrink from it. She had wanted to be his equal, hadn't she? And she wanted to be strong.

So show him that you're still there for him. Love him the way you really want to love him. Why let him shoulder this burden on his own, when you're more than willing to share it with him?

Her voice was low and trembling as her words came tumbling out. 'Do you have any idea of the history of Qurhah?' she demanded.

He looked at her as if this was the last thing in the world he had expected her to say. 'I can't see how that is relevant.'

'Can't you? Actually, it's *very* relevant. I'll have you know that my family is descended from mighty warriors and ruthless tyrants. There have been Al-Maisan sultans conquering neighbouring lands ever since our people first settled in the desert, and there has been much bloodshed along the way. Nobody's history is whiter than white, Gabe. Not yours and especially not mine.'

He shook his head. 'That's not the same,' he said stubbornly.

She laid her hand on his arm. 'It *is* the same—just different. Our baby isn't a clone of your father, you know. Nor of you—or me. Our baby is unique and I know for sure that the best and only legacy we can give him—or her—is love. We must love this baby with all our hearts, Gabe. Even if you don't feel that way about me—do you think you can find it in your heart to love our baby?'

He shook his head and for a minute his face was contorted with pain. 'What a brute of a man you must think I am,' he declared bitterly, 'that I would be incapable of feeling something for an innocent scrap of humanity.'

'Not a brute,' she said gently. 'A man who has been wounded—badly wounded. But I am your wife and I am going to help you heal, but I can only do that if you let me. If you can bear to open up your heart, Gabe—and let me in.'

She saw a muscle flickering at his temple as he caught hold of her wet shoulders and looked into her face.

'Only if you can you forgive me,' he said. 'Can you ever forgive me for what I have done, my darling Leila?'

'There's nothing to forgive,' she said softly, her hand reaching up to touch the hard contours of his face. She ran her fingertip along the high slash of his very Slavic cheekbones and the firm curve of his lips. She looked into the pewter eyes and her heart turned over with love. One day soon she would tell him to learn to understand his father, and then to let the bitterness go. That there was a little bit of bad in the best of people, and a little bit of good in the worst.

But not now.

Now she must be focused on the most important things.

'We're both very cold and very wet,' she said as she snuggled up against him. 'Do you think we should go home?'

Gabe stroked a straggly strand of damp hair away from her face and smiled, but the lump in his throat meant that it took a moment or two before he could speak. 'Right here is home,' he said unevenly. 'Wherever you are. I love you, my compassionate and passionate princess. I love you very much.'

He tapped on the glass and the car moved away, and that was when he started to kiss her.

EPILOGUE

'HE LOOKS VERY Qurhahian,' said Gabe as he gazed into the crib where the sleeping infant lay.

Leila smiled, giving one last unnecessary twitch of the snowy cashmere blanket which now covered the crescent curve of Hafez's perfect little foot. 'Do you know, that's exactly what Murat said to me today.'

'Did he?'

She nodded as she looked down at their tiny son. His skin was faintly tinged with olive and already he had a hint of the slightly too-strong nose which had been the bane of her life, but which Gabe always told her was the most beautiful nose in the world. Deep down she suspected that her husband was relieved to discover that their firstborn looked more like her than him. But Leila was confident that, with time, his few remaining reservations about his heritage would melt beneath the power of her love.

Today had been Hafez's naming ceremony, here in the palace in Simdahab where she'd grown up—and it had been the most glorious of visits. All the servants had clucked excitedly around the princess's new baby. That was when they hadn't been buzzing round the Western guests who had flown out for the occasion and who mingled with the dignitaries and kings from the neighbouring desert countries.

It had been a day of immense happiness and joy, but Leila thought that Murat seemed rather pensive and she wondered if it was because the woman he had been destined to marry had found happiness with another man.

She put her arms around Gabe and pressed her lips to his cheek. 'My brother said something very strange to me today.'

'Tell me.' He started to kiss her neck.

Leila closed her eyes as shivers of sensation began to whisper over her skin. 'He said that at least there was another generation of the Al-Maisan family, in case he never produced an heir of his own. He seemed to imply that he would never marry—and that he'd be contented with a long line of mistresses instead.'

Gabe smiled as he brushed his mouth over her scented skin. Hadn't he once thought that way himself? When his heart had been so dark and cold that it had felt as if a lump of ice had been wedged in his chest. 'All it takes is the right woman,' he said. 'And once she comes along, it seems that a man will happily change his entire life to please her. Just as I have done for you.'

'Oh, darling,' she said, closing her eyes with dreamy pleasure as she thought back to everything that had happened to them since Hafez had been born.

They had sold his apartment and moved to a large house overlooking Hampstead Heath, because Gabe realised that Leila had been right. That his minimalistic high-rise apartment was no place to bring up a baby—it had suited a phase of his life which was now over. Hafez needed grass and flowers, she had told him firmly. He needed a nearby nursery and hopefully a school he could walk to.

So a studio had been built for her in the basement of their new house, from which she would work as a freelance photographer. That way she got all the pleasures of working, but none of the regular commitment which would keep her away from their son.

Gabe lifted his hand and stroked back the glorious fall of hair from her face so that it streamed down over her shoulders in a cascade of ebony. The roseate curves of her lips were an irresistible invitation, and he kissed her with a steadily increasing hunger before drawing away from her.

'I love you,' he said.

'I know. The feeling is shared and returned.'

'And there's a spare hour to fill before the palace banquet,' he said a little unsteadily. 'Shall we go to bed?'

She opened her eyes. 'You're insatiable.'

'I thought you liked me that way.'

'I like you any way I can get you,' she whispered back. 'But preferably without any clothes on and nobody else around.'

'You are a shameless woman, Leila Steel.'

'Lucky that's the way you like *me*,' she teased.

'I know,' he said. 'I never stop reminding myself how lucky I am.'

And this was the greatest of the many truths he'd discovered in a life now lived without pretence, or fear or regret.

Next week was his birthday but he wouldn't be seeking to blot out the past with a bottle of Scotch and oblivion. He would be embracing the golden and glorious present with his wife and their beloved baby son.

And he would be telling Leila how much he loved her, just as he did every single day of his life. His beautiful Qurhahian princess who had brought his heart to life with the power of her love. Just as the rains fed the dormant flower seeds, to bring the desert miracle to the Mekathasinian Sands.

* * * * *

COMMANDED BY
THE SHEIKH

KATE HEWITT

After spending three years as a die-hard New Yorker, **Kate Hewitt** now lives in a small village in the English Lake District with her husband, their five children and a golden retriever. In addition to writing intensely emotional stories, she loves reading, baking and playing chess with her son – she has yet to win against him, but she continues to try. Learn more about Kate at www.kate-hewitt.com.

CHAPTER ONE

'I NEED YOU, OLIVIA.'

Olivia Ellis quickly suppressed the flare of feeling Sheikh Aziz al Bakir's simply stated words caused inside her. Of course he needed her. He needed her to change his sheets, polish his silver and keep his Parisian townhouse on the Ile de la Cité pristine.

That didn't explain what she was doing here, in the royal palace of Kadar.

Less than eight hours ago she'd been summoned by one of Aziz's men, asked unequivocally to accompany him on the royal jet to Siyad—the capital of Kadar—where Aziz had recently ascended the throne.

Olivia had gone reluctantly, because she liked the quiet life she'd made for herself in Paris: mornings with the concierge across the street sipping coffee, afternoons in the garden pruning roses. It was a life that held no excitement or passion, but it was hers and it made her happy, or as happy as she knew how to be. It was enough, and she didn't want it to change.

'What do you need of me, Your Highness?' she asked. She'd spent the endless flight to Kadar composing reasons why she should stay in Paris. She *needed* to stay in Paris, needed the safety and comfort of her quiet life.

'Considering the circumstances, I think you should

call me Aziz.' The smile he gave her was whimsical, effortlessly charming, yet Olivia tried to remain unmoved. She'd often observed Aziz's charm from a distance, had heard the honeyed words slide from his lips as he entertained one of his many female guests in Paris. She'd picked up the discarded lingerie from the staircase and had poured coffee for the women who crept from his bed before breakfast, their hair mussed and their lips swollen.

She, however, had always considered herself immune to 'the Gentleman Playboy', as the tabloids had nicknamed him. A bit of an oxymoron, Olivia thought, but she had to admit Aziz possessed a certain charisma.

She felt it now, with him focusing all of his attention on her, the opulent palace with its frescoed walls and gold fixtures stretching around them.

'Very well, Aziz. What do you need of me?' She spoke briskly, as she had when discussing replacing the roof tiles or the guest list for a dinner party. Yet it took a little more effort now, being in this strange and overwhelming place with this man.

He was, Olivia had to admit, beautiful. She could acknowledge that, just as she acknowledged that Michelangelo's *David* was a magnificent sculpture; it was nothing more than a simple appreciation of undeniable beauty. In any case, she didn't have anything left inside her to feel more than that. Not for Aziz, not for anyone.

She gazed now at the ink-black hair that flopped carelessly over his forehead; his grey eyes that could flare silver; the surprisingly full lips that could curve into a most engaging smile.

And as for his body…powerful, lean perfection, without an extra ounce of fat anywhere, just pure, perfect muscle.

Aziz steepled his fingers under his chin and turned towards the window so his back was partially to her. Olivia waited, felt the silence inexplicably tauten between them. 'You have been in my employ for six years now?' he said after a moment, his voice lilting as if it was a question, even though Olivia knew it was not.

'Yes, that's correct.'

'And I have been very pleased with your dedicated service in all of that time.'

She tensed. He sounded as if he were about to fire her. *And so now I'm afraid I have to tell you that I have no need of you any more...*

She took a careful breath, let it out silently. 'I'm very glad to hear that, Your Highness.'

'Aziz, remember.'

'Considering your status, it doesn't seem appropriate to call you by your first name.'

'Even if I demand it by royal decree?'

He turned around and raised his eyebrows, clearing teasing her. Olivia's mouth compressed. 'If you demand it, I shall of course comply,' she answered coolly. 'But in any case I shall do my best to call you by your first name.'

'I know you will. You have always done your best, Olivia, and that is exactly what I need from you today.'

She waited, unease creeping its cold fingers along her spine. What on earth could he need her for now, here in Kadar? She didn't like surprises or uncertainty; she'd spent six years creating something safe, small and good and she was terribly afraid of losing it. Of losing herself.

'In Paris you have done an admirable job keeping my home clean and comfortable and welcoming,' Aziz told her. 'I have another task entirely for you here, but it shall be short, and I trust you are capable of it.'

She had no idea what he was talking about, but if it

was short she hoped it meant that she'd be able to return to Paris, and soon. 'I hope that I am, Your—Aziz.'

He smiled, his gaze sweeping over her in approval. 'See what a quick learner you are?' he murmured.

Olivia said nothing. She ignored the little flutter of—something—Aziz's lazy murmur had caused inside her. In Paris their conversations were so mundane Olivia simply hadn't felt the full force of the Gentleman Playboy's charisma. That she should feel it here, now, was disconcerting but understandable. She was out of her element, in this beautiful yet overwhelming palace, and Aziz wasn't talking to her about house repairs or his social diary.

She gave him a quick, cool, professional smile. 'I'm afraid I still don't understand why I'm here.'

'All in good time.' Aziz flashed her an answering smile before walking over to a walnut desk inlaid with hand-tooled leather. He pressed a button on the side of the desk and within seconds Olivia heard a knock on the door.

'Enter,' Aziz said, and the same man who had escorted her to the room came in.

'Your Highness?'

Aziz braced one hip against the desk. 'What do you think, Malik? Will she do?'

Malik's gaze flicked to Olivia. 'The hair…'

Aziz snapped his fingers. 'Easily dealt with.'

'Eyes?'

'Not necessary.'

Malik nodded slowly. 'She's about the right height.'

'I thought so.'

The man turned to look at Aziz. 'Discreet?'

'Absolutely.'

'Then I think it's a possibility.'

'It's more than a possibility, Malik, it's a necessity. I'm holding a press conference in one hour.'

Malik shook his head. 'One hour—there won't be time.'

'There has to be. You know I can't risk any more instability.' Olivia watched as Aziz's expression shuttered, his mouth hardening into a grim line, turning him into someone utterly unlike the laughing, careless playboy she was familiar with. 'One rumour at this point will be like a lit match. Everything could go up in flames.'

'Indeed, Your Highness. I'll start making preparations.'

'Thank you.'

Malik withdrew and Olivia turned to Aziz. 'What on earth was all that about?'

'I apologise for speaking in such a way with Malik. I'm sure you are more confused than ever.'

'You're right,' Olivia answered, her voice coming out in something close to a snap. She hadn't liked the way the two men had discussed her...as if she were an object. She might be Aziz's housekeeper, but she wasn't his possession, and she had no intention of letting another person control her actions or attitude ever again.

'Pax, Olivia.' Aziz held up his hands. 'There would have been no point continuing our discussion if Malik hadn't approved of you.'

'*Approved* of me?'

'Found you suitable.'

'For what?'

Aziz let out a little sigh, the sound sudden. 'I presume you are not aware of the terms of my father's will?' he asked.

'No, I'm not,' Olivia replied. 'I'm not privy to such information, naturally.'

He shrugged, the movement careless, negligent, yet utterly graceful. 'It could have leaked out. There have been rumours of what the will requires.'

'I don't pay any attention to rumours.' She didn't even know what they were; she didn't read gossip magazines or tabloids.

Aziz lifted his eyebrows. 'You know I am engaged to Queen Elena of Thallia?'

'Yes, of course.' Their engagement had been announced publicly last week; Olivia knew the wedding was in the next few days, here in Kadar.

'You might have wondered why Queen Elena and I became engaged so quickly,' Aziz remarked, his dark gaze steady on her as he waited for her reaction.

Olivia gave a little shrug. Gentleman though he might be, Aziz was still a playboy. She'd seen the evidence herself in the women he'd brought home to his Paris house, had turned away more than one ardent admirer who'd received the diamond bracelet and bouquet of lilies that was Aziz's standard parting gift.

'I expect you feel a need to marry, now that you are Sheikh,' she said, and Aziz let out a little laugh, the sound hard, abrupt and utterly unlike him.

'You could say that.' He gazed out of the window once more, his lips pressed together in a firm line. 'My father has never approved of my choices,' he said after a moment. 'Or of me. I suspect the requirements of his will were put in place so he could keep me in Kadar, bound by the old traditions.' He lifted one shoulder in a shrug. 'Or perhaps he just wanted to punish me. That is perfectly possible.' He spoke easily, almost as if he was mentioning something pleasant or perhaps trivial, but she saw a coldness, or perhaps even a hurt, in his eyes.

Curiosity flickered and she quickly stamped it out.

She had no need to know about Aziz's relationship with his father, or with anyone. No need to wonder about what emotions he tried to hide, if any. 'What requirements?'

'In order to remain Sheikh, I must marry within six weeks of my father's death.' Aziz's mouth possessed a cynical twist, his eyes flinty. She'd never seen him look so bitter.

'It's been over a month already.'

'Exactly, Olivia. It has, in fact, been five weeks and four days. And my wedding to Queen Elena of Thallia is set for the day after tomorrow.'

'Then you will succeed,' she answered. 'You will marry within the time required and there'll be no problem.'

'But there is a problem,' Aziz informed her, his voice turning dangerously silky and soft. 'There is a big problem, because Elena has gone missing.'

'*Missing?*'

'Kidnapped by an insurgent two days ago.'

Olivia gaped before she managed to reassemble her features into her usual composed countenance. 'I had no idea things like this still happened in a civilised country.'

'You'd be surprised what can happen in any country, when power is involved. What secrets people keep, what lies they tell.' He swung away from her, the movement sudden, strangely defensive; again Olivia had the sense he was hiding something from her. Hiding himself.

In the six years she'd worked for him, Aziz had always seemed like nothing more than what he was on the surface: a charming, careless playboy. But for a moment, as he angled his face away from her, he seemed as if he had secrets. Darkness.

And she knew all about secrets and darkness.

'Do you know where this—this insurgent might be keeping Queen Elena?' Olivia asked after a moment.

'Somewhere in the desert, most likely.'

'And you're looking for her?'

'Of course, as best as I can.' Aziz turned around to meet her troubled gaze with an unflinching one of his own. 'I have not been back to Kadar in five years and I spent as little time here as a boy as possible. The people don't know me.' His mouth twisted. 'And, if they don't know me, they won't be loyal to me. Not until I've proved myself to them, if I can.'

'What are you saying—?' she began, only to have Aziz cut her off in a hard voice.

'I'm saying it is very difficult to find Queen Elena in the desert. Her kidnapper has the loyalty of the Bedouin tribes, and they will shelter both him and her. So until I find her, or come to some agreement with him, I need to make alternative arrangements.'

'What kind of alternative arrangements?' Olivia asked, although she had a horrible, creeping feeling just what they might be, or at least who they might concern. *Her.* Somehow he wanted to involve her in this debacle.

Aziz gave her a dazzling grin, his eyes flaring silver, his teeth blindingly white. Olivia felt her body involuntarily respond, her insides pulse with awareness of him, not as an employer or even an attractive person, a work of art, but as a man. A desirable man.

She blinked and forced back that rush of surprising, and completely inappropriate, feeling. Clearly it was just a basic biological reaction she had no control over. She had thought she was past such things, that she didn't have anything left in her to fizz or spark, but perhaps her body thought otherwise. Even so, her mind would prevail. 'Your Highness—'

'Aziz.'

'*Aziz*. What alternative arrangements are you talking about?'

'It is important that no one knows Elena is missing. Such knowledge would make Kadar more unstable than it already is.'

'*More* unstable?'

'Some of the desert tribes have rallied around this rebel.' Aziz's mouth twisted. 'Khalil.'

He spoke tersely, without emotion, yet Olivia still sensed something underneath his flat tone, something that seethed. Who exactly, she wondered, was Khalil?

'Why have they rallied around this Khalil? You're the legal heir.'

'Thank you for your vote of confidence, but I'm afraid it's a bit more complicated than that.'

He spoke lightly again, but Olivia wasn't fooled. 'How is it complicated? And what could I possibly have to do with any of this?'

'Since I can't let the public know my bride is missing,' Aziz said, turning the full force of his silvery gaze on her once more, 'I need someone else.'

Olivia felt as if someone had caught her by the throat and squeezed. For a moment she couldn't breathe. 'Someone else,' she finally repeated, her voice coming out flat and strange.

'Yes, Olivia. Someone else. Someone to be my bride.'

'But—'

'And that's where you come in.' Aziz cut her off smoothly, something almost like amusement glinting in his eyes. Olivia stared at him, disbelieving and appalled. 'I need you to be my bride.'

CHAPTER TWO

HIS COOL, CAPABLE HOUSEKEEPER, Aziz thought in bemusement, looked as if she was about to hyperventilate. Or faint. She swayed slightly, her lovely slate-blue eyes going wider, her lush, pink lips parted in a rather delectable *o*.

She was a beautiful woman, he acknowledged as he had many times before, but it was a cool, contained beauty. Sleek, caramel hair she always kept clipped back at the base of her neck. Dark blue eyes. Smooth skin and rosy lips, neither ever enhanced by make-up, at least that he'd seen. Not that she needed any cosmetics, particularly right now. A flush was rising up her throat, sweeping across her face as she shook her head and compressed her mouth.

'I'm not quite sure what you even mean, Your Highness, but whatever it is it's not possible.'

'To start with, you need to remember to call me Aziz.'

Temper blazed so briefly in her eyes he almost missed it. He was glad, contrarily, perhaps, that she actually possessed a temper. He'd often wondered how much passion lurked beneath that reserved exterior.

He'd known Olivia for six years, admittedly seeing her only a few times a year, and he'd had only a scant few glimpses of any deeper feeling. A silk scarf in deep reds and purples that he'd been surprised to see her wear.

A sudden rich, full-throated laugh he'd heard from the kitchen. Once, when he'd arrived in Paris a day early, he'd come upon her playing piano in the sitting room. The music had been haunting, full of grief and beauty. And the look on her face as she'd played… She'd been pouring her soul into that piece of music, and it was, he'd thought in that moment, a soul that had known anguish and even torment.

He'd crept away before she'd seen him, knowing how horrified she would have been to realise he'd been listening. But he'd wondered just what lay underneath her cool façade. What secrets she might be hiding.

And yet it was her cool façade, her calm capability, that had made him choose Olivia Ellis for this particular role. She was intelligent, discreet and wonderfully competent. That was all he needed.

He hoped.

'Let me rephrase,' he said, watching as her chest rose and fell in indignant breaths. She wore a white blouse that still managed to be crisp after a nine-hour flight from Paris, and her hair, as sleek and styled as ever, was held back in its usual clip. She'd matched her blouse with a pair of tailored black trousers and sensible flats. He knew she was twenty-nine but she dressed conservatively, like a woman who was middle-aged rather than in the prime of her youth. Though still stylish, he acknowledged. Her clothes, while staid, were of good quality and cut.

'Rephrase, then,' she said evenly, and the temper he'd seen in her eyes was now banked. He saw the old Olivia, the familiar Olivia, return now. Calm and in control. *Good.* That was what he needed, after all.

So why did he feel just a tiny bit disappointed?

'I need you to be my temporary bride. A stand-in for Queen Elena, until I can find her.'

'And why do you need a stand-in?'

'Because I want to dispel any rumours that she might be missing. I'm holding a press conference in one hour and we're meant to appear together on the palace balcony.'

She pursed her lips. 'And then?'

He hesitated, but only briefly. 'And then, that's all.'

'That's all?' Her eyes narrowed. 'If you only needed a woman for one balcony appearance, surely you could have found someone a bit more local?'

'I wanted someone I knew and trusted and, as I told you before, I have not been back to Kadar in many years. There are few I trust here.'

She swallowed and he watched the working of her slender throat. Then she gave a little shake of her head.

'I don't even look like Queen Elena. She's got dark hair and we're not the same height, no matter what you said earlier to your staff. I must be a few inches taller.'

He arched an eyebrow. 'You're familiar with Queen Elena's height?'

'I'm familiar with my own,' she answered coolly. 'And I have seen photos of her. I'm guessing, of course, but—'

'No one will concern themselves with a few inches.'

'And my hair?'

'We'll dye it.'

'In the next *hour*?'

'If need be.'

She stared at him for a long beat, and he felt tension gather inside him in a tight, hard knot. He knew he was making an unusual request, to say the least. He also knew he had to get Olivia to agree. He didn't want to threaten her, God knew, but he needed her. He didn't have any other woman in his life who he trusted to be discreet and competent, the way Olivia was. He supposed that said something about his own life, but at this moment all he could care about was achieving his goal. Securing the crown of a kingdom he'd been born to rule…even if many didn't believe it. Even if he'd never been sure he would.

Never sure if his father would change his mind and disinherit him, just as he had Khalil.

'And if I say no?' Olivia asked and Aziz gave her his most charming smile.

'But why would you?'

'Because it's insanity?' she shot back without a shred of humour. 'Because any paparazzi with a telephoto lens could figure out I'm not Queen Elena and plaster it all over the tabloids? I don't think even the Gentleman Playboy could charm himself out of that disaster.'

'So cutting, Olivia.' He shook his head in gentle mockery. 'If that happened, I'd be responsible. All the blame would fall to me.'

'You don't think I'd be dragged through the gossip mill, every aspect of my life dissected in the tabloids?' For a second her features contorted, as if such a possibility caused her actual physical pain. 'No.'

'If you were discovered, which you won't be,' Aziz answered calmly, 'No one would who know you are.'

'You don't think they could find out?'

'Possibly, but we're theorising to no purpose. There are no journalists out there. The country has been closed to foreign press for years. I have yet to change that decree.'

'The Kadaran press, then.'

'Have always been in the royal pocket. I've requested no photographs on this occasion, and they'll comply.' His insides tightened. 'I'm not condoning the way things are here, but it's how my father ran things, and currently it continues.'

She stared at him for a moment, her slate-blue gaze

searching his face. 'Are you going to do things differently now you're Sheikh?' She sounded curious but also a bit disbelieving, which Aziz could understand, even if he didn't like it.

He hadn't proved himself capable of much besides being a whiz with numbers and partying across Europe, at least to someone like Olivia. She'd seen his hedonistic lifestyle first-hand, had cleaned up its excesses. He could hardly blame her now for being a little sceptical of his ability to rule well, or even at all.

'I'm going to try.'

'And you'll start with this ridiculous masquerade.'

'I'm afraid it's necessary.' He cocked his head, offering her a smile that didn't even make her blink. 'It's for a good reason, Olivia. The stability of a country. The safety of a people.'

'Why has Khalil kidnapped Queen Elena? And how did he even do it? Wasn't she guarded?'

A hot, bright flare of anger fired his insides. Aziz didn't know whom that anger was directed at: Khalil, for taking his bride, or his staff, who had not been alert to the threat until it was too late. No, he realised, he was angry at himself, even though he knew he could not have prevented the kidnapping. He was angry that he couldn't have prevented it, that he didn't know this country or people well enough yet to command their loyalty or obedience—or to find Elena hidden somewhere in its endless, barren desert.

'Khalil is the illegitimate son of my father's first wife,' he explained tersely. 'He was raised as my father's son for seven years, until my father discovered the truth of his parentage. My father banished him, along with his mother, but he insists now that he has a claim to the throne.'

'How awful.' Olivia shook her head. *'Banished.'*

'He was raised in luxury by his aunt in America,' Aziz told her. 'You needn't feel sorry for him.'

She eyed him curiously. 'You obviously don't.'

Aziz just shrugged. What he felt for Khalil—when he even allowed himself to think of the man who shadowed his memories like a malevolent ghost—was too complicated to explain even to himself, much less to Olivia. Anger and envy. Sorrow and bitterness. A potent and unhealthy mix, to say the least.

'I admit,' he said, 'I don't have much sympathy for him now, considering he is destabilising my country and has kidnapped my bride.'

'Why do you think he believes he has a right to the throne?'

Because everyone else does. Because my father adored him, even when he learned he wasn't his son. Even when he didn't want to. 'I'm not sure he does believe he has a right,' he told her with a small shrug. 'This might just be revenge against my father, a man he thought to be his own father for much of his childhood.' Aziz glanced away from Olivia's inquisitive gaze. *Revenge against me, for taking his place.* 'My father was not a fair man. This extraordinary will is surely proof of that.'

'And so Khalil has kidnapped Queen Elena in order to prevent your marriage,' she stated slowly, and Aziz nodded, his jaw bunching. He hated to think of Queen Elena out in the desert, alone and afraid. He didn't know his prospective bride very well, but he could only imagine how terrifying such an experience would be for anyone, and especially for someone with her history. She'd told him a little of how her parents had died, how alone she'd been. He just hoped Khalil would keep her safe now.

'If you don't marry within the six weeks,' Olivia asked, 'What happens?'

'I lose the throne and title.'

'And who does it go to?'

Aziz hesitated. 'The will doesn't specify a particular person,' he answered. 'But a referendum will have to be called.'

'A referendum? You mean the people will decide who is Sheikh?'

'Yes.'

Her mouth curved slightly. 'That sounds nicely democratic.'

'Kadar has a constitutional monarchy,' Aziz answered, struggling to keep his voice even, dispassionate. 'The succession has always been dynastic. The referendum is simply my father's way of forcing me to jump through his hoops.'

'And you don't want to jump?'

'Not particularly, but I recognise the need.' He'd spent over three weeks trying to find a loophole in his father's will. He didn't want to marry, didn't want to be forced to marry, and certainly not by his father. His father had controlled his actions, his thoughts and desires for far too long.

Yet even in death his father had the power to control him. To hurt him. And here he was, jumping through hoops.

'Why not just call the referendum?' Olivia asked.

'Because I'd lose.' Aziz spoke easily, lightly, using the tone he'd taken for so long it was second nature to him—a second skin, this playboy persona of his. But talking about his father—about the possibility of Khalil being Sheikh because his country didn't want him—was making that second skin start to peel away, and he was afraid of what Olivia might be able to see through the tatters. 'Hazard of not spending much time in Kadar, I'm afraid,' he continued in a mocking drawl. 'But I'm hoping to remedy that shortly.'

'But not in time for the referendum.'

'Exactly. Which is why I need to appear with my bride and reassure my people that all is well.' He took a step towards her, willing her to understand, to accept. 'My father left his country in turmoil, Olivia, divided by the choices he made twenty-five years ago. I am trying my hardest to right those wrongs and keep Kadar in peace.'

He saw a flash of something in her slate-blue eyes—understanding, or even compassion. He was getting to her. He hoped. 'And if you don't find Queen Elena?' she asked.

'I will. I just need a little more time. I have men searching the desert as we speak.'

It had all been so cleverly, capably done. Khalil had planted a man loyal to him in Aziz's new staff, a man who had given Aziz the message that Elena's plane had been delayed by bad weather. He'd bribed the pilot of the royal jet to divert the flight to a remote desert location and he'd had his men meet Elena as she came off the plane.

That much he knew, had pieced together from witnesses: from the steward who had helplessly watched Elena disappear into a blacked-out SUV; the maid who had seen one of Aziz's staff looking secretive and shifty, loitering in places he shouldn't have been.

Aziz sighed. Yes, it had been capably done, because Khalil still had the loyalty of many of the Kadaran people. Never mind that he'd left Kadar when he'd been seven years old and had only returned to the country in the last six months. They remembered the young boy they'd known as Sheikh Hashem's beloved son—the real son, or so the whispers went.

Aziz was the interloper. The pretender.

He always had been, from the moment he'd been brought to the palace at just four years old. He remembered the way the staff had pretended not to hear his mother's humble requests, how they'd sneered even as they'd served them. He'd been bewildered, his mother desperate. She'd stopped trying to please anyone and had remained isolated in the women's quarters, rarely seen in public.

Aziz had tried. He had tried to win over the staff, the people and most of all his father. He'd failed in nearly every respect, and most definitely in the last. And so, finally, he'd stopped trying.

Except now. Now you want to try again. You're just afraid you'll fail.

He silenced the sly whisper of his personal demons and retrained his gaze on Olivia. They now had only forty minutes until his press conference. He had to make her agree.

'If I can't find Queen Elena, I'll arrange a meeting with Khalil. We might be able to negotiate.' Although Aziz didn't want to talk to Khalil, or even see him. Just the memory of the last time he'd seen Khalil made his stomach churn. The boy he'd thought was his half-brother had looked at him, all of four years old, as if he were something sticky and disgusting on the bottom of his shoe. Then his father had steered Aziz out of the royal nursery, dismissing him so he could be with the son he'd always favoured. The one he'd preferred, even when he'd learned that they shared no blood.

His father might have banished Khalil, but he'd chosen to cling to his memory and revile the son he'd made heir out of necessity rather than desire.

Now Aziz forced the memories back and turned to Olivia. 'In any case, none of that needs to concern you.

All I'm asking is that you appear on the balcony for about two minutes. People will see you from afar and be satisfied.'

'How can you be sure?'

'They're expecting Elena. They'll see Elena. I made the announcement that she arrived by royal jet this afternoon.'

She pursed her lips. 'When, in fact, I did.'

'Exactly. People will be waiting to see her. They're most likely lining the courtyard right now. Two minutes, Olivia, that's all I ask. And then you can return to Paris.'

She shook her head slowly. 'For how long?'

'What do you mean?'

'Will you really need a house in Paris with a full-time housekeeper once you're married and ruling Kadar, assuming you do find Queen Elena?'

He stared at her for a moment, nonplussed, before he realised she was worried about her job. 'I intend on keeping my house in Paris,' he told her, even though he hadn't actually considered it either way. 'And, as long as I have my house, you will have a job there.'

He saw relief flicker over her features, softening her eyes and mouth, relaxing the stiffness of her posture. She'd really been worried about her job.

'So? We are agreed?'

She shook her head, her eyes narrowed, the corners of her mouth pulled down. 'I don't…'

'I have forty minutes before I face the cameras and the reporters.' He took a step towards her, holding his hands out in appeal, offering the kind of wry smile he knew had melted hearts in the past, if not hers. 'You're my only hope, Olivia. My salvation. *Please*.'

Her mouth twitched before she firmed it into its usual

cool line. 'That might be laying it on a bit thick, Your Highness.'

'Aziz.'

She stared at him for a long moment and he could see the conflict clouding her eyes. Then she gave one brief nod, pulling herself up straight. 'All right,' she said quietly. 'I'll do it.'

CHAPTER THREE

WITHIN SECONDS MALIK had returned to the room and Aziz was speaking to him in rapid Arabic. Olivia felt as if she'd entered into some alternate reality. How on earth could she actually impersonate Queen Elena?

She'd been reluctant to agree, but she also saw the wisdom in going along with Aziz's outrageous plan. Aziz held her livelihood in his hands and, while he hadn't outright bribed or blackmailed her, Olivia had still felt the tit-for-tat exchange he was offering: *do this and you'll have a job for as long as you want.*

And her job, the life she'd built for herself in Paris, was all she wanted now. All she hoped to have.

She wasn't entirely self-serving, though, she told herself as she followed Malik down several marble-floored corridors. She understood Aziz's dilemma and she didn't want to exacerbate the instability of his country or rule. She didn't know if pretending to be someone else actually would help things, but she supposed it would at least buy Aziz some time.

And hopefully no one would ever know and tomorrow she would be back in Paris.

'This way, Miss Ellis.'

Malik opened a door and ushered Olivia into a bedroom decorated in peach and cream. She glanced around the sumptuous room, from the canopied bed with its satin cover and pile of pillows, to the brocade sofas and teakwood dressing table. It was a woman's room, feminine and opulent, and she wondered who had last stayed in it.

'Mada and Abra are here to help you prepare,' Malik said and two smiling, sloe-eyed women stepped forward shyly to greet her. 'I'm afraid they speak very little English,' Malik said in apology. 'But I trust you will be in good hands.' With a brief nod, he turned and left Olivia alone with the two women.

With smiles and shy nods they ushered her towards the *en suite* bathroom, which if anything was even more sumptuous than the bedroom, with a sunken marble tub, a two-person shower and double sinks with what looked like solid gold taps.

One of the women said something to her in Arabic, and Olivia shook her head helplessly. 'I'm sorry, I don't understand…'

Smiling, she indicated her own clothes and then gestured to the buttons of Olivia's blouse. The other woman held up a bottle of hair dye and belatedly Olivia understood. She needed to undress so they could dye her hair.

Why was she doing this again? she wondered as she slid off her blouse and trousers and then stood shivering in just her bra and pants. She felt embarrassingly self-conscious; she lived such a solitary life now, and she couldn't remember the last time anyone but her doctor had seen her in her underwear.

One of the women draped a towel around her shoulders and the other laid out the preparations for the hair dye.

'What is your name?' Olivia asked the woman who had given her the towel. She wished she knew a little Arabic. Did Queen Elena know any?

The woman understood her question, for she smiled and ducked her head. 'Mada.'

'Thank you, Mada,' Olivia said and Mada gave her a lovely, gap-toothed smile before leading her towards the marble sink.

Olivia leaned over the sink, closing her eyes as Mada ran warm water over her head and then worked in the hair dye. She realised she hadn't even asked if it was a temporary colour. She hadn't had time properly to consider the ramifications of this charade, she acknowledged as the other woman, Abra, snapped a plastic cover over her hair and eased her up from the sink.

She hadn't had time to ask Aziz if it was even legal. Was impersonating someone—and especially a royal someone—a *crime*? What if she was arrested? What if someone twigged she wasn't Elena and sold the story to the foreign press?

They might uncover other secrets. She couldn't bear the thought of the world knowing her past, raking over her secrets, judging her. She judged herself harshly enough, God knew. She didn't need everyone else doing it too.

And her father, she thought, would be disgraced. After selling her soul to keep him from disgrace ten years ago, the thought that he might end up humiliated anyway gave her a surprising surge of savage satisfaction, and then more familiar rush of guilt.

One appearance. Two minutes. Then it would be over.

A few moments later Mada indicated that she should rise from where she'd been seated, waiting for the dye to set, and Olivia returned to the sink and bent her head so the women could rinse the dye from her hair.

She watched the water in the sink stream blue-black with the dye. When it finally went clear Abra eased her up again, and she stared at herself in the mirror in shock.

She looked completely different. Her skin seemed paler, her eyes deeper, darker and wider somehow. Her hair, her smooth, caramel-coloured hair, now framed her face in a damp, inky tousle. She didn't really look like Queen Elena, but neither did she look like herself. Perhaps from a distance she really would pass as the monarch.

Mada took her by the hand and led her back into the bedroom where clothes had been laid out: a dove-grey suit jacket and narrow skirt paired with an ivory silk blouse.

She dressed quickly, sliding on the gossamer-thin, sheer stockings first, and then the blouse and suit. Four-inch black stilettos heels completed the ensemble. Olivia hesitated; she always wore plain, sensible flats. The heels, she thought as she gazed down at them, felt too…sexy.

And that was not a word she wanted to associate with herself…or Aziz.

Next came hair and make-up; the women styled her newly dark hair in an elegant chignon, then did her face with subtle eye shadow, eyeliner, lipstick and blusher, all of it more than Olivia ever wore. The clothes had been familiar but the shoes, make-up and hair made her feel strange. An impostor.

Which was exactly what Aziz wanted her to be—a convincing one.

A knock sounded on the door and then Malik entered. 'You are ready, Miss Ellis?'

She nodded stiffly. 'As ready I can be, I suppose.'

He glanced up and down her body and then nodded, seemingly in approval. 'Please come with me.'

As she followed him down the corridor, her heels clicking smartly on the marble tile, she remarked with a touch of acerbity, 'Clearly Mada and Abra are both in on this plan, and both of them looked far more like Queen Elena than I do. They have the right colouring, at least. Why couldn't one of them act as her stand-in?'

Malik slid her a sideways glance. 'Neither of those women possesses the confidence or ability to enact such a masquerade. In any case, they would not even be comfortable wearing Western clothes.'

'But you trust them? Aziz trusts them?'

Malik nodded. 'Yes, of course. Very few people know about this deception, Miss Ellis. Only you, Sheikh Aziz, myself, Mada and Abra.'

'And the crew of the royal jet,' Olivia pointed out. 'Plus the staff who escorted me here.'

He inclined his head in acknowledgement. 'True, but it is a contained group, and everyone in it is loyal to the Sheikh.'

'Aziz said he had not been in Kadar long enough to gain the people's loyalty.'

Malik gazed at her with an inscrutable expression. 'So he seems to think. But there are more loyal to Aziz than he knows, or allows himself to believe.'

Before Olivia could consider a response to that rather cryptic remark, Malik opened a door and ushered her into an ornate reception room. French windows led out to a wide balcony, and even from across the room Olivia was able to glimpse the courtyard below already filled with people pressed shoulder to shoulder, all of them craning their necks to catch a glimpse of their new Sheikh and his future bride.

Her stomach lurched and she pressed a hand to her mouth.

'Please don't be sick,' Aziz remarked dryly as he stepped into the room. 'That would ruin quite a lovely outfit.' He stopped in front of her, his silvery-grey gaze wandering up and down her figure, eyes gleaming with a blatant masculine approval that made Olivia's stomach tighten. He'd never looked at her like that before. 'Dark hair suits you. So do high heels.' His mouth quirked in a smile. 'Very much so. I'm almost sorry it's only a temporary dye.'

She lifted her chin, forcing the feeling back that Aziz stirred so easily up inside her. Why was she reacting to him now, when she never had before? 'As long as I look like Queen Elena. As much as I can, at any rate.'

'I think you'll pass. Very well, actually.' His smile turned sympathetic. 'I do recognise that I am asking much of you, Olivia. Your willingness to help me is deeply appreciated, believe me.'

Olivia met his compassionate gaze with a direct one of her own. 'I just want to return to Paris.'

'And so you shall. But first, the balcony.' He nodded towards the doors; even from here, with them closed, Olivia could hear the muted roar of the crowd below. She swallowed hard.

'You had the press conference?'

'Just a few moments ago.'

'Were the media concerned with why Queen Elena wasn't there?'

'A few asked, but I said you were tired from your journey and preparing to meet your new people. They accepted it. In any case, it would be unusual in this country for a woman to appear in front of the media and speak for herself.'

'But Queen Elena has spoken for herself many times,' Olivia observed. 'She's a reigning monarch.'

'True, but in Kadar she is merely going to be the wife of a Sheikh. There is a difference.'

Olivia heard a surprising edge of bitterness in his

voice and wondered at it. 'Why did Queen Elena agree to this marriage if she would have few rights in your country? It wasn't, I presume, a love match?'

'Indeed not.' Aziz flashed her a quick, hard smile. 'The alliance suited us both, for different reasons.'

A surprisingly implacable note had entered Aziz's voice, but Olivia ignored it. 'You speak in the past tense. Does it not still suit you?'

'It will,' Aziz told her. 'When I find her. But as for now...' He gestured to the balcony doors. 'Our adoring public awaits.'

Nerves coiled tightly in Olivia's belly and she nodded. There was surely no going back now. 'All right.'

'It is important for you to know,' Aziz said in a low voice as they walked towards the balcony, 'That, though my marriage to Elena was for convenience only, the public assumed it was a love match. They want it to be a love match.'

Olivia shot him a sharp glance, nerves leaping now, like a nest of snakes had taken up residence in her stomach. 'Even though you only became engaged a few weeks ago?'

Aziz shrugged. 'People believe what they want to believe.'

That, she thought grimly, had certainly been true in her own experience. 'So what does this mean for our appearance out there?'

Aziz gave her a teasing smile and reached out to brush her cheek with his fingers, sending a sudden shower of sparks cascading through Olivia's senses. Instinctively she jerked back. 'Only that we both need to act as if we are hopelessly in love. Try to restrain yourself from too much PDA, though, Olivia. This is a conservative country, after all.'

She opened her mouth in outrage, knowing he was joking yet still indignant. Aziz just chuckled softly then slipped his arm through hers and guided her out onto the balcony and the throng that waited below.

A cheer went up as soon as they both stepped outside; the hot, still air hit Olivia full in the face. She blinked, dumbfounded by the roar of approval that sounded from below and seemed to go on and on.

Aziz slid a hand around her waist, his fingers splayed across her hip as he raised one hand in greeting.

'Wave,' he murmured and obediently Olivia raised her hand. 'Smile,' he added, a hint of laughter in his voice, and she curved her lips upwards.

They stood like that, hip to hip, Aziz's hand around her waist, waving as the crowd continued to cheer.

'I thought,' Olivia said in a whisper, even though no one could possibly hear, 'That you said the Kadaran people were not loyal to you.'

He shrugged. 'They are a romantic people as well as a traditional one. They like the idea of my marriage, of a fairy-tale wedding, more than they like me.'

'It is indeed a fairy tale,' Olivia answered tartly and Aziz just smiled.

After another endless minute he dropped his hand. Olivia thought they would be finally, thankfully heading back inside, but he stayed her with his hand still around her waist, the other coming up to frame her jaw.

'What are you doing?' she hissed.

'The crowd wants to see us kiss.'

'What happened to no PDA?' she retorted through gritted teeth. 'And this being a conservative country?'

'Siyad is a little more modern. And we'll keep it chaste, don't worry. No tongues,' he advised, and as her mouth dropped open in shock he kissed her.

Olivia froze beneath the touch of his lips; it had been so long since she'd been kissed she'd forgotten how it felt—how intimate, strange and frankly wonderful. Aziz's lips were cool and soft, the hand that framed her face both tender and firm. Her eyes closed instinctively as she fought against the tidal wave of want that crashed so unexpectedly through her.

'There.' He eased back, smiling. 'You managed to restrain yourself.'

'Easily,' she snapped, and he laughed softly.

'It's so delightfully simple to get a rise out of you, Olivia. It makes your eyes sparkle.'

'How *delightful* to know,' Olivia retorted, and he just laughed again.

'Indeed.'

He was leading her back inside but Olivia was barely aware of her surroundings. Her mind spun with sensation and her lips buzzed, as if his brief kiss had electrocuted her. It had been an appropriately chaste kiss, little more than a brushing of mouths, yet her insides felt alarmingly shivery and weak. Why had a simple kiss affected her so much?

Because it hadn't been simple for her. When you hadn't been kissed in nearly a decade, Olivia thought, a little one like that could be explosive. Unforgettable.

It surely had nothing to do with *Aziz*. Although she had to admit that, in her limited experience at least, he seemed a very good kisser.

As soon as the balcony doors were closed, Olivia tugged her hand from Aziz's. 'There.' She fought the urge to wipe her mouth, as if such a childish action could banish the memory of his kiss and the unwelcome feelings it had stirred up inside her. 'We're done. I can go back to Paris.'

'And so you shall, in the morning.'

'Why not tonight?'

'It's a long flight, Olivia. The pilot needs to rest; the plane to be refuelled. Besides, I am meant to be having dinner with my bride, and I know you don't want to miss that.'

She ignored the teasing, even though part of her actually was tempted to smile. The man was incorrigible, determinedly so. 'You never said anything about dinner.'

'It must have slipped my mind.'

'Liar.'

'As Sheikh, I'm in control of how much information to disseminate at a given time, it's true.'

'Such big words.'

'I looked them up in the dictionary.'

And then she did smile, helpless to keep herself from it, knowing that she, like every other woman, was falling prey to his charm. 'And I'm meant to be Queen Elena at this dinner?'

'It's a private dinner, so you only have to pretend for me.'

'And the staff who see us together,' Olivia pointed out. 'Aziz, this is ludicrous. I might be able to pass myself off as Queen Elena from a balcony, but I can hardly do so face to face. One look at me and your staff will know.'

'You are assuming they will be suspicious,' Aziz answered calmly. 'And why should they be? Word went out that Queen Elena arrived by royal jet this afternoon. And so she did. Then she appeared with me on the balcony, as planned. Everything is going just as it should, Olivia. No one has reason to suspect otherwise.'

'Except for the fact that I don't look anything like her.'

'Do you think anyone here has seen Queen Elena in the flesh?'

'Photographs in the papers,' she argued. 'And, in any case, didn't she come here to discuss your marriage?'

Aziz nodded, still unruffled. 'Yes, but it was a private meeting, very discreet. At that point, neither of us wanted to make the negotiations public.'

'Even so.'

He smiled, laid a hand over hers, and Olivia had to fight the urge to yank her hand away. She'd been numb for so long, she hadn't thought she had any feelings or desires left for Aziz to stir up inside her. Yet he had. So easily, he had. 'Just dinner, Olivia. And then you can leave in the morning.'

She shook her head again, feeling as if she'd been caught in a riptide. She was being carried away from everything she'd known and wanted, everything *safe*, so quickly. She couldn't fight against it.

And yet she was honest enough to admit she was tempted—tempted to enjoy this fleeting time with Aziz, to let herself fall just a little bit under his spell. Just for a night. Then she'd go back to her little life.

'You need to eat, Olivia,' he murmured.

'I could have a sandwich in my room.'

'Fine, then I'll join you. Of course, then the staff might really gossip.'

She pulled her hand from his. 'You're impossible.'

He smiled and inclined his head. 'Thank you.'

'It wasn't,' she informed him tartly, 'A compliment.'

His smile just widened. 'I know.'

What point was there in resisting? Olivia wondered. Aziz would wear her down eventually with his tireless charm that masked a far more steely sense of purpose. She hadn't realised that before, hadn't seen how determined he could be, but then they'd never been at cross purposes before. And were they even now?

You are tempted...

Tempted to enjoy one evening with a beautiful man. Tempted to access those deadened parts of herself and feel like a beautiful, desirable woman, even if it was just pretend.

'Fine,' she said. 'I'll have dinner with you. But I leave first thing in the morning.'

She gazed at him in challenge and Aziz just smiled blandly. 'Of course,' he answered, and with a creeping sense of foreboding Olivia wondered if she dared to take him at his word—or if she even wanted to.

CHAPTER FOUR

THE PRIVATE DINING ROOM, one of the palace's smaller ones, had been set for a romantic dinner for two. Aziz raised an eyebrow at the snowy linen tablecloth, the creamy candles casting flickering shadows across the dim, wood-panelled room. Olivia, he knew, would not be pleased by any of it. He'd never met a woman so resistant to his charm.

Although, she hadn't been resistant when he'd kissed her. He'd felt her shock first, tensing her whole body as if a wire that ran through her had been jerked taut, and then he'd felt her compliance, even her desire, as her body had relaxed and her hand had come up to grip his shoulder. He wondered if she'd even been aware of the fullness of her response, how she'd drawn him closer, parted her lips under his. He'd teased her that she'd have to restrain herself but he hadn't thought she'd take him at his word.

And as she'd responded he'd felt, with a sudden, shocking urgency, a desire or even a need to deepen that kiss, slide his tongue into her mouth and taste her velvety sweetness.

Thank God he hadn't acted on that overwhelming instinct. The people of Siyad might want to see them kiss chastely; they would have been appalled by such a blatant display of sexual desire.

And what he'd felt for Olivia in that moment had been deeply, potently sexual. A complication, he mused, that he certainly didn't need right now.

'Your Highness.' A member of staff opened the doors of the dining room. 'Her Highness, Queen Elena.'

So she'd fooled at least one person, Aziz thought with satisfaction. Olivia stepped into the room, her dark hair styled into an ornate twist with a few tendrils curling around her face. She wore an evening gown of shimmering silver; the sparkling bodice hugged her tiny waist before flaring out around her legs in gossamer folds. She looked magnificent, radiant, and more beautiful than he'd ever seen her before. Lust reached out and caught him by the throat, left him momentarily breathless and blindsided.

The doors closed behind her and she stopped in front of them, fixing him with a defiant stare. 'I didn't choose this dress,' she told him. 'But Mada and Abra insisted. I don't even know where it came from.'

'I had some clothes ordered.'

'For the impostor or the real thing?' she retorted.

Aziz kept his own voice deliberately mild. 'Does it matter?'

'I don't know.' She looked lost for a moment, vulnerability melting the ice in her eyes, before she shook her head in weary resignation. 'This is all so strange.'

'I agree. But strange, in its own way, can be enjoyable.' Aziz walked towards her, wanting to touch her. He felt the entirely primal and primitive reaction of a man alone with a beautiful woman; he wanted to enjoy it, enjoy her, and not discuss how strange or wrong or dangerous it all was.

'You certainly look the part now,' he said as he gestured to her sparkling dress. 'You are lovely, Olivia.'

Her cheeks pinked and she arched one elegant eyebrow. 'I think you're a little more adept with the compliments than that.'

A smile tugged at his mouth. 'Oh, am I?'

'I've heard you compare a woman to a rose petal before.'

'Oh dear, that sounds rather uninspired.'

'She obviously fell for it. The two of you were upstairs before dessert was served.'

'Mmm.' He felt strangely disconcerted. He wasn't ashamed of his sexual exploits; he'd discovered at fifteen that women liked him, and after an isolated, unhappy childhood that had been a powerful aphrodisiac. So, maybe they only liked his body, his charm, but that was enough.

He wasn't looking to offer his heart. He knew what happened when you did that. He'd put his on a damn plate for most of his childhood, for anyone to shove away, to shatter.

Yet he was conscious now of how much Olivia knew about him. His housekeeper had turned a blind and clearly unimpressed eye to his goings-on in Paris; why she felt the need to remind him of them now, he wasn't sure. He didn't like it.

'I'll have to think of an apt comparison,' he said as he reached for her hand. Her skin was cool and soft. 'An icicle, perhaps? Glittering, perfect and rather cold.'

'That sounds more like a criticism.'

'Well…' Aziz answered with a hint of a wolfish smile. 'Icicles melt.'

Olivia melted just a little then, her fingers tightening on his, her cheeks pinking again as she looked away. Her reaction, Aziz decided, was delightful. 'Come,' he said as he drew her further into the room. 'Dinner is waiting.'

'This is all very romantic,' she murmured as she let him lead her to the table. Her fingers felt fragile and slender in his, and he let go of her hand with reluctance.

He knew, logically at least, that acting on the desire he felt for Olivia was out of the question. It would complicate what needed to be—for the sake of the monarchy, not to mention his marriage—very simple.

God willing, Olivia would be flying back to Paris tomorrow—and he would have found Elena.

Yet he still wanted to enjoy himself tonight.

As if she could read his mind, Olivia asked, 'Is there any news on Queen Elena?'

Aziz shook his head. 'I'm afraid not.'

'This Khalil wouldn't… He wouldn't hurt her, would he?' Concern shadowed Olivia's eyes and Aziz felt an answering clench of both worry and anger in the pit of his stomach.

'I don't think so. There would be no purpose to it and, as you said earlier, she is a reigning monarch. Kidnapping her is bad enough, but hurting her would have international consequences.'

'That's true,' Olivia said, frowning. 'But doesn't Khalil realise that? He could be brought before an international tribunal.'

'Kadar exists outside of such things.' Aziz gave her a bleak smile. 'At least, at the moment. My father ruled with an iron fist. The people loved him even so, because he was strong and he kept the country stable. But he did things his own way, and it means there are very few repercussions for what happens within its borders.'

'But surely someone from the Thallian government will protest?'

'If they find out.'

'You've kept it from them too?'

'From everyone, Olivia. I've had to. But I will find her.' He placed the heavy damask napkin in her lap, just an excuse to touch her. Her body quivered under the brush of his fingers. 'I understand you have questions,' he continued quietly. 'But I'd much rather talk about something else. Something pleasant, even.' He smiled, willing the tension and uncertainty of the last few hours, the last few weeks, away, if just for one evening.

'Something pleasant,' Olivia repeated, her long, slender fingers toying with the crystal stem of her wine glass. Her mouth curved and she glanced up at him, eyebrows raised. 'Nothing comes to mind at the moment, I'm afraid.'

His lips twitched in an answering smile. 'Oh dear,' he murmured. 'What a dilemma. Surely we can come up with something?'

'Do you really think so?'

'I'm sure, between the two of us, we could think of something pleasant indeed.' His voice had dropped to a husky murmur and his insides tightened with desire. He hadn't intended a sexual innuendo, but it was there all the same. He heard it and, from the way Olivia moistened her lips, he knew she did too. He wondered what she would do with it, how she would respond...and how he wanted her to.

'I'm sure you think of *something pleasant* all the time,' she answered. 'Although, that's a euphemism I haven't come across before.'

'Rather an innocuous one,' he answered, and her expression tightened.

'Don't flirt with me, Aziz. I know it's your default setting but you managed to keep yourself from it before.'

He let out a laugh. 'My default setting?'

She faced him directly, her gaze now resolute. 'You're a playboy. You can't help it.'

He smiled wryly. 'You make it sound like I have some condition. A disease.'

'One I'd hope you can control. I'm not going to be one of your conquests.'

She was going on the attack because their little bout of flirting had disconcerted her, Aziz decided. Had affected her. 'Default settings aside,' he said, leaning back in his chair, 'I like seeing you smile, Olivia, and hearing you laugh. I've only heard you laugh once before, and I wasn't even in the room.'

A wary confusion clouded her eyes. 'I don't know what you're talking about.'

'You were in the kitchen and I'd come into the house without you knowing it. I heard you laugh.' He paused, noting the way her face went pale, her eyes widened. 'It was a delightful laugh,' he continued. 'Rich and full, almost dirty. I wondered what you were laughing about.'

'I—I don't remember.'

'Why don't you laugh like that with me?'

'Maybe you're not funny enough,' she shot back, on the attack again, and he nodded, smiling.

'Ah, a direct challenge. I now have a mission.'

'One you'll fail at, Aziz. I'm your housekeeper. You don't need me to laugh. You don't even know me.'

'And is there very much to know?'

Her fingers tightened around her wine glass. 'Not really. I live a very quiet life in Paris.'

'Why is that?'

'I prefer it.'

'Yes, but why?' He realised he truly did want to know the answer, wanted to understand why a woman like Olivia Ellis—a beautiful, capable, intelligent, lovely woman—would hide herself away as housekeeper to an empty house for six long years.

'Why shouldn't I?' she challenged. 'Not everyone wants to live like you do, Aziz.'

He sat back in his chair, amused and still intrigued by her non-answer. 'And how do I live, Olivia?'

'You know as well as I do. Parties till dawn and a different woman in your bed every night.'

'You disapprove.'

'It's not for me to judge, but it's certainly not how I want to live my life.'

'Surely there's a balance? We're opposites, you and I, in our pursuit of pleasure, but don't you think we could find some middle ground?'

Her eyes flashed. 'And where would that be?'

In bed. He had a sudden, vivid image of Olivia lying on top of tangled satin sheets, her glorious hair spread out on the pillow, her lips rosy and swollen from his kisses. His libido stirred insistently. He knew he had no business thinking like this, feeling like this.

And yet he did.

'It's up for discussion, I suppose,' he said easily, and Olivia just shook her head.

A waiter came in with their first course and they both remained silent as he laid plates of salad before them. Olivia kept her head bowed, her face averted, although she murmured a thank you as the man departed.

'I don't think he suspected,' Aziz murmured as the door clicked shut.

Olivia glanced up at him. 'Like you said, people believe what they want to believe.'

She sounded hard, Aziz noted, and cynical. 'Has that been your experience?'

'More or less.'

'Which one?' he asked lightly, and she stared at him, her whole body going still, her face turning blank.

'More,' she said flatly, and then looked away. He wanted to ask her what she meant but she didn't give him the chance. 'Will you miss your old life?' she asked. 'The parties, the whole playboy routine? I suppose things will be very different for you, getting married, living in Kadar.'

'Yes, I suppose they will.' He picked up his fork and toyed with a piece of lettuce. 'But in answer to your question, no, I won't miss my old life.' He glanced up, taken aback by his own honesty, striving for nonchalance. 'Which I suppose is a confession of how shallow I really am.'

She cocked her head, eyeing him thoughtfully. 'A shallow person wouldn't be fighting for his throne.'

'Maybe I just want power.'

'Why *do* you want to be Sheikh?' she asked. 'You never even seemed interested in Kadar before. You hardly ever returned here, by your own admission.'

'It isn't a question of want,' Aziz answered after a moment. 'It's my duty.'

'A duty that didn't concern you before,' she pointed out and he pretended to wince.

'You don't pull your punches, do you, Olivia?'

'Why should I?'

He chuckled softly. 'No, I don't suppose you should. It's a fair question, anyway.' One he didn't particularly want to answer, yet he felt the surprising need to be honest. So much of his life was pretence and prevarication. Olivia, with her direct gaze and no-nonsense attitude, was someone he knew he could trust and confide in, at least a little. 'My father never really wanted me to be

Sheikh,' he said after a moment. 'I was always a disappointment to him.'

'But why?'

Because he'd wanted Khalil. Even when he knew he wasn't his son, when he'd rejected him, Hashem had longed for the son he'd loved, not Aziz. Not his son by blood. Honesty only went so far, though, and Aziz wasn't about to admit any of that. He couldn't stand it if Olivia ended up pitying him and the desperate-for-love boy he'd been. 'We just didn't see eye to eye on a lot of things.' Which was putting it mildly.

Even now he could remember the way his father had sneered at his every attempt to please him. He could feel the scorching shame he'd known when Hashem had marched him into a meeting of royal aides and staff and asked him to recite Kadar's constitution. Aziz had stumbled once, *once*, and Hashem had mocked him ruthlessly before slapping his face and dismissing him from the room.

Just one memory among dozens, hundreds, all of them equally cringe-worthy. Until he'd been fifteen and he'd lost his virginity—to one of his father's mistresses, no less—and he'd realised there was another way to live. A way not to care.

'Is that why you've stayed away from Kadar? Because of your father?' Olivia asked, and Aziz blinked back the memories and stretched his lips into an easy smile.

'Pretty much. Our meetings were—acrimonious.'

'But you still haven't told me why you've chosen to return to Kadar and be Sheikh.'

'I suppose,' he said slowly, 'It's a bit of perversity on my part. I want to prove my father wrong. I want to prove I can be Sheikh, and a damned good one at that.' He heard the passionate intensity throb in his voice and felt a shaft of embarrassment. He sounded so *eager*.

'So your decision is still about your father,' she said after a moment. 'You're still letting him control you. Letting him win.'

He jerked back, stung more than he liked by her assessment, yet knowing she was right. His choices were still dictated by his father. He might not wear his heart on his sleeve any more, but he still wanted his father's approval. *His love.*

'I never thought of that before,' he said as carelessly as he could. 'But, yes, I suppose you're right. It's still about my father.' And maybe it always would be.

'It's hard,' Olivia said quietly, 'When someone has so much power and influence in your life, to let go of it. Even choosing to ignore that person still makes them the centre of your life, in a way. You're spending all your energy, all your time, trying not to think about them.'

'You're speaking from experience,' Aziz observed and she shrugged.

'Like you, I'm not very close to my father. He's still alive, of course, but we haven't spoken in years.'

'I wasn't aware of that.' He thought of her father, an easy-going, affable man who had climbed high in the diplomatic service. 'He recommended you for the position as housekeeper,' he recalled and she nodded stiffly.

'I think he felt he owed me that much, at least.'

'Owed you?'

She shook her head and he could tell she regretted saying even that much. 'It doesn't matter. Ancient history.'

But he saw how her hands tightened in her lap, her features became pinched, her eyes darkened with remembered pain, and he knew it wasn't that ancient. And it did matter.

She looked down at her plate, her expression clearing, Aziz suspected, by sheer force of will. 'Anyway, we should be talking of the future, not the past,' she said briskly. 'Assuming you find Queen Elena in time, do you think you will come to love her?'

Aziz stiffened in surprise. *No, never.* Because he wasn't interested in loving or being loved, didn't want to open himself up to those messy emotions, needless complications. Look where it had got him; you loved someone and they let you down. They didn't love you back or, worse, they hated you.

But he wasn't, thank God, a needy, foolish boy any more. He was a man who knew what he wanted, understood what he had to do, and love didn't come into it at all.

'Queen Elena and I have discussed the nature of our marriage,' he informed her. 'We are both satisfied with the arrangement.'

'That isn't really an answer,' Olivia replied, and Aziz smiled and spread his hands.

'We barely know each other, Olivia. I've met Elena twice. I have no idea if I could love her or not.' 'Not' being the operative word. 'In any case, I'd rather talk about you. I'm sure you're far more interesting than I am.'

She shook her head rather firmly. 'I most certainly am not.'

'You're the daughter of a diplomat. You must have grown up in all sorts of places.' She conceded the point with a nod and Aziz pressed, 'Where would you call home?'

'Paris.'

With a jolt he realised she meant his house. No wonder the job meant so much to her. It was probably the longest she'd lived anywhere.

'Not just because of now,' she explained. 'I spent some

time in Paris as a child—primary school years. I've always liked it there.'

'And where did you spend your teenaged years?'

The slightest hesitation. 'South America.'

'That must have been interesting.'

A tiny shrug, the flattening of her tone. 'It was a very small ex-pat community.'

Which was a strange response. She had secrets, Aziz thought. He thought of that rich laugh, the anguished piano music. She hid all her emotion, all her joy and pain—why?

Why did he hide his?

Because it hurt. It hurt to show your real self, to feel those deep emotions. They were both skimming the surface of life, he realised. They just did it in totally different ways.

'And if I recall your CV, you only spent one year in university?'

'One term,' she corrected, her voice giving nothing away. Her face had gone completely blank, like a slate wiped clean. 'I decided it wasn't for me.'

Her knuckles were white as she held her fork, her body utterly rigid. And even though he was tempted to press, to know, Aziz decided to give her a break. For now. 'I'm not sure if it was for me either,' he told her with a shrug. 'I barely scraped a two-two. Too busy partying, I suppose.'

He saw her relax, her fingers loosening on her fork. 'A playboy even then?'

He shrugged. 'It must be in my genes.' And there could be some truth to that, considering how many women his father had had. But Aziz knew that, genetics aside, his decision to pursue the playboy life had been deliberate, even if it was empty. Especially because it was empty.

'You're clever, though,' Olivia said after a moment. 'You started your own consulting business.'

'I'm fortunate that I have a way with numbers,' he said dismissively with a shrug. In truth, he was rather fiercely proud of his own business. He hadn't taken a penny from his father for it, although people assumed he had. In reality he hadn't accepted any money from his father since he'd left university. Not that he went around telling people that, or about the percentage of his earnings that he donated back to Kadar to support charities and foundations that helped women and children, the vulnerable and the oppressed. He wasn't going to brag about his accomplishments, or try to make people like him more.

Except, maybe he needed to, if he wanted to keep his throne.

'What about you, Olivia? Did you ever want to be anything other than a housekeeper?'

Her eyes flashed ire. 'There's nothing wrong with being a housekeeper.'

'Indeed not. But you're young, intelligent, with the opportunity of education and advancement. The question, I believe, is fair.' He waited, watching the play of emotions across her face: surprise. Uncertainty. Regret.

'I intended to study music,' she finally said, each word imparted with obvious reluctance. 'But, as you know, I dropped out.'

He thought again of her playing the piano, the passion and hopelessness he'd seen on her face. 'You never wanted to take it up again?'

She shook her head, decisive now. 'There was no point.'

'Why not?'

She pressed her lips together, her gaze turning distant. 'The music had gone,' she finally said. 'The desire, along with the talent. I knew I couldn't recapture it even if I tried, which I didn't want to do.' She sounded matter-of-fact but he felt her sadness like a palpable thing, like a cloak she was wearing that he'd just never seen before, never seen how it suffocated her.

For beneath that cool, remote exterior, Aziz knew there hid a beating heart bound by pain. A woman who had suffered…but what? And why?

He wanted to know but he kept himself from asking. She'd shared enough, and so had he. They both had secrets, and neither he nor Olivia wanted them brought to light. Yet he could not keep himself from wondering. He'd touched something dark and hidden in Olivia, something he shouldn't let himself feel curious about, yet he was.

He wanted to know more about this woman.

Olivia shifted in her seat, avoiding Aziz's penetrating stare, and focused on her salad. He was asking too many questions, questions that felt like scabs being picked off old wounds.

She'd put her memories in a box in her mind, sealed it shut and labelled it 'Do Not Open. Ever'. Yet with his light questions, his curious tone, Aziz was prying off the lid.

She didn't think about her dreaded term at university when she'd been like a sleepwalker, only half-alive, if that. She didn't think about her music, although she'd surrendered to the desire and even the need to play a couple of times in the last few years. Playing the piano was like a blood-letting, all the emotions and agonies streaming out along with the notes.

She'd needed the release because the rest of the time she kept herself remote, distant, from everyone and everything, even her own feelings, her own heart.

Life was simpler, and certainly safer, that way. She'd fallen apart once, overwhelmed by emotion, by grief, guilt and pain, and she had no intention of letting it happen again. If she gave those dark feelings so much as a toe-in they'd take over everything. They'd swamp her soul. And she might never come up for air again.

So she stayed numb, safe. She kept a tight rein on her emotions, let herself be content with a half-life.

Yet in the few hours since she'd been with Aziz too many of those emotions had been stirred up. Grief. Joy. Guilt. Hope. Aziz stirred up everything inside her. He asked questions, he made her smile, he touched her with his teasing in a way she hadn't expected and couldn't let herself want.

She'd thought she was dead inside but when Aziz had kissed her she'd felt gloriously, painfully alive.

Out there on the balcony she'd almost responded to his barely there kiss and turned it into something else entirely. She'd felt as if she'd been teetering on a wonderful precipice and part of her had wanted to swan-dive into that chasm of feeling and see if she really could fly.

She would have dropped like a stone. That life, a life of wanting, feeling, *loving*, was over.

'What will you do if you don't find Queen Elena in time?' Olivia asked. No more talking about herself.

'Failure is not an option.'

'And I assume Khalil feels the same way.' She didn't want to involve herself in complicated Kadaran politics, yet part of her was curious, intrigued by the sudden spike of bitterness she'd heard in Aziz's voice, the surprising darkness she'd seen in his eyes when he'd spoken of Kadar or his father—or this illegitimate son who was now trying for the throne. 'Did you ever meet him?' she asked. 'Khalil?'

Aziz smiled, but it belied the sudden coldness in his eyes. 'Yes. Once.'

'When?'

'When I was a child. He was living at the palace, and I was the pretender then.'

'You were? How?'

'I was the son of my father's mistress, an acknowledged bastard. My father legitimised me when he banished Khalil. It was not a terribly popular move, I'm afraid.' He spoke as if it didn't really matter, but Olivia knew it did. It had to.

'Is that why people support Khalil now?'

'They've always supported him. He left the country when he was seven, but he's remained in everyone's hearts—the poor little prince who got booted out. And I've always been the smug brat who took his place.' He still spoke lightly, but his eyes were like iron.

'It sounds like your father didn't think through his decision very wisely,' Olivia said quietly, and Aziz let out a laugh, the sound harsh and abrupt.

'My father,' he answered, 'Wanted to have his cake and eat it too. And he didn't even like cake.'

'So he loved Khalil,' she said slowly, 'But he still banished him.'

'I've often wondered why he did, since he made it clear what a disappointment I was compared to Khalil.' Aziz's mouth twisted in something like a smile. 'I suppose he did it because he was so angry that he'd been made a cuckold. Or maybe he was furious with himself for loving a son who wasn't actually his. Or maybe he just reacted out of anger and pain.' He took a breath and let it out slowly. 'I think he made this will because he wanted to give Khalil a chance.'

She met his gaze directly. 'A chance you don't want to give him.'

Aziz jerked back as if he'd been slapped. 'Why should I? He's not the ruler by right. *I* am.'

'But do you even like Kadar?' Olivia pressed. 'You've spent so little time here by your own choice.' She shook her head slowly, realisation dawning. 'You're only doing this to spite your father, and he's dead.'

She saw anger blaze briefly in Aziz's eyes before he gave her a rather sardonic smile. 'What an astute psychological assessment, Miss Ellis.'

'Sarcasm is the lowest form of defence.'

'I thought the expression was the lowest form of humour.'

'That too,' she conceded. 'I'm not saying you don't deserve to be Sheikh, Aziz, although—' She stopped and his gaze narrowed.

'Although…?'

'Although I wonder if you think you do,' she finished quietly.

He stared at her, breathing hard, as if he'd been running. Olivia held his gaze, wondering why she'd pushed him yet also glad that she had. 'You're right,' he finally said. 'I do wonder if I should be Sheikh. If the people don't want me to be, if my father didn't…'

'And yet you're still here.'

'When I first read my father's will I thought about just giving it up to Khalil. Turning my back. I think plenty of people were expecting me to.'

'But you didn't.'

'No, I didn't.' He spoke heavily, as if he doubted the wisdom of his choice. Doubted, Olivia suspected, himself.

'Well, I think that says something,' she said and Aziz glanced at her with a hint of his old humour.

'Oh? And what does it say? That I'm stubborn and bone-headed?'

'And determined and strong,' Olivia answered. 'Aziz, you're the Gentleman Playboy.'

'As you keep reminding me—charming, shallow, feckless and so on. Yes, I know.'

'Forget shallow and feckless for a moment,' Olivia said. 'You're charming. You have most of Europe eating out of your hand, and I don't just mean the women. Why shouldn't you be able to win the hearts of your own people? You just haven't tried before.'

He pressed his lips together as if to keep from saying something, then after a moment gave a little smile. 'Thank you for that pep talk. It was obviously needed.'

So he was reverting to lightness, Olivia thought. She was disappointed and yet she told herself it was just as well. They'd had enough emotional honesty for one evening, surely.

'Enough talk about Kadar and politics,' he said, pouring them both more wine. 'Let's talk about something else.'

'Such as?'

'What do you like to do in your spare time?'

'What?' Startled and more than a little discomfited, she simply gaped at him. Aziz smiled back, his teeth gleaming white in his tanned face, his eyes like silver. Her insides tightened in helpless, yearning response. Why had she never responded to him like this before?

Because you never let yourself. Because she'd never spent so much time with Aziz that hadn't been mundane and perfunctory. Because she'd never got to know the man behind the persona before—a man who was more thoughtful, sensitive and appealing than the Gentleman Playboy but with all of his charm and charisma.

'Hobbies, Olivia. Pastimes. Do you like to read? Go to the cinema? Crochet?'

'Crochet?'

He shrugged. 'A shot in the dark.'

An unwilling bubble of laughter escaped her, surprising her. She was enjoying this silly banter, she realised. She liked how it made her feel. 'I don't crochet, I'm afraid.'

'No need to be afraid. I'm not disappointed.' She laughed again and Aziz's eyes flared. 'There it is. That lovely sound. I will find out why you laughed in the kitchen.'

She shook her head slowly, still smiling. 'It was nothing.'

'It was a wonderful laugh.'

'I was laughing at a squirrel,' she told him. 'A little red one. He was trying to pick up a nut and it was too heavy for him.'

She'd watched that little squirrel for several minutes, had been absorbed in his little drama, and when he'd finally managed to pick up the nut she'd laughed. It had been such a silly little thing, but it had taken herself out of her own head for a little while, and she'd needed that.

'No big mystery,' she told Aziz lightly and he smiled.

'But now you intrigue me even more. You make me wonder why I've never been able to make you laugh before, yet now I can.' He held her gaze then, still smiling, but with a certain steadiness in his eyes that made Olivia's mouth dry—for wasn't this far more dangerous, this emotional connection, than a merely physical one?

A man who could make her laugh as well as burn.

She looked away.

'Olivia?' Aziz said quietly.

'I suppose laughter doesn't come easily to me any

more,' she said after a moment. She was amazed she was telling him this much, yet part of her wanted to tell him, to unburden herself, if only just a little.

'Why is that?'

She just shrugged. She didn't want to unburden herself that much, to admit that she'd thought the carefree, laughing girl she'd once been had died when she'd been just seventeen and it had felt like her soul had been ripped from her body. It *had*.

Aziz reached over and placed his hand gently on top of hers. 'Whatever has made you sad,' he said quietly, 'I'm glad to see you happy, even if just for a moment.'

She nodded jerkily, her throat so tight she knew she couldn't manage any words even if she'd known what ones to say.

Aziz removed his hand and sat back. 'Are you finished?' he asked, gesturing to her half-eaten salad. 'I'll call for the next course.'

Olivia nodded, grateful for the reprieve from their conversation, and a few minutes later the waiter returned to clear their plates and then bring the main course. Aziz asked for some mundane details about the Paris house, and by silent agreement they kept the conversation about various issues concerning the house and nothing else for the rest of the meal.

Yet, even though Aziz wasn't asking her personal questions any more, Olivia couldn't keep her mind from wandering to places it shouldn't go. She couldn't keep her gaze from roving surreptitiously over him, or from noticing the way the candlelight gave his hair a blue-black sheen.

He wore an evening suit that emphasised the breadth of his shoulders, the trimness of his hips, the overall perfection of his body.

Everything about him was graceful and elegant; Olivia was mesmerised just by the way he held his knife and fork. He had lovely fingers, she thought: long and slender, yet with so much latent strength. There was, she decided, a leashed and stealthy power about him that she hadn't noticed before, at least not consciously. Perhaps now that he was ruler of a country she felt it, had the sense that he was more than a man of wealth and charm.

A dangerous man.

A desirable man.

And that was something she had no business thinking about. Aziz was getting *married.* Determinedly she yanked her gaze away from those long-fingered hands. He was getting married in just two days, if he found Queen Elena.

And if he didn't?

Not her problem. Not a question she needed to answer, or even ask. Yet her heart lurched all the same.

The candles had burned down to waxy stubs by the time they had their coffee, thick and syrupy, brewed in the Arabic manner that made Olivia pucker her mouth.

Aziz laughed when he saw her expression. 'It does take some getting used to.'

'You're obviously used to it,' she said, for he'd drunk his without so much as a grimace, or even adding any sugar.

'It took a while,' he admitted as he finished the last of his coffee. 'But the taste of it has grown on me.'

'So you don't miss your Americanos?' Olivia asked with a little smile. She'd made his coffee on the machine he'd had installed in the kitchen of the house in Paris.

'Oh, I miss them,' Aziz assured her. 'But I've made a point of having only Kadaran food and drink since I've been here.'

'To show your loyalty?'

'Something like that,' Aziz agreed, and Olivia sensed the brush-off. He was, she realised, constantly playing himself down. She thought suddenly of what Malik had said: *there are more loyal to Aziz than he knows, or allows himself to believe*. She thought she understood a little of what the older man had been saying; she'd felt it from Aziz tonight.

He didn't believe in himself. He didn't believe he would be accepted by the Kadaran people *as* himself. And maybe his careless, playboy attitude was just a cover-up for the fear and doubt he felt inside.

Or was she being fanciful because she knew how much she hid herself? This was *Aziz*, after all, the darling of Europe, a confident, charismatic man who had women constantly fawning over him. How could he possibly doubt *anything*?

Yet she wanted to know, wanted to know who the real Aziz was, and that was a foolish, dangerous thing to want, because he affected her too much already, and in any case he wasn't hers to know.

With effort she swallowed her questions down. She didn't need to know more about this man. She couldn't allow herself to, or let the attraction that had leapt to life today turn into something even deeper and more powerful, something she hadn't even thought she was capable of any more.

No, it needed to end here and now. Tomorrow she would be back in Paris and Aziz, hopefully, would have found Queen Elena.

She rose from the table and gave him a cool smile. 'Thank you for dinner.'

Aziz arched an eyebrow, and just that one little quirk made her feel sure he knew what she was doing and why. That he knew she was afraid and attracted all at once, but of course the Gentleman Playboy would never say so.

'Thank you for humouring me and continuing this charade,' he answered, rising also. He stepped closer to her and her heart seemed to stutter. She was achingly conscious of his nearness, even the smell of him, a citrusy aftershave that she must have smelled a thousand times before but now made her feel dizzy with longing. She knew she should move back and yet she didn't. She couldn't.

Aziz dipped his head and his gaze seemed to heat her from within, kindling feelings and needs that she'd thought were no more than cold ash. 'I'm sorry to have put you to such trouble, but you were the first person I thought of, Olivia. The first person I knew I could trust.'

The sincerity in his voice made the flames inside her rise higher. Logically she knew this had to be mere flattery. She was his housekeeper, for heaven's sake, and of a house he only visited on occasion, one step up from a maid—and he *trusted* her? *She* was the person he'd first thought of in a time of trouble?

Yet the warmth of his gaze and the seeming sincerity of his tone caused a maelstrom to whirl inside her. Desire and something deeper, something fiercer—the longing to be needed, to be important to someone again, to *matter*.

Ridiculous.

She barely knew Aziz. And this whole thing, on both their parts, had been nothing more than an act. Everything that had happened between them had been fake.

Even if it didn't feel fake.

'I'm glad to have been of service,' she said crisply and took a step away from him. The gauzy skirt of her dress caught on the stiletto heel she wasn't used to wearing and she tripped backwards, her arms windmilling as she desperately attempted to right herself, even as she braced herself to land on her backside.

Aziz stepped forward in one fluid movement and caught her in his arms. He brought her body into close, exquisite contact with his. She felt their hips and thighs collide and desire shot through her as if she'd been injected intravenously with lust. It sizzled through her whole body, pulsed between her thighs. She let out a ragged gasp and Aziz's gaze darkened, came to rest on her parted lips.

Olivia could only wait. Her heart had started a heavy, insistent thud and, despite her resolutions of a mere moment ago, her whole body yearned and strained for him to kiss her, to feel so much, even more than she already had. *So much more.*

For a second, no more, she thought he might kiss her. He leaned forward, drawing her body even closer to his so she felt the hard press of his arousal, and that electric pulse of want jolted her yet again, right down to her toes.

Then he stepped back, steadying her, and dropped his hands. She swallowed, fought for composure and tried to arrange her expression into something neutral and bland, as if the whole world hadn't tilted on its axis and all her certainties hadn't scattered. As if she hadn't suddenly realised how stark, dull and empty her life had been and how she now wanted so much more.

Wanted Aziz.

Aziz smiled but now it seemed like a mere stretching of his lips. His eyes, Olivia saw, were dark and fathomless.

'Thank you,' she muttered and Aziz nodded in acknowledgement. 'I should— It's late.' She stopped, took a breath and let it out slowly. 'Goodnight,' she said, the single world coming out with far too much finality.

'Goodnight, Olivia,' he said softly, and with a jerky nod, lifting her dress up so she wouldn't trip again, Olivia hurried from the room.

CHAPTER FIVE

AZIZ GAZED GRIMLY at the dawn sky. The sun was a huge, orange ball peeking above the horizon, spreading its morning rays over the courtyard, bathing the palace in brilliant, golden light.

His mood, however, was as dark as a moonless night. He'd spent most of the night awake, surveying satellite printouts of Kadar's desert, searching for a possible camp-site for Khalil and his band of rebels. From a satellite it was possible to discern various settlements, but neither Aziz nor any of his aides had been able to determine whether such settlements contained Khalil—or Queen Elena.

He'd sent another troop of soldiers, the few he felt he could trust, to investigate the most promising settlement which, when compared with printouts from the last few weeks, had shown the most activity. But it was three hundred miles from Siyad and the men were going by Jeep, as a helicopter would surely alert Khalil…if he was even there.

And if he *was* there? How far would his once-believed half-brother go to gain the throne? Would he risk his life and, more importantly, would he risk Elena's?

Aziz had told Olivia that he didn't think Khalil would be so foolhardy, but the truth was he didn't know. He didn't know Khalil at all.

He had, since taking the throne, read all the information the Kadaran intelligence service possessed about him. Khalil had been banished, along with his mother, at the age of seven, and his aunt had taken him to live with her in America. He'd gone to an elite boarding school and university, worked in business for a while before serving in the French Foreign Legion for seven years.

Aziz suspected it was while in the army that Khalil had made the contacts that had enabled him to return to Kadar. To return to the people who had wanted him back, had embraced him. The people of Siyad might like having a cosmopolitan man with European ways and a head for numbers as their ruler, but the heart of Kadar, its desert tribes, wanted Khalil. And it was the heart Aziz was concerned about.

Once more you're trying to win someone's heart, he thought cynically. *Trying to make someone love you. When will you realise you can't? You never will.*

Except he hadn't even started trying, because he was afraid he'd fail.

Olivia had been amazingly astute about it all. Her observations still stung him hours later. She'd seen how he still wanted to please his father, knew that he was afraid to try. How had she seen so much? How had he revealed it?

It was incredibly unsettling, to be understood in that way, yet there was something strangely, intrinsically good about it too—because Olivia hadn't rejected or judged him because of his fears. She'd encouraged him by insisting he could win the Kadaran people to his side...if he just tried.

The trouble was, he didn't think he believed her. From behind him Aziz heard the door softly open and close.

He glanced over his shoulder and saw Malik standing to attention, waiting for his order.

Malik had been on his father's staff, had known him as a boy. He knew how Aziz had been sneered at and mocked by his father and most of the palace staff. He'd stepped in more than once to deflect his father's contempt and, even though Aziz was grateful, he also felt the squirming shame of having his weaknesses exposed in front of another person.

'We're no closer to finding Elena, are we?' he said, a statement rather than a question.

'On the contrary, Your Highness, the settlement we viewed earlier on the satellite photograph looks promising. There has been an extraordinary amount of movement to and from it, as you saw, and just now we were able to find a photograph from the day Queen Elena was taken. It shows several vehicles on the outskirts of the camp.'

Aziz swivelled in his chair. 'That is promising, Malik,' he said. 'But, even if the soldiers I deployed enter the camp and Queen Elena is there, there is no guarantee as to what might happen.'

'No, indeed, Your Highness.'

Aziz sighed wearily and raked his hands through his hair. 'Can I even blame Khalil?' he said, only half-asking. Sometimes he felt furious at Khalil for endangering not just his bride, but his whole country. Did the man he'd once thought was his half-brother actually *want* war? Would that be his revenge for Sheikh Hashem's rejection of him?

Yet for seven years Khalil had believed himself to be his father's son, his country's heir. And he must know that Aziz had stayed away from Kadar for years; maybe he assumed Aziz didn't want to be Sheikh.

Maybe he believed he'd be a better one.

'It's my father I really blame,' Aziz told Malik. 'For making marriage a condition of my rule. For not naming a successor and inciting dissent with this damned referendum.' He shook his head, fury and despair warring within him. 'He was trying to create instability. He wanted it both ways.'

'You don't know that, Your Highness.'

'Don't I?' Aziz turned to give Malik a shrewd, bleak look. 'You know, Malik, that he never wanted me as his heir. He never—' He swallowed down the pathetic words 'loved me' and said instead, his voice rough, 'Really accepted me as his son.'

'But you are his son. His only son. And those in Siyad, and in the palace, know that. They believe you are the rightful ruler.'

'But many others don't. Many wonder if Khalil was treated unfairly. If my father banished him simply because he'd grown tired of his mother and preferred mine.'

'They will learn the truth.'

'Will they? Or will my entire rule, however long it even is, be dogged by such rumours?' He turned to stare out of the window; the courtyard was now shimmered in the morning heat. 'Damn my father,' he said in a low voice. 'Damn him to hell.'

'Perhaps he is already there,' Malik answered quietly.

'I'm not normally quite this negative, am I?' Aziz said, smiling at his aide, the action both false and familiar. *Smile. Laugh. Joke. Act like you don't car, and then maybe you won't.*

It didn't seem to fool Malik, however, for the older man gave a small, sorrowful smile and inclined his head. 'Your sentiment is understandable, Your Highness. Much of this current trial is your father's doing, I know. But there are more loyal to you than you realise.'

'I can't gamble on the people's loyalty, Malik. Not when I've been away for so long.' Aziz shook his head. 'I have two days to find Elena,' he stated. 'Two days before the six weeks are up and I lose my throne.'

'You have men looking for Elena, Your Highness,' Malik said. 'There is no more you can do now. They should have a report back to you by tonight.'

'Which gives me one day to make an alternative plan.'

'Speaking of alternative plans...' Malik cleared his throat. 'You are meant to attend the opening of the Royal Gardens in Siyad's city centre with Queen Elena today.'

Aziz closed his eyes. 'Damn it, I forgot. Can I cancel?'

'It's not advisable.'

'I'll go alone, then.'

Malik hesitated. 'Again, not advisable. Yesterday's appearance on the balcony was very popular.'

'You mean they want to see Elena again.' *Olivia.* Malik nodded. 'I don't think she can pull it off, Malik—even if she agrees, which she won't.'

'She could be veiled.'

'Veiled? Siyad is more modern than that.'

'It would be a nod to tradition, a way to show the more conservative parts of the population that you and your queen will respect the old ways.'

'Even if I want to change them?'

'Respect can exist with change.'

'I don't know.' He didn't like the thought of yet more pretence. More lies.

'Her eyes would be visible,' he said at last.

'Coloured contact lenses,' Malik answered swiftly.

Aziz shook his head slowly. 'It's too dangerous. They might ask her to speak.'

'Nothing beyond a murmured pleasantry, probably in Arabic.'

'I doubt Olivia knows any Arabic.'

'She can learn a few phrases.'

'It's madness.' Aziz rose abruptly from his chair and strode to the window, bracing one hand against the ancient stone arch. '*Madness*. What happens if they find Elena at the camp? How do I explain that?'

'You don't. We fly her in discreetly and have her replace Miss Ellis, who returns to Paris as she wished, no one the wiser. It's the ideal outcome, Your Highness.'

'And what if we don't have the ideal outcome?' Aziz queried grimly. 'What if we can't find Elena, or we find her and she's hurt, or—' He swallowed down the words, the awful possibility he did not want to give voice to. Fury towards Khalil surged inside him. Damn the man who had made his life hell, even when he'd been thousands of miles away. 'What then?' he demanded of Malik. 'How do we explain the fact that I've been posing with my bride for the last two days?'

'Not easily,' Malik acknowledged. 'But we've already taken this risk by having you appear on the balcony. It was a gamble, Your Highness, even a desperate one, but necessary. You know that.'

Yes, he knew that. He knew how unstable and insecure his reign really was. How one more whisper could start a firestorm of doubt and rumour that would ravage his entire kingdom...or even start a civil war.

'I'll go speak to her,' he said, and turned from the room.

Olivia lay in the massive bed, staring up at the silk canopy above her. Morning light filtered through the slats of the shutters Mada had drawn over the windows last night. It couldn't be much past dawn, and already the room was hot, the air still.

Today she'd return to Paris, to familiarity and safety. She felt a wave of relief mixed with a treacherous flicker of disappointment.

She didn't want to leave. She'd enjoyed herself with Aziz, enjoyed the attention and interest of a gorgeous, sexy man whose touch made her whole body tingle. A man who made her laugh, made her wonder, made her *feel*.

After so many years of numbness she knew now that some contrary part of her yearned for more from her life. From Aziz. She longed for his attention, his teasing, banter and sense of fun—and for his kiss. For that rush of sensation that had fired up her whole body, had made her senses sing.

Trying to banish the desire that rushed through her just at the memory of Aziz's lips on hers, Olivia threw off the covers just as a knock sounded on the door. 'Come in,' she called, and then froze in shock when the door swung open and Aziz stepped into the room.

They stared at each other wordlessly for a long, suspended moment. Olivia was suddenly, horribly conscious that she was wearing nothing but a frothy nightgown of lace and silk that ended mid-thigh; Mada and Abra had given it to her last night. Her hair was tousled about her shoulders and she'd frozen, half-risen from the bed, so the nightgown rode up on her thighs and low on her breasts. She glanced at the nightgown's matching robe laid out on a chair a few metres away. Would it be better to grab it and put it on, flimsy as it was, or to dive beneath the covers again?

She watched Aziz's gaze rove slowly over her, saw

his eyes flare and then darken with desire. Felt her body tingle treacherously in response.

'I thought...' Her voice came out in a croak and she tried again. 'I thought you were one of the women who had helped me last night.' She glanced at the clock and saw it was only a little past seven. 'Has something happened?'

'As much as I would enjoy discussing such matters with you in this moment, I fear I would be far too distracted.' His gaze dipped meaningfully to her scanty nightgown, his mouth curving into a teasing smile. 'Perhaps you could meet me for breakfast?'

Olivia felt a prickly flush spread over her whole body, even as a pleasure at his little bit of flattery stole through her. She'd distract him? She liked the sound of that... even if she shouldn't.

'Yes, of course,' she managed, willing her body-blush to fade.

'I'll send the women to you,' he said and with a last wicked smile he withdrew from the room.

Quickly Olivia rose from the bed and stripped off the nightgown, flinging it into a corner of the room before hurrying to the shower. Why had Mada and Abra given her such a ridiculously frothy, *sexy* thing to wear? It occurred to her then that the clothes she'd been wearing might belong to Queen Elena. Perhaps Aziz had bought them for her. Maybe that frothy nightgown was meant for their wedding night.

She blanched at the thought, hating that such a thought made her feel jealous. This was nothing more than pretend. Aziz was getting *married*, she reminded herself yet again.

Pretend or not, she knew she'd enjoyed herself more, *lived* more, in the last twenty-four hours than she had in ten years. And, even though she knew nothing could happen with Aziz, she didn't want this time with him to come to an end.

By the time she got out of the shower, Mada and Abra were waiting in the bedroom with a fresh set of clothes. Olivia tried to explain to them that she wanted her old clothes back, but they didn't understand and kept insisting she wear the sky-blue silk dress they'd brought.

With a sigh of defeat Olivia acquiesced; the dress was simple and elegant, belted at the waist and swirling about her knees. Pearl earrings and a necklace, along with a pair of low suede pumps, completed the outfit. Mada did her hair in a coil low on her neck, and Olivia felt a jolt of surprise as she looked in the mirror. She still wasn't used to her dark hair.

'Thank you,' she murmured, and the two women smiled and nodded, clearly pleased with their effort.

Malik was waiting outside her bedroom when she opened the door. 'Good morning, Miss Ellis. May I escort you to Sheikh Aziz?'

She nodded and followed him through the maze of the palace to a pleasant room at the back. The French windows were thrown open and a table had been set for two on a private terrace overlooking the palace gardens. Aziz rose from the table as she approached.

'I hope you don't mind eating outside. It's early enough not to be hot.'

'It's lovely,' she said. The air felt fresh and the view of the terraced gardens, lush and green, even though Siyad was in the middle of a desert, was beautiful.

'Coffee?' Aziz asked with a glinting smile as he proffered the little brass pot.

Olivia gave a little grimace. 'I admire your tenacity in getting used to it. I suppose I should do the same.'

Too late she realised that she'd made it sound as if she intended to stay in Kadar. She reached for her napkin and laid it in her lap. 'Are the pilot and plane ready to return me to Paris?'

'Yes, as soon as you are.'

Again she felt that mingled rush of relief and disappointment. 'Good. Thank you.'

'It is I who should be thanking you,' Aziz answered. 'You have helped me immeasurably, Olivia.'

There was something about the way he said her name that made her insides shiver. She suppressed the reaction and took a sip of the strong coffee. 'Is there any further news of Queen Elena?'

Aziz put down his coffee cup, his narrowed gaze on the horizon. 'We've had some progress. My men are investigating a desert settlement that has had some unusual activity, according to satellite photographs. I'll know by tonight if Elena is being kept there.'

'I hope she's found.'

'As do I.' Aziz turned to look at her; there was something so solemn and steady about his grey gaze that Olivia stilled. The Gentleman Playboy looked awfully serious, but then she knew now there was more to him than what he showed to the world.

'What is it?' she asked, because even though he hadn't said anything she felt there was something.

'I have no right to ask anything more of you, Olivia,' Aziz said. 'But I am a desperate man in desperate circumstances.'

Nothing about Aziz, Olivia thought, seemed desperate. From the moment she'd met him he'd been powerful, confident, assured. So much so that she still had trouble believing he could ever doubt himself. 'What do you want?' she asked, although she had a feeling she already knew.

'To stay one more day. I'm meant to open the Royal Gardens in the city centre with Queen Elena this afternoon. They've been redesigned. It would be no more than cutting a ribbon—'

'Cutting a ribbon?' Olivia shook her head in disbelief, even though happiness rippled through her at his request and at the realisation that she might be able to stay longer. 'It would be a lot more than that, Aziz. I'd have to talk to people, stand right next to them… I wouldn't fool anyone for a minute, or even a second.'

'That was my concern as well,' Aziz replied easily. 'But you'd be veiled and wearing traditional Arabic dress. It's not necessary in Siyad, but it would be seen as a sign of respect for the old ways, and happily it would be convenient for us. The only thing people would see of you is your eyes.'

'And my eyes,' Olivia pointed out, 'Are blue. I don't know what colour Queen Elena's eyes are, but I'm quite sure they're not blue.'

'They're grey. And we could use coloured contact lenses.'

'Coloured—' She stopped abruptly and shook her head. This was getting too deep, too dangerous, even if part of her wanted to stay. To be with Aziz. That, she thought darkly, was even more dangerous than any masquerade. 'No, I can't. I'm sorry. It's too risky.'

'You think I'm not aware of the risks?' Aziz answered, one eyebrow arched. He spoke casually enough but she felt the suppressed tension and even anger in him.

Olivia sat back, still shaking her head. 'You must be, of course,' she said slowly.

'I have far more to lose than you do, Olivia,' he told her quietly. 'Surely you see that. Even if we were discovered, your part in this plot would be easily explained and dismissed. You're my employee, after all. I could have coerced you, or threatened you with dismissal.'

'But you wouldn't!'

'Of course not!' He shook his head, smiling, yet clearly a bit affronted. 'What kind of man do you think I am?'

'I don't know what kind of man you are, Aziz,' Olivia answered, although she certainly felt she knew him better now than she had twenty-four hours ago—and she knew he was not the kind to blackmail or threaten. She knew him better than she knew anyone else in her life, which was a sad commentary on how isolated she'd been. Even so, she made herself state, 'I barely know you.'

'You've been in my employ for six years.'

'And in all that time I've seen you only a few times a year, for a few minutes at a time, to discuss the house or your social calendar. I don't *know* you.'

She stared at him; her words seemed to echo through the room, taking on a new, deeper meaning.

Aziz stared back at her, his eyes glittering like gun metal. 'I think you know me well enough to know I would never mistreat you or anyone,' he said, and his voice once again held that wry lightness Olivia now suspected hid other, darker emotions. Hurt or anger or even despair.

'I don't think you would mistreat anyone,' Olivia told him quietly. 'And I don't think you'll fire me if I refuse to continue with this charade.'

'No, I won't. Your job is secure, Olivia, if that's what you're really worried about.' He paused, watching her thoughtfully for a moment. Olivia tried not to squirm under that silvery gaze. No, she wasn't just worried about her job. She was worried about her heart. Her soul.

'All I'm asking for is a favour,' Aziz resumed. 'And, yes, I know it is a big one. Come to the Royal Gardens with me today and you can fly home to Paris tonight.'

He made it sound so simple. And it felt so tempting. To be someone else for a day, to *feel* like someone else, light, happy and free…

Desired.

Olivia gazed out at the stunning view and tried to resist. 'And what will you do if Queen Elena isn't found?' she asked after a pause. 'Tomorrow is meant to be your wedding day, Aziz.'

She looked up to see him do a mock double-take. 'Wait, *tomorrow*?' She gave a small, answering smile as his smile turned bleak. 'I have to find her, Olivia. And I will.'

'But if you don't,' Olivia pressed, even she knew she shouldn't—shouldn't ask, shouldn't know, shouldn't care. 'What will you do? The six weeks run out tomorrow.'

'I'll have to think of something else.' Aziz met her gaze directly. 'But that is not your concern, Olivia. All you need to do is accompany me to the gardens today.'

'Couldn't you just say Queen Elena is indisposed, or tired?'

He shook his head. 'Our appearance on the balcony yesterday was very popular, and things are unstable enough as it is. If people found out she is missing…'

'Why hasn't Khalil said anything?' Olivia asked suddenly. 'Surely he knows how dangerous the situation is, just as you do? Why hasn't he admitted he has Queen Elena?'

'Because even in Kadar kidnapping is illegal,' Aziz answered with a grim smile. 'And Khalil is gambling that I won't want people to know she is missing.'

'And he's right.'

'Yes.'

'Couldn't you talk to Khalil? Reason with him?'

'Possibly, if I could reach him. At the moment he

doesn't want to be found. In any case, I'm not sure either of us is in the right frame of mind for a nice chat.'

Aziz turned away to gaze once more out at the garden; Olivia could hear the tinkling of a fountain in the distance. 'I know this is a risk, Olivia,' he said quietly, his gaze still on the gardens. 'But it is my risk, not yours, and one I must take—not just for duty's sake, but because I need to.' He turned to her, his gaze grim, yet blazing.

'And not just for the sake of my country but for the sake of my own soul. You told me I was insisting on claiming my title because of my father, and you were right. Part of my desire to return to Kadar is bound up in that. But a bigger part is about reclaiming my country's past. Healing it, and healing my own soul.' The smile he gave her seemed sad. 'I spent my entire childhood feeling inferior. I want to prove to myself as well as my people that my father was wrong. That I can be a good ruler.' His smile turned wry, mocking. 'And now you can cue the triumphant violins. Find a handkerchief to dab the tears from your eyes.'

'I'm not teary,' Olivia told him, although she actually was, a little. She'd heard such sincerity, such raw honesty, in Aziz's voice. 'But I understand, Aziz. Maybe more than you even realise.'

Wasn't her own soul at stake too? Aziz was bringing her back to life, painful as that was. Maybe, when she returned to Paris, she'd be strong and alive enough again to want; to feel; to try, just as he was trying.

They were helping each other, in a strange and totally unexpected way.

Aziz nodded slowly. 'If you choose to return to Paris today, I will respect your decision.'

He waited, silent and still, for her answer. An answer,

Olivia knew, that she should give immediately and un-equivocally.

No. Of course not. This dangerous charade had gone on long enough. She owed Aziz nothing, no matter what she felt for him now. And it was too dangerous to stay here, to spend time with him. Dangerous in a way that had nothing to do with impersonating Queen Elena…and all to do with her contrary, alive-again heart.

'Well?' Aziz asked softly.

Olivia didn't speak. She stared at Aziz, saw a faint smile curve his lips, yet his eyes, those lovely, grey eyes, were filled with a sorrow that cut right to her heart.

She drew a breath and let it fill her lungs. She shaped her mouth to form the words, *'No. I'm sorry, Aziz, but I can't'.*

They filled her head, echoed through her, yet the ones that came out of her mouth were different.

'All right, Aziz,' she heard herself say. 'I'll do it.'

CHAPTER SIX

OLIVIA STARED AT her reflection in a kind of incredulous wonder. If she'd thought she looked different with dark hair, she looked like an utter and complete stranger in the Arabic dress Abra and Mada had put her in. Unfamiliar grey eyes stared back at her in the mirror from above a black gauzy veil that covered her nose and mouth. A *hijab* hid most of her hair, save for a bit peeking out on her forehead, and her figure was swathed in a voluminous Arabic dress of grey shot through with silver thread.

She could not imagine elegant Queen Elena wearing such a get-up, but she supposed she would have had to, if she were here.

Instead, Olivia was wearing it. And, even though she'd agreed to this, she still felt disbelieving that it was actually happening.

She'd felt a kind of dazed incredulity all morning, from the moment she'd told Aziz she'd do it. The smile he'd given her had been dazzling, melting the last of her inhibitions even as she'd tried to caution herself. Aziz might have woken up feelings inside her, but those feelings didn't have to be about him. For him.

Yet so many of them were. She *liked* this man, more than she'd ever expected to. And she was poised to feel a whole lot more, if she let herself.

Which she wouldn't.

The rest of the morning had been given over to getting her ready: touching up her hair, putting in the coloured contact lenses that made her eyes itch, donning these clothes. Turning herself into a stranger. Yet she'd agreed to it because she wanted to help Aziz.

Because she wanted to be with him. She didn't just like him; she liked being with him. She liked who she was when she was with him. She felt, amazingly, more like herself. Like the girl she used to be: lighter; happier. More hopeful, and when she'd thought hope had long passed her by.

Don't you realise how dangerous this is?

A knock sounded on the door of her room and then Malik appeared. 'Miss Ellis.' His dark gaze swept over her and he nodded in approval. 'Well done.'

'I don't think anyone would be recognisable under all this,' Olivia said and Malik's normally stern face cracked into a small smile.

'And that is good for us. Are you ready?'

'I suppose.'

'Sheikh Aziz would like to go over the particulars of the afternoon with you before you depart. I'll take you to him.'

Olivia's robe whispered along the floor as she followed Malik out of her bedroom. She felt so strange, as if she were wearing a costume for a fancy-dress party. She half-expected someone to come up to her and rip the veil away from her face, laughing that she hadn't fooled anyone.

'Sheikh Aziz,' Malik announced, opened a set of double doors and ushered Olivia into an elegant salon. He closed the doors behind him, leaving her alone with Aziz who she saw was also wearing traditional robes and a turban.

'The dark hair and high heels suited you,' Aziz said after a moment. 'And, amazingly, so does this ensemble.' He smiled, his eyes crinkling at the corners, his good humour utterly infectious so that Olivia smiled back, even though she knew he couldn't see it beneath her veil.

'Should this be my new housekeeper's uniform, do you think?'

'I'll think about it,' Aziz replied thoughtfully, and Olivia's smile widened.

'I feel rather ridiculous.'

'You look lovely, even so. I wonder, how can a woman still look beautiful when she is completely covered?'

'You tell me.'

He walked towards her, his gaze sweeping slowly over her. 'You are beautiful, Olivia. You are very beautiful.' He smiled, his eyes glinting, inviting her to share his good humour. 'I should be comparing you to flower petals, I suppose.'

She let out a little gurgle of laughter. 'Now, that would be a bit stale. I think you need to find some new flattery, Aziz.'

'Is it flattery if it's the truth?'

Pleasure flared deep inside. The truth was, she did feel like a flower, like something once dormant and dry that had finally found sunlight, sought water. 'That's not saying much,' she bantered back. 'Considering I've changed my hair and eye colour and am currently covered from head to toe.'

'True. I must admit, I prefer you in the evening gown you wore last night.'

Another flare of pleasure, deeper, fiercer.

She nodded towards his own robes, a turban covering most of his dark hair. 'And is your outfit part of this plan to show respect?'

'Indeed, yes.' Wryly he glanced down at his *thobe*. 'This get-up is just about as strange to me as yours is to you.'

'You look good. You should wear it more often,' she teased, half-amazed at herself, at the humour and happiness Aziz brought out in her, even in the midst of all that was going on. Aziz smiled back, his eyes sparkling.

'Maybe I'll surprise you.'

You already do. Aziz's devotion to his country, his determination to rule, hinted at depths she'd never even guessed at. He was a man she'd thought careless, judged as shallow. And yet, to her surprise, the light, laughing man known as a playboy enchanted her now as much as the deeper, more thoughtful man she was beginning to realise hid underneath. She liked laughing with him, teasing and being gently teased, especially when she now knew there was more to him than his charming façade.

'So what now?' she asked. 'When are we meant to appear at the gardens?'

'In a short while.' He smiled and took a step towards her. 'But first I need to teach you a few phrases in Arabic.'

'Arabic?' Olivia stared at him in alarm. 'Why?'

'Because the people will expect it, and it will please them to hear you speaking their language.'

'Except I can't speak their language,' Olivia pointed out, unable to keep a high note of panic from entering her voice.

'No one will expect you to speak it well, or even understand what you are saying,' Aziz assured her. 'Elena had learned a few phrases only.'

'Which is a few more than I've learned.'

His mouth curved in the kind of smile that invited her to share the joke. Jump right into it. 'Hence, our lesson,' he said, his voice nearly a purr, and then he took her by the hand, causing those sparks to race up her arm, and drew her towards him. 'Come.'

He led her to a private alcove with a velvet divan and, sitting down, he drew her by the hand so she sat next to him, the folds of her robe spilling over his own. She could see the outline of his powerful thigh beneath the fabric that had drawn taut when he'd sat down, inches from her own leg. She was mesmerised by the sight of his leg; she couldn't stop staring at it. It was if her brain had slowed down; everything in her focused on Aziz and this incredible, unbearable awareness of him.

Why hadn't she felt like this when she'd sat with him in the drawing room of the Paris house, going over accounts?

Because she hadn't been truly alive then. Aziz hadn't woken her up, made her want.

Want him.

She drew a shaky breath and smoothed her robe over her lap, just to give her hands something to do. She forced her gaze upwards, away from his thigh. His eyes were dancing. 'So; Arabic. What do I need to say?'

'Let's start with hello: *"assalam alaykum".*' His voice, as soft and rich as velvet, caressed the syllables of the unfamiliar words, making them sound as if they were an endearment, even though Olivia knew he was only saying hello. *Hello*. Her body didn't seem to grasp that fact.

'Olivia?' He raised his eyebrows, expectant, and she realised she'd just been gawping at him, her brain and body both on overload from the simple presence, the sheer masculinity, of him.

'*Assalam alaykum,*' she repeated, fighting a flush, half-afraid that Aziz would be able to guess the nature of her thoughts. Surely he could see her body's reaction to him? She felt as if everything in her both tingled and ached, and she was afraid she might not be able to control the overwhelming need to touch him. What would he do if she did touch him? If she just reached out and stroked his face, or touched that taut and powerful thigh? *Squeezed it...*

'Let's try it again, shall we?' Aziz murmured, his smile seeming to wind around her heart, which thumped harder.

'I'm nervous,' she muttered, and he nodded.

'It's understandable.'

Except that she wasn't nervous for the reason he thought: the upcoming appearance; the charade. She was nervous because of him: because of his nearness and this all-consuming attraction that was getting so very hard to fight. Because of these feelings and desires that were flowing up and out of her, impossible to ignore or resist.

'Assalam akaylum,' he said again and she forced herself to repeat it as best as she could. Aziz gave a little nod. 'Good. Now this one is a little longer.' He smiled, his gaze warm and encouraging. *'Motasharefatun bema refatek.'*

Olivia's eyes widened. *'Motashar*—what?'

Aziz laughed softly, the sound no more than a breath. 'I know, I know, it's a mouthful. Try again.' He said the words again, and Olivia did her best to repeat them. 'Good. One more time.' She did and he smiled and nodded, reaching over to squeeze her knee covered by the heavy gown.

Olivia felt as if she'd been branded. She lurched upright, sparks zinging through her system, making her feel more agonisingly alive—all because he'd touched her knee.

Aziz glanced down at his fingers, still wrapped around

her knee. 'Sorry,' he murmured but he didn't sound at all repentant. 'I guess I got carried away.'

He was teasing her, Olivia knew. He was a playboy, after all, hidden depths or not. How many women had he taken to bed? How many had he kissed? He probably didn't even remember their names, and here she was, quivering because he'd touched her knee through a thick robe. He must think she was pathetic. Her desire for him must be horribly, humiliatingly obvious.

'What does it mean?' she managed, and was thankful her voice came out sounding normal—almost.

'"Pleased to meet you".' Aziz paused and Olivia braced herself for him to say something embarrassing, like *I know this is difficult, when you're so obviously attracted to me*. Not, she acknowledged, that Aziz would ever say such a thing. She didn't think he'd ever intentionally humiliate her. But the knowledge she saw in his eyes was bad enough. The moment passed and he just smiled and asked, 'Shall we try it again?'

Olivia nodded.

They went through a few more Arabic phrases, no more than pleasantries that Aziz assured her she wouldn't be expected to say faultlessly—which was a good thing, because she was still having trouble concentrating on anything at all.

'Did you speak Arabic growing up?' Olivia asked when they'd finished. 'Is that why you're so good at it?' Her head was buzzing from all the words she was afraid she wouldn't remember, and also from this impossible awareness of Aziz. During their little lesson her heart rate, thankfully, had begun to slow, and it had been easier to breathe. Now, however, she felt everything kick into overdrive for he'd moved closer to her and his thigh nudged hers.

'Yes, I spoke it as a child.' He smiled, but she saw that hardness enter his eyes, and sadly she wondered whether he had a single happy memory from his childhood.

'But you didn't speak it much as an adult, did you?' she asked. 'In Europe?'

He shrugged. 'Not often. But I think you always remember the language of your childhood.'

'Well, I'm still impressed,' Olivia told him. 'I'm rubbish at languages, always have been. Perhaps you could tell?'

His eyes gleamed with amusement—and maybe something else as well. 'Not at all.'

'Every time we moved somewhere new, my father tried to get me to learn the language,' Olivia continued. 'But I was hopeless, no matter how hard I tried.'

'You seem like someone who always does the best she can.'

Except she hadn't done the best, not when it had mattered the most. She'd been too afraid, too hurt, too weak. Her throat went tight and she shook her head, not wanting to say any more, wondering why she'd said as much as she had.

She kept *saying* things to Aziz, things she'd kept to herself for so long, and even though it scared her part of her actually wanted to say them. Wanted someone to understand her in a way she'd never let herself be understood.

And more than that: she wanted not just to be understood, but to be resurrected. To be the laughing, carefree girl of her youth; to have her innocence. To be the girl she'd thought dead and buried, whom Aziz had called back to life.

And maybe that was his gift to her, giving her that desire. Even when they reverted back to their usual roles when she left Kadar, perhaps she could still be thankful that he'd woken her up.

Except she knew waking up meant feeling everything: not just the joy and lightness but the darkness, the despair. The feeling that you weren't whole, that you were sleepwalking through life, soulless and empty...

'Olivia?' Aziz took her by the shoulders and gave her a gentle shake. 'Where did you go?'

She blinked up at him, the memories receding, even though that awful feeling of emptiness remained. 'I'm right here.'

Aziz frowned. 'For a few seconds there you looked as if you were lost in your memories, and they weren't good ones.'

Somehow she managed to summon a smile. 'I'm okay,' she said, which was no answer at all, and wasn't even true.

Aziz stared at her for a long moment, his hands still on her shoulders. Olivia stared up at him, and even with the emptiness echoing inside her she felt her heart start to thud, her bones start to melt. She didn't want him ever to let her go, and for a heart-stopping second she thought he might actually draw her closer, whether for a kiss or just a hug. In that moment it didn't even matter; she just wanted him to touch her.

A knock sounded at the door and slowly, reluctantly, Aziz released her. Olivia sat back against the divan, her heart still thudding so hard she thought Aziz might be able to hear it.

'Enter,' he called, and Malik came into the room.

'Your Highness, the car is ready.'

'Thank you, Malik.' Aziz turned to Olivia with his usual charmingly wry smile, the intensity of the previous moment seemingly completely forgotten, though its aftershocks still rippled through her. 'Your chariot awaits, madam.'

Smiling back, trying to stuff all the feelings and memories back down inside, Olivia rose from the divan and followed Aziz from the room.

A dark sedan with tinted windows was waiting in the palace courtyard. The gates were closed, but spectators still lined the other side of the fence, and when they emerged from the palace a cheer went up that nearly sent Olivia reeling backwards.

Aziz steadied her with a firm hand on her lower back. 'The crowd already loves you.'

Olivia gave a shaky laugh. 'You mean they love Queen Elena.'

'How could they,' he murmured, dipping his head low so his breath fanned her cheek, 'When she's not even here?'

'It's the idea of her,' Olivia answered as she slid into the car, arranging the voluminous folds of the robe around her. 'The idea of your bride. I suppose,' she mused, 'It doesn't really matter who it is.'

She'd just been thinking aloud, but from the sudden stillness, the arrested look on Aziz's face, Olivia felt as if she'd said something momentous. 'What is it?' she asked warily, but Aziz just shook his head.

'Nothing. Nothing at all.'

It doesn't really matter who it is.

The words echoed through him. *It doesn't really matter... It doesn't really matter... It doesn't really matter who it is...*

All he needed was a bride, a willing wife. Elena had been suitable, certainly, but she wasn't here now. And, if he couldn't find her, she wasn't suitable at all.

But Olivia was.

Part of Aziz was appalled at how quickly he was willing to discard one bride for another; another part of him was amazed he hadn't thought of it before.

He had two days. Olivia was here. Suddenly it seemed simple.

Of course, Aziz knew it wasn't really remotely simple. He was considering marriage and, while it had been expedient for both him and Elena, it certainly wasn't for Olivia. She had no reason, and perhaps no desire, to marry him.

He glanced at her; the headdress and veil were hiding most of her face. Her grey eyes and Arabic clothing might make her look like a stranger but he saw something familiar in the curve of her cheek, the fullness of her lips.

Lips he'd touched and tasted...

There was an attraction between them, even if she wanted to deny it, as well as a friendship, or at least the beginnings of one. Surely both were a good basis for marriage? At least for the kind of marriage he wanted: one without any emotional risk.

And he suspected Olivia might want that kind of marriage too.

Maybe it could work.

'Aziz?' Olivia was peering out of the window and nibbling her lip. 'Look.'

He looked and saw that the narrow streets of the Old Town were lined with people. Distantly he registered the roar of the crowd. The people were throwing flowers onto the car. He watched a single blood-red rose hit the window and fall to the ground.

His people loved his bride.

His fake bride. The bride they thought was Queen Elena of Thallia, not a nobody, a housekeeper from Paris.

What the hell was he going to do?

'We're very popular,' he said lightly, giving Olivia a reassuring smile. Her face had gone pale.

'This could all go horribly wrong,' she said, her voice low, her gaze still on the crowds outside the window. The car had slowed to a crawl.

'Not for you,' Aziz answered. 'Only for me.'

'You know I'd be affected.' She leaned back against the seat and closed her eyes. 'I must have been mad to agree to this. *Mad.*'

Aziz gazed at her, wanting to reassure her but knowing he couldn't, at least not now. They were in the car; she was dressed as Queen Elena. Calling a halt to the charade now would be disastrous to them both.

'I'm sorry,' he said suddenly, and she opened her eyes and looked at him. He held her gaze; it felt as if they were somehow connected.

'Thank you for saying that,' she said quietly. Her mouth quirked into a tiny, teasing smile. 'Even if there's nothing you can do about it.'

'Too true.' He nodded towards the street; they'd left the Old Town and were entering the central square of Siyad's more modern district. The square was filled with people too, all of them proffering bouquets and gifts. Crowds and flowers. 'Those people aren't just going to go away.'

'No, I don't suppose they are.'

He leaned over and touched her hand, wanting the contact, needing it, and suspecting she needed it too. 'You'll be fine, Olivia. You'll be wonderful. You're elegant, lovely and gracious, and you're warm and friendly when you let yourself relax.'

'Was that your pep talk?' she answered with raised eyebrows, but she was smiling. 'How am I supposed to relax in front of about a thousand people?'

'If anyone can do it, you can.' He squeezed her fingers before withdrawing his hand. 'We're here.' The car had pulled up in front of the main gates to the public gardens and several security personnel jumped out of the car in front and cleared a path to their door. Aziz took a breath and gave Olivia a reassuring smile. 'Are you ready?'

'As ready as I'll ever be,' Olivia said with an attempt at flippancy that almost worked. Aziz felt a swell of admiration for this woman whom he was coming to realise was courageous, not just capable. She was strong, sweet and incredibly, amazingly, sexy.

'That's my girl,' he murmured and she looked away, trying to hide her smile.

One of his staff opened the door. 'Let's go,' Aziz said and, taking her hand, he helped her out of the car.

CHAPTER SEVEN

FLASHBULBS BLINDED OLIVIA for a moment and flowers fell at her feet, causing her to stumble as she exited the car

Then Aziz slid his hand around her waist, steadying her, and she felt her confidence come back. Someone spoke to her in Arabic, an incomprehensible babble, and Aziz murmured in her ear. 'Steady, now. *Assalam alaykum.*'

'*Assalam alaykum,*' she repeated, and managed to force her lips into something like a smile, even though she realised belatedly that no one could see it behind her veil. '*Assalam alaykum.*' There. That sounded slightly more natural. And the people around her obviously understood what she meant, because their smiles grew wider and another cheer went up.

Olivia kept smiling and nodding; her head felt light and her heart was beating so hard it felt as if it would jump right out of her chest. Aziz stepped slightly away from her and she felt the loss. She needed his strength now. She needed *him*.

He spoke to someone else in Arabic and an old woman, her face almost completely hidden by her veil, reached for Olivia's hand and patted it, murmuring something in Arabic. Olivia felt tears spring to her eyes.

She was touched, humbled and ashamed all at once.

She felt like such a fraud. She wanted this to be real. Her emotions rose like a tidal wave inside her, drowning out practical thought, capable action.

From somewhere she found the unfamiliar words. *'Motasharefatun bema refatek.'* She mangled the phrase but the woman understood and beamed. Aziz slid a sideways smile at her, his eyes so warm with approval that Olivia blushed.

Then he took her hand and led her through the crowd to the gates of the Royal Gardens. A red silk ribbon ran across them; someone handed Aziz a rather wicked-looking knife. He made some joke about it in Arabic, for several people laughed and nodded. Then he raised the knife high over his head and slashed the ribbon in two. Everyone cheered. Olivia clapped her hands and smiled at the people around her, who beamed back.

They wanted to like her, she realised, just as they wanted to like Aziz. How could he not see that? How could he not see that his people were ready and waiting to accept him?

Because he doesn't accept himself.

Someone spoke to her in Arabic, smiling and gesturing to her veil, which Olivia guessed had met with people's approval. They wanted to see Aziz's bride, but appreciated the sign of respect for the old ways, as Aziz had said they would.

She smiled wryly back and patted her hijab, trying to convey how strange and yet acceptable it was to wear it. Somehow this actually worked, for the woman she was talking to clapped her hands and crowed with laughter.

Olivia felt something unfurl in her soul. *Hope.* Happiness. She'd cut herself off for so long, she'd actually forgotten how much she missed being with people. Besides talking to workmen and the concierge across the

street, she'd lived the last six years in virtual isolation—
and by choice.

Maybe now she would finally have the strength to
choose differently. Maybe that would be Aziz's legacy
to her, his gift.

Finally Aziz reached for her hand and drew her towards
the garden. They stepped through the gate and it closed
behind them, leaving them blissfully alone in an oasis
of beauty and scent.

'Is no one coming in with us?' Olivia whispered and
Aziz smiled and shook his head.

'No, this is our private time. As a couple.'

'Oh. Well, that's a relief, I suppose.'

'I think you fooled them.'

Olivia bit her lip, remembering the way the old woman
had smiled at her and touched her hand. 'I feel like such
a fraud. Like a liar.'

Aziz was silent for a moment, his gaze on the brick
walkway in front of them. 'I know,' he said finally. 'I
do too.'

'You shouldn't,' she said impulsively. 'You're not pretending to be someone else.'

'Aren't I?'

She shook her head. 'I think you believe you are somehow, but your interest is genuine, Aziz. I can tell. So can
they. You may not see it, but the people want to accept
you. To love you.'

His mouth twisted. 'The people of Siyad, maybe. And
only because they think I'm sophisticated and glamorous.'

'Well,' she answered, daring to tease, 'You *are* sophisticated and glamorous. You're the Gentleman Playboy, after all.'

'On the surface, maybe. That's not who I really am.'

She stopped walking and nearly stopped breathing. 'Then who are you, Aziz? Really?'

He paused mid-stride and for a moment she thought he'd say something real, something important. Then he turned to her with a teasing smile. 'Well, I'm not answering that question until you answer it too.'

'What do you mean?'

'You can't tell me *you're* an open book, Olivia. You're hiding something.'

'Not hiding,' she answered stiltedly, unnerved by his perception. 'Just—not thinking of it. Why dwell on bad memories?'

'Why indeed? I'm in a beautiful garden with a beautiful woman.' His eyes glinted teasingly. 'What should I compare you to? Not rose petals, since you've heard that one before.'

'You'll think of something, I'm sure,' Olivia answered.

'Just give me a moment.' He strolled down the path, his hands behind his back. 'In any case, I actually mean it, Olivia. You don't act as if you know it or believe it, but you really are a beautiful woman.'

'Is that another line?' Olivia answered back, unnerved by the sincerity in his voice, and he turned to face her, all levity and artifice gone from his face.

'No, it's not.'

He looked so serious, so *intent*. Olivia's mouth dried and her mind spun. She licked her lips and shook her head. 'Aziz…' She didn't know how to articulate what she felt, all the hope and fear. She loved being with him, loved his attention and interest, but she was also afraid. Being woken up to all these feelings was scary. It meant you could get those same feelings hurt.

'Just a simple statement of fact,' Aziz said with a smile. 'I can't help but notice.'

'Always charming,' Olivia answered, half-teasing, glad to retreat back to banter. 'No wonder you're called the Gentleman Playboy.'

'Such a silly nickname.'

'How did you come to get it, then?'

He studied a crimson flower intently while Olivia waited. 'One of the gossip magazines gave me the nickname a few years ago and it stuck.'

'Why did they give you it?'

'Because they interviewed one of my former lovers and she said I'd been a gentleman throughout our relationship.' He spoke matter-of-factly but Olivia still flushed. *One of my former lovers*. Images, provocative and craven images, danced through her head.

'And what did she mean, you'd been a gentleman?'

He turned to her with a gently mocking smile. 'So curious, Olivia.'

'Maybe I am,' she answered boldly. 'Maybe I can't understand how "gentleman" and "playboy" go together.'

'It's simple. Just choose women who don't want anything from you but sex.' As he spoke his voice hardened. He turned away, leaving Olivia even more curious.

'Isn't that all you've wanted?' she asked after a moment. It certainly seemed as if it had been, judging from his many casual affairs she'd witnessed over the years.

'Yes, of course it is. How could I ever want anything more?' There was something mocking and bitter about his words, his voice, and Olivia didn't understand it. By his own admission he'd chosen his lifestyle; he didn't want serious relationships... Yet in that moment she wondered if at least part of him did.

Just as part of her did—that awake, alive part of her that was now clamouring for more.

'We should look at these flowers,' Aziz said, his good humour clearly and purposefully restored. He tugged her along by the hand. 'I'll have to say something about them when we leave the garden.'

That moment of intensity broken, Olivia gazed round at the unfamiliar shrubs and blooms. The placards indicating what everything was were in both English and Arabic, and she stepped closer to read one.

'This is certainly beautiful,' she said, indicating a deep red, overblown rose. 'How do you say "beautiful" in Arabic?'

'Jameel,' Aziz said quietly, and when she turned she saw he was staring right at her, with the same intent look as before, only more so. There was more heat in his gaze. More obvious, unashamed desire.

Her heart started to thud. Her body swayed. She wanted him to kiss her, wanted it so badly her body shook. She wondered, distantly, if he could see how she trembled.

'Let's walk,' Aziz said, his voice thick. Taking her by the elbow, he led her along the twisting walkways, vibrant blooms and bushes on either side of them.

Another intense moment had been thankfully broken, but Olivia couldn't keep the ache of want from pulsing insistently through her.

'What will you do as Sheikh?' she asked when they were deep in the heart of the garden, the sounds of the city having long faded away. Time to be sensible and have a normal conversation. 'I mean, what do you want to do? What do you hope to accomplish?'

'That's a good question.' Aziz walked alongside her for a few moments, his contemplative gaze on the path in front of them. 'I told you before that I wanted to be a good ruler—an honest and fair one.' He glanced up at her with a wry smile that also seemed a little vulnerable. 'Which is ridiculous, I know, considering the lie I've ensnared us both in now when I've barely started my rule.'

Olivia didn't reply. She might not like the charade she'd got involved in, but she understood now how Aziz had been driven to it. And who was she, really, to talk about secrets and lies? She'd been harbouring both for ten years. 'I understand why you've done what you did,' she said. 'Desperate times call for desperate measures, I suppose.'

'Yes, I suppose they do. But I hope I'll be able to put all this behind me. I want to bring Kadar into the twenty-first century in so many ways.' She heard a raw note of passion and purpose enter his voice, fuelling it. 'I want to give women more rights and I want to nationalise health-care and bring more international business and trade to Siyad.' He let out a rueful laugh. 'And now I'm really sounding ridiculous.'

'No, you're not. Those are all admirable things.'

'And how do you suppose I will accomplish them?' Aziz stopped and stared up at the hard, blue sky. 'The people might never accept me as Sheikh.'

'You say that, but I don't see why they wouldn't, in time. They certainly loved you out there.' She swept an arm back towards the garden gates.

'They loved the idea of my marriage, which might not even happen. I'm supposed to marry tomorrow and I'm no closer to finding Elena.'

She put her hands on her hips. 'What do you want, Aziz? Do you want people to fall at your feet? Work with what you have. Go out to the desert tribes and visit them. Talk to them. You can do it.' She stepped closer to him and heard the raw passion in her own voice. 'You already are doing it, even if you don't realise it. You were natural out there with everyone, chatting and laughing and listening. People like your sincerity, not that you're some sophisticated playboy. The people of Siyad want a leader who listens and the people of the desert will want it too.'

He turned to look at her, almost seeming surprised by her impassioned speech. Olivia realised she had sounded rather fierce, but that was because she believed what she'd said. She believed in Aziz.

'You sound like my school matron, back when I was sent to boarding school when I was seven,' he said ruefully. 'She told me to stop snivelling too.'

'I didn't tell you to stop snivelling,' Olivia protested.

'No, you didn't. You said some very nice things, Olivia, and I thank you for them.'

'It wasn't just flattery. I meant it.'

For a moment he looked truly touched and at a loss for words. Olivia felt her throat close up with answering emotion. Aziz nodded once. 'Thank you,' he said simply.

They walked for a little longer, listening to the birds twittering in the trees above them, the silence between them companionable rather than tense .

'So, your turn,' Aziz finally said. 'You gave me a another pep talk. I can give you one.'

'I don't need one.'

'Don't you?' He turned to her with far too much perception in his silvery gaze. 'Why have you hidden yourself away for so long, Olivia? What sadness is tying you to the past so you feel you can't have a future?'

'It's not like that,' she began feebly and he shook his head.

'Why else would a lovely young woman like you hide herself in an empty house, tidying rooms that hardly anyone ever sees? That's not what you want to do with your life, Olivia. It's not who you want to be.'

'You don't know anything about it,' she began, and Aziz took a step towards her, his expression suddenly fierce.

'Then tell me.'

'We were talking about you.'

'And now we're talking about you. Why do you hide from life, Olivia? What happened to make you so afraid?'

'I'm not afraid,' she protested. 'It's just…easier this way.'

'Why?'

She took a deep breath, let it out slowly. 'I lost someone,' she finally said, and her voice sounded strange and distant. 'Someone who was incredibly—incredibly—' She stopped, her throat so tight she couldn't get any more words out. She *never* talked about Daniel. 'Important to me,' she finally managed. 'And when you lose someone like that… Well, it keeps you from trying ever again. It keeps you from feeling like you could try, even if you wanted to.'

She couldn't look at Aziz, not without crying, which was something she had absolutely no intention of doing. But she could feel him looking at her, felt his hand skim her cheek, slide under her veil. 'Did you love him very much?' he asked quietly, and she knew he thought she was talking about a man. A lover.

'I loved him more than life itself,' she answered, because to say anything else would be a betrayal of Daniel and she'd already betrayed him once. She wouldn't again. 'I still love him and I always will.'

Aziz's fingers lingered against her face and Olivia resisted the urge to lean into his hand, to take comfort from his caress. 'I'm sorry for your loss,' he said, and Olivia managed a trembling smile.

'It was a long time ago.'

'Even so.' His hand was still on her face and Olivia risked a glance upwards. The sympathy and kindness she saw in his eyes felt like a blow to the chest, to the heart.

'Aziz,' she whispered, although she didn't know why she'd said his name, what she was asking him for.

But Aziz must have, for his eyes darkened and his hand tightened against her cheek as he lowered her veil and brushed his thumb over her lower lip. He took a step closer to her so she could feel the heat of his body, could inhale the dizzying scent of his aftershave.

'Olivia…' he said softly, and the way he said her name made those newly wakened parts of her surge and ache. *Demand.*

And then somehow—Olivia didn't know who moved first—he was kissing her. She was kissing him. And it felt incredibly tender, wonderfully sweet, finally to be touching him as she'd wanted to for what felt like for ever. To have him touch her.

His lips moved over hers and her nails dug into his shoulders as she pressed closer to him. Sweetness gave way to urgency, a sudden, overwhelming need clawing its way out of her.

'Olivia,' Aziz said again, muttering her name against his mouth as his hands roved over her body, pulling at the shapeless robe, his fingers seeking the curves hidden underneath the heavy fabric. His tongue slid into her mouth, sweeping its softness, and Olivia moaned.

Aziz's touch was like a drug; she was instantly addicted, immediately craving more and more of him. She *needed* him with an urgency that was shocking and total.

He brought his hands up to frame her face, pulling the

hijab completely away as his fingers tangled in her hair. Pins fell on the walkway with a tinkling clatter and still Aziz kissed her, each kiss acting as a brand on her soul, ensuring she would never, ever forget this. Forget him.

He'd changed her, affected her in a way no one else ever had. He'd reached deep inside her with his laughter, his understanding and his kiss.

Oh, his kiss…

She slid her hands under his *thobe*, felt the heat of his skin through the thin linen of his shirt and pressed closer. Somehow Aziz had managed to get his hand through the front opening of her robe and he brushed his thumb over the peak of her breast, causing Olivia to let out a sharp gasp of wonder and surprise.

The noise startled them both; Aziz yanked his hand away from her and stepped back quickly, a look of appalled realisation coming over his face that might have been comical in any other situation.

As it was, Olivia felt suddenly, cringingly conscious of her undone hair, her disordered robes and fallen *hijab*, her swollen lips. Of the hunger inside her that now roared to life, demanding satisfaction.

She stared at Aziz, too incredulous about what had just happened even to be embarrassed—yet. Reality was rushing in to fill all the aching, empty places inside her, reminding her that this man was about to marry someone else; that she hadn't kissed anyone in over a decade; that what she'd just done was beyond stupid.

Somehow she managed a shaky, ragged laugh. 'Well. If anyone had seen that, they would have been convinced of your fairy-tale wedding, I'm sure.' She turned then, because she didn't trust the expression on her face, and she didn't want to see Aziz's pity. Had she kissed him first? He'd responded, but maybe only because that was what a *Gentleman Playboy* did if a woman threw herself at him. Is that what she'd done? So much for staying cool, calm, remote and *safe*.

'Olivia…'

'I need to do something about my hair.' Her voice trembled and she put shaking hands up to her head as she blinked hard.

'Let me help.' Aziz knelt on the path and began to pick up her hairpins. Olivia smoothed her robes and picked up her *hijab*. Anything to keep herself occupied. She prayed Aziz wouldn't see how her hands shook. How affected she was.

'Here.' Gently Aziz took her hair in his hands and began to rearrange it into a neat coil.

It felt almost as intimate as their kiss, to have him standing behind her, his breath fanning the nape of her neck, as he arranged her hair. She stayed still, her body taut with tension yet still aching with desire, an impossible combination, as he carefully replaced all the pins, sliding them through her hair with a slow gentleness that was nearly her undoing. He wrapped the hijab around her head and adjusted her veil.

'There. I think you're presentable.'

She kept her head bowed, still unable to look at him. 'What if people guess?'

'They'll be pleased. Like you said, it's all part of the fairy tale.' She tried to move away but he stayed her, his hands on her shoulders. 'Olivia.'

'What?' Her voice came out high and strained.

'I didn't mean for that to happen.'

So she *had* kissed him first. She closed her eyes, fought the tidal wave of humiliation and hurt that threatened to overwhelm her. 'Neither did I, as it happens.'

He laughed softly, no more than a breath of sound. 'I know you didn't.'

He *did*? She opened her eyes. His hands were still on her shoulders, his body still so close to hers. He dipped his head so his lips nearly grazed her cheek. 'That wasn't for show,' he said quietly. 'No one was watching. That was just me kissing you, Olivia, because I wanted to. Because, for a moment, it felt as if I had no choice. As if I *had* to kiss you.'

Just as she had had to kiss him. She should have felt gratified by his admission, but she only felt confused. Scared. This couldn't go anywhere, at least anywhere good. Caring for Aziz, letting him in at all, would just end in her being hurt.

'Clearly you have poor impulse control,' she said, her voice thankfully tart, and she slipped from his loose embrace. He let her go. She kept her back to him, fussing with her appearance, even though she knew she looked as put together as she was ever going to, at least without a hairbrush or mirror. 'How did you get so adept at styling a woman's hair?'

'Experience, of course,' he answered, and his voice was light again. The intimacy of the moment had been broken and Olivia was both glad and ridiculously, helplessly disappointed.

'We should go back,' Aziz said. He twitched her veil better into place, his expression shuttered. 'They will be waiting for us.'

Wordlessly, Olivia followed him through the gardens. The stillness and silence felt oppressive now, rather than peaceful, the tension tautening between her and Aziz. The gates loomed before them and with them the crowds. Olivia knew that once they entered the melee she wouldn't be able to talk to Aziz. And tonight she would leave for Paris.

Yet what could she say to him? She didn't know what had happened back in the garden; who had kissed whom or why. She didn't know how tenderness had kindled so quickly into the kind of raw, urgent passion she hadn't felt in years, decades—if ever. She didn't even know if she wanted to feel it, if she wanted to give into that kind of hunger even as her body insisted that she did.

So she said nothing.

They moved through the crowds and she mumbled the Arabic phrases Aziz had taught her, keeping her eyes lowered, her face hidden.

He helped her into the car and then they were speeding back towards the palace, still not having exchanged a word since they'd left the garden.

She snuck a glance at Aziz and saw he was looking out of the window, his eyes narrowed, his arm braced on the window frame, his fingers pressed against his temple. He looked, Olivia thought, as if he had the weight of the world on his shoulders, or at least of a country.

'Perhaps there will be news of Queen Elena when we return,' she said and, seemingly startled out of a reverie, Aziz glanced at her.

'Yes,' he said tonelessly. 'Perhaps.'

He hadn't meant to kiss her. Guilt churned sourly inside him as they headed for the palace. He hadn't meant to kiss her, Aziz acknowledged, but the kiss itself had been surprising. *Amazing.* What at first had seemed like it was going to be no more than a brush or buss had turned into something deeper and fiercer, something more *real*, than he'd ever felt before.

He might have had many lovers, plenty of mutually

satisfying experiences in the bedroom, but that was all they'd been: experiences. Not relationships, not even emotional connections. Just the soulless, pleasurable joining of bodies—which was what he'd always wanted. What he'd chosen. Anything else brought with it the possibility of pain.

Yet when he'd kissed Olivia in the garden he'd felt something different, something deeper, and for a moment he'd wanted the kind of life, the kind of love, he'd never let himself have before. .

But love had no place in any relationship he chose, any marriage. Not the marriage he'd intended with Elena, and not the one he now contemplated with Olivia.

The sedan pulled into the palace courtyard and the security personnel jumped out of the other car and opened the doors. Aziz helped Olivia out of the car while his mind buzzed with possibilities.

Tomorrow was his wedding day. *But with which bride?*

They gave one last wave for the crowds lining the courtyard and then headed into the palace.

As they walked together, Aziz noted that Olivia seemed to have recovered her composure. In the garden he'd seen how shaken she'd been by their kiss—and how desperately determined she'd been not to show him.

'Perhaps a cup of tea after you've changed? I do have English tea here.' He spoke as if their meeting would be no more than a farewell, knowing he needed to handle their next conversation carefully. Olivia hesitated and he knew she was torn between wanting to spend time with him and wanting to stay safe.

Just as he was torn. They were very similar; he was realising that more and more. Both of them safeguarded their hearts. Hid their true selves, their deepest desires. They just went about it in completely different ways.

'Very well,' she said, and after she left Aziz headed for his study where he knew Malik was waiting to debrief him.

'Well?' he asked as he strode into the room. He yanked off his turban and ran his hands through his hair. 'Any news?'

'I'm afraid not. She was at the camp, but everyone had gone by the time your men arrived.'

'Gone? Did they have warning that someone was coming?'

'It is hard to say. I suspect Khalil has gone to one of the tribes for shelter. They will hide him.'

'I know that.' Aziz pressed a fist to his temple; his head had started to throb. 'How can he command the loyalty of people he has never even met before?' he demanded, and Malik shrugged.

'He represents something to them, perhaps. The old ways, from before Hashem showed disrespect for tradition and banished a wife to take another.'

'Even though his first wife was unfaithful,' Aziz answered. He heard the bitterness in his tone but could not keep himself from it. He did not have it in him to feel sorry for Khalil or his mother, not after everything he and his own mother had endured as their replacements.

He sighed wearily and dropped his hand. 'So now Khalil has taken Elena to some other desert camp and we start all over again.'

'He can't have gone very far.'

'He could be anywhere, as far as we're concerned. We're running out of time, Malik.' Aziz swung away to stare at the window. 'My wedding is tomorrow. The six weeks are up then. If I have not married, referendum or not, this country will descend into chaos and civil war.

I will not be able to prevent it. The people's loyalties are too divided.'

'You have Siyad, Your Highness.'

'But nowhere else.' Determination hardened his heart. He would not, he acknowledged starkly, find Elena before the six weeks were up. He could not allow Khalil to put forth his claim to the throne and he was not willing to call the referendum. Whether he won or not, a civil war could still ensue, causing rebellion, insurgency and unrest.

'I must marry,' he said aloud.

'We could still find her.'

'No. It will be too late.' He turned around and gave Malik a grim smile. 'Time has run out, Malik. I must marry, and I will do so tomorrow.'

'But—'

'You know it is true.'

He was going to have to convince Olivia to marry him, whether by charm, reason or perhaps even the coercion she'd been worried about. His heart and soul rebelled against the idea, but his will prevailed. He smiled bleakly at Malik. 'My bride, after all, is right here.'

Olivia donned her plain white cotton blouse and dark trousers with a rush of relief, feeling as if she were reassembling herself, equipping herself with a kind or armour and banishing the memory of Aziz's kiss and the restless desire it had stirred up inside her.

She was going back to Paris. Yet she knew she couldn't go back to the person she'd been, that cold, lifeless husk of a human being. She didn't even want to, not after being with Aziz. After talking to him, laughing with him.

Kissing him.

The memory of that incredible kiss, impossible to suppress, made her heart beat harder. She closed her eyes, tried once more to exorcise the feel of Aziz's lips on hers, the memory of the urgent need that had spiralled inside her, spiralled out of control so hard and fast. Another few minutes and who knew what would have happened?

She took a deep breath and willed her heart rate to slow. Whatever might have happened *hadn't*. They'd stopped, and tonight she'd return to Paris.

And, even though she couldn't go back to her old life, or lack of it, she could still find comfort in the safe routines of keeping Aziz's house. She could start slowly, perhaps, in wanting more for herself—take a class, try to make some friends; nothing too big or too scary.

The thought depressed rather than encouraged her. She didn't want to learn photography or make a new pal. In that moment, she only wanted Aziz.

She shoved the thought away as she put her hair in its usual clip and, with one last resolutely satisfied glance at her reflection, headed out of her room to find Aziz. She'd get their last meeting over with and move on, whether her heart wanted to or not.

A member of staff directed her to a suite in another wing. Two sofas faced each other and a silver tea tray had been set between them. Olivia was just debating whether she should pour when a door to an adjoining room opened and Aziz strode into the room, dressed in faded jeans and a button-down shirt that had yet to be buttoned. A towel was slung round his shoulders and his hair was wet and spiky.

Olivia felt her body stiffen, her eyes pop. She could not draw her gaze away from the tantalising glimpse of bare flesh his open shirt provided. His skin was bronze, the muscles of his chest taut and defined—Michelangelo's *David*, indeed.

'Sorry,' Aziz said, 'I didn't realise you'd arrived.' He tossed the towel onto a chair and began to button up his shirt—leisurely, Olivia thought. She forced her gaze upwards.

'I just came in. When is the plane scheduled to leave?'

'That depends,' Aziz answered. He went over to the tea tray and began to pour. Olivia remained where she stood, an unease caused by too many different feelings creeping through her. 'Here.' Smiling, his eyes silver in the afternoon light, he handed her a cup of fragrant tea. 'Milk, no sugar, yes?'

'Yes… Depends on what, Aziz?' She took the cup and sat down across from him, sipping the tea without really tasting it. Her sense of unease deepened, settled in her bones.

'Depends on the conversation we're about to have,' Aziz answered as he took a sip of his own tea.

Olivia put her cup down with a clatter. 'You want me to stay longer, don't you? What is it now— another appearance? A dinner?' She spoke accusingly, but she couldn't deny the anticipation, the excitement, she felt at the thought of staying. Of being with Aziz for longer.

'No. I don't want you to pretend to be Queen Elena again. Ever.'

The finality of his tone made her head spin, her mouth gape. 'What, then?'

'I want you to be yourself, Olivia,' Aziz continued steadily. 'I want you to stay here as Olivia, not as Elena.'

'Why?'

'Because,' Aziz answered, 'I want to marry you.'

CHAPTER EIGHT

'DON'T FAINT,' AZIZ SAID, laughter lacing his voice, and Olivia shook her head as if to clear it. The dizziness still spiralled inside her, along with a thousand feelings. Shock. Hope. Fear. *Joy*.

'I'm not going to faint,' she said, and her voice sounded strange to her own ears. 'I just can't believe you said what you said.'

'That I want to marry you?'

'Yes.'

'Well, I do.'

Still she just stared, shock making speech or even thought virtually impossible. Finally she found the sense to string some words together. 'What about Queen Elena?'

'She's not here.'

'You're *engaged* to her, Aziz. Doesn't that mean anything to you?'

The lightness left his face and his eyes and voice both turned steely. 'Of course it does. But we became engaged because it was convenient for both of us. I have accepted the fact that I am not going to find her before the six weeks set out in my father's will are up. Therefore I must find another bride.'

'And you suppose I'll do.'

'I think,' Aziz said, his voice dropping to a knowing murmur, 'Based on the kiss we shared earlier today, you'll more than just do, Olivia. There's an attraction between us—'

'That doesn't mean I want to get *married*.' Olivia swung away, her whole body trembling with the shock of Aziz's proposal. Although, she acknowledged as she swallowed a near-hysterical laugh, he hadn't actually *asked*. He'd just told her his intention.

'I can't believe you'd actually suggest such a thing,' she muttered. 'It's crazy.'

'I'll admit, this whole situation has an element of madness to it. But needs must.'

'For you.' Olivia turned around, her body trembling, this time with indignation and even hurt. 'Needs must for *you*, Aziz. But I have no need to get married. Unless— unless you're going to threaten to fire me if—'

'I told you before I'd never do that, Olivia.' His voice was hard, but then his expression lightened as he offered her a wry smile. 'I'm not the kind of man who resorts to coercion or bribery. I have better strategies than that.'

'Which are?'

'I simply intend to convince you of the benefits of marriage to me.'

'The benefits,' she repeated. Already she could imagine all too well just what some of those benefits might be: waking up next to Aziz every morning; sleeping in his arms every night; sating that wild need she'd felt for him in the garden again and again…

'I think,' he murmured, his smile turning sleepy, 'Judging by your blush, you might be aware of some of them?'

'Damn you,' she choked, and turned away again, if only to hide her flushed cheeks.

'Olivia.' She felt his hand on her shoulder, the heat of his body behind hers. 'I'm not trying to embarrass you. Trust me, the attraction we feel for one another, as unexpected as it might be for both of us, is something I certainly consider a benefit.'

'You don't marry someone just because you're attracted to them,' Olivia managed to get out. Her voice sounded suffocated.

'No, of course not. But it's better to be attracted to the person you marry, don't you think?'

'Were you—are you—attracted to Elena?' Olivia asked and Aziz didn't answer. She turned around, rubbing her arms as if she was cold. And she was cold, despite the still, drowsy air in the room. She was cold with shock—not just over Aziz's proposal but her own reaction to it. For when he'd told her he wanted to marry her, as disbelieving as she'd been, a part of her had already answered with a resounding *yes*. A part of her had clamoured that this, *he*, was what she'd been waiting for, what she needed.

'I didn't spend enough time with Elena to discover whether we were attracted to one another,' Aziz finally said. 'The two times we met were akin to business meetings. Neither of us was interested in anything else.'

'But weren't you curious if you'd even like each other, never mind desire—?'

Aziz sighed. 'Why are we talking about Elena?'

'Because you were planning to marry her,' Olivia shot back. 'And, if by some miracle she walked through the door right now, you'd still marry her.' She shook her head, scrambling for self-preservation. 'Although, you're right, I'm not sure why we're talking about Elena, or any of this. I'm not going to marry you, Aziz. I can't.'

He raised his eyebrows, a small smile playing about his mouth. 'Can't or won't?'

'Both.'

Aziz gazed at her thoughtfully, his face calm, his whole being utterly unruffled. 'Are you happy in Paris, Olivia?'

'What?' Her nails dug into her arms as she hugged herself then, realising what she was doing, she dropped her arms and glared at him. 'What kind of question is that?' A good one, she thought with something close to panic. And one whose answer she refused to give.

'Because you admitted to me in the garden today that you chose the life you live because it's safe. Because anything else is too hard.'

'So?' she demanded, her voice raw, and Aziz smiled gently.

'So I'm offering you an alternative. One that is still safe but might be more pleasant, more enjoyable, than the life you currently lead. Aren't you ever lonely?'

'You don't marry someone just because you're lonely.'

'I'm sure lots of people marry for precisely that reason.'

'Well, I don't.' He didn't respond, just sat there, watching her. Waiting. 'Your suggestion is absurd,' she burst out. 'As if I would marry you simply because I'm a little lonely sometimes!' She shook her head, furious now. 'You're unbelievably arrogant.'

'Arrogant? But I don't mind admitting it, Olivia. I'm lonely too.'

'The Gentleman Playboy?' she scoffed. 'Lonely?'

'None of the liaisons I've had have been remotely satisfying except in the most basic way.'

'And you want more than that?'

'Not exactly, which is why I think we'll suit each other so well.'

'I don't understand.'

'Don't you?' Aziz gave her a fleeting, almost sad smile. Olivia shook her head, not wanting to understand. Not wanting to concede any point to Aziz.

'We're friends, I hope,' he resumed. 'And we're attracted to each other—both a solid basis for a marriage.'

'Maybe,' she allowed, but even that felt like conceding too much. Was he going to argue her into agreeing? Knowing how persuasive he could be, and how tempted she was, he just might.

Rather frantically she reminded herself of all the reasons she shouldn't entertain this idea: she barely knew him, for one. He was a playboy, for a second. And third, he was ruler of a country. She'd have to be a queen, a public figure, and just that thought nearly had her breaking out in hives.

There was no way she wanted to bind herself to a life like that, never mind the man involved.

Of course she wasn't thinking of it. Not for one second.

She shook her head again and Aziz smiled. 'In a moment,' he said teasingly, 'I think I'm going to see smoke coming out of your ears.'

'I just find it so incredible that you would ever suggest such a thing,' Olivia forced out.

Aziz tilted his head to one side, his gaze sweeping over her. 'Do you really find it incredible, Olivia?'

'You mean because you're desperate,' she answered flatly. 'I'm the only choice you have.'

'That's not quite true. I'm sure I could find someone else at short notice if I really needed to.'

'Am I meant to be flattered that you chose me?'

'Flattered, no. But I would like you to seriously consider the idea instead of rejecting it out of hand, outraged that I even suggested such a thing.'

She felt some of her anger leave her, and she missed the certainty it had given her. When you were so busy being angry you didn't have time to think, to wonder.

To want.

She took a breath, let it out slowly and then sat on the sofa across from Aziz. 'All right, fine. Tell me what you're thinking, Aziz. Tell me just how you envision a marriage between us working.' If she couldn't dissuade him through outrage, Olivia thought, she'd do it through cold, hard logic. She'd argue him into rescinding his offer.

Liar. The only person who was likely to change her mind was her. She was playing with fire, having this conversation. Entertaining the idea of marriage to Aziz even for a moment made it far more likely that she'd end up with burned fingers—and a broken heart.

Because, while Aziz was waking her up to ideas of life, love and happiness, she was under no illusion about what he still wanted: a convenient marriage. A cold one.

'I confess, I haven't thought through every detail,' Aziz told her, his voice low and steady. 'But that's something we can do together.'

'Don't jump ahead,' Olivia answered sharply. 'I just want to hear what you're thinking, Aziz. For curiosity's sake.'

'For curiosity's sake,' he repeated, his eyes and smile both gleaming. 'Very well. I imagine it would look something like this. Tomorrow we both show up in the Gold Salon here in the palace. We say some vows. We become husband and wife.' He spread his hands. 'The rest is up for discussion.'

Not everything, Olivia thought. Although, why she even

cared she didn't know. She'd been thinking about taking a *class*, for heaven's sake. Not getting married.

'Don't make light of it,' she told him. 'It's a serious thing. I'd take any vows I said seriously.'

'So would I, Olivia. But are you seriously thinking about saying them? Or are you really just curious?'

She stared at him, unwilling to answer. *Why* was she pursuing this conversation? *Actually thinking...* 'It's mad,' she said finally and he nodded.

'I know.'

'I don't want to be a queen, a public figure.'

'Your appearances could be kept to a minimum. Your privacy and comfort would be paramount.'

She shook her head. 'The last thing I want is to live in a strange country, far from everything I've known.'

'Something we can discuss. If you married me, you could divide your time between Paris and Kadar.'

'But you would be in Kadar.'

'Yes.'

So he really was suggesting the kind of arrangement he'd had with Elena: convenient, cold, coming together only for special engagements or state functions.

And yet in the space of about five minutes, against all sense, not to mention her better judgement, she had been spinning some other fantasy. Picturing herself waking up in Aziz's bed, halfway to falling in love...

'I'm not sure,' she said as crisply as she could, 'What I am meant to gain from such an arrangement.'

'Companionship, for one. Physical affection.' His smile was gently teasing but Olivia just stared him down.

'Companionship, Aziz, with half the world between us? Besides, what kind of companionship can two strangers really hope to have? I said it last night and I'll say it again—you don't really know me.'

He tilted his head, his smile almost sad, somehow. 'Don't I?'

He knew her better than anyone else did, but that still wasn't saying all that much. 'No,' she said, her voice still crisp. 'You don't.'

'I know you prefer coffee in the mornings but tea in the afternoons. You can't stand the smell of fish. You dress in dark colours but you like bright ones. You jiggle your left foot when you're nervous.' Both of their gazes moved to her jiggling foot and with an exasperated breath she placed both feet flat on the floor.

'I commend your powers of observation, but none of that is really knowing me.' Although she was more shaken than she would ever admit at how much he'd observed about her. How did he know all those things? She didn't think she could say she knew the same about him, and she had a feeling Aziz liked it that way.

'Fine.' His expression was bland and yet somehow challenging. Or perhaps she was just feeling remarkably raw. 'You like a quiet life.'

'I *told* you that.'

'But you didn't always. You loved someone once, and you don't ever want to love again. You have secrets but you want to pretend you don't. You have a deliciously dirty laugh but no one ever hears it.'

'Stop,' she whispered.

'You bought a red and purple scarf but you won't wear it out of the house. You hum pop songs from ten years ago when you're working, but you couldn't tell me a single hit song from today. You don't play the piano very often, but when you do your soul and all its sorrows pours right out of you.' He sat back on the sofa, his arms folded, one eyebrow arched. 'Well? How am I doing so far?'

'If you think,' Olivia said in a shaky whisper, 'That

knowing all that about me will convince me to marry you, you're dead wrong, Aziz.'

'Because you don't want to be known.' He nodded, as if he'd expected as much, his gaze blazing and so very certain. 'So you can't use that as an argument, can you, Olivia? That I don't know you. Because you don't even want me to.'

Except she didn't know *what* she wanted any more. She looked away from him, unable to bear the certainty she saw in his eyes. 'So why,' she demanded, 'Would I want to marry you?'

'I told you. Companionship. Attraction.' He paused. 'Sex.' That one word seemed to sizzle in the air like hot grease on a griddle. 'Closeness,' Aziz continued, 'But not too close.' He leaned forward and reluctantly Olivia looked back at him. 'That's what we both want, isn't it? Enough, but not too much?'

'I'm not even sure what that means.'

'Then let me enlighten you. It means I'll let you keep your secrets, and I'll keep mine. It means I'll make love to you every night, but I won't ask you questions or press you for answers. I won't fall in love with you and I won't break your heart.'

Olivia pressed one hand against her thundering heart. The words, she knew, were meant to comfort her, but they just sounded cold. Maybe it was more than the half-life she'd had, but would it be enough? Did she even dare to want—and try for—more? 'And you assume I want that kind of—arrangement,' she stated numbly.

Aziz arched an eyebrow. 'By your own admission, you're not looking for love. And neither am I.'

Disappointment was like a stone in her stomach. 'Why aren't you?'

He shrugged. 'Same reason as you, I suppose, except I never got as far as actually loving someone.'

'If you haven't had your heart broken, why are you so afraid of getting hurt?'

'A child's heart, perhaps,' he answered after a moment. 'Not the same thing.'

'You mean your father.'

'My experience with him made me reluctant to love or trust anyone else.'

'Was he—was he cruel to you?'

'It doesn't matter,' he dismissed. 'We're talking about the future, Olivia. What we can gain from each other.'

She folded her arms. 'And what if…?' *What if I told you I wanted more?* No, she couldn't ask that. Couldn't reveal that much. 'What if I told you I like my life the way it is?'

'You could tell me, but I'm not sure I'd believe it.'

She opened her mouth to tell him off for his arrogance, but nothing came out. She was suddenly and utterly tired of the posturing. The pretence. *The lies.*

'Fine. Maybe I'm missing something, but I'm not sure what you're offering will fill that emptiness.'

'You could try.'

'And if it doesn't work?'

'Then you can go back to Paris and live the life you had before. You'll be married to me, I admit, but I won't trouble you.'

Which just made her feel sadder than ever. Sudden tears stung her eyes and she turned away, hiding her face from him, trying to hide all of herself, but she knew it was too late. He'd seen too much.

'You've been hurt before, Olivia,' Aziz said quietly. 'I understand that and I respect it. I promise you, I won't hurt you.'

'You can't make promises like that.'

'To the very best of my ability.'

'It's not enough.' She dragged a breath into her lungs. 'You've got the wrong end of the stick anyway,' she forced out. 'I haven't had my heart broken in the way you think, by some *man*.'

Aziz stilled, his expression turning watchful, alert. 'Who was it, then?'

Olivia blinked back more tears, her gaze unfocused, her mind spinning. She remembered the last time she'd talked about Daniel, when her father had told her to forget him. *For ever.* Yet now, incredibly, she wanted to talk about him. She wanted to tell Aziz, to have him understand...

Madness.

'Olivia,' he said, and just the way he said her name made her feel he understood, or at least that he could understand if she let him. And she wanted to let him; she craved another person's compassion.

'His name was Daniel,' she said clearly. She lifted her head to meet Aziz's concerned gaze. 'And he was my son.'

CHAPTER NINE

IT WASN'T WHAT he'd been expecting. A son. A *child*. Aziz stared at Olivia, at the grief he saw so clearly in her eyes, on her face, and thought, *of course*. Of course she hadn't had some standard, run-of-the-mill love affair. Of course her pain was deeper than that.

He leaned forward and put his hand over hers; her skin was icy cold. 'I'm sorry,' he said quietly, and she let out a sound that was close to a sob. Everything in Aziz ached. 'Tell me?' he said, a question, and she stared down at their hands, his skin brown and hers so pale. He thought she wouldn't say anything but after a moment she began to speak.

'I was seventeen.' She took a deep breath and looked up at him, her eyes glassy with tears, her face pale. 'I've never told anyone this,' she said in a low voice. 'Not one person.'

'You can tell me, Olivia,' he told her quietly. 'If you want to. If you think it might help.'

'I don't know.' She withdrew her hand from his and wrapped her arms around herself, as if she was cold. Aziz felt the sudden, fierce need to put his arms around her, to warm her and comfort her in a way that had nothing to do with desire but rather with compassion—or even some deeper emotion. 'I don't even like to think of Daniel,' she whispered. 'It hurts too much.'

'What happened to him?'

He thought she wouldn't answer. Her gaze had become distant and unfocused, her slender arms still wrapped around her body as if she were holding herself in; keeping herself together. 'I gave him away,' she whispered, and her voice broke on the last word. She bowed her head, her shoulders shaking, and Aziz didn't even think then. He just acted.

He pulled her into his arms, felt her slender body shaking with sobs. She didn't pull away; if anything, she pressed closer against him, needing him in a way that flooded Aziz with a longing to comfort and protect her.

When had someone needed him, wanted him, for anything other than a casual sexual encounter? He'd chosen things that way, had told himself he preferred it, but as he held Olivia close he began to grasp just how much he'd been missing.

And still would miss. The kind of marriage he'd suggested to Olivia wasn't meant to be about this kind of intimacy: sharing secrets, offering each other comfort. Already they were both breaking the rules and Aziz knew that couldn't lead to anywhere good.

'It was an accident, of course,' Olivia said after a moment, her voice muffled against his chest. He could feel the dampness of her tears through his shirt. 'I didn't even have a boyfriend at the time. I went to a party and had too much to drink. I didn't normally drink at all, besides wine sometimes at a family dinner. But I was feeling grown up—I'd just been offered a place at university— and there was a boy there I'd always had a secret crush on. Maybe not so secret, though.' She let out a laugh that held no humour and shook her head.

Aziz felt all his protective instincts rear up. 'You're

saying this boy took advantage of you while you were drunk? That's rape, Olivia.'

'No, I wasn't that drunk,' she told him. 'Honestly. I'd just had enough to feel prettier and funnier and more confident than I actually was. And when one thing led to another...' She sighed, the sound heavy, even defeated. 'I regretted it, of course, in the morning. Terribly. I never even thought about falling pregnant, though. Stupidly.'

'And when you found out?' Aziz asked in a low voice.

'I didn't find out. My mother did. She suspected before I did, at least. I was sick in the mornings, and I thought I just had stomach flu. She confronted me and my first thought was that I just *couldn't* be. But, of course, I was.'

'And what happened then?'

'My mother was furious. We lived in South America then, and the country was conservative, the ex-pat community very small. She insisted I get a termination. She told me it was for the best, as I already had a university place, my whole life in front of me. And I convinced myself she was right.'

'But you didn't get a termination,' Aziz stated quietly. 'Did you? Because you said you gave him away.'

Olivia let out a shuddering breath and nodded, her hair brushing against his chest. 'No, I didn't, but I almost did. My mother had arranged it all. We had to go to New York, because terminations were illegal where we living. She made up this big story about a mother-daughter shopping trip. She didn't want my father to know.'

'Why not?'

'She said it would kill him.' Her voice choked. 'Not literally, of course. But I was always a daddy's girl. Spoiled, probably, but I—I loved my father so much. I couldn't bear the thought of disappointing him, so I agreed not to tell him.' She was quiet for a moment, so he could hear the soft draw and tear of her breaths. 'He used to have me play piano whenever he was tired. He said my music always soothed him. My mother said he wouldn't be able to bear hearing about what I'd done. And she wouldn't let me tell Jeremy—the father—either. Not that he would have even cared, but…he should have known. I should have been strong enough to tell him.'

Aziz couldn't bear to hear the throb of grief in Olivia's voice. He sensed her sorrow had more than one cause: the loss of her son, the secret from her father, her mother's fury, the stupid boy's rejection of her; all of it had tangled together, choking her, keeping her from truly living.

'So we went to New York,' Olivia resumed after a moment, her voice flat now. 'And I made it all the way to the clinic. All the way to the examining room, even. The whole time I felt as if it were all happening to someone else, almost as if I were watching a film, wondering what was going to happen next. And then the doctor came in—she was very kind—and asked me if I understood what was happening. I've never known if she asked that of everyone, or if I just looked particularly terrified.'

'I imagine,' Aziz murmured against her hair, 'It was a terrifying experience.'

'I told the doctor that I understood, but I couldn't go through with it. My mother was out in the waiting room and when I came out after just a few minutes she was furious. *Furious.*'

'Your mother sounds like a fearsome woman.'

'I can't blame her, really. She was doing her best for me—trying to protect me, I suppose, along with our family's reputation. My father's career.' Her voice choked again and she took a few even breaths before she continued. 'My father has always been such a dreamer. He needs someone like her, I think, although…' She stopped, and Aziz wondered what she was thinking. Remembering.

'What happened then?' he asked after a moment.

'I told her I wanted to keep the baby. She told me I was wrecking my life. We were at a stand-off for a while, the rest of my first trimester anyway. I remember because I felt him kick for the first time and I still didn't know what was going to happen to him or me.'

Aziz's chest hurt as he imagined her with one hand pressed to her gently rounded belly, overwhelmed with both wonder and despair. 'Oh, Olivia.'

'My mother wanted me to give him up for adoption. She still insisted on hiding my pregnancy from everyone—she planned to tell people I was recovering from stress and send me to a clinic in America to have the baby.'

It sounded like a selfish, heartless decision and inwardly he railed against the woman who had bullied her daughter in such a way. 'Is that what you did?'

A small hesitation, a telling pause. 'Yes,' she finally said. 'I gave in eventually, so I went.'

He wondered what she'd chosen not to tell him, but decided not to ask. 'How long were you there?'

'Six months. The longest six months of my life in some ways, and the shortest in others. Because I knew I'd have to give him up when it was over. I wasn't…I wasn't strong enough to have him on my own. I should have been, but I wasn't.'

'You were so young, Olivia.'

'Yes, but other girls have done it. I could have—I don't know—applied for benefits or childcare help at university. I could have stood up to my mother and insisted. But I didn't do any of that. I just felt so numb, so dead inside. I didn't have the strength.'

His arms tightened around her. 'Tell me what happened next.'

'He was born. He was so beautiful...' She swallowed hard. 'I held him after he was born. He was so tiny, he fitted right in the crook of my arm. He looked like a little old man.' She let out a sound that was half-laugh, half-sob. 'I kept him overnight. I even fed him myself, though the nurses told me it would better if I didn't. I remember staring down at his face. He kept looking at me with these huge blue eyes when I fed him. He was so alert.' She drew a shuddering breath. 'I named him, even though I knew it would be changed. Daniel.'

She pressed her face into Aziz's chest once more. 'And then I let him go.' She drew a quick, sharp breath, her words coming faster, tumbling over themselves. 'I believe he's happy now. I pray he is. An American couple adopted him. I met them, and they seemed very nice. Very kind. He'll be well looked after.'

'But you didn't want to give him up.'

'No.' She subsided then, still leaning against him, and Aziz wondered if she was even aware that he was holding her—that he *wanted* to hold her. 'I never did, but I tried to convince myself it was for the best. I told myself I had university to look forward to, a career as a musician. My mother kept telling me to forget about it, him, because I still had my whole life in front of me. It just didn't feel that way. It felt like my life had gone. And it was my own fault.'

'It wasn't, Olivia. You were young—'

'So? Does that really make a difference? If you want something badly enough, you should be strong enough to fight for it.'

He didn't argue with her any more, because he understood how she felt. He knew how you could tell yourself the truth so many times—*it's not my fault my father doesn't like me; I'm worthy and deserving of love in my own right*—and yet you still didn't believe it. Maybe you never could.

And Olivia, he surmised, had been devastated by this experience. *Losing her son.* No wonder she hid herself away, longed only for a quiet life. She'd been hurt badly and she didn't want to try again. Could he blame her? He was the same, and he hadn't even been as hurt as she had. He hadn't lost as much.

'So what happened after?' he asked. 'You went to university...'

'For one term. I don't remember much about it, actually. I was kind of—numb.' She eased herself away from him then, and he missed her warmth and softness pressing against him. She scooted across the sofa, her arms folded across her chest, her head bent and her hair hanging down so he couldn't see the expression on her face.

'I dropped out after Christmas,' she continued. 'And I drifted around for a while. Then my father arranged the housekeeping position. He was trying to help me.'

Again Aziz sensed there was something she wasn't saying but he had no idea what it was. 'And you haven't wanted anything else?' he said after a moment.

'No.' She rose from the sofa and paced restlessly to the window, one slender hand resting on the sill, her back to him. 'I don't know why I told you all this. The point of anything between us was that we'd get to keep our secrets, wasn't it?'

He sat back against the sofa and watched her; her narrow back seemed almost to quiver with tension. 'Maybe not the *point*. More like a side benefit.'

'And yet I just told you mine.'

'Are you sorry you did?'

She turned to him, one hand still on the sill, her eyes dark and wide. 'No, I'm not. Which is kind of frightening.'

Yes, Aziz agreed silently, it was. For both of them. Hearing someone's secrets meant they trusted you to keep them. Not to let them down. And, while he'd promised he wouldn't hurt her, suddenly it seemed harder now and far more fearsome. He really didn't want to hurt her, not even a tiny bit. He cared about her, more than he'd expected. More than he wanted to.

'And this kind of soul-baring certainly isn't part of any arrangement we might have, is it?' she asked with a humourless smile. 'Have I freaked you out?'

'No, of course not. And, in any case, I said everything was up for discussion,' Aziz answered as lightly as he could.

She raised her eyebrows. 'You still want to marry me?'

'Yes.' And he knew he meant it, even if nothing had happened quite as he'd expected. Even if he wasn't sure what a marriage between them would look like now or what he really wanted from it.

She shook her head and turned back to the window. 'It's just so crazy,' she murmured. 'So, so crazy.'

'I completely agree. But my father's will is crazy.'

'Would you ever have married,' she asked, 'If the will hadn't dictated it?'

He hesitated, not sure what she wanted to hear, and uncertain how much truth to share. 'I don't know,' he finally said, which was, at least, honest.

'What about an heir? You'll need one eventually, I suppose?'

'Yes.'

She tensed then, her fingers curling around the windowsill, knuckles whitening. 'So this marriage—it would mean children?'

And that, Aziz realised, was a bit of a loaded issue. 'Yes, Olivia, it would.' Something he hadn't mentioned before—hadn't even thought of, really, except in the abstract. He waited for her to say something, but she just stared out of the window. 'How do you feel about that?' he asked after a moment.

'A baby,' she murmured, then shook her head again. 'I—I don't know.'

'Do you want more children?'

'I never thought…' She lapsed into silence and Aziz just waited. Just like Olivia, he was starting to realise just all a marriage between them would entail. He'd thought he'd understood and accepted it all after having discussed it with Elena; they'd laid out all the relevant points in a twenty-page legal document. He'd accepted that a cold business arrangement was what he wanted for himself, never mind what he needed to fulfil the terms of his father's will.

But now…with Olivia… When he'd wiped away her tears, when he'd held her in his arms, when he'd felt her pain…

He couldn't let himself want more. Olivia didn't want to love him, and he didn't want to love her. They needed to keep it that way. Keep it simple. Keep it safe.

'I can't give you an answer now,' she said finally. 'It's too big a decision. I know you have to marry by tomorrow, and I can tell you later today, perhaps. But I can't…' She shook her head, biting her lip.

'I understand,' Aziz said quietly. It was a huge decision, for both of them. And, just as Olivia had pointed out earlier, it was a case of needs must for him, but not for her.

She turned to him. 'What will you do if I say no?'

'That's not your problem to worry about, Olivia. And frankly I'd rather you didn't agree just because you're trying to save me.' He smiled wryly, although he felt a certain heaviness inside. He couldn't stand the thought of her pity. 'This isn't a mercy mission.'

'I know that.'

'Any marriage between us would, I hope, benefit you as much as it would me.' Although he wasn't sure if he believed that. What did he really have to offer Olivia? Sex? She could get it somewhere else if she wanted it. Friendship? If she wanted friends, she could make them. She didn't need to get *married*, for heaven's sake.

So what would motivate her to agree? What was making her think seriously about it now?

And then he knew. Of course—a child. She wanted a child.

Not him; not his friendship or even just his body. Only a child. A child of her own.

'Think about it,' he said, and his voice sounded strange, stilted. He forced a smile. 'You know where to find me when you have your answer.'

She nodded slowly, and after an endless moment she turned and left the room.

Aziz remained seated, staring, his mind spinning emptily. Distantly he wondered how he would feel if Olivia now agreed to marry him. And with a heaviness inside he knew it wouldn't be the unadulterated relief he'd been anticipating just a few moments ago—and he didn't even want to figure out why.

Olivia walked slowly down the corridor, barely aware of where she was going. Somehow she found her way back to her bedroom, which thankfully was empty. She didn't think she could face seeing anyone just now, not even Mada or Abra with their kind, smiling faces.

She sank onto the bed, her mind still spinning, emotional and physical exhaustion crashing over her in a tidal wave.

What had just happened?

The events of the last few hours swirled through her mind, from her passionate kiss with Aziz in the royal gardens, to his shocking marriage proposal, to her own just as shocking admission. *She'd told him about Daniel.* She'd cried in front of him, had sought his comfort, had revelled in the feel of his arms around her. *She was seriously thinking about accepting his marriage proposal.*

She'd said it was madness, and he'd agreed. It *was* madness. She barely knew him. She'd have to be a *queen*, appearing in public, photographed by newspapers when all she'd ever wanted was a quiet, solitary life.

She'd have a child.

Another child—not one to replace Daniel, because no baby could ever do that, but one to keep and love, one to redeem both her past and herself. One to cherish…

Olivia told herself she could have a child without getting married. Women did it all the time; you didn't even need a man any more, just a sperm bank. She was half-amazed she hadn't thought of it before, yet the prospect held no appeal now. She wanted a child, yes, but she knew she wanted more than that. She wanted an equal, loving partner to support her and help raise their child.

And how on earth could that be Aziz? He'd just laid out all the reasons he didn't want a real, loving marriage. She was heading for heartbreak at a hundred miles an hour and the only way to stop was to get on a plane to Paris.

But the thought of going back to Paris now felt like regression. Defeat. She couldn't go back, not to the life she'd once had, and not to the little better than that life she'd been thinking of.

She wanted more. She wanted it all. But it was madness to try for it with Aziz.

Wasn't it?

Aziz had made it clear he wasn't looking to love or be loved. *Enough and no more*, he'd said. But how much was enough?

A tremor ran through her body as she once again remembered that incredible kiss…and imagined being with Aziz as a wife, a lover. The feel of his hands on her body, his mouth on hers…

With a shuddery breath Olivia lay down on the bed and stared at the canopy above her. Could she really be thinking about marrying Aziz?

She rolled onto her side, tucked her legs up to her chest and closed her eyes. *Madness*, she told herself. *Madness*. He'd already stirred up so many feelings and desires inside her. How much more of a maelstrom would he create in her if she married him?

Even if they set limits on their relationship, kept to simply being friends, it wouldn't work.

Would it?

Or could she keep herself from feeling too much, from falling in love with him? She'd kept herself from feeling anything at all for ten years. Surely she could manage it?

Did she really have any choice?

With a jolt Olivia realised she'd already decided. Of course she had. She wasn't going to go back to a half-life of safety, numbness and fear. Aziz had changed her too much already for that. And, if she wasn't going to go back, she had to go forward. She wanted what Aziz offered: friendship, physical affection, *a child*.

It was so much more than she'd ever had in her adult

life and it would have to be enough. She would make it be enough, Olivia told herself. She would choose joy.

A sudden bubble of incredulous wonder rose up inside her, escaped in a gurgle of sound—although whether it was a laugh, a sob or something in between Olivia didn't know.

Because, while she was choosing life, hope and happiness, she had no idea what that would actually look like. Feel like. And even more alarmingly, she was quite sure that Aziz wasn't choosing the same things.

Aziz paced the confines of his study, as he'd been doing for the last hour since Olivia had left him. He was going to wear the carpet to threads, he thought wryly, then let out an impatient sigh as he glanced at the clock.

How much time should he give her? And what the hell was he going to do if she said no?

He walked to the window, bracing his hands on the sill as the evening breeze, only just beginning to cool, blew over him. The trouble was, he didn't just want some nameless bride to fulfil the terms of his father's will any more. If Olivia refused his proposal, he could most likely find someone else to marry him. He'd sign another legal document that covered every eventuality; he'd work hard to make sure his bride was accepted by his people.

But he didn't want to do that any more; he was amazed that he'd ever wanted it, that he'd been willing to enter an utterly soulless agreement with Elena.

And what are you going to have with Olivia, if she agrees?

Aziz pushed away from the window and paced restlessly once more. The afternoon with Olivia had blown all his preconceptions, all his priorities, to hell. Their passionate kiss. Her heartbroken confession. The feel of her in his arms, her hair brushing against his cheek, her tears wetting his shirt.

Just the memory made him ache in a way he hadn't ached since he was a boy desperate to gain his father's approval. *His love.*

Was he going to be so phenomenally stupid as to go down that path again? Try to make someone love him, someone who didn't, and didn't even want to? Who had *said* as much?

No, of course not. He'd learned his lesson, surely. And, while he might feel tender and protective towards Olivia when she was obviously in a vulnerable state, he wasn't about to love her. Of course he wasn't.

If he married her, he'd give her what he'd promised. Companionship. Children. Loyalty.

But not love. Never love.

A sound at the doorway startled him and he turned, his heart seeming to leap into his throat and then still completely as he saw Olivia standing there. She still wore the plain trousers and tailored shirt she'd had on earlier, but they looked slightly crumpled now, and her hair was loose and dark about her face. The dye, Aziz noticed, was already starting to fade; he could see streaks of caramel through the black, the real Olivia coming through.

'Good evening.' He cleared his throat and forced a light smile as he raised his eyebrows in teasing query. 'You look rather serious, Olivia.'

'I feel rather serious,' she answered quietly. She stepped into the room, closing the door behind her. 'Malik said I could find you here. I hope I'm not disturbing you?'

'No, of course not.' He'd just been waiting for her to find him for the last hour. 'Have you made a decision?'

'Yes.'

He smiled, shoved his hands into his trouser pockets and rocked on his heels. 'Well, don't keep me in suspense.'

'I don't mean to. It's just—it's a bit like leaping off a cliff, isn't it, Aziz? And you have no idea what waits for you at the bottom.'

His heart lurched, although whether in relief or hope or even fear he didn't know. Wouldn't consider. 'Is that a yes, Olivia?'

'Yes.' Her lips trembled even as she smiled. 'It is a yes. But I have a lot of questions, Aziz. A lot of concerns.'

'Of course you do. And, like I said, everything is up for discussion. We can make this work for both of us, I promise.'

'I told you before, you can't make promises like that.'

'I can.' He stepped towards her; the emotion rushing through him, he realised, was more than relief or hope. It was something frighteningly close to joy. 'I can and I will. We'll discuss anything you like. But not just this minute.'

She blinked up at him; he'd stepped closer so he was standing right in front of her. 'Why not?'

'Because right now I just want to kiss you. My bride.'

Her lips parted in both surprise and expectation and Aziz placed his hands on her shoulders, drawing her gently towards him. Her hair whispered against his face and her breath came out on a sigh as he dipped his head and brushed his lips against hers.

Oh, he'd wanted this again. He'd been waiting for it, dreaming of it, since he'd last kissed her. Both kisses reached a place inside him he'd thought had been closed off for ever. His heart. His soul. Everything in him wanted her, needed her, with an urgency that shocked him even as it made him bolder, deepening the kiss, pulling him against her so she could feel his arousal.

'Aziz…' His name was a moan as his tongue swept the softness of her mouth, his hand sliding down to cup the gentle swell of her breast.

He felt her sudden indrawn breath against his mouth and he broke the kiss, his heart thudding as he managed a wry smile. 'I don't think we'll have any problems in that department,' he murmured. 'You drive me wild, Olivia.'

'It's mutual.' She flushed as she straightened her clothes then gazed up at him, searching his face with a worried, wide-eyed gaze. 'Can we really do this?'

Aziz cocked an eyebrow. 'To what, exactly, are you referring?'

Olivia let out a hiccupy laugh and shook her head. 'You know what I meant. This *marriage*.'

'Of course we can.'

He drew her back into his arms, needing her to be there. Right now he didn't want to discuss the practicalities, or make promises about how they wouldn't hurt each other. Wouldn't love each other.

Right now, he just wanted to kiss her again, so he did.

CHAPTER TEN

OLIVIA SAT AT the head of a large mahogany table, Aziz next to her, a pack of lawyers at the other end, a host of legal documents spread out on the table before them.

Her wedding was in one hour.

After Aziz's kisses last night, he was all business this morning, dressed in a grey silk suit, a pair of glasses perched on his nose as he scanned a legal document whose endless tiny type had blurred in front of Olivia's eyes.

Looking at him now, he seemed forbiddingly remote. A stranger. She hadn't even known he wore glasses. Such a small thing, so unimportant, and yet in that moment it seemed critical. It reminded her rather painfully how little she knew this man, and yet after spending just forty-eight hours with him she was willing to pledge her life to him. Be mother to his child.

Which was what she needed to remember now, she told herself. Forget fairy tales, the castles in the air she'd been building in her head for the last twenty-four hours. She needed to remember what she was getting out of this bargain: companionship. Affection. *A child.* She would have a child.

Aziz, she thought suddenly, would make a good father. He would laugh and tease and tickle.

Do you really know what kind of father he'll be? What

kind of husband he'll be? What on earth are you doing, Olivia?

'Looking at point five...' one of the lawyers said, clearing his throat, and Olivia snapped back to attention.

'Yes,' she murmured, gazing blindly down at her copy of the agreement, although she had no idea what point five, or any of the points, was.

Aziz leaned over and flipped the page over, tapping one lean finger in the relevant place.

'Thank you,' Olivia murmured, flushing. Point five, it turned out, dealt with her royal appearances, 'as and when required'.

'We can put a limit on them,' Aziz said, turning to her. 'No more than once a month, if you prefer.' He spoke calmly, unemotionally, as if this was no more than a normal business meeting. It made Olivia feel like screaming.

She should be reassured by all the provisions Aziz was putting in place, she told herself. He was looking out for her, protecting her interests. She should want all these safeguards, because then she would know just what she was getting into.

Except she didn't know what she was getting into, didn't even know what she *wanted* to get into. Last night she'd told herself she'd chosen joy. She'd acknowledged how alive and whole and happy Aziz made her feel, and had made herself believe a marriage with him could work because it was still more than she'd ever had before. Had ever dared to have.

This morning she didn't know anything.

'Olivia?' Aziz prompted.

'Once a month is fine.'

'Very well.' He turned towards the team of lawyers. 'Could you add that, please?'

'As for point six...' one of the lawyers said, and Olivia

forced herself to focus on the next point, even though her mind was buzzing and the words blurred. She made out 'issue resulting' and she turned to Aziz.

'Issue?'

'Children,' he murmured and her fingers tightened on the papers.

'What is the provision for our children?'

'We can discuss it, of course. This document is based on the one that was drawn up for Elena and me, but naturally things are different now.'

Not that different, Olivia thought with a clawing panic. This was still a convenient marriage. A cold-hearted business arrangement.

Was she selling her soul for a little happiness? Settling for a little more than a half-life, but still not enough?

The questions screamed inside her head so loudly she felt like covering her ears. That wouldn't help. Nothing would help.

She forced herself to look at Aziz. His expression was impossible to read. 'What was your agreement with Elena, with regards to children?' she asked. Her voice sounded distant and strange.

'We both needed heirs, so that was our priority. The first son would be the heir to Kadar, the child after the heir to Thallia.'

'What if you didn't have a son?'

He gave a small shrug. 'Just about every king has faced that possibility. Perhaps by the time a child of mine accedes the throne, a woman could rule Kadar. I certainly hope so.'

She took a deep breath. 'Any child of ours would remain in our home and not be sent away to school.'

Aziz nodded calmly. 'Make a note, please,' he told the lawyers.

'No nannies or governesses.'

'We would need some childcare provision, Olivia. You will have some royal responsibilities, even if they are kept to a minimum.'

'Fine. Any childcare provider must be approved by me.'

'And me,' he answered lightly. 'Fair?'

She nodded jerkily, hating that everything had to be a negotiation. Hating how cold it all felt, when all she wanted to do was throw herself into Aziz's arms and beg him to love her.

Love her? Was that what she really wanted now? Was that why she was so panicked?

He gazed at her thoughtfully for a moment, his eyes narrowed, and then he nodded towards the lawyers. 'Could you leave us for a moment?'

With murmured apologies and assents they left, the door clicking shut behind them. Aziz rose from the table.

'What's wrong, Olivia?'

She clenched her hands, her nails biting into the skin of her palms. 'Nothing's wrong.'

'Are you having second thoughts?' He stood there quietly, his arms folded. He didn't look angry or uncaring, just…calm. Too calm. As if he was in a business meeting, which Olivia knew he *was*.

'Not second thoughts,' she said after a moment. 'Not exactly. But this is so *strange*, Aziz. And now that we're talking about all these details it makes it seem even stranger. More real and less real at the same time.'

'So you *are* having second thoughts.'

'I—I don't know!' She whirled away from him, suddenly near tears. Her emotions were so close to the surface now. They'd been buried deep for a decade, yet now the feelings bubbled up, impossible to suppress.

'Olivia.' Aziz came to stand behind her, his hands resting gently on her shoulders. 'I know this is strange. It's strange for me, too. But that doesn't mean it can't work—'

'Like a washing machine?' she filled in. 'Like a…a *blender*?' She let out a laugh that sounded half-wild and jerked out of his arms. He stared at her, frowning slightly.

'That's not the analogy I would have chosen, but I suppose it is appropriate.' She shook her head, the movement as wild as her laugh, and his gaze narrowed. 'What's really going on here, Olivia? Analogies aside, what's bothering you? What are you afraid of?'

'I'm not afraid.' Except, she was. She was afraid of all these feelings inside her, feelings Aziz had called up. Afraid of caring too much, of getting hurt.

Afraid of falling in love with him.

Last night, when he'd been kissing her and making his promises, caring about Aziz hadn't seemed so scary a possibility. Today, when he stood in front of her in a business suit and with a narrowed gaze, it was terrifying.

'There's just so much uncertainty,' she said after a long, tense moment when Aziz just gazed at her with that inscrutable expression. 'What if the people of Kadar don't accept me? They think I'm Elena right now. What if they really want Elena? What if they decide they want Khalil because you lied to them about this?'

Aziz's jaw went tight. 'Distinct possibilities,' he bit out.

'You said your country was already unstable,' Olivia continued recklessly. It was so much easier to focus on the politics than what she felt, what she was afraid to feel. 'You said that if people found out Elena was missing it could cause unrest, even a civil war. What if our *marriage* causes one, Aziz?'

'It's a risk I have to take.' His voice was cool, as cool

as she'd ever heard it. 'But I'm aware that it's not a risk you have to take. You don't have to marry me, Olivia. You pointed that out yesterday, and it still holds true today. If the risks are too much for you, then you can back out now. Better now than in an hour, after the vows have been said. Kadarans do not look kindly on divorce.'

He gazed at her evenly, almost indifferently, and with a terrible lurch inside Olivia wondered if he even cared whether she married him. Maybe he had a substitute waiting in the wings. Maybe any woman at all would do.

'And if I backed out now?' she whispered. 'Our wedding is in less than an hour, Aziz.'

'Forty-five minutes, actually,' he answered. 'I confess, it will be difficult to find someone else in that amount of time.'

'I don't want to be just a willing body,' she blurted, her voice breaking. 'I don't want you to be just as happy to choose someone else. I want more than that from a marriage, Aziz. From life.'

He stared at her, his gaze still narrowed. 'What more do you want, Olivia?'

Love. I want you to love me. No, she couldn't say that. She didn't even want to think it. 'All this legal talk just seems very cold,' she said after a moment. 'It makes me realise what I might be missing.'

'Such as?'

'I—I don't know. I sound ridiculous, I know. It's just nerves.' She forced a smile. She was a coward, but she couldn't admit that she wanted more now. She had to focus on what she already had, what she could have. 'I do want this marriage, Aziz. I realised last night how much I want a child, to be a mother again. It won't bring back Daniel, I know, but the thought of having a baby to love… I want that very much.'

For a second, no more, she thought he looked almost disappointed, or maybe even hurt. Or was she just wishing he did? Then he shrugged and said, 'Not to point out the obvious, but you don't need me to have a child, Olivia. You could have one on your own if that's all you really want.'

But it wasn't all she wanted. She didn't just want a baby to love; she wanted a partner to support her. She wanted to be part of a family. 'I want this marriage,' she said firmly. 'And I think you'd be a good father, Aziz.'

His lips curved in a humourless smile. 'Would I? I must admit, I didn't have a great example.'

'Yes, you would. You're fun and kind and easy to—' She swallowed and quickly filled in, 'Like. Besides, lots of people with less than stellar parents have been good ones themselves.'

'Thanks for that vote of confidence.'

Olivia heard a note of bitterness in his voice, and as he turned away she wished she'd been more honest with him. She wished she'd risked her heart a little more and confessed that she wanted so much more than what she'd said. That she wanted a child with him.

And do you remember the last time you risked your heart? You laid it all on the line, confessed all your hope, fear and need, and your father just looked away and asked you to play the damn piano.

Just the memory of that betrayal, and her own reeling reaction, had the power to keep her silent now. It was better this way. She might not feel like it now, but it would be better to keep within the limits of their agreement. To keep herself from wanting it all. *Enough and no more*, just like Aziz had said.

An hour later, it was done.

Aziz jerked off his tie, letting out a weary sigh. He

was married, and within the six weeks dictated by his father's will. He should feel relieved—overjoyed, even—but instead he felt only unsettled and restless, as he had since that confrontation with Olivia.

She'd made it perfectly clear she was only in this marriage to have the child she longed for, nothing else, and certainly not because of any finer feelings she possessed for him.

Feelings he shouldn't even want her to have. He wouldn't beg for love again. He wouldn't debase himself like that, not for anyone. Not even for Olivia. Really, everything had worked out just as he'd wanted. He should be glad now, elated, even.

Not somehow disappointed.

The bathroom door to the bedroom suite they'd been given in a secluded wing of the palace opened and Olivia stood there, dressed in a white silk negligee. It was modest enough, the straps scalloped with lace, but Aziz's mouth still dried and every thought flew from his head.

Every thought but one: his wife was beautiful and he had every intention of making love to her. Tonight.

Now.

He smiled, his gaze sweeping over her lovely, slender form. He could tell just from looking at her, observing her pale face, that she was a little nervous. 'You look beautiful, Olivia.'

'The nightgown is a bit much, isn't it?' she said with a shaky smile. 'Or maybe it's not enough.'

'It's quite enough from my point of view,' he told her, and took a step towards her so he was close enough to slide his hands over her bare shoulders. 'I wouldn't want you any more covered up.' He pressed a kiss to her bare shoulder and she shivered.

'I know we don't need to be—be romantic with one another.'

'Why shouldn't we?' He pressed another kiss to the hollow of her throat and her breath came out in a soft rush.

'Because we...we don't love each other.'

Words that once would have reassured him; now he felt something crystallise inside him, something cold and hard and *hurt*. He didn't like hearing her state it so plainly and he didn't want to think about why. 'Isn't this a kind of love?' he answered. 'Don't dismiss it out of hand, Olivia. Not when you know what I feel for you.' His voice had thickened with need and he pulled her to him, slid his arms around her slender waist, wanting to draw a response from her. Show her just how much she needed and wanted him.

And he felt that need in her answering kiss, in the way her body yielded to his, her curves moulded against him. Aziz eased away just enough to unbutton his shirt, wanting to feel her bare body against his own.

Her gaze roved over his bare chest and her tongue darted out to moisten her lips. A primal triumph surged through him at the obviousness of her desire.

'You should know...it's been a long time for me, Aziz.'

He drew her back towards him, revelling in the way her breasts brushed against his bare chest. 'You don't need to be nervous with me. We can go slowly, Olivia. As slowly as you like.' With a smile, he tugged on her hand and drew her to the bed. The sky was darkening to indigo with violet streaking across the horizon, the minarets and towers of the Old Town silhouetted against the sky.

Olivia lay on her back, her cheeks flushed pale pink, her eyes dark and luminous. The swell of her breasts above the negligee was almost more than Aziz could bear.

Her skin was creamy and perfect, the colour of ivory. He tucked a tendril of hair behind her ear, skimming her cheek with his fingers. He'd always thought her beauty was cold and contained, but seeing her lying here, all flushed and rosy and ready to love, he had to amend his opinion. She was like a flower seeking sunlight, shyly bending towards it. He leaned down and pressed a kiss to her temple. Olivia let out a soft sigh.

Encouraged by her response, Aziz pressed another kiss to her cheek, and then to her lips. Olivia brought her hand up to rest it against Aziz's cheek, and everything in him expanded and ached.

He deepened the kiss, taking his time to explore the softness of her mouth, the fullness of her lips. He slid his hand from her shoulder to her waist, splaying his fingers across her hip, the silk slippery beneath his hand.

Olivia moved restlessly under him, her hand tightening on his cheek, her mouth opening under his. She tangled one leg with his so his fierce arousal was brought into exquisite contact with her thighs and he let out a little groan.

He slid his hand from her waist to her breast, his thumb brushing over its tightened peak as he watched her pupils flare and heard her breathing go shallow. 'You like that?' he asked softly and she nodded.

He bent his mouth to her breast, dampening the silk with his tongue as he took the peak into his mouth. Her hands clutched in his hair. 'Oh…no one's ever…'

'No one?' He drew back, even though he longed to continue, ached to do so much more than that. Still he studied her; her hair was a soft cloud around her face, her face so deliciously flushed, her lips parted. 'You've had lovers, though.'

'Not many. Well, two.' She bit her lip and looked away. 'The boy from high school, of course—'

'In a drunken fumble you barely remember?'

She shrugged. 'And once, when I'd left university, just to see if I could still feel anything.'

His heart twisted inside him. 'And could you?'

She glanced back at him, her eyes heartbreakingly wide. 'No. Not then.'

'And now?' He cupped her breast again through the damp silk and she let out a breathy sigh of pleasure.

'Now, sometimes I wonder if I feel too much.'

An admission that gave him a primal feeling of pleasure, of power. *He'd* made her feel again. He'd been the one to wake her up. 'I think I might need to challenge that assertion,' he murmured and kissed her again, deeply this time, holding nothing back.

He felt her brief hesitation and then she responded, kissing him back with just as much passion, just as much wild, raw feeling that it made him want her even more simply because she wanted him. Olivia's response to him was the most powerful aphrodisiac he'd ever known.

She slid her leg between his, drawing him closer, and he slipped a hand between her thighs, pushing the negligee up so she was bare to the waist.

She stilled, but only for a moment. Then her hands went to his belt buckle, trembling as she fumbled with the clasp. Aziz helped her and then he drew off her clothes as well as his own so they were both wonderfully naked.

'You're perfect,' he murmured. He leaned down and kissed her tummy and then, because he wanted to, *needed* to, he moved lower.

Olivia stilled, her hand still tangled in his hair. 'Aziz…'

'Perfect,' he said again, and kissed her between her thighs.

Olivia felt her body arch up of its own accord, her

breath coming out on a ragged gasp as he kissed her again, spreading her legs open with his hands.

The feelings rushed through her like colours, an intense rainbow of sensation that blurred her thoughts into one single, shining realisation of how much Aziz was showing and giving her.

She felt his mouth on her again and once more she reared up, her breath now coming in shallow pants. She'd never known anything like this, felt anything like this, ever, and it made her want to cry and laugh and sing all at once.

'Aziz,' she choked, because that was the only word she could form. The only thought she could think. She was teetering on a precipice of pleasure, longing to tumble right into it but a little afraid as well. This was so much.

It felt like everything.

'I'm right here,' he said, his voice ragged, and he drew back for one heart-stopping second before he slid inside her, filling her right up.

She'd never felt so close, so connected to another person. Never felt so loved.

This has nothing to do with love.

Her mind made one last, frantic insistence but her body refused to agree; her body sang with the joy of Aziz's touch, everything in her opening up, seeking light.

Aziz began to move, his hands on her hips to encourage her to match his rhythm, which she did instinctively, easily, both of them climbing higher and higher, *reaching…*

And then she did reach that apex of pleasure, all the tightly held parts of herself seeming to loosen and spin away so all she could do was *feel*. Feel every emotion she'd denied for so long. It was so intense and amazing, she cried out, tears starting in her eyes, her body wrapped around Aziz's. In that moment she never wanted to let him go.

As the wave of pleasure subsided to ripples she lay back against the pillows, her skin slick and damp, Aziz's weight a comforting heaviness on top of her. He kissed her forehead and then her lips before rolling off her, one hand still across her stomach, as if he didn't want to let her go.

And she didn't want him to. She thought she'd been changed before, had been opened up, her feelings stirred to life, but she'd had no idea. No clue as to what she'd been missing, what she needed.

She turned to Aziz, wanting to say something of all she felt but unable to put it into words. He must have seen some of it in her eyes, however, for he drew her to him once more, fitting her body so easily to his, and kissed her softly.

Olivia kissed him back, felt his heart beat against hers. Sometimes, she thought, you didn't need words. Sometimes they weren't enough for something that had been so emotional, so incredible.

So wonderful.

She laid her head on Aziz's shoulder and eventually they both slept.

CHAPTER ELEVEN

'A HONEYMOON?' OLIVIA repeated in surprise. 'Is that really…necessary?'

'I'm afraid it is.' Aziz sat across from her at the breakfast table in one of the smaller dining rooms of the palace. Dressed in a navy blue suit, his hair still slightly damp from the shower, it was hard to believe he'd made love to her until nearly dawn last night. Their wedding night.

Now, in the cold light of day, Olivia felt all her old uncertainties return. Once again, Aziz felt like a stranger. And, even though her body burned to remember his touch, her mind scurried for self-protection. She couldn't let him know how much last night had affected her. He'd probably be appalled if he found out.

'Why?' she asked as Aziz poured them both coffee.

'It's best if we both stay out of sight for a few days. My marriage has been announced, but not the name of my bride.'

'But everyone will assume—'

'It's Elena. Yes, I know.' He gave her a rather grim smile. 'This is going to a very delicate diplomatic manoeuvre.'

'So how do you intend to announce it?'

'I want to speak to Khalil first and arrange for Elena's release.'

'You make it sound easy.'

'No, just necessary. Now that I'm married he has no reason to keep her. I hope he'll be able to see sense and put aside this desire for revenge.'

'Maybe it's not revenge motivating him,' Olivia said slowly, and Aziz swung his gaze back to her.

'What, then?'

'Maybe, like you, he wants to redeem the past. You were both treated badly by Hashem, in different ways.'

Aziz felt himself bristle. 'He was banished because he was not Hashem's son.'

'But he thought he was, and that had to have hurt him terribly. He lost everything he ever knew, Aziz, and he was just a little boy.'

'He lived a life of luxury in America,' he said stiffly. 'I'm sorry if I can't feel sorry for him.'

'I'm not asking you to feel sorry for him,' Olivia answered after a moment. 'I don't care about Khalil, to be honest. But…' She let out a soft breath. 'I care about how he affects you. Maybe there is a way to put this conflict to rest, to find peace, not just for Kadar but for you and Khalil.'

He let out a hard laugh. 'Peace with Khalil? Never.'

'It's not like you to be so bitter or unforgiving, Aziz,' she protested.

'You don't know—'

'What? Tell me.' She held her breath, wanting him to share something of himself. Wanting to understand him, to help him.

Because she was falling in love with him. And she didn't know how to stop.

Her fingers gripped her fork and she laid it down on the table; she couldn't eat anything anyway.

'Nothing,' Aziz said, his tone final. 'It doesn't matter.

In any case, we don't need to talk politics now. We can enjoy ourselves, for a few days, at least.'

She nodded, knowing she needed to let it go, at least for now. 'Where are we going?'

'To another royal palace, this one on the coast. It's in a very remote and beautiful spot. I'm sure you'll love it.'

'I don't have any clothes or cosmetics.'

'Everything you need will be provided.' He hesitated, his face so very bland. 'Unless you wish to return to Paris for some reason? The terms of our agreement allow—'

'I don't,' she said, hating the thought of that legal document that defined their marriage in such businesslike terms. 'Although I probably should at some point. I'd like to get my things.'

'Of course. You can go back whenever you like, assuming you have no royal duties.'

She stared at him, half-wanting to ask him if he'd miss her, or if he wanted her to go. Maybe he'd rather have her out of the way. She had no idea what he felt, and it seemed absurd to think he'd feel anything, when they'd been no more than employer and employee for six years. This relationship, this marriage, was so very new and strange.

'It's settled, then.' Aziz rose from the table. 'I'll meet you in the grand foyer in an hour. We'll travel to the coast by helicopter. There's a helipad at the back of the palace.'

She nodded, her mind still whirling, and Aziz strode from the room.

An hour later they were in a helicopter high above the desert, the Arabian Sea jewel-bright in the distance and sparkling with sunlight.

Aziz had told her it would only take an hour to get to the palace, and Olivia spent the time gazing out of the window, entranced by the starkly beautiful scenery. The desert terrain was scattered with huge, black boulders, like misshapen marbles tossed from a giant's hand. As they drew closer to the sea, the craggy, forbidding coastline came into view. The palace, Aziz had said, was hidden in its own private cove, inaccessible except by helicopter or boat.

As they landed, the sight of the palace took her breath away. Made of the same mellow, golden brick as the palace in Siyad, this coastal retreat was still completely different, built right into the rock, its elegant towers pointing towards the sky.

'It's quite something,' Aziz said with a small smile. 'I've only been here once before myself.'

Olivia followed him from the helicopter towards the steps cut into the cliff side that curved steeply up to the palace. 'Why only once?'

Aziz shrugged. 'As you know, I spent as little time in Kadar as possible. I think we went here once for a family holiday—my father's birthday, if I remember.' He sounded indifferent, as if he barely remembered when or why he'd been, but Olivia still wondered.

'Tell me about your father,' she said quietly and, even though he was several steps ahead of her, Olivia *felt* him stiffen.

'Why on earth would I want to talk about him?' he answered after a pause.

Olivia waited until they'd reached the top of the cliff-side steps, the palace's ornate wooden doors in front of them. 'Because I know your relationship with him was a troubled one, and it affects you even now. I want to understand.'

'There's nothing to understand.' Aziz turned to open the doors and then began greeting the staff who were lined up in the mosaic-tiled foyer.

Olivia followed him, murmuring her own greetings,

and then they were shown to their private quarters, a beautiful suite of rooms with balconies overlooking a garden with cascading pools, the sea visible beyond. She decided to let the personal questions go for now. There would be time later, she hoped, to get Aziz to open up to her.

'This is amazing,' she said as she stood on a balcony, gazing out at the magnificent view. 'I can hardly believe I'm here.'

Aziz stood in the doorway, the latticed shutters open to the wind and sun. 'It's been a whirlwind few days.'

'Yes.' In the space of just seventy-two hours she'd gone from impersonating a queen to marrying a Sheikh. No wonder her head was still spinning.

Her hands curved around the stone railing, her gaze still fixed on the sea shimmering under the noonday sun. She wanted to tell Aziz something of what was in her heart. She wanted to tell him that in the space of just a few days he'd changed her. And, even though it was scary, she was glad she'd changed, grateful that he'd opened her up.

And she wanted to change him too, to show him that you could risk your heart again, that love was worth it. But how could she explain any of that when she wasn't even sure if she believed it? When just the thought of telling him, never mind living it out, scared her senseless?

Why couldn't she just be satisfied with what Aziz had offered? *Enough and no more.* He didn't want to go deeper with her, even if she now thought she might want to. She'd already told him her secrets; he had no call to tell her his.

You haven't told him everything. No, she hadn't gone into much detail about those awful, endless years after she'd given up Daniel. Hadn't admitted just how low she'd sunk, how she hadn't thought she'd ever crawl out of that dark, dark hole. Hadn't admitted how it wasn't just losing

Daniel but losing her parents', and especially her father's, trust that had made her retreat into isolated numbness.

And he probably didn't want to hear it all now.

He came to stand behind her and rested his hands lightly on her shoulders. 'How about a swim?'

She glanced down at the cascading pools and then smiled up at him. *Enough.* She'd let this, him, be enough. 'That sounds good.'

They spent three days at the coastal palace, chatting and laughing, swimming and making love. With every day she spent in Aziz's company, every hour, Olivia knew she was falling deeper and deeper in love with him. She also knew he wasn't falling in love with her.

She saw how, even when he was right there with her, he kept some part of himself removed. Remote. Even when she lay in his arms, when he kissed her, when he buried himself inside her, he held something back.

And as the days passed she knew with an utter certainty that she wanted that part, wanted to reach all of him. Love all of him. Even if it was scary. Even if it hurt.

She just didn't know how to *begin.*

'I love hearing you laugh,' Aziz said as they lay on the sun-warmed tiles by the main pool's waterfall one afternoon, another pool shimmering below them. 'It makes me realise how little I heard it in Paris. How sad you seemed, but I don't think I quite realised it then.'

Olivia rolled onto her stomach. 'Why should you have? I was just your housekeeper.'

'And you're my wife now.' He stroked her cheek and Olivia took a deep breath. For the last three days she'd been telling herself that she shouldn't push, yet now she couldn't keep herself from it. She wanted to know more about this man she cared about. This man she loved.

'Aziz, will you tell me more about yourself? About your past and your childhood and what made you leave Kadar?'

His fingers stilled on her cheek then he dropped his hand and turned onto his back, staring up at the cloudless blue sky. Olivia waited, hoping he might tell her at least a little.

'There's not all that much to tell, really,' he said after an endless moment. His voice sounded almost disinterested, but Olivia knew now how Aziz hid himself from her and from everyone with a light tone, a raised eyebrow, a teasing smile. His mask.

'Everyone has something to tell,' she answered, matching his light tone. Deliberately she reached out and skimmed one hand along his bare chest, running her fingertips through the water droplets that beaded there. Touching him still felt a little strange, and filled her with wonder. She liked it and wanted it to become familiar, easy. Natural. 'And, whatever your story is,' she continued, running her fingertip along the defined muscles of his abdomen, 'I want to hear it.'

Aziz trapped her hand against his stomach and twisted to look up at her with a wicked smile. 'Are you sure you wouldn't rather do something else instead?'

'*Aziz.*'

'You want to hear me blather on about my childhood?' He moved her hand a little lower. 'I'd like to hear you moan with pleasure.'

She flushed, desire already coursing through her veins in a molten river. She wanted that too, just as much.

Almost.

'Aziz, I'm serious.'

'So am I.' But he let go of her hand with a sigh and stared up at the sky once more. 'So, what do you want to know? My favourite subject in school? My hobbies? I liked maths and making paper aeroplanes.'

'That's a start, I suppose,' Olivia answered with a little smile. 'I could have guessed the maths, considering what a financial whiz you are now. The paper aeroplanes are a bit of a surprise.'

'I used to drive my mother mad, with all the crumpled sheets of paper lying around.'

'Were you very close to your mother?'

He shrugged, the movement easy, yet his face had gone still, blank. Olivia sighed.

'Do you not want to tell me *anything*, Aziz?'

'I thought,' he said after a moment, 'That wasn't the kind of relationship we were meant to have.'

Stung, she blinked a few times, forcing the hurt back. He was right, she knew that. She was the one who had changed, not him. 'I told you my secrets.'

He gazed at her, his face bland, inscrutable. 'Do you regret it?'

'No, I don't. It felt good to open up like that. Scary and surprising, but good.' She hesitated, then made herself add, 'Maybe you'd find it was too.'

'Cathartic soul-baring? Hmm, I'm not so sure.' He was back to being teasing, masking the evasion with a playful smile. 'I can think of a few other things I'd like to do,' he added, and reached out with one hand to toy suggestively with the strap of her swimming costume.

Olivia pulled away slightly. 'I'm not asking for your deepest secrets,' she said, trying to sound as casual as he did. She had a feeling she hadn't quite managed it. 'I just want to know you a little better. We are married, after all.'

Aziz was silent for a moment; he slid one hand up and down her arm almost absently, his brow furrowed. 'All right,' he finally said. 'What is it you wanted to know?

Was I close to my mother? Yes, as a small child. But when we moved to the palace she withdrew more and more from everyone, even me, and then I hardly saw her after I went away to school.' He flipped onto his stomach and reached for her again. 'Now, let's get back to the more important issue…'

And, with a little laugh, Olivia let him draw her towards him. She didn't think she'd get much farther with Aziz's confidences just then, and in any case she had neither the willpower nor the desire to resist him any longer.

Later, the shuttered windows open to the sun setting over the Arabian Sea turning the placid water to gold, they lay on the huge canopied bed, legs entwined, heart rates slowing.

A sleepy satisfaction was stealing through Olivia, making her feel almost boneless. Aziz pressed a hand to her flat stomach.

'Do you think we made a little prince or princess already?' he asked in a lazy murmur, and pressed a kiss to her navel.

Olivia's insides jolted with surprise; she hadn't even been thinking about babies since Aziz had first made love to her, which was a bit ridiculous, considering how she'd made it her main reason to marry him.

Not quite your main reason.

She might have presented it to him as her main reason, so she wouldn't scare him off, but, cocooned in the intimacy of a sleepy afternoon's love-making, Olivia knew she hadn't agreed to marry Aziz just for the sake of a child, or for the promise of companionship or sex.

She'd married him because she'd been falling in love with him, had been falling in love with him since she'd first come to Kadar—or perhaps even before then.

Maybe she'd been fooling herself all along. Maybe Aziz had been waking her up slowly with his gentle teasing and easy smiles. It had taken coming to Kadar and moving right out of her comfort zone, out of herself, to bring her fully to life. To make her realise she loved him.

'What are you thinking about?' Aziz asked as he kissed his way up her belly. Olivia glanced down at his tousled ink-dark hair, saw his glinting eyes, his teasing smile. She knew he didn't want to hear what she'd been really thinking about. He'd be horrified if he knew just how much she felt for him.

'Nothing too serious,' she said lightly and touched his hair.

'You look awfully serious,' Aziz answered. He pressed one last kiss to her stomach and then rolled onto his back, his hand linked loosely with hers.

Olivia gazed down at their joined hands and knew she couldn't keep from pushing to know more about him, at least a little. 'I was thinking about you, Aziz.' She smiled, although it felt wobbly. 'I was imagining you running through the halls of the palace, paper aeroplanes whizzing through the air.'

He gave her a small smile back, but Olivia saw his expression had turned wary.

'Perhaps our son, or our daughter, for that matter, will do the same.'

Was he reminding her why she was here at all? Olivia wondered. For the sake of a child. Suddenly her admission that she was only marrying him so she could be a mother again seemed incredibly cold. She wanted to tell Aziz she didn't feel that way any more, maybe had never even felt that way, but somehow the words wouldn't come.

'Maybe,' she answered, even though it seemed no more than a distant dream. She could be pregnant, she reminded herself. They hadn't used protection and her cycle was irregular. But she didn't want to think about a baby just now. She wanted to think about Aziz.

'You said you were close to your mother,' she began, and Aziz rolled into a sitting position.

'Why are you digging, Olivia?' he asked as he reached for his shirt.

'Digging? Is that what it feels like? I just want to know—'

'Why? What difference does it make? It's a little late for second thoughts.'

'*Second thoughts?* I'm not having second thoughts.'

'If you're worried about what kind of father I'll make,' Aziz clarified with a shrug, as if this conversation was already boring him. Olivia watched him slip on his shorts. He raked a hand through his hair and reached for his watch.

'Aziz,' she said slowly, 'This has nothing to do with what kind of father you'll make. I want to know about you for your sake, and mine. Because you're my husband and, regardless of what we agreed or signed, we're married and we have a relationship that is meant to last a lifetime.' She took a breath and ploughed on. 'Are you going to push me away for ever?'

'I wasn't aware you wanted to get closer.'

Her heart seemed to still and then beat harder. 'And if I did?' she asked after a moment.

Aziz's back was to her, so she couldn't see his face— not that she'd be able to tell what he was thinking or feeling if she could see it. He was, Olivia knew, amazingly adept at hiding his feelings. Just as she'd once been.

Aziz remained with his back to Olivia. He didn't know what to say to her, had no idea what she wanted from him. He'd been evading her questions all day, unwilling to open up, as she now seemed to want him to do. *And for what?* She'd made it clear what she wanted from him and this marriage.

A child. Nothing more.

'I don't really see the purpose of some kind of heart-to-heart,' he finally said, his back still to her. 'We agreed we didn't really want to know each other that way.'

'We also agreed that everything was up for discussion,' Olivia reminded him. 'Has that changed?'

'No,' Aziz answered after a moment. He turned around to see Olivia sitting cross-legged in the middle of the bed, her hair, now almost back to its caramel colour, spilling over her shoulders. She had a sheet wrapped around her and her skin was creamy and flushed pink. She looked, Aziz thought, utterly beautiful and happier than he'd ever seen her before, despite the faint shadows in her eyes. Shadows he suspected he was putting there with his reticence.

He sat on the edge of the bed and stared down at the rumpled sheets.

'My father,' he said slowly, each word emerging from his tightened throat with effort, 'Always resented me and the fact that he needed me as his heir.'

'Because of Khalil?' she asked softly.

His throat went tighter as he nodded. 'He always loved him. Always preferred him.'

'But he banished him.'

'I know, and he hated that he'd had to do it. Khalil was his adored first son, the pet of the palace, of the whole damn country—' He broke off, hearing how ragged his voice had sounded, feeling his heart start to thud, the old anger and bitterness rising up inside him in an unstoppable tide.

He hadn't wanted to rake all this up, to remember it. Being back in Kadar was hard enough without trawling through all the awful memories of his childhood. Yet now that he'd started he found he couldn't stop. He didn't even want to stop.

He drew his hand away from Olivia's and rose from the bed, his back to her. 'You want to know about me, Olivia? Fine, here's the unfiltered version: my father hated me. *Hated* me, from the moment I entered the palace, or maybe even before.'

He took a shuddering breath, let it out slowly. 'Although, I suppose he didn't care enough to hate me before he had to make me his heir. But when he did, he resented me for it. Resented the fact that he needed me, so he made my life a complete misery.'

He heard how his voice shook and self-loathing poured through him, as corrosive as acid. He hated remembering this. Talking about it was even worse and yet, even though he'd spent most of his life pretending his childhood hadn't happened, hiding himself and all his fears and deficiencies from everyone, now he felt a compulsion to come clean.

It was like that impulse you had to throw yourself off a bridge or under a train, he thought darkly. The death instinct, Freud called it, and he was feeling it now.

Perversely, stupidly, he wanted to tell Olivia everything. He just didn't think he could bear the look he'd see on her face when he did.

Right now, however, when he risked a glance towards her sitting there on the bed, she looked calm. 'How old were you when you became the heir?' she asked.

'Four.'

'Oh, Aziz.' Her voice and face both softened with a sympathy he couldn't stand. It felt like pity. 'Tell me about it,' she entreated, her voice so soft and sad it wound around him with its silken strands, made him trapped, furious and desperate.

'You really want to know all the ugly, pathetic details? We were despised, my mother and I. Loathed and ridiculed from the moment we stepped through those hallowed doors—by my father, by the palace staff, by everyone. It just about killed my mother. She was a village girl, chosen to be the Sheikh's mistress with no say in the matter. She'd never wanted to be queen.'

'Aziz,' Olivia whispered, but he barely heard her. Now that he'd started, he didn't think he could stop, not until it was all out, every last, terrible detail.

'At first it was just little things—forgetting to bow or give her the respect she deserved as queen. She ignored it, because it seemed easier. Safer. Then, encouraged by my father, people grew bold, taunting her and me. Tripping us as we walked by. Starting rumours in the palace, in the city bazaar. My father went along with it all.' Aziz swallowed, the taste of acid on his tongue, churning in his stomach. 'He made a mockery of us both. My mother stopped making any public appearances. She lived in her private rooms, terrified that she would be banished like Khalil. Just as I was terrified.' He swallowed, his throat working, his breath coming in pants, before he calmed himself by sheer force of will.

When he spoke again, his voice was flat, dispassionate. 'My father lived to show everyone how deficient I was in every respect. He'd drag me into his chambers, ridicule me in front of all his cabinet members.' And still he'd tried to please him. He'd spent hours memorising anything his father might quiz him on: his times tables, facts about Kadaran history, every law of the Kadaran constitution. If he failed on one point, his father branded him a failure. Slapped his face and told him to get out.

'Oh, Aziz,' she said, 'I'm so sorry.'

'You know the worst part?' he said in a low voice, unable to look at her now. 'I still loved him. Why, God only knows. But I loved him and—' He stopped, hating that he was telling her this. That he *needed* to tell her this. 'I wanted him to love me. I did everything I could, every single thing, to try and make him love me.' His voice choked and he swore, turning furiously away from her. 'I even asked him once. I asked him, point-blank, why he didn't love me.' He shook his head, the memory twenty years old, yet still possessing the power to make him feel like that desperate, cringing boy. 'Do you know what he said?'

'No,' Olivia said, her voice quiet and sad.

Aziz stared blindly out of the window. 'He said, "why would I?"' He let out a defeated, weary laugh. 'I've never been able to answer that question.'

'I can answer it, Aziz,' Olivia whispered and he realised just how pathetic he must sound, whinging about how no one loved him.

'Not another one of your pep talks, please,' he said, trying to keep his voice light, to reassemble his armour. The Gentleman Playboy in full force. 'It's ancient history now anyway.'

'It still matters.'

'Well, yes, because it's affected my choices now. That's why you don't need to worry that I'll fall in love with you, Olivia.' He forced himself to smile at her, as if this was actually reassurance he wanted to offer. 'I'm not interested in wearing my heart on my sleeve ever again.'

'I know you're not,' she said quietly. 'But just because your father rejected you doesn't mean other people will.'

'Not a risk worth taking, in my opinion. And not in yours either, I thought.' He spoke sharply, reminding himself as well as her just what the terms of their marriage were—and why.

Because you could never convince someone to love you, no matter what you did. Better not to try. Not then and not now.

Olivia drew her knees up to her chest, circling them with her slender arms. 'And the Gentleman Playboy,' she said after a moment. 'Where did that come from?'

He tensed. 'What do you mean?'

'How did a little boy longing for love from his father became the playboy of Europe?'

He flinched at her assessment, hating how she'd put it into words. That was who he'd been, who he still was.

'When I was fifteen, I discovered women.' He raised his eyebrows, forced another teasing smile. 'My father's mistress, actually. She seduced me and at first I went along with it just to lash out at him. Then I realised I could please women, and focused on that rather than the impossible task of trying to please my father.' He'd meant to sound light but it just came out bitter.

'I see,' she said quietly, and he knew she did. She saw far, far too much.

'I don't know why we're talking about this.'

'Because I want to know you. Understand you.'

'Satisfied?' he demanded, his voice ringing out, and she just looked at him. He saw pity on her face, in the dark eyes and turned-down mouth, and he hated it.

He swung away from her, stalking to the window, his hands curling around the sun-warmed stone as he stared out at the sky that had darkened to deep indigo.

'So,' he finally managed, and his voice sounded a little

more like his usual self, the self he'd chosen to be. 'You really felt better after that kind of confessional?'

She laughed softly, sadly. 'Not right away. Mostly I felt shell-shocked and emotionally exhausted.' He heard the whisper of sheets as she rose from the bed and came to stand behind him. She rested a hand on his shoulder. 'But in time, Aziz, I hope you'll feel better. Stronger. And I hope you'll be glad you told me.'

He doubted it. Already he was regretting having revealed so much, shown so much weakness.

'Aziz,' she murmured, and slid her arms around his waist, drawing her gently back to him. His back collided with her bare softness, but in that moment he didn't feel desire.

He felt something deeper, something more overwhelming; his throat tightened and his eyes stung. He reached for her hand, not even knowing what he felt, only that he didn't want her to leave him then.

Or ever.

'Aziz,' Olivia said again softly, her arms still around him, her fingers threaded through his. 'Aziz, I know you might not think you want to hear—'

A knock sounded on the door and Olivia fell silent. With a sad little sigh, she slipped away from him and reached for a robe.

Aziz turned, waiting until she'd belted it and was covered before saying in a clipped voice, 'Come in.'

To his surprise, it was Malik. He didn't look at Olivia, but kept his rather grim gaze trained on Aziz.

'Aziz, we've received a message from Khalil. He wishes to speak with you.'

Stunned, for a few seconds, he could only stare. 'Speak with me?'

'He is in Siyad and can come here by helicopter in an hour.'

An hour. Aziz's mind spun with this new revelation as well as everything that had just happened between him and Olivia.

'You'll speak to him?' Malik confirmed, and he nodded.

'Yes. Prepare one of the rooms downstairs for our meeting, please.'

Malik left and he turned to glance at Olivia; he saw she looked white-faced and apprehensive. He probably looked the same. He certainly felt it. He had no idea what Khalil wanted to say to him; he doubted his former half-brother was coming to renounce his claim. As for anything between him and Olivia...

'What do you want me to do?' Olivia asked, and he almost reached for her hand, almost asked her to stay with him, because he needed her. Needed both her strength and her sympathy, her understanding and compassion.

And he didn't want to need her. Didn't want to need anyone, to open himself up to that weakness.

And yet he knew it was already too late. He'd been trying to protect his heart and he'd failed. He loved her. He loved her so much it hurt.

He imagined asking Olivia if she loved him and having her say the same words his father had once said to him.

Why would I?

She'd phrase it more nicely, of course. She might even apologise. But she'd make it clear that she didn't love him, couldn't love him, and there was no way in hell he was ever going to let himself in for that kind of rejection and pain again.

'Just wait here,' he said and left the room.

CHAPTER TWELVE

Aziz walked away from Olivia, still reeling from everything he'd confessed and felt. And now Khalil was coming here. With that coming on the heels of his conversation with Olivia, he felt as if his nerve-endings had been scraped raw.

'This could be a good thing,' Malik said quietly, and Aziz shrugged.

'Or he could be declaring his intentions.' Khalil might demand he call the referendum. No matter that he'd fulfilled the terms of his father's will; the people still supported Khalil, or at least most of them, and Khalil could argue that Aziz should let the people decide.

And maybe he should. Maybe clinging onto a title nobody wanted him to have was foolish. He'd never earned his father's love; why did he think he could earn his country's?

Yet Olivia believed he could. The memory strengthened his resolve. He wasn't going to give it all away now.

Half an hour later, showered and dressed in a pair of dark trousers and a button-down shirt, Aziz prowled the elegant confines of one of the palace's smaller receiving rooms. He could have stood on ceremony as ruling Sheikh and been seated on a throne of gold and silver but such petty tactics seemed both obvious and pathetic. He was above them, he hoped.

He hadn't spoken or seen Olivia since Malik had entered the bedroom. He just thought of her, remembering how she'd drawn him against her, her arms around him, how good he'd felt...

He knew she'd been going to tell him something. Something he probably didn't want to hear, because it would just make him love her more.

Aziz whirled around, stalked the length of the room. He loved her, but he was utterly afraid to tell her. If that made him a coward, then so be it. He couldn't risk offering his heart again. Couldn't bear to see the look on her face as she tried to let him down gently, reminded him of their awful arrangement...

It was better this way, he told himself. Better to face Khalil alone, to keep the feelings in. Eventually they would fade. He'd learn not to feel so much for her.

A thought which felt like an even worse agony.

In the distance he heard the hectic whirring of a helicopter's blades and his gaze met Malik's steady one.

'Why don't you meet him, Malik? I'll wait here.'

The older man nodded and Aziz resumed pacing as he waited for the man he'd once thought was his half-brother to arrive.

Five seemingly endless minutes later, a knock sounded on the door. Aziz turned around, his heart thudding. 'Enter.'

The door opened and Khalil stood there, Malik behind him.

Aziz stared at the man he had no blood relation to, yet whose life had been twined with his since birth. Khalil stood tall and proud, but without any anger in his eyes.

Aziz had expected a rebellious firebrand, but Khalil seemed too calm and composed for that.

He nodded tersely. 'Come in.' Khalil took a step forward and Aziz glanced at Malik. 'You may leave us.'

His aide nodded and closed the doors behind Khalil, leaving the two men alone. Neither of them spoke for a long, taut moment.

Finally Aziz broke the silence. 'I forgot how still and quiet you can be.'

Khalil arched an eyebrow. 'You remember me?'

'I remember meeting you when I was four.'

'That was weeks before Hashem banished me.'

'Was it?' The memories were blurred in Aziz's mind. 'I suppose it was.' Enough reminiscing, he thought with a sudden surge of impatient anger. 'Why are you here, Khalil? What have you done with Queen Elena?'

'She is safe.'

'Where is she?' Aziz's voice came out like the crack of a whip. 'Don't you realise you could face imprisonment for kidnapping?'

'Elena won't press charges.'

Aziz grimaced. 'Did you terrify her into agreeing to that? What did you threaten—?'

'Enough, Aziz.' Khalil held up one hand. 'I regret my actions now.'

Aziz bared his teeth in a smile. 'I'm afraid that's not quite good enough for me.'

'I wouldn't expect it to be. We have been enemies a long time.'

'You still haven't told me where Elena is.'

'She is waiting for me in Siyad.' Khalil paused, his expression still so very composed. 'We're married, Aziz.'

Aziz's breath came out in a rush. 'You forced her!'

'It was not forced.'

Aziz didn't speak for a moment. So Elena had changed sides, abandoned him. Could he really be surprised? He'd abandoned her too, after all. 'Why did she agree?' he finally asked, his voice flat and hard. 'Did she actually believe your claim?'

'She did, as I did. All my decisions have been based on believing I was the rightful heir to Kadar's throne.'

'Even though you have no blood relation to my father.'

'I thought I did.'

Aziz stared at him, utterly nonplussed. 'What?'

'I thought I did,' Khalil repeated, his voice a low throb. 'My whole life, I thought Hashem had banished me simply because he preferred your mother. Preferred you.'

Aziz let out a choked laugh of disbelief. *Preferred him?* Did Khalil really have no idea how absurd a notion that was? 'And then what happened?' he asked.

'I found out two days ago that Hashem wasn't my father. My mother had an affair with one of the palace guards.'

Aziz stared at Khalil, saw how his jaw bunched and his throat worked. It must have been, he realised, a hard fact to accept. 'How did you learn of this?'

'My mother's sister told me. She kept it from me for many years because she didn't want to tarnish my mother's memory. But when she saw that I'd—that I'd found Elena, she thought maybe I'd changed enough to hear it. To accept it.'

'Found Elena,' Aziz repeated neutrally. 'What does that mean, exactly, Khalil?'

'We love each other.'

He swung away, jammed his hands in the pockets of his trousers. 'I see.'

'Elena has made me realise how much more there is to this life than cold, hard ambition. My whole existence was oriented towards reclaiming my birthright. Every decision, every choice—' Khalil broke off. 'Aziz, I accept the throne is not mine. It was never mine. I'm renouncing my claim.'

Aziz knew he should feel something: joy; relief; satisfaction *something*. He felt nothing at all. He turned back, stared at Khalil and felt empty. 'You really think it's that simple?' he finally asked evenly. 'You renounce your claim and everything becomes easy?'

'No,' Khalil answered. 'Nothing about this is easy.'

'More than half the country supports you,' Aziz stated. 'If we called the referendum right now, you would still win, whether you had a claim or not.'

'Maybe,' Khalil allowed. 'But I've been travelling through the desert for six months, rallying support. You haven't even been in Kadar.'

Although Khalil spoke neutrally, Aziz still felt the accusation, even the contempt. 'So the Gentleman Playboy has been carousing through Europe?' he proposed cynically. 'Is that what you think?'

'Tell me differently.'

'Why should I? I don't owe you anything, not even an explanation.'

'No, I don't suppose you do.' Khalil regarded him evenly. 'I'm sorry,' he said after a moment, 'For kidnapping Elena and making things harder for you.'

'And I should just accept your apology?' Aziz answered incredulously.

'No,' Khalil answered, 'You probably shouldn't. But I don't know what else to do. I want to make this right, Aziz. You are the rightful Sheikh. I've spent months— hell, a lifetime—acting otherwise. But I recognise it now and my hope is that we can work together for the sake of

Kadar.' He paused, his gaze shuttered. 'But I'll understand if you feel we can't.'

Olivia's words, her soft voice, echoed through him. *I care about he affects you. Maybe there is a way to put this conflict to rest, to find peace, not just for Kadar but for you and Khalil.*

It felt impossible, yet Olivia believed it could be so. She believed in *him*, that he might be strong enough to move beyond the past. His throat was thick with emotion as he bit out, 'My life was hell because of you.'

Khalil blinked, clearly surprised. '*Your* life was hell? I spent three years in the desert being whipped like a dog.'

'What?' Aziz gaped at him. 'You went to America—'

'Only after my aunt found me. Hashem had me sent to the desert, to my mother's tribe. The sheikh hated me and he let me know it every day of my life.'

Just as Hashem had done to him. Aziz's mind spun with his new information. 'I'm sorry,' he said after a moment, knowing anything he said now would be inadequate. 'I didn't know.'

Khalil let out a hard laugh. 'You thought I was living the high life in America?'

'You've assumed I was living like a spoilt prince.'

'Hashem *chose* you,' Khalil said emphatically. 'Over me. He chose you, he made you his heir, so—'

'So what do I have to complain about?' Aziz filled in. 'Poor little playboy? Maybe I am.' He swung away once more, hating that he was raking this all up *again*. 'Maybe I am,' he repeated quietly, and neither of them spoke for another long, tense minute.

Finally Khalil broke the silence. 'Why was your life hell, Aziz?'

'My father might have banished you from the palace,' Aziz said after a moment, 'But he never banished you from his heart. He loved you, Khalil.' He turned around, realising how Khalil needed to hear this. To know it. 'He always loved you. He banished you, I suppose, because he felt he had no choice, but in his mind and heart you were his real son. Not me.'

Khalil's jaw bunched and he blinked rapidly. 'He had a funny way of showing it.'

Aziz nodded; his anger was leaving him in a rush, leaving him only sad and weary. 'Yes, I suppose he did.'

'You actually expect me to believe Hashem loved me and still threw me to a man like Abdul-Hafiz? Let me be beaten and starved and shamed for three years?'

'I'm not defending his actions,' Aziz answered. 'I don't know why he did what he did. Maybe anger won out over love. Maybe he didn't know how to deal with his disappointment. Maybe he was just what he's always seemed to me—a cruel, petty, sadistic bastard.'

'Maybe he was,' Khalil agreed after a moment. 'But if he really loved me so much,' he continued in a low voice, 'He could have accepted me. Found a place for me.'

'I know. Trust me, I know. Coming to the palace and being made his heir was the worst thing that ever happened to me.'

Khalil shook his head slowly. 'Whenever I thought of you, I pictured you as a spoilt little prince being fawned over by everyone, given your every heart's desire.'

Aziz let out a hollow laugh. 'That was far, far from the truth.'

Khalil nodded again. 'So we both suffered.'

'Yes. Hashem has a lot to answer for.'

'And he's not here to pay the price. We are.' They were both silent, but Aziz felt the tension between them had eased a little. He had no idea what kind of relationship, if any, he could have with Khalil, but he knew this man was no longer his enemy.

Olivia had helped him to see that now, he realised. Olivia had changed him, made him want to move on. *Made him love.*

'Let me help you,' Khalil said quietly. 'Let me help our country. Together we can repair the damage our father caused to Kadar's very fabric. We can unite the people—'

Aziz eyed him with a weary scepticism coupled with the most fragile hope. 'How?'

'By telling the truth. By being united ourselves. You are the rightful Sheikh, Aziz, and I accept that.'

'Even if you don't want to.'

'I do not have the liberty to indulge my desires. Accepting I do not have any right to the throne is difficult. I am still coming to terms with it.'

'And what of Elena?'

'We love each other. She has accepted I will not be Sheikh, although I am still ruler of my mother's tribe, and as such I give my obeisance to you.'

To Aziz's shock Khalil sank to one knee, his head bowed. Aziz's eyes stung and he blinked rapidly.

'Get up,' he said, his voice choked. 'I've never stood on ceremony.'

Khalil rose slowly, his gaze steady. 'People like you, Aziz. You have charmed most of Europe. You can win the affection of the people of Kadar.'

'Thank you for your vote of confidence.' Except, Aziz acknowledged, he'd won the love of people by not being himself. By play-acting a role he was already tired of. *And when people learned the truth...*

Olivia knew the truth. He'd spilled his sad, sorry secrets to her and she was still here, still supporting him.

Loving him?

Was that what she'd been going to tell him? Could he dare believe that she felt even a little for him what he felt for her?

Could he risk baring his heart to another person, begging someone to love him back?

Aziz blinked the questions back. 'You must have heard, I've married myself,' he told Khalil.

'Yes.'

'Since it's not Elena, the people may have trouble accepting my bride.'

'Then it is up to you to show them how capable she is.'

And Olivia was certainly that. She was calm, strong and dignified, yet with so much heart and warmth. He hadn't seen it at first, not when she'd just been his cool, capable housekeeper. But he saw it now and he felt his heart swell with pride. She would, he thought, make an excellent queen.

'You can do this,' Khalil said quietly. 'You can do it on your own, but it would be my honour to help you.'

Aziz stared at Khalil for a long moment, his thoughts whirling through his mind like leaves in a storm. Then slowly he nodded and reached out to shake the other man's hand.

The past was, at least in part, forgiven. Healed. He had Olivia to thank for it; he knew that. Olivia had helped him and healed him in so many ways.

He needed to tell her that, needed to tell her so much. If only he could find the courage.

Two hours had passed since Aziz had left their bedroom and the sky was inky-black and spangled with stars. Olivia had been staring at it through the window, the shutters thrown open to the night, her mind first blank and paralyzed, then seething with questions and fears, and back again.

At some point she dressed, and Mada brought food in that she couldn't eat. She paced the room restlessly and then picked at a salad, nearly threw it up and went back to the bed, sitting on its edge as she clutched a pillow to her chest.

In her mind she went over that last exchange with Aziz. He'd looked so cold, so closed. She'd wanted to be with him, to share this with him and support him in whatever happened with Khalil, but he hadn't wanted her. That had been all too painfully obvious.

She clutched the pillow hard, felt the first threat of tears. Maybe she should just give up. Admit defeat. Accept what Aziz was offering, or even try to live apart if it would hurt too much.

Or you could tell him you love him.

The thought flooded her with terror. What would happen if he told her he didn't love her? If he looked appalled or horrified? She might slide into the kind of endless despair she'd felt after losing Daniel. Losing Aziz, she knew with heart-sickening clarity, would be just as painful.

She heard the snick of the door opening and closing and Olivia glanced up, the pillow still clutched to her chest.

Aziz stood there, his expression impossible to read. Olivia swallowed hard.

'What happened?' she managed in a whisper and Aziz walked slowly into the room. He turned to gaze out of the window, his back to her.

'Khalil has renounced his claim.'

'*Renounced—?*' Olivia stopped and stared at Aziz

who was still facing away from her. 'But that's good news, isn't it?' she asked uncertainly because he didn't seem happy.

'Very good news.' Aziz's voice was flat. 'Apparently he'd always believed he was the rightful heir. He didn't think his mother had ever been unfaithful to my father.'

'And he learned...'

'The truth. Yesterday. His aunt told him. He's officially withdrawing his claim. There will be no war, no referendum. He wants to support my rule, help heal our country.' He stated all this so matter-of-factly, his back still to her.

Olivia stared at him in confusion and then with a terrible, dawning realisation: his throne was essentially secure. If he wanted to, he could end their marriage. After all, he'd told her that he'd never wanted to be married in the first place.

She hadn't even been introduced to the public, Olivia thought sickly. And, if Khalil had renounced his claim, he would have let Elena go. Aziz could marry Elena, if he wanted to. If he wanted to be married at all.

She licked her lips, felt her heart beat with slow, hard, painful thuds. 'Do you...do you want to annul the marriage?'

'Annul?' Aziz turned around, his expression still so very blank. 'Is that what you want, Olivia?'

'I'm asking because you seem so...so strange, Aziz. And I know you never wanted to be married in the first place.'

'No,' he agreed after a moment. 'I didn't.'

'So...' She spread her hands, not wanting to be the one to say the words. She didn't want to offer him an out. Only hours ago she'd wanted to tell him she loved him. She'd wanted *more*, not less.

She still wanted more.

'So?' he repeated. 'So you want me to release you from our marriage vows? Is that it?' His voice rose, surprising both of them. 'So much for taking them seriously, then.'

'I thought it's what you wanted!' Olivia cried, her voice breaking. 'Tell me what you want, Aziz.'

He stared at her, his chest heaving with emotion, his eyes full of anguish she didn't understand. 'I want you to love me,' he whispered. 'God, I'd never thought I'd say that again. I never thought I'd let myself beg for someone's love ever again.'

'You don't need to beg—'

'But after I left you to see Khalil I realised how much I wanted you with me. How much I loved you.'

Olivia blinked back tears, amazement and hope unfurling inside her. 'You did?'

'Yes. I love you, Olivia, so much. I've been fighting it since you came to Kadar or, hell, maybe even before then. Maybe since I first started wondering about you, about the woman with the wonderful laugh who played music that made me want to both weep and sing. I just haven't wanted to tell you, haven't wanted to admit it even to myself, because it was so frightening to think of being rejected again—and this time even worse.'

'You wouldn't—' Olivia began, but he continued, the words coming faster.

'I don't expect you to love me back. I'm not asking for a miracle. But I needed to tell you, and I hope—' His voice wavered before he continued. 'I hope that maybe in time you might come to feel for me as I feel for you. At least a little.'

'Oh, Aziz.' A tear slipped down Olivia's cheek as she realised how much this beautiful, broken man was risking for her. He'd told her he loved her without any idea of how she felt in return. Without even hoping that she might love him the way he loved her.

He loved her.

'Is that too much to ask?' he whispered. 'In time? I know you've been hurt, Olivia. So badly. But I want to help you get over that pain, at least as much as you can. I'd never minimise how much losing Daniel affected you, but—'

'Aziz.' She smiled through her tears as she walked towards him. 'Stop talking.'

'What—?'

'I love you,' she said simply. 'I already love you. Now, here, so much. I wanted to tell you earlier but I didn't have the chance, and the truth is I was afraid you wouldn't want to hear it. Afraid of what I'd do, how I'd feel, if you told me you didn't want my love.'

Aziz was staring at her as if he couldn't make sense of her words. 'But a few minutes ago you asked if I wanted to annul our marriage.'

'Because I was *afraid*.' She knew she needed to explain more. 'I didn't tell you everything about when I gave up Daniel,' she began. 'Or just how badly it affected me.' She closed her eyes for a second, heard her father's determinedly cheerful voice in her head. *Do what your mother says, Olivia, it's for the best. Now, come on, darling, let's have no more unpleasantness. Play the piano for me, eh? Just like old times.*

As if she hadn't just spilled her guts right there in front of him, torn out her heart and offered it to him, begging him to help her. Support her.

It had been that fear, the memory of how hurt she'd been, how *destroyed* after confessing her heart, that had kept her from telling Aziz she loved him. But she was telling him now. She'd tell him everything.

'I told my father about Daniel,' she went on quietly.
'I asked, I *begged* him to support me. Sort of like you
begged your father to love you, Aziz. And my father,
my adored father, turned away from me. He didn't want
to know. He didn't even want to look at me. And when I
pleaded with him to help me keep my baby he just patted my head and told me to do what my mother said.' Her
voice cracked. 'And then he asked me to play the piano
for him.' She shook her head, half-amazed that such an
old memory could still hurt so much. 'And you know
what I did right then?' she finished sadly.

'You played the piano,' Aziz said softly and she nodded jerkily. 'It's what I would have done. What I *have*
done, trying endlessly to please someone who didn't care
about me. Trying to earn his love a thousand times over.'
He reached for her then, pulled her into his arms and
buried his face in her hair. 'When you asked if I wanted
to annul the marriage I felt as if you'd just yanked my
heart right out of my chest. I was trying to work up the
courage to tell you I loved you—'

'And I made you think I wanted out. I'm sorry, Aziz.'

'We've both let old fears and hurts control our actions,'
Aziz said, holding her tightly. 'But not any more. This is
a new start for both of us, Olivia.'

'I want that. I want that so much.'

He eased back, framing her face with his hands as
he gazed down at her. 'Tell me what happened after you
told your father.'

She swallowed past the tightness in her throat. 'I did
what he said. I went to the clinic and gave up my baby.
And then I went to university and pretended nothing
was wrong.' She still remembered how surreal it had
felt, going to lectures and writing essays as if her world

hadn't fallen right off its axis. Her stomach had been saggy, milk still leaking from her breasts just three weeks after giving birth. And she'd been in a fog, pretending it was normal, that she was okay. 'When I went home for Christmas, my parents acted as if nothing had happened,' she told Aziz. 'They seemed so jolly, pretending this was a normal Christmas. Or maybe they weren't even pretending. Maybe they really believed it was.'

'People believe what they want to believe,' he reminded her quietly. 'You told me you knew that was true. Were you thinking of them?'

'Yes.' She sniffed, let out another shuddering breath. 'I flew back to England and took a train to my university, but when it was time to get off I just didn't. I stayed on the train until the last stop and ended up in a run-down seaside town. I got a job working in a bed and breakfast for a while, then kept moving from place to place over the years, just existing. Anything to keep from feeling.'

'But you feel now.'

'I feel so much, and you made that happen, Aziz. You're like Prince Charming, waking me up with a kiss.'

He kissed her then, sweetly and softly. 'And you woke me up, Olivia. You took away my mask and kept me from hiding myself. My fears. And you believed in me, even when I didn't believe in myself.'

'Do you believe now, Aziz? Because I know you'll be a good ruler. A wonderful ruler.' She gazed at him seriously. 'Malik told me when I first arrived in Kadar that you didn't believe the people would support you. I see now it's because you haven't given them the chance.'

'I've been afraid to,' Aziz admitted quietly.

'You need to give them that chance, Aziz. I think you'll be surprised at how they take it.'

He lifted her hand and pressed a kiss to her palm. 'With you by my side, I feel like I can do anything.'

She reached up on her tiptoes and kissed him. 'You can,' she said. 'We can.'

Together, she knew, they could do anything.

EPILOGUE

Sun streamed through the palace windows as Olivia gave her reflection one last final check. Nerves fluttered in her stomach, but excitement did too. It had been six weeks since her wedding to Aziz and they were making a formal appearance on the balcony of the palace in Siyad, along with Khalil and Elena.

As soon as they'd left the coastal palace, Aziz had issued a press statement announcing the news. There had been a few whispers, a few raised eyebrows, but things were thankfully starting to settle down. When people had realised he and Olivia loved each other, just as Khalil and Elena did, they'd been enchanted. There were two happily-ever-afters instead of one.

Aziz had made Khalil his chief advisor and together they'd travelled around Kadar, visiting the desert tribes, sowing loyalty and support rather than discord.

The country was becoming united. Strong.

The door opened and Aziz stood there, smiling with an ease and sincerity that shone out of him. No longer the Gentleman Playboy, his charm was still devastating and not a mask. He was his real, wonderful self…just as she was. Aziz had helped her to recapture her hope, her joy. He'd brought out the best in her, made her see and feel the happiness and wonder of life again, and for that she would always be thankful.

Together they made each other stronger and more whole. *Complete.*

'Ready?' he asked. 'They're waiting for us to go out.'

'What about Khalil and Elena?'

'They're waiting, too.'

Khalil and Elena, Olivia knew, were just as happy as she and Aziz were. They divided their time between Thallia and Kadar and, if Olivia wasn't mistaken, they would be making an announcement about a future prince or princess some time soon.

Just as she hoped to, one day.

She slid her hand into Aziz's and they left the room for the salon that led to the palace's main balcony. Khalil and Elena were already there, heads bent together as Khalil whispered in Elena's ear. She giggled and smiled and Olivia's heart swelled with the happiness she knew they all felt.

Aziz and Khalil had found a solid, working relationship; they'd become allies and perhaps even friends. Almost brothers—bound by so much, if not by blood.

And Olivia liked Elena; they'd become friends too, as well as sisters-in-law of a sort.

'Ready?' Aziz said and everyone nodded. Olivia could feel the expectation in the room, the tension in Aziz. This was the first time they would all be appearing together in public.

An aide threw open the doors to the balcony and Olivia stepped out with Aziz, both of them blinking in the bright sunlight.

Below them the palace courtyard was thronged with people and the noise was incredible. They were chanting, Olivia realised, although it took a few seconds for her to realise what they were saying.

Sheikh Aziz! Sheikh Aziz!

She turned to her husband with a radiant smile. 'They love you,' she said softly, and he smiled back.

'They love us both. Shall we satisfy them?' She nodded and he drew her towards him for a kiss of both promise and thanksgiving, the sweetest kiss she'd ever known.

On her other side Khalil and Elena had come out, and they were both smiling and waving to the crowds.

Drawing back, his heart in his eyes, Aziz kept his hand tightly in hers as he turned to address his people.

* * * * *

*If you enjoyed this book,
don't miss Khalil's story in
CAPTURED BY THE SHEIKH by Kate Hewitt*

THE LAST PRINCE
OF DAHAAR

TARA PAMMI

*For my brother—I'm so proud
of the man you have become.
With such real-life inspiration,
no wonder the hero of this book
is such an awesome son and brother.*

Tara Pammi can't remember a moment when she wasn't lost in a book—especially a romance—which was much more exciting than a mathematics textbook at school. Years later, Tara's wild imagination and love for the written word revealed what she really wanted to do. Now she pairs alpha males who think they know everything with strong women who knock that theory and them off their feet!

CHAPTER ONE

PUMP HIS BODY full of narcotics and fall into blessed oblivion? Or suffer a fitful sleep and welcome the madness within to take over?

Abuse his body or torture his mind?

It was a choice Ayaan bin Riyaaz Al-Sharif, the crown prince of Dahaar, faced every evening when dusk gave way to dark night.

After eight months of lucidity, and he used the term very loosely, he had no idea which he would favor on a given day.

Tonight, he was leaning toward the drugs.

It was his last night as a guest in Siyaad, the neighboring nation to his own country, Dahaar. He would be better off knocking himself out.

You did that last night too, a voice whispered in his ear. A voice that sounded very much like his older brother, who had spent countless hours toughening up Ayaan.

Stepping out of the blisteringly hot shower, Ayaan dried himself and pulled on black sweatpants. He had run for three hours straight tonight, setting himself a pace that lit a fire in his muscles. His body felt like a mass of bruised pulp.

He had kept to lighted grounds, to the perimeter of the palace. And every time he'd spotted a member of the royal guard—both his own and Siyaadi—his breath had come a little more easily.

Walking back into the huge bedroom, he eyed the bottle of narcotics on his bedside table. Two tablets and he would be out like the dead.

The option was infinitely tempting. So what if he felt lousy tomorrow with a woozy head and woolen mouth?

Another night would pass without incident, without an *episode*. Another night where he accepted defeat, accepted his powerlessness in his fight against his own mind.

Defeat...

He picked up the plastic bottle and turned it around, playing with the cap, almost tasting the bitter pill on his tongue.

A breeze flew in through the French doors, blowing the sheer silk curtains up. Dark had fallen in the past half hour, the heat of the evening touched by its cold finger.

Peaceful, quiet nights were not his friends. Peaceful, quiet nights *in a strange place* were enough to bring him to his knees, reducing him to a mindless, useless coward.

He was still a bloody coward, afraid of his own shadow.

Powerless fury roared through him, and he threw the painkillers across the empty room. The bottle hit the wall with a soft thud and disappeared beneath an antique armoire.

A quiet hush followed the sound of the bottle, the silence beginning to settle over his skin like a chilly blanket.

He grabbed the remote and turned on the huge plasma TV on the opposite wall. He had specifically requested the guest suite with the largest TV. Flipping to a soccer game, he turned the volume up so high that the sounds reverberated around him. Soon, his skull would hurt at the pounding din of it, the echoes ringing in his ears. But he welcomed the physical discomfort, even though at this rate, he would be deaf by the time he was thirty.

Walking around the room, he turned off the lights.

As his eyes became accustomed to the dark, he got into bed. A pulse of distress traveled up his spine and knotted up at the base of his neck. He curled his fists, focusing on the simple act of breathing in and out. He willed his mind to understand, to stop looping back at its own fears and feeding on them.

Sleep came upon him hard, a deceptive haven capable of snatching control from him and reducing him into a cowering animal.

Zohra Katherine Naasar Al-Akhtum slowly made her way through the lighted corridors toward the guest suite that was situated in the wing farthest from the main residence wings of the palace.

Her feet, clad in leather slippers, didn't make a sound on the pristine marble floors. But her heart thumped in her chest, and with each step, her feet dragged on the floor.

It was half past eleven. She shouldn't be out of bed, much less roaming around in this part of the palace where women were expressly forbidden. Not that she had ever heeded the rules of the palace. She just hadn't needed to be in here until now.

Now…now she had no choice.

She straightened her flagging spine and forged on.

The fact that she hadn't encountered a guard until now weighed heavily in her gut instead of easing her anxiety. It had been easy to bribe one of the maids and inquire which suite their esteemed guest was staying in.

Suddenly there she was, standing in front of centuries-old, intricately carved, gigantic oak doors. Zohra felt as if cold fingers had clamped over her spine.

Behind those doors was the man in whose hands her fate, her entire life, would lay if she didn't do something about it. And she couldn't accept that. If she had to give offense for it, take the most twisted way out of it, so be it.

Sucking a deep breath, she pushed the doors and stepped in. The main lounge was quiet, the moonlight from the balcony on the right bathing it in a silvery glow. But the bedroom in the back, the sounds of a…soccer game boomed out of it.

Was the prince having a party while she was getting cold sweats just thinking about her future?

Straightening her shoulders, Zohra set off toward the bedroom. Flashes of light came and went, the sounds so loud that she couldn't distinguish one from the other.

She neared the wide entrance, crossed the threshold and came to a halt, her gaze drawn to the huge plasma screen on the opposite wall. It took her a moment to see through the flashes of light, to realize that there was no crowd in the room.

Scrunching her face against the loud noise from the speakers plugged in overhead and around the room, she searched for the remote. It was enough to give a person a pounding headache in minutes.

Flinching every time another roar went up, she walked around and found the remote on the bedside table. She quickly muted the television, the light from the bright screen casting enough glow to let her see the outline of the room.

With silence came another sound she hadn't heard until now. A sound that turned her skin clammy. The hairs on her arms stood up. It began again. A low, muffled cry, tempered by the sheets. Like a scream of utter pain, but locked away in someone's throat. She shivered, the agony in that sound crawling up her skin and latching on to the warmth.

Every instinct she possessed warned her to turn around and leave. She half turned on the balls of her feet, her neck cricking at the speed of it.

But the next sound that came from the bed was pure suffering. This time, it wasn't locked away. Neither was it loud but more gut-wrenching for the accompanying whimper it held.

The sound ripped through her, breathing the anguish of an unbearable pain into the very air around her.

She wanted to curl up, brace herself against it. Or at least run far from it.

And yet the agony in that cry...she would never forget it in this lifetime.

Zohra turned around and reached the bed. She almost tripped on the heavy stool that lay at the side of the bed in her hurry. Clutching the silk sheets with her fingers, she hefted herself onto the high bed.

Her blood running cold in her veins, she pushed through the sea of crumpled sheets, until her gaze fell on the man.

For a moment, she could do nothing but study him. His eyes were closed, his forehead bunched into a tight knot and his hands fisted on the sheets with a white-knuckled grip.

White lines fanned around his mouth, a lone tear escaping from his scrunched eyes. His forehead was bathed in sweat, as he thrashed against the sheets.

Pushing the sheets away, Zohra reached for his hands and gasped. He was ice-cold to the touch. Another soft whimper fell from his mouth.

A wave of powerlessness hit her. Shoving it away, she grabbed his shoulders, even knowing that trying to move him would be truly impossible. With strength that surprised even her, she tucked her hands under his rock-hard shoulders when his muscled arm shot out.

That arm hit her jaw with a force that rattled her teeth. She half slipped, half tumbled to the edge of the bed. Darts of pain radiated up her jaw. She swallowed the lump in her throat and pushed herself back onto the bed.

This time, she was prepared for him. She moved to the head of the bed, avoiding his arms and placing her hands either side of his face. A groan escaped his mouth again, and his fingers clamped over her wrists.

His grip was so tight but she ignored it and shook him hard. And then tapped his cheek, determined to break the choking grip of whatever stifled him.

She couldn't bear to hear that tortured sound anymore, not if there was any way she could wake him up.

"Wake up, *ya habibi*," she whispered, much like she had done with her brother Wasim when her stepmother had died six years ago. "It's just a nightmare." She ran her hands over his bare shoulders, over the high planes of his cheeks. She kept whispering the same words, much to her own benefit as his, as he continued to turn his head left and right.

"You need to wake up," she whispered again.

Suddenly his thrashing body stilled. His gaze flew open, and Zohra was looking into the most beautiful golden bronze gaze she had ever seen.

Her heart kicked against her ribs. With his hands still gripping her, she stared at him as he did her.

He had the most beautiful eyes—golden pupils with specks of copper and bronze, with lashes that curled toward angular cheekbones. But it wasn't the arresting colors of his gaze that made her chest tighten, that made it a chore to pull air in.

It was the unhidden pain that haunted those depths. His fingers caressed her wrists, as though to make sure she was there.

He closed his eyes, his breathing going from harsh to a softer rhythm and opened his eyes again.

It was as though she was looking into a different man's eyes.

His gaze was cautious at first, openly curious, next sweeping over her eyes, nose, lingering on her mouth, until a shadow cycled it to sheer fury.

It lit his gaze up like the blazing fire of a thousand suns.

He released her, pushed her back and she fell against the headboard with a soft gasp. He pulled himself up to his knees, his movements in no way reminiscent of the nightmare he had been fighting just moments ago. "Who are you?"

His words sounded rough, gravelly, which meant he had been screaming for a while before she had arrived.

Her chest tightened. "Are you okay?" she whispered, taking in the sheen of sweat on his forehead, the infinitesimal tremble in the set of his lean shoulders.

"How is that any of your business?" he roared. "I dismissed the guards hours ago. I was informed no one would be allowed into this wing per my orders. So what the hell are you doing here?"

That's why no one had stopped her. And he had the volume on the TV set to that earsplitting level as if he had known...

Zohra frowned. "I saw you thrashing on the sheets. I had to help."

"I could have hurt you."

She instantly tugged the sleeves of her tunic over her wrists.

His face could have been poured from concrete for the tightness that crept into it. Only the slight flare of his nostrils and the incandescent rage in his gaze said he was still a man and not one of the concrete busts of long-gone emperors and warriors scattered around the palace. "Turn on the lamp."

She leaned over and turned it on, her entire body feeling strangely awkward. The lamp was on her side and cast just enough glow to illuminate his face.

Ayaan bin Riyaaz Al-Sharif, the new crown prince of Dahaar was not what she had been expecting. The *Mad Prince*, that's what she had heard the Siyaadi palace staff whisper about him. Yet there was nothing remotely mad about the man staring at her with incisive intelligence in his eyes.

There had been only a single picture of him, a grainy one, eight months ago when Dahaar had jubilantly celebrated his return. He had been pronounced dead five years ago along with his older brother and sister—victims of a brutal terrorist attack.

But nothing more about him had been revealed, nor had he appeared anywhere in public. Even the ceremony where he had been declared crown prince had been private, which had only fueled the media and the public's hunger for information about him.

He had remained a shapeless, mindless figure at the back of her mind.

Until she had visited her father this afternoon. Weakened by a heart attack, the king had sounded feeble and yet his words had rung with pride and joy.

Prince Ayaan has agreed to marry you, Zohra. You will be the queen of Dahaar one day.

Suddenly, the Mad Prince had become the man who could bind her forever to the very world that had taken everything from her.

The reminder, however, did nothing to stem the quiet, relentless assault his very presence wreaked on her. She could no more stop her gaze from drifting over him than she could stop breathing.

He had a gaunt, chiseled look that added to the rumors swirling about him.

His face was long with a severe nose, a pointed chin, with cheekbones that were sharp enough to cut. His wavy, black hair curled onto his high forehead in an unkempt way. As if he had threaded his fingers through it and tugged at it viciously. The moment the thought crossed her mind, she knew it was true.

The tendons in his neck stood out. He was lean, bordering on thin and yet what flesh there was to him looked as if it had been carved out of rock.

A pale, inch-wide scar stretched from his left shoulder all the way to his ribs on the right side and beyond to his back. What could wield such a painful-looking scar?

Her empty stomach rolled on itself. How could a man withstand so much without...*going mad*?

The thought swept through her like a fierce cold wave, and she shivered.

His scrutiny as intent as her own, he said, "Hold out your hands," in a tone that held raw command.

Zohra sucked in a breath and tucked her hands behind her.

He moved on the bed with lithe grace that would have been beautiful to savor if her heart hadn't crawled into her throat. She was taller than the average Dahaaran woman and yet he towered over her.

The scent of him had a tang to it that made her suck in a quick, greedy breath even before she knew it. He tugged her hands forward in a sudden move.

Her skin stung where he had gripped her at even the slight friction of his fingers. He sucked in a deep breath.

As though he was bracing himself. His fingers gentled as he pushed the sleeves of her tunic back.

Dark impressions framed each wrist. A chill surrounded them, and she had the strangest feeling that his emotions were at the center of it.

She tugged at her hands but he didn't let go. "How long were you here before I woke up?"

The tension emanating from him rendered her mute.

"*How long?*"

He didn't shout the words yet they radiated with utter fury. "Five, maybe six minutes. I didn't know what to do."

He let go of her hands with a jerk. "You were not supposed to be in here in the first place. And if you're reckless enough to be, the minute you saw me, you should have turned around and walked out."

She shook her head. "I would loathe myself if I just walked away."

He ran a hand through his hair again, his movements visibly shaken. But he didn't get off the bed, blocking her escape. "It is a quarter to midnight. I have asked you twice why you are here. If you will not answer me, I will summon the guard. Before you realize it, you will be out of a job, out of a livelihood. All for what? To get a little information on the Mad Prince? A quick photograph, is that it? Tell me who sent you here and I will show lenience."

He thought she was a servant paid to gather information about him? "No one sent me here, Prince Ayaan."

He became stiffer, if possible, the rigid line of his shoulders obvious in the feeble light. The bones at the crook between his neck and shoulders stood out in stark relief.

She didn't want to antagonize him any more than she already had. She didn't want to ponder about his nightmare, his reaction to her being a witness to it. If she did this right, she wouldn't need to see him ever again nor hear the gut-wrenching pain she had heard in his cries.

"I…came here of my own volition. It was important for me to talk to you before you left tomorrow morning."

Slowly, the annoyance in his expression shifted to watchfulness. And she fought the need to shy away from it, to hide from his intense scrutiny.

He knew.

She could pinpoint the exact moment he realized—the watchfulness turned into realization, a flare of color in those beautiful eyes.

That gaze moved over her in a slow sweep, lingering over her face for the longest time, seeing her with new eyes. This time, it wasn't mere anger that colored it, but wariness, almost as if she had suddenly become dangerous to him.

"Of course you're not a servant."

He stepped off the bed as though he couldn't breathe the same air for another moment. She stared at the broad expanse of his back. The scar streaked through his back too, like a rope bound around his body.

He pulled on a T-shirt and stood by the foot of the enormous bed, his hands behind him, as though waiting for her to come to her senses.

Heat spread up her neck and she gritted her teeth.

She had nothing to feel guilty or ashamed about. She had seized the only opportunity available to her. She had seen a man in the throes of a violent nightmare and tried to help.

She slid to her feet, the muscles in her legs trembling.

"What was so important that it had to be said in the middle of the night?"

This was it. This was why she had risked coming into

his suite. And yet, her tongue felt as if it was glued to the roof of her mouth.

"Should I send word to King Salim?"

She stared at him, the sudden threat in his words, the raw command showing a different man. "There's no need to involve my father in a matter that concerns me...*us*. I'm sure we can settle this between ourselves and come to a conclusion that is agreeable to both of us."

CHAPTER TWO

SHE WAS HIS *betrothed*.

Ayaan felt the world tilting at his feet as what he had guessed curdled into undeniable reality.

This slip of a woman, who had the nerve to climb onto his bed and hold him through a nightmare, this woman, who was even now meeting his gaze with an arrogant confidence, was the woman he had agreed to marry just a few hours ago?

He hadn't given her a moment's thought. She was nothing more than a bullet point in the list of things he had agreed to in the name of duty.

He stood unmoving, the need to vent his spiraling frustration burning his muscles.

Her light brown hair was combed away into a braid. Her eyes were brown, huge in her long face. A strong nose and mouth followed, the stubborn jut of it saying so much about the woman.

She wore a light pink tunic over black leggings, a flimsy shawl wrapped loosely around her torso. Her outfit was plain for a princess, giving no hint as to what lay…

With a control he had honed tight over the past few months, he brought his gaze back to her face. He had indulged himself enough. How the woman looked, or what kind of a body she had, held no significance to him.

Her mother had been American, someone had mentioned it to him. But she was a copy of King Salim. The same no-nonsense air about her, the proud chin, the dogged determination it must have cost her to be near him during his nightmare.

He had no doubt about how violent he could get when caught in one of those nocturnal episodes. It was the reason he detested having anyone even within hearing distance. And despite every precaution he took to hide the truth, to spare his parents, they had already earned him the title of Mad Prince.

If only the world knew what a luxury madness was compared to his lucidity.

He didn't want to marry this woman any more than he wanted the mantle of Dahaar. The latter, he had been able to postpone. The former…?

The people of Dahaar need reassurance that all is well with you, they need a reason to celebrate. They haven't had one in five years. And Siyaad needs our help. King Salim stood by me when I had no one else to rely on, when I was crumbling under the weight of Dahaar.

Now it is time we return the favor.

Ayaan wasn't prepared for it. He would never be.

How could he be, when he didn't trust himself, when he didn't know what could break him again, when he was constantly hovering over the thin line between lucidity and lunacy?

But he couldn't refuse his father, not after everything he had gone through to rule and protect Dahaar, after losing his eldest son and daughter, losing Ayaan to insanity.

His parents had lost everything in one night, but they hadn't broken. They hadn't failed in their duty. He couldn't either.

But suddenly, King Salim's profuse excuses at tonight's

dinner made sense. His daughter's absence had been an act of defiance. Not that Ayaan had cared that she was absent. On the contrary, he had been glad that he didn't need to give the concept of his betrothed a concrete form until that moment was absolutely upon him.

And now here she was, pushing herself into his mind in a way he couldn't just undo. Within five minutes spent in her company, he already knew more about her than he wanted to learn in a lifetime. She was stubborn, she was brave and the worst? She wasn't conventional.

"I understood you were too ill to be out and about, Princess Zohra," he said, forcing utter scorn into his words. "And yet here you are, walking around the palace at night, disrupting a guest's privacy, offering insult."

"Do not call me a princess. I have never been one."

He was too...*irritated* to even ask her why.

He was chilled to the bone, as he always was when he woke up from one of his nightmares. "Fine. Please tell me why you are in my bed, in my suite, in the palace wing that is strictly forbidden to women, at the stroke of midnight. What was so important that you had to—"

"You were thrashing in the bed, crying out. I couldn't just stand by and do nothing. Nor could I walk away and come back at a better time."

"Are you deaf? Or just plain dense?" The words roared out of him on a wave of utter shame. He gritted his teeth, fighting for control over a temper that never flared. "Why are you here in the first place?"

The brown of her eyes expanded, her mouth dropping open on a soft huff. His uncivilized words chased away the one thing he couldn't bear to see—her pity.

"If you think you can scare me into running away by behaving like a savage, it won't work."

He could have laughed if he wasn't so wound up. Every

inch of her—her head held high, the deprecation in her look, the stubborn jut of her chin—she was a princess no matter what she said. "If this were Dahaar, I would have—"

"But it's not Dahaar. Nor am I your loyal subject dependent on your tender mercies," she said, steel creeping into her words. "This is Siyaad. And even here, all those rules, they don't apply to me." Her eyes collided with his, daring him to challenge her claim. When Ayaan said nothing, her gaze swept over his features with a thoroughness that she couldn't hide. Did she feel the same burn of awareness that arched into life suddenly? "I came to inform you that it's not worth it."

Ayaan had known only one woman in his life who had had the temerity and the confidence to speak to him like that—Amira, his older sister. A sliver of pain sliced through his gut. Amira had never let Azeez or him get by with anything. And it had been more because of her core of steel than because she had been born into an extremely powerful family.

He had a feeling the same was true of the woman who met his gaze unflinchingly.

"What is not worth it?"

"Marrying me."

"Why are you telling me this instead of your father?"

She blinked but it didn't hide the pain that filled her eyes. "I… He is not well. I could not…take the chance and risk making him worse."

"Being here with me, persuading me why you are not *worth it* does not harm him?"

A shrug of those slender shoulders. "If you refuse me, he would be disappointed, yes. But not surprised."

He frowned at her conclusion. "So you want me to do your dirty work for you?"

She took a deep breath and his curiosity mounted. "I'm not shy, willing, happy to be a man's shadow—the kind of woman whose only mission in life would be to spew out your heirs every other year. I have never been and it's not a role one grows into."

Ayaan smiled, despite the irritation flickering through him.

The woman had gall. And even without her mission statement just now, it was clear she wasn't a woman who could tolerate the traditional marriage their countries dictated.

Then why was King Salim pushing for this marriage? He had to know that Ayaan and his father would stand beside him without this marriage clause, and yet he had shown more enthusiasm for it.

"If you had attended the dinner and did your duty, I could have told you what I want in my wife."

She shook her head, her breath quickening. "What is there to learn? The wives—they are nothing but bloodlines and broodmares. Even a harem girl probably has it better than the dutiful wife of the king. At least, she gets good sex out of the…"

He burst out laughing. His chest heaved with it, the sound barreling out of him. Even his throat felt raw in a strange way.

He couldn't help taking a step toward her.

Pink stole into her cheeks, and she looked away from him, something unintelligible falling from her mouth.

Her long lashes cast shadows onto sharply fragile cheekbones, her mouth—unpainted and pink. The slow burn under his skin gathered momentum. He had never liked the scent of roses growing up, it had pervaded the palace, his own chamber and sometimes, even his clothes. Yet the scent of her skin danced beneath it, teasing, tempting, coated with her awareness of him.

"So you would prefer to be part of my harem instead of my wife?"

Her gaze widened, her mouth opening and closing. "This is my life we're talking about."

He came to a stop near her and leaned against the bed, enjoying the proximity of her presence. It didn't fill him with the suffocating tension that everyone else's did since his return. "You haven't said a single word that would make me take you seriously, Princess." She opened her mouth but he didn't give her the chance. "All I see is a woman throwing a tantrum like a petulant teenager instead of doing her duty. What if someone had seen you come into my suite? You risk exposing yourself to ridicule and scandal, adding to your father's burden."

She didn't like that. He could see it in her eyes. "Of course, you wouldn't want someone petulant like me to be the future queen of Dahaar, would you?"

"So, this is all to prove a point?"

"I don't have any duty toward Siyaad. And nothing will make me feel anything more for Dahaar either." She took a deep breath, as though bracing herself. "Marrying me will only bring shame to you and the royal house of Dahaar."

He covered the distance between them, knowing that she was baiting him yet unable to resist. "Why does that sound more like a threat and less like a warning?" he whispered.

"I'm simply telling you the truth. Whatever expectations you have of your bride, I will fail them."

Ayaan frowned, regretting not learning more about her before he had given his word. "If this is about *your* expectations of this marriage, state them."

Zohra tamped down the scream building inside her chest looking for an outlet. He wasn't supposed to ask her what she wanted out of this marriage. He was supposed to sputter in outrage, call her disobedient, scandalous…

Any other man in his place would have called her behavior an insult. He would have gone straight to her father and broken the alliance.

"The only expectation I have of you," she said, feeling as though she was stepping over an unknown threshold, "is that you use the power you have to refuse this marriage."

A neat little frown appeared between his brows. "Unless I have a strong reason for it, it would be termed as an insult to your father, to you and to Siyaad."

"Isn't it enough that you have zero interest in marrying me?"

"I have zero interest in marrying anyone. But I will do it for—"

"For your country, yes, I know that," she spat the words out, feeling that sense of isolation that had been her constant companion for eleven years. She had never belonged in Siyaad, never felt as if she was a part of it. "But I'm not duty bound as you are. All I want is the freedom to live my life away from the shackles of this kind. And if it is a crystal clear reason that you want, then I will give you one."

"You have my full attention, Princess." There was a dangerous inflection in his voice where it had been void of anything else before.

She wet her lips, praying her voice would hold steady when she was shaking inside. "I'm not future queen material. I don't give a fig about duty and all that it entails. I'm educated *and* I'm smart enough to have my own opinions, which, I have been informed, are enough to drive a man up the wall. I'm a…*bastard*." She had to breathe through the lump growing in her throat. "My father lived with my mother until I was seven but he…never married her. He became my guardian when she died."

Not even by the flicker of an eyelid did he betray his reaction. "Is that all?"

Curse the man to hell and back. Desperation tied her insides into painful knots. "No, there's one last reason—the most important of all."

"Don't stop now," he said, his voice laced with mockery.

"I'm not a chaste virgin with an unblemished reputation." Her chest was so tight she wondered if she was getting any air. "I would rather you refuse me now than claim that you've been cheated when you…find out."

He ran his forefinger over his temple, his expression betraying nothing. Her heartbeat ratcheted up. "When I find out that you're not a virgin?"

Fierce heat blanketed her, even as shock stung her. Why wasn't the man throwing a royal fit even now? "When you find out that I was in love with another man, when you find out that I have spent four summers with him in a desert encampment…" She swallowed painfully, just the thought of Faisal slashing pain through her.

"That is…a valid reason for me to refuse you," he finally said.

Zohra felt the most perverse disappointment. He had been unlike anything she had imagined until now.

"So are you prepared for your father's reaction when I present him with this…reason?"

Her gut dropped to her feet. "What do you mean?"

"I told you. I have no wish to insult your father after everything he has done to stand by mine. You might not feel any duty to your country. But are you so selfish that you would put your father through this? He will not only be shamed by his daughter's behavior but he will be so in front of an audience."

She flinched at the distaste in his words. He hadn't intended to back out for a second. Her gut churned with a powerless clawing. "I have no wish to weaken my father. I merely gave you the truth."

His gaze was filled with a bitterness that cut through her. "Your 'truth' is only useful to me if I can quote it to your father's face. Our fates are sealed no matter what you or I wish, no matter what skeletons we have in our closets."

Zohra's palms turned clammy. He was not backing out. Marrying a stranger, being locked forever into the cage of duty and obligation—the same duty that had ripped her family apart? She would take an uncertain future over that.

She sought and discarded one idea after the other, panic gripping her tight.

"Fine," she said, her mind already jumping ahead. It had been a waste of time to come here. "I have only one choice left then."

She turned around, determined to act before the night was up. She couldn't stay in the palace, in Siyaad for another minute.

She was about to step over the threshold when a hand on her arm pulled her back. A soft gasp escaped her mouth as she was pushed against the wall with sure movements. The muscles in her arms trembled, her senses becoming hyperaware of every little detail about him.

Like the strong column of his throat as his chest fell and rose. Like the tingle in her skin where his fingers touched her.

"I suddenly have great sympathy for your father, Princess. My sister Amira is just as headstrong as you seem to be, but at least, she listens when Azeez or I…"

A dark shadow fell over his face. He had spoken of his sister as though she was still alive. She shouldn't care about his pain, but it pierced through her anyway.

"Your sister? The one who died five years ago?"

He met her gaze. The pain in it flayed her open. "Yes."

His hands landed on either side of her face. He bent until she could see the light scar over his left eyebrow. Any grief she had seen a moment ago was gone. "Now, tell me what the only choice you have left is."

She pushed at him, but he didn't relent. "I've not given you the liberty to touch me, Prince Ayaan, neither to haul me around."

"You should have thought about that before you barged into my room, Princess." Mockery gave his mouth a cruel slant. "Whatever you do now, I will hold myself responsible for it."

"You wouldn't have even laid eyes on me until the wedding if I hadn't forced my way in here. No one is responsible for my actions or my life but me."

"I became responsible for you the minute I said yes to this alliance. And I won't let you cause any more problems for your father."

"This…" she couldn't speak for the outrage sputtering through her "…this kind of archaic behavior is what I'm talking about. Your claim just proves how right I am in wanting to get out of this marriage, out of Siyaad."

"So you're going to run away in the middle of the night and expose your father to a scandal?"

"I owe my father nothing. *Nothing.* And I'm not running away, I'm going to exercise my right as an adult and leave. Neither my father nor you can force me into a marriage that I don't want, nor can you stop me from leaving."

He took his hands away from her. Not trusting his actions even for a second, Zohra straightened from the wall. Her knees shook beneath her.

"Fine, leave," he said, displeasure burning in his gaze. "But you leave your father no choice either except to announce my betrothal to your sister. I understand she will be eighteen in a year."

Bile crawled up Zohra's throat and pooled in her mouth. How dare he? "*Sixteen and a half.* My sister is sixteen and a half."

Only silence met her outburst.

She covered the gap between them, fury eating away at reason. She pushed at him, powerless anger churning in her gut. Saira would never go against their father. She had been born and raised in Siyaad, exposed to nothing but the incessant chatter about duty and obligation despite Zohra's presence.

"You cannot do that. She…I won't let my father or you…"

She fisted her hands and let out the cry sawing at her throat.

There was nothing she could do to stop her father from promising Saira in her place. And he would, without blinking. Zohra knew firsthand the lengths to which her father could go for Siyaad.

Her chest felt as if there was a steel band around it, the shackles of duty and obligation sinking their claws into her.

"Saira is innocent, a teenager who still believes in love and happily ever after."

"And you?"

"They do exist. Just not in this world, in your world. And I will do anything before I let Saira's happiness be sacrificed in the name of duty."

"So you're not completely selfish then." He moved closer. "What is this world that I belong to, Princess, to which you don't?"

"It's filled with duty, obligations, sacrifice…what else? If Saira marries you, you will shatter her illusions, bring her nothing but unhappiness. You would marry a mere girl in the name of duty?"

Disgust radiated from him. "The very thought of betrothal

to a sixteen-year-old makes my skin crawl. But Siyaad needs this public alliance. Your father's heart attacks in the last six months, your brother's minor status, the latest skirmish at the border? It has made Siyaad weak. This wedding means that the world knows that Dahaar stands by Siyaad. It's the best chance your father, your people, have of retaining their identity. If something should happen to your father, your brother will have our protection.

"Knowing all this, you refuse this alliance? You risk your country's future, your brother's future by acting so recklessly?"

Zohra crumpled against the wall, the fight leaving her. She owed nothing to her father, nor to Siyaad. But Saira and Wasim…if not for them, she would have been so alone all these years. A stranger among her father's people at thirteen—shattered by her mother's death and the devastating truth that her father was not only alive, but that he was the sovereign of Siyaad and had a wife and six-year-old son and daughter.

If not for her brother and sister, she would have had nothing but misery. "I had no idea this would benefit Wasim."

"Why am I not surprised?"

His derision felt like a stinging slap. But this was all her fault.

She had always made it her mission to learn as little as possible about the politics in Siyaad, she had rebuffed her father's attempts to educate her, to make her active in the country's politics. If she hadn't sunk her head in the sand like an ostrich, she would have been better equipped to deal with this situation.

She ran a trembling hand over her forehead, shaking from head to toe. She was well and truly caught, all her hopes for a future separate from duty and obligation crumbling right before her eyes.

"If this is all for Siyaad's benefit, why are you agreeing to this? You can snap your fingers and find a woman who will be your silent shadow. You clearly already dislike me. You can still refuse this, you can help Siyaad without—"

"*Enough!*" Bitterness rose up inside Ayaan, burning in his blood like a fire unchecked. He reveled in the anger, in the way it burned away the crippling fear that was always lurking beneath the surface eating away the weight of what his lucidity meant to him. "You think you are anything like the woman I would want to marry if it wasn't for duty, if it wasn't to repay the debt my father owes yours?" he said, filling his every word with the clawing anger he felt.

Every inch of color fled from her face and she looked as if he had struck her. And Ayaan crushed the little flare of remorse he felt.

It would have been better if his unwanted wife had been a woman who would scurry at the thought of being in the same room with the Mad Prince. But this defiant woman was what fate had brought him.

There was no point in railing against it. "There is very little that matters left to me, Princess. Except my word. And I would rather be dead than lose that, too."

"Then, send me back when Wasim turns eighteen, when he doesn't need your protection anymore, however long that might take. The world will still know that Siyaad has your support. You can claim that I was an unsuitable wife and I will not contest you. You can sever all connections with me and no one will point a finger."

He shook his head, surprised at the depth of her anger toward their way of life.

To be rid of her when there was no need anymore was an infinitely tempting offer. But there would be no honor in it. "If I send you back, you will become the object of speculation and ridicule. That is a very high price for your freedom, Princess. It will always be tainted in Siyaad."

He saw the tremor that went through her, the fear that surfaced in her gaze. But of course, she didn't heed it. He already knew that much about this woman. "Anything is better than being locked in a marriage whose very fabric is dictated by duty and nothing else."

"Marriage to me doesn't have to be the nightmare you are expecting."

"What do you mean?"

"I have very little expectations of my wife. She will live in Dahaar. She will do her duty in state functions by my side. She will be kind and thoughtful to my parents.

"I will not love her nor will I expect her to love me. I don't even want to see her except in public. This marriage is purely for the benefit of my parents. And I don't care what you do with your time as long as you don't bring shame upon Dahaar. Our lives can be as separate as you or I want."

She frowned, her gaze studying him intently. "What about an heir? Isn't that part of the agenda that's passed down to you? Produce as many offspring, male preferably, as soon as possible?"

"How old are you, Princess?"

"Twenty-four."

"I thought I was too bitter for my age. I have no intention of fathering a son or daughter, Princess, not with you or anyone else, not until…" *Not ever if he didn't find control over his own mind.* "How about we revisit the invigorating subject of procreation in say…two years from now?"

She swallowed, drawing his gaze to the delicate line of her throat. "How do I know you won't change your mind… about everything?"

"I have enough nightmares without the added ones of forcing myself on an unwilling woman. Believe me, the last thing I want is to sleep with you."

Her gaze sparked with defiance. "If I'm to be stuck in a marriage that will save my sister and benefit my brother, then I might as well be in one with a man who's just as indifferent to it as I am."

Ayaan frowned, something else cutting through the pulse of attraction swirling around them. Not only had she elicited a reaction he had thought his body incapable of, but she had annoyed, perplexed and downright aggravated him to the extent that she had so easily banished the backlash from his nightmare, the chills he would have been fighting for the rest of the night.

That she was able to do that when nothing else had worked in the past few months rendered him speechless, tempted him to keep her there, even if it was only to…

Shaking his head, he caught himself. Whatever relief she brought him would only be temporary. "If you have had enough of an adventure, I will walk you back, Princess."

The smile slipped from her mouth, her gaze lingering on him, assessing, studying. She tucked her hands around her waist, loosened them and hugged herself again. Her indecision crystal clear in her eyes, Ayaan waited, willing her to let it go, willing her to walk away without another word.

Her gaze slipped to the bed and back to him, a caress and a question in it. Every muscle in him tightened with a hot fury. "Will you be okay for the rest of the—"

Forcing his fury into action, Ayaan tugged her forward. "Remember, Princess. You will be my wife only in front of the world. In private, you and I are nothing more than strangers. So stay out of things that don't concern you and I will do the same."

CHAPTER THREE

THE WEEK LEADING up to the wedding was the most torturous week that Zohra could remember, even though the wedding day dawned bright and sunny.

Prince Ayaan had left the next morning while Zohra and her family had traveled to Dahaara the day after that, renewed vigor seeping into her father who had been ill for the past month.

It was as though she could hear the ticking of the clock down to an unshakeable chain binding her to everything she hated.

With each passing moment, her confidence in her betrothed's words faltered, the midnight hour she had spent talking to him becoming fantastic and unreal in her head. Especially as Queen Fatima, Ayaan's mother, spent every waking hour regaling Zohra about Ayaan's childhood.

The contrast between the charming, loving boy his mother mentioned and the dark stranger she spoke to in the middle of the night was enough to cast doubt over everything.

Would he not expect anything from her? What kind of a man didn't even want to lay eyes on his wife?

She tugged the gold-and-silver bangles on to her wrists as the celebrations around the city blared loudly on the huge plasma-screen TV in her suite. The capital city of

Dahaara had been decorated lavishly, very much a bride itself, albeit a much happier one, ready for a celebration unlike Zohra had ever seen or heard of.

The gold-and-red-hued flag of Dahaar with the sword insignia flew on every street, from every shop. A holiday had been declared so that the people of Dahaar could enjoy the wedding. Gifts had been flowing in from every corner of the nation—breathtakingly exquisite silk fabrics, handmade jewelry boxes, sweets that she hadn't heard of before—each and every gift painstakingly overflowing with Dahaar's love of its prince.

The telecast of the celebrations, the crowds on the roads, the laughter on the faces of adults and children alike revealed how much this wedding mattered to Dahaar. The whole world was celebrating. Except the two people who were irrevocably being bound by it.

"Zo, look now. There he goes," Saira exclaimed, looking beautiful in a sheer silk beige dress that sparkled in the sunlight every time she moved. Zohra couldn't help but smile at the innocence in her half sister's voice. "Wow, Zo. I didn't realize he was so…handsome."

Unable to resist, Zohra turned and there he was.

Displayed in all his glory on the monstrous screen. The cameras zoomed in on him, and Zohra's breath halted in her throat.

Handsome was too tame a word for the man she was about to marry.

The motorcade transporting him and his parents weaved through the main street with ropes and security teams holding off the public.

Shouts and applause waved out of the speakers. It was almost palpable, the din of the crowd, the joy in their smiling faces. King Malik sat with Queen Fatima by his side, Prince Ayaan opposite them, resplendent in a dark navy

military uniform that hugged his lean body, the very epitome of a powerful prince.

She could no more stem her curiosity about him than
she could stop staring at him on the screen. Zohra shivered
despite the sun-drenched room. He looked every inch a
man who was used to having his every bidding done before it was given voice. Until she saw the detachment in
his gaze.

Even through the screen, she could see the tension in
his shoulders, in the tight set of his mouth, in the smile that
curved his mouth but never reached his eyes.

He was standing in a crowd of people that loved him,
next to parents who adored him, seemingly a man who
had the world at his feet. And yet she could sense his isolation as clearly as if he were standing alone in a desert.

The joy around him, the celebrations, the crowds—
nothing touched him. It was as though there was an invisible fortress around him that no one could pierce.

Did no one else but her see his isolation, the absolute
lack of *anything* in that gaze? Would she have seen it if she
hadn't seen him incoherent, and writhing in pain?

She swallowed and turned away from the screen. There
it was—all the proof she had needed so desperately.

The truth of what he had said to her—that this wedding was solely for the benefit of his people, for his parents, was all laid out on the screen to see. Nothing but his
sense of duty was forcing him to stand there, as it was
forcing him to marry her.

The realization, instead of appeasing her, gave way to a
strange heaviness that pervaded through her limbs.

She turned around, just as her father stepped into the
room, dressed in the dark green military uniform of Siyaad.

She had done everything she could to avoid him once
they had left for Dahaara. Busy as he had been in nego-

tiations with King Malik and Prince Ayaan, it had been easy enough.

But, suddenly facing him in her bridal attire, the knot of anger she kept a tight hold on threatened to unravel. "Have you come to make sure I have not run away?"

Saira's gasp next to her checked the flow of bitterness that pounded through her veins. Passing a worried look between them, Saira excused herself, having never understood Zohra's antipathy toward their father.

"I know you're not happy with this alliance, Zohra. But I never doubted that you would do your duty."

There it was, that word again. It had broken her family apart, it had thrust her into an unknown world, and it had taken the life of her mother, who had done nothing but pine after the man she had loved.

She stood up from the divan and met his gaze. "I'm doing this for Saira and Wasim. I don't want Saira to be sacrificed in the name of duty, too."

He ventured into the room, and she braced herself for the impact of his presence. In the eleven years that she had lived in Siyaad, she had always stayed out of his way, made sure she spent the least amount of time with him.

"Is that what this marriage is to you? Can you not view it as anything else but sacrifice?"

"What else could it be? You didn't ask me if I wanted this. That man," she said, pointing her finger toward the screen, "didn't ask me if I wanted to be his wife. You have reduced my life to an addendum clause on a treaty."

His jaw tightened. "You will be the future queen of Dahaar, a woman who can have just as much power as she wants in the tri-nation region. Your education, your intelligence, they can be used to do good in Dahaar, Zuran and Siyaad, to pave way for new things, to change old ways, ways you have always called archaic. No one will ever dare question your right to rule along with Prince Ayaan. You will live the rest of your life with the utmost—"

"This alliance is nothing but a way to secure Siyaad's future."

He nodded, sudden exhaustion seeping into his face. "I am glad that Saira and Wasim mean something to you." *Unlike me*, the words hovered in the air between them. "That means you will at least keep an eye on them."

Zohra refused to feel guilty, refused to let him put her in the wrong when he had made an irrevocable decision all those years ago, when he continued to show again and again that Siyaad would always come first with him. "They are my family. I will do anything for them," she said, forcing herself to speak the words. "They are the only reason I've stayed—"

"In Siyaad all these years, I know."

The knot in her throat cut off her breath. She held herself absolutely still as he neared her, her gut twisting on itself. The sandalwood scent of him knocked her sideways, unlocking memories she had forcibly buried. Maybe if he had always been an absentee father, maybe if she didn't remember her mother's desolation, her own aching grief when she had been told one fine morning that her father was dead...

Only to learn after her mother had died that he had just walked away from them to take up the crown of Siyaad, that he had already had a wife.

His whole life with her mother and her had been a lie.

He pressed a kiss to her forehead, and the longing she fought broke free. But she couldn't let it out. If she did, it would hurt her like nothing else could. So she turned the emotion engulfing her into a bitterness that had already festered for so long.

"I always wondered why you took custody of me when

mom died instead of sending me to her brother. Living in Siyaad all these years, being a daughter, a bastard at that, I realized I have no consequence for you, no importance in your life. But now... Is this why? You knew I would come in handy for one of your many obligations toward your country?"

His mouth compressed into a tight line, a flash of anger in his gaze now. "When will you realize that Siyaad is just as much a part of you as it is of me?"

"Not in this lifetime."

Resignation settled over his features. And suddenly, he was the man who had had two heart attacks in the space of six months. "Whatever I say is immaterial because you've already decided the answer."

He clasped her cheek with his palm, his gaze drinking in every feature, every nuance in her expression. *He is remembering my mom.* Zohra knew that as clearly as if he had said her name out loud. Ever since he had suddenly reappeared in her life when she had been thirteen and dragged her to Siyaad, she had always understood one thing.

He had loved her mother just as much as her mother had loved him. And yet, he had walked out of their lives and put duty first.

"Ever since you were a little girl, you've always been stubborn. Incredibly strong but also stubborn.

"You've always decided your own fate, Zohra. You decided why I had left without ever asking me. You decided to hate your stepmother when you came to live in Siyaad, even though she had been nothing but kind to you. You decided you would have nothing to do with Siyaad or your heritage.

"You decided to love your half brother and half sister, *you* decided to stay in Siyaad for them when you turned

eighteen. No one has or will ever tell you how to live your life.

"What you make of this marriage, whether you view it as a cage or your freedom is, as always, up to you."

Saira came bursting into the room, pink high in her cheeks. "He's arrived in the Throne Hall."

Zohra didn't need to be told again who it was that was waiting for her.

Her gaze anxiously shifting between Zohra and their father, Saira handed Zohra the bouquet of white lilies. Her palms were clammy as though she were walking to her execution rather than her wedding.

As the sweet scent of the flowers tickled her nose, Zohra took her father's offered hand. For a moment, she couldn't get her legs to move, couldn't shake off the sudden fear that descended over her.

In the next, she was standing at the entrance to the Throne Hall, a vast chamber with a high, circular dome ceiling. The moment Zohra and her father crossed the threshold, traditional Dahaaran music blared to life from their left and right. The festive sounds set her heart thumping in tune.

A gasp fell from her lips. The whole setting could have been torn out of her worn-out copy of *One Thousand and One Arabian Nights*. Back when she had still been enchanted enough to believe the magical stories spun by her father, before the reality of duty and obligation had shattered her world, before the truth of a princess's life had forced her to grow up too fast.

The hall was huge with at least a thousand gold-edged chairs on either side, leaving a carpeted path between for her to walk. The floor was cream-colored marble with inlaid jewels.

The carpeted path was strewn with red rose petals.

Zohra followed the path with her eyes to the other end of the hall, where there was a wide dais. Sheer gold-and-beige-colored fabrics draped across the dais which was built of steps leading to a gold-edged throne, wide enough for two. Thousands of cream-colored roses, with bloodred roses here and there, adorned every step and surface of the dais.

And standing next to the throne, his navy uniform contrastingly starkly against the richly romantic background, a blur to her panic-stricken gaze, was her bridegroom.

Never for a moment had she imagined such a lavish wedding, or such a forbidding-looking man waiting for her at the end of it. She had imagined the same day with Faisal so many times. A simple wedding free of obligations and duty with the man she loved, both of them able to live the life they had wanted.

How had such a simple dream turned into dust?

Her heart thudded hard against her rib cage, her chest incredibly tight.

Across the vast hall, her gaze met Prince Ayaan's. And held.

She had expected him to be just as isolated from her as he had been through the parade. And yet, she could swear he was tuned to her every step, every breath, as if they were the only two people in the huge hall.

Her nerves stretched tight at the intensity of that gaze. It burned hot, alive, intense and she realized she was the cause of it. That awareness between them, it had a life of its own across the vast hall.

Was he anchoring her or was she anchoring him onto a path neither wanted to go on?

Sucking in a breath, she severed the connection, and focused on something beyond his shoulder. An uncontrollable shaking took root in her.

She did not need his strength, imagined or real, nor did he need hers.

The setting of the wedding, the festivities and joy around her, it was all getting to her.

This marriage will be whatever you make of it.

For once, Zohra agreed with her father's practical advice and she intended to set the tone for it from the beginning. And that meant remembering the prince and she were nothing but strangers brought together by duty.

Ayaan heard Zohra's answer to the imam's question, her voice crystal clear with no hesitation in it. The second time and then the third time, she gave her consent to the wedding.

Whatever doubts she'd had, no one would detect even a hint of it in her voice right then.

Or that she was, in any way, not fit to be the future queen of Dahaar. After she had left that night, he had wondered not only at his father's decision to choose a woman with tainted birth—even if it wasn't her fault—but even more, someone as impulsive and hotheaded as her.

But had his father seen the strength and poise she radiated with her very presence as she did now? Had he seen the assertiveness, the intelligence that shone from her gaze? Had he thought Ayaan needed an educated, even an unconventional wife to compensate for...

Suddenly it was his turn to give consent and the imam's words washed over him.

He gave his consent, his promise to cherish, protect and love Zohra Katherine Naasar for the rest of his life, the words sticking in his throat.

Protecting her—that was the only promise he could keep and to do that, he needed to keep his wife as far from the reaches of his darkness as possible. He slipped an emerald ring, seated among tiny diamonds, onto her finger. And extended his own hand for her to do the same.

Her fingers trembled when they touched his, her movements betraying the anxiety she hid so well.

From everything he had learned about her, his bride belonged in a category of her own. And despite every warning aimed toward himself, he couldn't tamp down his curiosity about her. Especially as, for the first time in eight months, he could remember every sensation, every scent— every minute of his encounter with her in exquisite detail.

His days, especially hours spent in someone else's company, were usually a blur to him. Yesterday's groom's ceremony that his mother had observed with happiness glittering in her every movement was already a vague memory.

He'd had only silence to offer when his mother had told him how happy she was that he had accepted this alliance. For every hundred words she said, he had only one.

This morning had been the first time he'd faced Dahaar's people since his return.

He had choked in the face of the joy, in the expectations of the people of Dahaar and the crushing weight of it. They cheered him on, they called him a survivor, a true hero when the truth was he was fighting every waking and sleeping moment to stop his reality from turning into a nightmare.

It was how he saw his life stretch in front of him. Isolated during the day and fighting his demons each night.

Until his bride had stood at the entrance to the hall.

He had sucked in a sharp breath, feeling as though a fog was falling away from his eyes. Suddenly, he had become aware of the reverent hush of the crowd as they watched her walk toward him, the festive strains of traditional music and the scent of the roses around the dais wafting up toward him.

Instead of the pristine white that tradition demanded, her dress was of the palest gold color with intricately heavy embroidery. It draped her torso in a severe cut, even the neckline revealing nothing but the palest hint of her skin. Thousands of tiny crystals stitched into the bodice twinkled every time she moved. It was cinched at her tiny waist and then showed off her long legs. Her hair was piled high and atop it sat a diamond tiara.

He had no doubt as to what statement she was making with that dress. Subtlety in any shape or form was apparently a strange concept to his bride.

His mouth curved, a lightness filling his chest.

The severity of the style did nothing but highlight the shape of her body—every curve and dip neatly delineated to satisfy his spiraling curiosity from that night.

Her skin glowed. She wasn't the most beautiful woman he had ever seen. Her features were too distinct and determined to play well with each other, but in that moment, there was no woman who would have suited better to be the future queen of Dahaar.

The longer he took in her beautiful face, the faster his heart beat.

His gut tightened in the most delicious way, a slow curl of heat unraveling in his muscles. He shuddered at the strangely dizzying sensation.

When the imam completed his prayer and she turned to look at Ayaan, the scent of her skin—rose attar and something else—teased his body into rising awareness.

She was his wife, his woman.

In name only, but in that moment, the primitive claim washed away everything else.

The music climbed a crescendo and the imam pronounced them man and wife.

She was now Princess Zohra Katherine Naasar Al-Sharif, the future queen of Dahaar.

Cheers and good wishes swept up through the hall. He let it all flow over him, fighting the inimitable weight of it, willing himself to focus on the happiness flowing around.

Hooking her hand through his, he led her down the steps of the dais and toward the area on the right to where the next ritual would take place. She had asked for the ceremonies to be completed the same day.

"What was the reason for this request?" he whispered at her ear, noticing her eyes light up as her brother Wasim hugged her. She said something to him and immediately the young prince of Siyaad cheered up.

It was the only time she fully smiled—when it was her half sister or half brother. For the rest of them, including her father, there was never a smile, at least not one that reached her eyes. Only a distance she clearly projected between her and the outside world.

Pity, because her smile held inexplicable warmth, almost a promise to chase away the shadows from the person she bestowed it on.

She stilled and turned toward him, her hand going to the sheer, gold-colored veil that fluttered from beneath the tiara. He leaned in and tugged it from where it had caught on the tiny crystal on her bodice. His fingers grazed the curve of her breast. She jerked back just as he did.

Her beautiful brown eyes flared. "I have no love for rituals that take three days. This way, my father can return to Siyaad tomorrow morning instead of waiting for another three days and spend energy he doesn't have on—"

"I thought you didn't care about your father."

"I don't. But it doesn't mean that I want him to suffer. That would just…"

"Finally break through your stubborn head and show you what an ungrateful daughter you are."

Zohra came to a sudden halt and stared at the man who was now her husband. They were surrounded from all sides by her father's family and his own. And yet the scorn that had rattled in his words was just as obvious in his gaze. "Have I done something to upset you, Prince Ayaan?"

"No, Princess," he said, lingering a second too long on the title. "Just telling the truth as I see it. It seems very few people dare to."

"And you do?"

"I have taken an oath just now that I would protect you. Even if it has to be from yourself."

"And of course, being a man, you have all the correct answers without knowing anything about my relationship with my father, right?"

One corner of his mouth turned up in mockery. "Have you noticed how every argument with you comes down to the fact that I am a man and you are not? One would think beneath all this contempt you show for duty and Siyaad, you're just annoyed that you are not allowed to rule."

His arrogance rendered her mute for a second. "I have never coveted the crown of Siyaad," she said, angry with herself for letting him rile her so easily. "All it entails is that you endlessly sacrifice either your or your loved ones' happiness at its feet."

"As you are apparently unable or unwilling to see, I will spell it out for you, Princess. It seems your father has given you unfettered freedom while you didn't even blink at the idea of betraying his trust. A princess of Siyaad, spending her summers in the desert, falling in love, the very life you have led is a testament to it. You're standing here," he said, laying his arm so casually against her waist that for a moment she lost track of what he said, "for no other reason than because *you* think you're protecting your sister from a horrible fate."

Her father and now Prince Ayaan, had both said the same thing to her.

Did they not see that it was their devotion to duty that had left her with no choice?

After more than an hour of mingling with guests, either strangers or her father's family, who snubbed her or the courageous ones that veiled their insults cleverly, Zohra was to ready to escape when she found herself next to her new husband.

His nearness unsettled her, an extra layer of awareness sparking to life. Or maybe it was that he had a habit of saying things that burrowed under her skin.

A ten-layered white glazed cake that looked like a castle perched on the edge of a mountain was wheeled in front of them.

She laughed and turned toward him. "This has to be the best part of wedding a prince."

His gaze lingered over her mouth a fraction too long before he responded. "A lesser man would take offense at that, Princess."

His hand was callused and warm over hers as they cut the cake, his breath an unwanted caress against her skin. Maintaining her smile took more effort than it should have. "It's a good thing you're not a lesser man, or even the average. I didn't think it was possible for anyone to be so…"

The cheers around them should have fractured the intimacy of the moment. Instead, a web wove around them and neither could dispel it. His long fingers brought a piece of cake to her mouth, and Zohra's skin prickled. "So…?"

Swallowing the cake past a tight throat, Zohra mirrored his actions. His mouth, opening and closing over her fingers, sent a shiver up her spine. Shaking her head, she struggled to find her voice. "So unaffected, untouched by…everything around you. You seem to want nothing for yourself, you…"

"Who said I don't want anything?" he whispered.

His words washed over her like warm honey. Her gaze flitted to his lips as if drawn by a force she couldn't fight.

He really had the most sensuous mouth—full and lush, in perfect contrast to the sharp angles of the rest of his face. Longing, unbidden and powerful, reached and held tight inside her muscles.

With that awareness also came a gut-clenching realization. This man, despite all his promises of expecting nothing from her, was more dangerous to her than a traditional prince could have been. Because she didn't know what to predict from him. Like now.

Suddenly, a flicker of such unbearable pain filled his gaze and she lost track of her thoughts. He hadn't been fully smiling before—he never did—but at least there had been a gleam of indulgent humor in his expression. Now, his features were frozen into a cold mask.

A servant approached them with a long, rectangular silver tray in hand, the contents of it hidden under the Dahaaran flag.

Zohra could see the gleaming silver hilt of a sword encrusted with emeralds peeking from under the cloth.

"It is yours now, Ayaan," Queen Fatima said, her eyes filling up with tears.

Zohra turned toward him when no response came from Ayaan.

He looked at the sword as if it were something expressly

sent to torture him. There was a deathly pallor to his skin while his gaze remained glued to the tray.

Unease fluttering in her belly, Zohra looked to her new mother-in-law. For once, she was irritated at her own decision all these years to learn nothing of rituals and culture.

"Queen Fatima, what is the significance of this sword?"

"It was my brother's sword." The answer came from Ayaan, who was still staring at it. "The one he was honored with when he was announced the crown prince of Dahaar."

"I think Azeez," the queen began, "would have been happy to see you take it for yourself, Ayaan. And what better occasion—"

"What Azeez would have wanted was to be alive. As he deserves to be."

The words from Ayaan sounded like an anguished growl to Zohra. And she was sure she was the only one who had heard them.

In the next moment, Ayaan walked away without looking back, leaving a hall full of state dignitaries and distinguished guests staring after him with a mixture of curiosity and shock.

CHAPTER FOUR

AYAAN DRIED HIS hair roughly and threw the towel aside. He was bone-tired after his rigorous exercise regimen. It was the only way he knew of knocking himself out. Drown his body in so much physical strain that there was nothing for his mind to do but bathe him in sleep.

Sometimes it worked, sometimes he woke up screaming in the middle of the night.

At least he was in good shape. Khaleef, his bodyguard, a man he had known all his life, hadn't let Ayaan run to fat and utter worthlessness in five years. His mind might be out of his control, but Ayaan intended to retain every ounce of control over his body.

He came to a halt, facing the doors of his suite. He hadn't seen Zohra since he had stormed out of the Throne Hall.

He had been caught up in her beauty. But more than that, he hadn't been able to stop himself from pushing past her prickly armor and boundaries. The same boundaries that he had forbidden her to cross with him. And yet with her by his side, the joy of the festivities had made a mark even on him, reminded him of who he used to be five years ago.

And then he had seen his brother's sword. A stark reminder of why he was the one standing.

Several hours later now, the image of it refused to leave him alone. He pushed through the doors, came to the head of the bed and turned the light on. And stopped.

Wearing a gown made of the silkiest chiffon in the color of turquoise, Zohra lay sleeping against the pillows on his side. Instant heat swirled low in his gut. It was his wedding night, and his bride was sleeping in his bed. Even half the man that he was, he couldn't remain immune to the breathtaking beauty of the woman.

She slept on her back, her hands raised above her head. The swirls of henna across her skin were beautiful and his gaze swept over her body.

Her delicately arched feet were also decorated in the same deep red intricate design disappearing beneath the gown at her calves.

The dress swirled around her slender form and yet managed to drape silkily over every curve and dip. Over her legs and her thighs, over the indentation of her waist and finally over her breasts.

Hundreds of golden threads were worked around the neckline, the weight of which pulled the fabric down. Giving him a view of the upper curve of one breast. They were small and rounded and he couldn't move his gaze from the sight.

Desire ripped through him and even the simmering anger he felt at her presence couldn't wash it away. He moved closer without knowing it. She smelled divine, like roses and attar and a rich, erotic fusion of both with her own scent.

In eight months of lucidity, he had never once felt so alive, felt desire as sharp and focused as now. And he couldn't easily dismiss this sharp hunger at the sight of her, or view it with distaste.

Her long hair was fanned over his pillow, her mouth

pink. Long lashes lent her an air of vulnerable feminin-
ity that was missing when her eyes were open. Because
she was busy studying, assessing, challenging with that
intelligent gaze.

Suddenly, her gaze flew open. It stayed unfocused,
muddled with sleep. A slight flush lit her skin with a rosy
hue. Her gaze traveled over him lazily. Ayaan felt the force
of it down to his toes. For a second, all he could think of
was to climb into the bed.

Irritation flickered hot inside him. But he waited silently
for the heat of his desire to subside, even as he wondered
what had brought that smile to her lush mouth.

Shock flickering through her brown eyes, she shot up
and pushed her hair from her face. "Prince Ayaan, what
are you doing here?"

He raised a brow at her indignation. "That should be
my question. You're in my bed, in my suite, in my wing
again, Princess. If I were the jealous, possessive kind of
husband, I would take offense at how often you end up in
a man's bed."

Pulling herself up against the headboard, she looked
around, her gaze wide. It swept over his suite. Pink crept
upward from her neck. And the glare in her eyes went to
full-blown anger. She half slipped, half jumped from the
bed, her movements panic-stricken. "If you had been the
normal, entitled, king-of-everything-I-survey kind of man
like I had hoped, you would have rejected me and I would
be nowhere near this palace or you."

She turned around and started pulling the cushions and
pillows here and there. Bent over the bed like that, she gave
him a perfect view of the curve of her bottom draped by
nothing but the sheerest silk. The woman was capable of
pushing him over the last edge he was already standing on.

He grabbed his robe from the foot of the bed and threw it at her. "Cover yourself and get out of my chamber."

Zohra clutched the robe out of pure instinct while, she was sure, mortification turned her face bright red. "You think I want to be here, half-naked and incoherent, laid out like a feast for you?"

His silence in the face of her mounting fury chafed at her. She shrugged into the overlarge silk robe, the sleeves doubling over past her hands. "This is all because of your mother and her army of…"

The roaring blaze in Prince Ayaan's gaze, the concrete set of his jaw curbed her words. He took a menacing step toward her, his mouth flattened with fury. "Do you have no filter between your brain and your mouth, Princess?"

Mortification heated her skin like fire, but Zohra was damned if she left before she cleared his assumption that she wanted to be in his bedroom. "I have been awake since before dawn, going through a million rituals that mean nothing to me. I nearly fell asleep in that monstrous tub of perfumed oil before being led here," she said, meeting his gaze.

His hands folded at his chest, he stood there like a block of ice, unwavering, unfeeling. As though nothing mattered to him except his imposed isolation from everyone around him, as if his very survival was hinged on it. Frustration and curiosity turned Zohra inside out.

"I have no interest in how you arrived here, Princess. I do not want to see you in my quarters ever again. Is that understood?"

Zohra nodded, her own anger coming to her aid. It was what they had agreed upon for their marriage. But his cutting attitude, as if she polluted the very air around him by breathing it, reminded her of things she never wanted to remember. She lifted her chin, infused steel into her words. "I have no wish to remain here and bear the brunt of your uncivilized behavior. But I have no idea where I am supposed to go."

Her legs shook beneath her, a gaping void opening up in her gut. But she refused to let him see the nagging hurt his words evoked. He was not the cause of it, she knew that, but his words were a reminder of the most painful fact of her life. Since her mother had died, she had not belonged anywhere. Her life felt as if it was a repeat telecast of the worst moments; indifference and resentment. "Unless you want me to make a spectacle of myself and roam around the palace at this hour of the night in the inconsequential gown underneath this robe, I suggest you get off your high horse and find yourself a different bed for the night."

He reached her before she could blink, his hold on her wrist inflexible, leaving Zohra no choice but to follow. "As you might already be guessing with that smart head of yours," he said, his jaw so tight that she wondered that she could hear his words, "not only is the man you married uncivilized but he is also a coward who loathes sleeping anywhere but in his quarters."

Because of his nightmares?

Her chest tight, Zohra stared at his profile as he tugged her through the door. She swallowed the question, shrugging off the instant concern that stole over her.

She had no idea how far they had gone until they were standing in front of another set of doors. But by the thick silence around them, Zohra knew they were still in the same wing.

"This has to work for tonight."

With that curt statement, he turned and left, leaving Zohra speechless in his wake. Tucking her arms around her, she ventured into the huge room. Now that she was awake, the scent of attar and rose that clung to her skin cloyed through her, the sensitive rub of her thighs making her aware of her state of undress.

Using the velvet-covered footstool, she lugged herself onto the antique bed and lay down. She shivered, even though the room was comfortably warm. Silver threaded white cotton sheets rustled as she settled in, the silence creeping into her skin.

She stared up at the canopy of the bed, shameful tears pooling in her eyes.

Hadn't she lived through this same lonely moment too many times to be still weighed down by a stranger's indifference to her?

Zohra had known what she was taking on for Saira's sake and yet she couldn't shake the loneliness that twisted inside her, the crippling fear that she was bound to spend her entire life alone.

Stepping over the threshold of the State Hall, Zohra smiled for the first time in the week since the wedding. She was wearing an extremely comfortable and stylish pink pantsuit thanks to her personal stylist, and, for once, Zohra felt she could handle the day ahead.

It was the first official public event that Ayaan was attending since the wedding. Her gaze focused on Ayaan who, Zohra had noticed, rarely met his mother's eyes. Queen Fatima had walked them through every event that had been planned for the day. Even Zohra knew that it was a job for a political aide but she had a feeling the queen had taken it on so that she could spend some time with her son.

A small crowd had already gathered, including Ayaan's parents. Clad in a slate gray suit that hugged his wide shoulders, Ayaan stood at the opposite wall. His jaw clean-shaven, the unruly waves of his hair combed back, he looked every inch a commanding prince who had come back to Dahaar and its people against all odds.

He stood near his father and two other suit-clad men, but the way he stood, slanted away from the group, with a smile that curved his mouth but didn't touch his gaze, Zohra felt his isolation like a live thing, almost as if there were a fortress around him.

A hush fell around her as everyone noticed her entrance. Her skin prickled with awareness like a warning beacon just as those golden eyes landed on her. And she saw the infinitesimal tightening of his shoulders, the long indrawn breath, as if he were bracing himself.

Frowning, Zohra struggled with the overwhelming urge to turn tail and disappear. She already had a healthy amount of dislike for any state affairs, and Prince Ayaan's long-suffering attitude toward her presence on top of that grated at her.

She reached his side and the group widened to include her. Her nerves tightened at the press of Ayaan's hard muscle beside her and all she could hear was the amplified thud of her heart, the whistle of every hard-fought breath, as he introduced her.

Ayaan's palm lay against her lower back. She shivered, wondering if there was a brand on her skin in the shape of his palm. Zohra couldn't remember the names of the two men and their wives a second after they fell on her ears.

How could she react so strongly to his presence while he barely tolerated hers?

He turned her toward him slightly. "I hope you have recovered from the wedding, Princess."

A stinging response rose to her tongue. Pulling a deep breath in, she looked around and checked her impulse to shout at him in a very unprincesslike way. "You are actually deigning to speak to me?" she whispered.

He blinked at the animosity in her tone.

"Of course, state functions. That was in the rule book, wasn't it?" She was acting like a child, but she couldn't dismiss the image of Ayaan bracing himself to face her. Indifference and resentment had wounded her more than she had thought. And facing the same again...

"One of the times you will sigh deeply and suffer my company instead of banishing me from your presence."

His hands locked behind him, he studied her with an intense gaze as if he could drill into her head and read all her secrets and fears. His mouth flattened, his ire nothing but a spark in his golden brown gaze. "And here I was afraid that you were far too clever than I ever wanted my wife to be, Princess."

Rooted to the spot, Zohra stared at his back and spent the next two hours wondering what he meant. The informal social gathering complete, they were led through a narrow entrance, flanked by uniformed guards dressed in Dahaar's navy blue.

Surprised by the security measures, Zohra was about to ask Ayaan when huge, ancient doors opened in front of them.

It was a scene unlike Zohra had ever seen.

A roar went up instantly at the sight of Ayaan. They were in a marble-tiled hall, ten times bigger than the huge throne room with at least a thousand people standing upon the wide staircase on the other side and more falling into a single line behind security ropes around the perimeter of the hall.

With every cheer and greeting that came from the crowd, Zohra felt Ayaan freeze next to her, inch by painful inch as if someone was injecting ice into his very veins. She heard Queen Fatima whisper Ayaan's name, saw the king's concerned pat on his shoulder but Ayaan didn't budge.

He could have been the statue of a centuries-old warrior for all the life she felt in him.

Seconds merged and a tiny ripple of shock spread through the group around them. The cheers from the crowd began to pale into something else. Zohra stole a look at Ayaan and her breath hitched in her throat. His face looked as if someone had poured concrete over his features, his nostrils flaring as he fought to breathe.

Was this what he faced every time he walked in front of a crowd?

Her throat tight, Zohra reached for his hand. He didn't budge. She moved closer, clasped her fingers around his.

He turned and the distress in his gaze shook her insides. Shadows upon shadows flickered in the golden depths, mocking her petty insecurities and peevishness. She knew he wanted to leave, but she also knew he would castigate himself later.

Words came and fell away from her mouth, every one more trite than the previous. She couldn't even begin to imagine what he saw, or felt at that moment.

She shook her head with a tsk-tsk sound, strove to fill her words with a lightness that she was far from feeling. She tugged at his fingers, forcing him to focus on her touch, her words. "Is it because of my illegitimate birth or the fact that I lack a certain important organ that I have never been treated with half such enthusiasm in Siyaad?"

A lick of humor came alive in his gaze. "I would say a combination of both." The tight lines around his mouth relented. His gaze swept over her, wide, intense. "And more importantly, what they show you or not show you is only a reflection of your own interest in them, Princess."

Even with the black cloud of whatever it was that

haunted him, he didn't hold back his punches. She nodded, even though the truth stung. "Whereas you, they have known you your entire life."

He nodded. She heard him release his breath, felt him move closer to her until their sides grazed. "Except for the last few years."

"I thought turning back on something like this was nothing for a prince but it is not, is it?" she ventured.

She felt his gaze move over her, but stared straight ahead. Their fingers were still laced together, and yet there was no getting used to the feel of his rough fingers against hers. "No," he said after a long pause.

"What about this…bothers you, Prince Ayaan?"

He clamped his fingers tighter around hers. She must have made a sound because he instantly loosened his grip. "I'm not the man they think I am. I am not the man I thought I was long ago."

Zohra took in the eager anticipation on every face in the crowd. Standing so close to him, feeling the heat from his hard body, seeing him fight his fears with every inch of him, she had never been surer of a man's strength. "I have spent many moments in the past week accompanying you to various state functions that hold no meaning or significance for me, I have witnessed their celebration in your name. And I have come to understand one thing. They know exactly who you are, what it takes for you to be here and they accept you, Prince Ayaan. Even *I* know how rare that is."

It was only after the words had left her mouth that Zohra realized the very truth in them. Still, she braced herself for his mockery, expected him to laugh at her. Because, in reality, she was beginning to see how very little she knew about this life, and what it entailed.

He leaned down toward her, and she was enveloped by

the scent and heat of his skin. "You are a contradiction in yourself, Princess. I cannot quite decide whether the selfish, defiant version is the real you or this quiet, regal, perceptive one."

Shock robbing her senses, Zohra just stared at him. *Was she both or was she neither?*

She was still wondering the answer to that when Ayaan took a step forward and waved at the crowd. Their roaring response was earsplitting.

He turned around and looked at her. His gaze studied her as if solving a puzzle. And then instead of asking her, he tugged her forward until she had no choice but to walk by his side.

Be my wife at state functions.

It was one of the few things he had asked of her, and in this moment, Zohra couldn't shake off the feeling that it was her that Prince Ayaan saw and not a faceless, nameless woman he had married in the name of duty. And try as she did, the feeling wouldn't leave her alone.

They spent the entire day greeting Dahaarans who had traveled long distances to meet their prince and his new bride. And the hardest part was that all through the day, he kept touching her. He never completely relaxed but after the first hour, he became less tense.

Of course, Queen Fatima had warned her that there were eyes and ears watching their every move, hungrier than usual about the crown prince who was finally entering the political arena of Dahaar and his first formal ceremony with his new Siyaadi bride.

The little touches of his palm at her back, the brush of his hand against hers, were more for public display than anything else, but they affected her strongly nonetheless.

Her fingers tingled when he clasped them with his own, her heart thudded, every inch of her body thrummed as if they were alone instead of in a sea of people, as if he touched her because he craved it, because he needed to.

And despite her best efforts, Zohra kept forgetting that the man she had married sought nothing for himself. Not pleasure or power or fame.

The prince of Dahaar did everything he did in the name of duty.

CHAPTER FIVE

AYAAN ENTERED THE vast hall and took his seat opposite his mother while his father sat at the head of the centuries-old dinner table. And just as it did for the past few months, instantly his throat closed up, an unbearable stiffness setting into his shoulders.

The ancient, handcrafted table that probably weighed a ton, the colorful walls hanging with handmade Dahaaran rugs that showcased historical Al-Sharif events, the high circular ceilings... Every time he entered the hall, he felt as if he entered a tomb, as if he was being slowly but surely smothered by every inanimate object in the room.

Not to mention the fact he couldn't even look at his parents. Nodding at them, he settled into his chair. The weight of their attention was like a heavy chain on his shoulders.

Shying his gaze away from her, he answered his mother's inquiries about his day with single word answers, wondering why today felt even more painful than the past week.

The whole family together for dinner. Even before their family had been broken by tragedy, it had been a tradition his mother had enforced as much as possible. But never had it been such an exercise in pain as it had become since his return.

"Where is Princess Zohra?" his father asked, and Ayaan frowned.

Two weeks since their marriage, two weeks of countless political dinners and public appearances, and Zohra had somehow become the buffer between him and the outside world, even between him and his parents. Because whatever else his wife was, she was not a silent creature.

Listening to either her questions about the various ceremonies or her perceptive inquiries about state affairs and watching her struggle to curb her temper and her tongue—sometimes successfully, sometimes not—had become a daily ritual in itself. And looking at his father, Ayaan realized it was not just him that had become used to the princess's presence.

"Princess Zohra is completing the final wedding ritual and should be joining us any minute," his mother announced.

The uncomfortable silence descending again, Ayaan fidgeted in his seat, restless to leave. "Can we begin dinner?"

"No." An implacable answer from his mother which meant she was in full queen mode. It was a term his siblings and he had coined together.

His chest tightened at the recollection as Ayaan turned to the side and froze. One by one, the entire palace staff was entering the hall. The senior ones took their seats on low-slung divans along the perimeter of the wall while the rest of them stood in between. Almost a hundred of them and they were all dressed in their best, their pride and joy at being included shining in their gazes.

Another group of servants laid down numerous empty glass bowls with tiny spoons all over the huge table.

Straightening in his chair, Ayaan turned back to his mother. The restlessness in his limbs shifted, curiosity now rooting him to his seat. "What is the ritual, mother?"

"Every new Al-Sharif bride has to cook dessert for the family," his mother said, a hint of complaint in her tone. "Zohra somehow managed to postpone it until now."

Ayaan smiled. He could very well imagine Princess Zohra stomping with frustration somewhere. "But why is the entire palace staff here?"

His mother glanced in the direction of the entrance, the lines of her mouth tight. "They are all here to taste the dessert she cooks along with us, Prince Ayaan. It is a centuries-old tradition to give the staff a way to welcome the new bride, to give them a chance to feel that they are an integral part of the royal family."

Blinking, Ayaan leaned back against the chair. He had no idea if the Siyaadi princess could cook. For the first time in months, a strange anticipation filled him. But no matter what, he knew he was in for an interesting couple of hours.

Not just today, any time spent with his unconventional wife was always interesting. At the least.

He looked over to his right just as Zohra arrived at the entrance to the hall accompanied by fanfare and an army of excited servants.

Spying the anxiety in her gaze, the slight sheen of sweat on her forehead, Ayaan felt the most uncharacteristic surge of concern. From the corner of his eye, he could see Zohra approach the table with dragging footsteps that clearly said she wanted to be anywhere but here. In her hands was the centuries-old, gleaming silver bowl he remembered seeing long ago. Behind her, similar bowls were being carried by the kitchen staff and laid beside the low-slung divans where the palace staff were seated.

"Place the bowl on the table by Prince Ayaan's side, Princess Zohra." His mother's voice rang clearly in the deafening silence of a hundred and more curiously waiting gazes.

Her reluctance a tangible thing in the air around them, Zohra placed the bowl on the table next to Ayaan. A distinctive smell, sweet and...*burned*, wafted into the air around them.

His nostrils flaring, Ayaan glanced into the silver bowl. He gasped when he saw the contents, hearing the same sound fall from his mother's mouth and his father's cough. The dark brown, charred substance in the bowl looked like no dessert he knew.

His mouth twitched, and a sudden lightness filled his chest. Raising his head, he chanced a look at his mother. Her forehead tied into a frown, she was looking at the bowl with a shocked expression that had him clamping his mouth tight.

Whispers emerged from the staff around them, the more senior members even slanting a quick puzzled look at the bowl, but Ayaan couldn't help himself. Clearing his throat, which felt really hard, he looked up and met Zohra's gaze. "What is this, Princess?"

Her dark gaze fiery enough to burn him, she answered from tightly clamped lips, "*Halwa,* Prince Ayaan."

He didn't heed the warning in her voice. "You mean this is carrots and nuts?"

"Yes."

Fidgeting in his seat, he met his father's eyes at the head of table. Seeing the twinkle in his aged eyes, the tight set of his twitching mouth made Ayaan lose the tenuous hold on himself.

He laughed, the very act of it shaking his body from head to toe. And heard his father's peal of laughter alongside his own. His throat raw, Ayaan covered his face with his fingers but to no avail. His jaw and stomach hurt, but in the best way.

His body had no memory of what it felt like to laugh. Every face around them, including his mother's, watched him and the princess alternately, torn between the desire to laugh and bone-deep propriety.

Every time he looked at his father, it started again. He had no idea how long they laughed, but soon, he had tears in his eyes. "This is…" he choked, "*Ya Allah*, exactly like…"

His lean frame shaking with laughter, his father nodded, his mouth curled into a wide smile. "When Amira made—"

"When Amira made *Awwameh* on her twenty-first birthday," his mother finished, tears in her own eyes. Swallowing at the sight, Ayaan nodded, glad that her eyes were full of remembered laughter rather than the familiar shadows of grief.

"She hated every moment of it, too," his father said, looking at Zohra with a fond smile. "And Azeez and Ayaan teased her mercilessly for months."

A smile still curving his mouth, Ayaan met Zohra's gaze.

"Queen Fatima," Zohra's crystal clear tones rang through their laughter, laden with the promise of retribution, "who did you say tastes the new bride's dessert first?"

His laughter cut short, Ayaan shook his head and met his mother's gaze. "No."

Her mouth was still compressed but a spark of something wicked lit up his mother's gaze. "The husband, Princess Zohra," she said, studying him with an intensity that twisted his gut.

Zohra reached for a silver spoon, and scooped up a little of the charred *halwa* with it. "Traditions, of course, have to be followed. Do they not, King Malik?" she said, throwing the challenge at his father across the table.

Chuckles and approvals rang around the huge room, followed by his father's comment, "Of course, Princess Zohra," laden with laughter.

Knowing that he was well and truly caught, Ayaan looked up at Zohra. And opened his mouth when she brought the spoon to his mouth, victory dancing in her beautiful gaze.

When was the last time the palace walls had heard laughter like that? The last time his mother had smiled even if it had been buried under affected displeasure? The last time they had remembered the past with a smile?

With his chest feeling amazingly light, Ayaan reached Zohra's suite. The scent of scorched carrots and burned pistachios lingered in the air, bringing a smile to his mouth. He closed the huge doors behind him, suddenly craving the very privacy he usually avoided with her.

Leaning against the closed doors, he lost himself to the sheer pleasure of watching her. Cinched tight at her rib cage with a jeweled belt, the copper-sulfate-colored silk caftan she wore billowed from her tiny waist, highlighting the long line of her legs. The puckered sleeves showed off slender arms, the intricately designed diamond bracelets on her wrists twinkling in the light thrown by the lamps around the room.

She turned around, her hennaed hands tugging at the pearls threaded into her hair. The silky material cupped her breasts like a lover's hands, her stark sensuality robbing his breath.

Feeling like a teenager getting his first sight of a beautiful woman, he pushed away from the door.

He would ensure she was all right—a small courtesy

after the past two weeks—summon a maid, and leave. "Do you require help?"

She threw a quick look at the closed doors behind him and the slender line of her shoulders tensed up. "Have you not had enough fun at my expense, Prince Ayaan?"

He crossed the room and took her hands in his as she went to pull another pearl from her hair. Sensation skittered up his fingers, like a spark of fire. She wrenched them back right as he dropped them. "You do that a lot," he said, before he could think better of it.

"What?"

"Take your temper out on your beautiful hair."

It was a personal comment that shocked them both, instantly filling the air around them with tension. He had not intended to touch her, either.

"Why are you here?"

She had every right to question him and yet he couldn't turn around and leave. "I wanted to make sure you were all right."

"I am fine." Struggling with the clasp of the necklace at her nape, she glared at him. "Except for the small fact that I am now the laughingstock of the Dahaaran palace."

"I will pass a law that enforces the strictest punishment on anyone who dares laughs at you," he said, surprising himself again.

"Will it apply to the king and the crown prince?" she challenged. "Because as much as I would like to forget that image, it was your father and you that were laughing." Her gaze stayed on him, surprise in it, as if she couldn't quite believe what she had seen. "That sound is still ringing in my ears."

She dropped onto a divan with her feet stretched in front of her. Scrunching her nose, she grabbed the sleeve of her caftan, sniffed it and made a face. Ayaan clamped his mouth shut and rocked on his heels. She looked up at him, her mouth turned down. "Oh please, go ahead and laugh. I know you are dying to."

Ayaan laughed, the sound barreling out of him again. "I wouldn't have believed it if I hadn't been sitting there. You should have seen my mother's face when you put that silver bowl on the dining table. Centuries old, studded with intricate handwork, encrusted with rare gems and inside…" He hummed a dramatic tune.

Hunched over with her head in her hands, she groaned. "*It was not that bad.*"

He dropped down onto the divan, still smiling at the expression on his mother's face, the twitch of his father's mouth. Silence in the grand hall had never held that much repressed laughter. "It was black and it tasted like soot, Princess."

She swatted him, her lower lip caught between her teeth, her beautiful brown eyes glimmering with laughter. "Have you seen the size of that palatial kitchen? How can anyone be expected to cook dessert for a hundred people? Of all the things I thought would make me unsuitable to be your wife…" Her eyes glittered like precious stones. "I…I thought I would be reduced to ash by Queen Fatima's glare."

"Even she cracked a smile at the end," he said, and Zohra doubled over laughing.

"For thirteen years, the palace staff at Siyaad were shocked by what I did but I think the faces of the staff here today…this is what they are going to remember for the rest of my life, aren't they?"

"I think it will be recorded as one of the most significant events in the history of Al-Sharifs." He stretched his hands wide, announcing the title. "*Princess Zohra and the Tale of the Burned Halwa.*"

"As if this was the first humiliating ritual I have been forced to endure." She slid lower on the couch. "Even the ritual where I have to spend a week with you in the desert is—"

Cold skittered down his spine and Ayaan looked away. He had lost everything in the desert the night they had been attacked. He couldn't bear to go there again, not even for his mother and one of her rituals. "We are not going."

Noticing the shadows that entered his gaze, Zohra wondered what it was that she had said. Standing up from the divan, she tugged the pearls again, cursing the elaborate hairstyle.

"Stop that," came Prince Ayaan's voice closer than she had expected.

"I need to—"

His hands were suddenly in her hair, and Zohra's breath caught. The companionship of their shared laughter left the air around them and was replaced by something else. Her scalp prickled as Ayaan's long fingers untangled her hair with sure movements. She held herself rigid, so rigid that her back ached. The heat of his body behind her became a beckoning caress.

Closing her eyes, she took a bracing breath. How was she going to spend the next few years with this man when his simplest touch provoked this kind of reaction in her?

She was about to move away when his hands landed on her shoulders and pressed her toward him. Her pulse drummed in her ears, her skin shivering with a new awareness. Zohra gasped and turned around. His touch had been there one minute and gone the next, the pressure infinitesimal. But in that second, she had felt the shudder that had passed through his lean, hard body, heard the long inhale of his breath, as if...

"Forgive me, Princess," he said stepping back,

color riding those sharp cheekbones. "I shouldn't have touched you."

She clutched her arms against her body, frowning. His beautiful eyes were darkened like she had never seen before, his jaw tight. "Why did you?" she blurted out.

"You have known a man's touch, understand a man's hunger. Do you not know what a temptation you present, especially to one who hasn't been near a woman in six years?"

He muttered the last part softly, almost to himself. Yet the words landed in Zohra's ears with the same force of an earthquake. He was attracted to her and she'd had no idea.

"Six years?" she said, still reeling at the impact of his words.

There was a banked fire in his gaze, but the heat of it was still enough to send a delicious, feverish tremble into every muscle in her body. No wonder she felt so drawn to him, no wonder the air charged the moment they laid eyes on each other. "I never had a chance to fully explore what life had to offer a prince seeing that I was captured just before my twenty-first birthday."

Fierce heat tightened her cheeks. "Does that mean you've never…"

He frowned. "I was twenty-one when I was captured, not sixteen. I was never the one that women flocked to, like Azeez had been, but I have vague memories. The first time, it was…"

She slapped her palm over his mouth, loath to hear all the details. Desire bloomed at the sensitive skin of her palm, spreading through her entire body. "I don't want to know," she whispered, past a dry throat.

He pulled her hand off his mouth. "I didn't realize what else my madness had robbed from me until you showed up, Princess." He slowly peeled his fingers off her skin.

And Zohra realized with a thudding heart how much he didn't want to, what it cost him to let go of her.

A shiver shook her from within. For the first time a tendril of fear uncurled itself. A fear of the tightly leashed desire in him, and worst of all, her own reaction to that all encompassing hunger.

Tugging her hand back, she stepped away from him. And his unblinking gaze took in everything.

He moved toward the door, coming to a stop and turned back. The right corner of his mouth tilted up into a lopsided smile that wound itself around her. "I recommend a bath to get rid of that burned smell, Princess. Probably a rose-scented one." He looked gorgeous, the ever-present shadows of pain and grief temporarily gone. The tension in the room broke even as her body still remembered the imprint of his fingers on her. "As for all the rituals you have to suffer through, I appreciate you humoring my mother. The last few months…have not been easy on her."

Zohra had to grip the bed behind her to steady her legs. "I must admit, it's worth smelling like burned carrots to see you smile, Prince Ayaan. I see why the queen mentions it so much."

"Does she?"

There was such naked hope, such a hunger for more, in his gaze that Zohra couldn't draw breath for a second. It was a glimpse into the boy he must have been, the one his mother couldn't stop talking about. "Why do you sound so surprised? You are all she talks about."

He gave a tight nod, and leaned against the closed door, the levity gone from his face.

Hundreds of questions pummeled through her head. "Did she not know you were alive?"

The look he shot her was scorching.

She pushed off the bed.

The quiet swirled and snarled around them. His jaw tightened; his hands turned into white-knuckled fists. The silence went on for so long that she wondered if he would answer. It felt as if she was standing on the shifting, sinking floor of a desert. The more she tried to hold herself at a distance, the more Prince Ayaan and Dahaar wove into the fabric of her very life.

"Only my old bodyguard, who found me, and my father knew that I was alive. Khaleef roamed the desert for months without giving up. Even after the rescue efforts had been called off. I think he wanted to find our bodies for my parents."

The image those words conjured twisted her gut. "Did he?"

"No, but he did find me." He met her gaze then and Zohra heard the thread of anger in his. "Is this just puerile curiosity, Princess, or is there a point to this conversation?"

Her breath hovered in her throat, an intense tightness in her chest. She could give the easy answer—lie and face his scorn at what he termed curiosity. But she couldn't be a coward while facing the truth of her own feelings or fear.

Maybe if she heard what had happened to him from his own mouth, if she knew what tormented him, she could stop speculating. Maybe she would fear him and this... rampant, unwise curiosity about him would die away. Still, it was the hardest truth she had ever given voice to. "I think, as your wife, irrespective of our...true relationship, I have a right to know what I'm dealing with," she replied, not holding her punches back. "That sounds like I'm hinting something like the rest of the world is, but I would rather know the truth."

A flash of something lit up his eyes. She released the breath she was holding. "Hint, Princess? I don't think you know the meaning of the word."

He smiled, a genuine curve of his mouth, a banked firework in his eyes. It cut grooves in his hollowed-out cheeks and sent a pang through her gut. "I—"

"It's the first sensible thing you have said since you stormed into my suite." He turned away from her. "Khaleef found me in the desert, a couple of months after the attack. According to him, I..." She saw him swallow with great effort. "I was incoherent and violent when he approached me. He didn't let me out of his sight until he could personally alert my father. My father took one look at me and sent me off to a castle in the heart of the Alps, where I was conveniently and blissfully mad for five years."

His words were so matter-of-fact, even when they held so much pain, that Zohra couldn't even speak for a few minutes. "Mad?"

He stared at her, as if suddenly realizing that she was there. "Mentally ill, violent, incoherent."

"Do you...remember what happened after you were captured?"

This time, there was no hiding the pain even in his stark face. "Most of it has come back to me."

"In your nightmares?"

He nodded, a flash of surprise in his gaze.

"So your mother had no idea that you were alive all these years or what...you have been through?"

He shook his head.

What had happened to him in the desert? What horrors did his mind revisit in those terrible nightmares?

Zohra hugged the strange fear that gripped her gut. She didn't want to know, not because the truth of what had been done to him would scare her. Maybe it would, maybe it wouldn't. But she was terrified of her own reaction, of crossing over a threshold and stepping into a path from which there was no return. Instead, she asked him something that had been bothering her, something that needed to be said even if it meant incurring his wrath.

"You said you were doing this—" she moved her hands to encompass them "—for your parents. But what's the point if your behavior is hurting your mother?"

He looked genuinely shocked, his frown deepening. Pure anger flattened his mouth and he took a step toward her. "*You* are lecturing me about duty toward one's parents? You've got a nerve."

Zohra refused to back down, even though his words hit her hard. "I've spent the better part of two weeks humoring your mother, seeing everything she hides from you and your father. Do you know that she hasn't spoken to him since you….*returned*? She feels so…"

Every time she looked at Queen Fatima, at the repressed pain in her eyes, Zohra's own pain, her mother's desolation after her father had left, it all rose to the surface. Lies, even told with the best intentions, caused pain much more terrible than truth itself. "I have seen the tears she hides from you and your father."

His skin lost pallor as though she had delivered him a physical blow.

"And yet you…*avoid* her. You barely exchange two words with her. She is standing on the outside, looking at you, wondering what she has done that you won't even—"

"How can she think she has done anything wrong?"

"Then why won't you speak with her, why won't you even meet her gaze?"

"*Because I'm not my brother.*"

It was a low growl that made the hairs on her neck stand up. His lean frame trembled as though he struggled to contain his emotions within. "I can't bear to look at her because when she sees me, she's looking for Azeez. She's remembering him, searching for something of him in me."

Zohra swallowed at the anguish in his words. "She thought all three of you were dead. She made peace with it until...suddenly five years later, she's told you're alive and..."

"Half-mad and haunted?"

"Your father had no right to lie to her."

His gaze flashed at her daring. "My father was protecting her. For all intents and purposes, *I was dead*."

"He lied because it would not serve Dahaar's interests. This is what I hate about this life...about..." She had to stop to breathe through the tightness in her chest, to swallow the rage sputtering through her. *This was not about her.* "Resenting her for remembering your brother only makes you human. It doesn't mean she—"

"You think I resent her for remembering her firstborn? My brother was the golden prince, the perfect heir. Passionate about Dahaar, smart, courageous, a man who was everything the future king needed to be.

"I'm not him. He should have been the one that survived. That's what my parents think when they see me, that's what the cabinet, the high council think when they see me."

It was what he thought, why he was so isolated from everything and everyone, Zohra realized, shaking. How could anyone live with so much self-loathing, with so much pain tied into their very existence?

"Who gets to decide who should survive—"

He clasped her cheek, his hand gentle in contrast to his face, a stony mask. "You think I should be grateful that I'm alive? A broken man, a coward afraid of the dark? If it had been Azeez who had survived, he wouldn't have lost his mind for five years and hid in some Swiss castle, leaving my father to deal with the catastrophe. He wouldn't have regained his lucidity only to be haunted by memories."

The bitterness in his words leeched every ounce of heat from the room. The hairs on her neck stood up, her gut gripped by the tight fist of pain.

His pain. She could feel it seep into her, enveloping her.

"My brother would have taken up the mantle of Dahaar instead of still hiding behind our father. He would have chosen a woman like you for his queen instead of being forced into it by duty." His gaze swept over her mouth with a hunger that shocked her. "He would have been man enough to make you his wife in every way instead of hiding under a sham.

"Do you understand why I can't bear to look at her, Princess, why I can't bear to be near you? Because I'm not fit to be a son, or a husband, much less a prince."

Pushing away from her, he left the suite, leaving the echoes of his anger and pain swirling around her.

With her knees buckling under the weight of his confession, Zohra slid to the seat behind her. He was like a tornado, and as much as she wished to stay out of his path, she had a feeling he would suck her into him.

His laughter and pain carved places inside her. The truth of his desire that she hadn't been able to see until now thrummed through her. How could she have when she had been mourning Faisal's loss, when she was nothing but a figurehead in Prince Ayaan's life?

She needed to escape from him, from everything he unraveled within her by his mere presence.

CHAPTER SIX

ZOHRA TOOK A sip of the sherbet and forced herself to savor the cool slide of the liquid.

It was hard with a dozen pairs of eyes trained on her from every corner of the vast hall, each speculating why she was attending the first gathering in Siyaad after her wedding alone. If it had been up to her, she would have canceled it. But of course, the traditional Al-Akhtum gathering was even more important this year as her family needed to meet the crown prince of Dahaar and understand that he was now an integral part of Siyaad's politics.

Only she had left Dahaara without waiting to know if Prince Ayaan could fit it into his busy schedule or not.

There was something about being near him, even for a limited time, that unsettled her. Something that had burrowed beneath her skin and refused to dislodge. And it wasn't just the explosive desire that he had let her see.

By sheer force of will, she forced a smile as another of her father's cousins took in her attire from top to toe and made his displeasure the known. Although she wore a designer pantsuit with a long-sleeved jacket that covered up every inch of skin, it was still not the traditional caftan that Siyaadi women wore.

She'd heard the whispers behind her father's back, seen the sneers beneath the smiles, felt their snubs for eleven years. But her wedding the future king of Dahaar and the absence of her father today meant the claws that were usually sheathed were now out.

She could just imagine the whispers if Ayaan let her go in a few years. Whether her father was alive or not, whether Wasim was crowned the prince or not, her life would not change.

Would she resent Wasim and Saira as the years went on because her love for them held her back? Shuttling between Siyaad and Dahaar, a daughter but not a true one, a wife but not a true one. Nothing in her life held any significance, not to her, not to anyone else.

She was so tired of having no one to laugh with, no one she could even call a friend, of living each day with no sense of purpose or hope for a fleck of future happiness.

The depth of her loneliness choked her.

Zohra stiffened as the son of her father's cousin, Karim, came to a stop beside her. He was the most vicious of them all, hungry for the power of the throne, unhappy that her father had formed an alliance with Dahaar.

He blocked her against the table and leaned in a little too close.

"My sympathies, Zohra." The false sympathy in Karim's words coupled with that ever-present seediness made the hairs on her neck stand to attention. She knew what he thought of her. Easy. Whether it was the accident of her birth or the fact that she didn't simper and bow like a traditional Siyaadi woman didn't matter.

"I knew this would happen," Karim said, standing scandalously close. "I warned Uncle Salim that no one could be expected to accept *you* as his wife, even the Mad Prince."

Her stomach churned just hearing Ayaan spoken of like that. "You're not fit to utter his name."

Shaking his head, he smiled. "Tell me, Zohra. Why

did he parcel you back to Siyaad after only three weeks of marriage? Has he already figured out you are...*unfit* to be even a madman's wife?" He made a tsk-tsk sound that scraped her nerves. A deathly silence fell around her. Could everyone hear the filthy words that fell from his mouth? "Is this because he discovered you are the result of your mother's affair with a married man or because he has discovered your own...*adventures* into love?"

The not-so-veiled threat in his gaze curled into dread she couldn't shake. That her past could sully Prince Ayaan's family's name sent feral fear pulsing through her. Not when he had been nothing but honorable toward her, offered her nothing but respect. Ayaan had challenged her, pushed her buttons, surprised her with his sense of humor, but not once had he treated her with anything but honor. The realization stupefied her even as Karim leaned in closer.

"All I ask is that we be mutually beneficial to each other." Bile scratched her throat. "And remember, Zohra, I am always here when you need comfort, comfort that the Mad Prince should be—"

Long fingers that looked extremely familiar curled around Karim's shoulder, cutting off his words. Zohra turned so hard that she had to grab the table behind her to keep her balance.

Ayaan stood next to her, cold fury stamped over his features. He bent his head toward Karim, but his gaze collided with her own, unasked questions in its golden depths. "Stand within a mile radius of my wife again and you will regret it. Deeply."

He hadn't spoken loudly yet his voice carried around the room. The color fled from Karim's face, leaving pasty whiteness beneath the dark skin. "Prince Ayaan, allow me to welcome—"

"Run as fast as you can, Karim."

The older man cast one last look at her and left the hall. Prickly silence shrouded the hall. Zohra breathed hard, her gut twisting and untwisting.

When had she become everything she detested? A useless princess waiting for her prince to do the saving?

She had known there was a chance Ayaan would be here. But she had been so caught up in her own misery to answer Karim back.

And now she was beholden a little more to the man she wanted to maintain distance from.

Standing so close that she could smell the scent of his skin beneath his faint cologne, Ayaan clasped her wrist gently. Their gazes met and held, the ever-present currents of desire arching into life. She could see the puckered scar over his eyebrow, hear the slightly altered tempo of his breathing.

His gaze missed nothing, the banked need in it reaching out to her. "Are you okay, Princess?"

This isn't about you, Zohra reminded herself sternly. If she had learned one thing in three weeks of marriage, it was that Ayaan bin Riyaaz Al-Sharif would have come to any woman's aid in the same situation. Honor was in his blood.

"I am fine," she finally managed to mumble. "And please, will you stop calling me that?"

He bent closer to her, the whole room watching them with bated breath. His brows pulled together, his gaze held a question.

"If you are waiting for me to thank you for coming to my aid so heroically," she said jerkily, hating that the crushing loneliness she had felt mere minutes ago disappeared in his presence, "you will be waiting for a while."

Leaning against the table by her side, he folded his hands. "Would you like to leave?"

She blinked. He was smiling. It was a wacky, co-conspirators kind of smile that barely curved his mouth. And yet it was there. The beauty of it was enough to scramble her already frazzled wits. "I...You are here to bestow all these people with the gloriousness of your exalted presence." She looked around the hall. "Leaving now would hardly accomplish that goal."

He turned away from her and she took the chance to study him greedily.

He wore black jeans and a white, long-sleeved tunic with a Nehru collar, handspun with the utmost care by the craftswomen in a small village near Dahaara specifically for their prince. The sleeves were folded to just below his elbows, a gold-plated watch adorning his wrist.

The collar was open at the neck, giving her a view of a strip of golden bronze skin. Feeling a flush creep up her neck, she turned away.

He was the most casually dressed man in the hall and yet a thrumming energy vibrated around him. It was a cruel joke indeed that he didn't realize the sense of power he wielded with his very presence. And it had nothing to do with being a prince either. From all the stories she had heard from his mother, Zohra knew he had once been laid-back, the one who had made everyone laugh, the one who had been the palace staff's favorite.

But he was more than that boy had ever been. Whether it was the torture he had been through or the responsibilities that lay on his shoulders now, Prince Ayaan was a formidable force in his own right.

He extended his hand toward her, palm up, cutting through her thoughts. She stared at the long fingers that always felt sinfully abrasive against her skin. "Princess?"

She raised her head and his gaze drank her in hungrily, as though he had been just as starved for the sight of her as she had been of him. "What is the point of being the Mad Prince if you can't at least postpone meeting the people you dislike?"

She laughed. The exaggerated arrogance in his gaze, the to-hell-with-it attitude of his words, it was knee-buckling. This was how he must have been before he had been captured.

A cocky, fun-loving prince who had been loved by everyone.

He straightened, his gaze unmoving from her face. "Why didn't you shut his filthy mouth?"

What could she say? That being amid her father's family made her feel like a lost and heartbroken thirteen-year-old girl again? That they had a way of punching her in the gut with the saddest truth of her life?

She didn't belong anywhere.

"You're the daughter of a king, wife to a crown prince. And more than that, you are…" Her heart crawled into her throat as he raked his gaze over her, "…*you,* Zohra."

You are…you, Zohra.

He hadn't mocked her or called her princess.

His words washed over years of hurt, warming the cold, hard pain that had become a part of her. Her heart swelled, even the shadow of Karim's words, the bitterness of being here couldn't dilute what Ayaan's simple words meant to her.

Blinking back tears, she placed her hand in his. Her steps faltered, the strong clasp of his fingers around hers felt incredibly good, in more than one way.

She held her head high. It was borrowed courage, she knew that. But in that moment, she took everything the man next to her lent her.

The aunts and uncles and cousins were people who were related to her by blood, who should have been a source of comfort to a grieving girl but saw nothing past the circumstances of her birth. She finally had a chance to turn her back on them.

The moment they entered the corridor, the walls lined with portraits of the esteemed ancestors of the Al-Akhtum family, he stopped her. "I want an answer to my question, which you very cleverly evaded."

She shrugged. "They have called me names for eleven years, much nastier than today. Nothing I say or do today is going to change that. My stepmother's family hates me because I represent the pain my father caused her. And now they think I have stolen Saira's chance to be the queen of Dahaar. To my father's family…I am nothing but a taint on their lineage, a taint he dared bring to Siyaad. My father is responsible for whatever I face today."

"Does he know how they speak to you?"

"What would he do even if he did? Go back in time and stop having an eight-year-long affair with my mother? Change his mind about walking out on her when it was time to be king? Change his mind about taking custody of his bastard?"

His fingers tightened over her arms. "Stop referring to yourself as that."

She felt a hot sting at the back of her eyes. She was not going to cry just because someone finally had a glimpse into what eleven years of her life had been. She didn't need his pity. It only weakened her. "Powerful as you are, you cannot change the truth."

"What about the threat that Karim made? This man you were involved with…do I need to find Faisal? Is he the kind to—"

Foreboding inched tight across her skin. "How do you know his name?"

"You are my wife. Knowing everything about you, especially—"

"Especially what?" she said, swallowing the distaste his words brought back.

His expression intractable, his aristocratic features reminiscent of centuries of powerful lineage, he was every inch the arrogant prince in that moment. "Especially anything that could come back and cast a bad light on you and Dahaar, I have to know about it. I have to be prepared."

The same past that she had shamelessly used to try and get out of this marriage to him now curdled in her stomach. "Are you regretting your decision to not listen to me when I warned you? Wondering if you should sever all ties with me and leave me here in Siyaad?"

"I made my vows. Nothing will make me turn my back on them."

His words cut through her sharper than if he had said he had regrets. "Of course, your blasted word. Nothing in the world is allowed to interfere with it. How much detail do you want? How I met Faisal? Why I fell for him? How many times he—"

He thrust his face closer, bracing his hands on the wall on either side of her. His breath fanned against her skin. "My lucidity is nothing but the barest veil over my madness as you very well know, Princess." His words were low, gravelly, and instead of scaring her, they incited the most dangerous tingle in her blood. "Do not provoke me. You don't want to see what an animal I can become." He pushed back from the wall, as though he found her nearness suddenly distasteful. "All I need to know is if he is a threat."

She laughed, bitterness tinged into the sound. "He is not. I'm not the woman he wanted me to be."

His frown deepened. "You're pining after a man who cared

about the circumstances of your birth? I'm disappointed in you, Princess."

She shook her head. It was tragic how she was surrounded by men with highest codes of honor and yet they inevitably hurt her. "He didn't. As luck would have it, Faisal was nothing if not full of honor. When he learned who I was, he thought I should be grateful that my father acknowledged me as his daughter. He thought I should become this paragon of virtue and spend the rest of my life proving to Siyaad and its people that I was worthy of being a princess.

"He thought I should embrace my duty. He wanted to live in Siyaad, wanted to earn a place by my father....the list was endless. When I suggested we leave Siyaad as he had been planning before he met me, he looked at me as though I had committed the greatest sin. He left without saying goodbye."

The corridor echoed with the bitterness in her words, the silence filling up with her anger.

"Then you're the one responsible, aren't you?" he said, a hard edge to his words. "Not your father, or anyone else. *You* ruined your happiness."

A dark fear inched its fingers around her heart. "All I wanted was to leave this place," she said, speaking past the thick lump in her throat. "I would have gone anywhere with him."

"Maybe he realized your hatred for this life was more than your love for him? That he was just the excuse you needed to finally leave?" Ayaan delivered the words with a quiet ruthlessness, leaving her with nothing to hide under.

"Why are you being deliberately cruel?" she said, tears coating her throat.

His mouth curved, a bitter mockery of a smile. "I am returning a favor. Truth. It is the only real thing between us, isn't it? You tell me the truth that everyone else around me is too scared to voice for fear of making me mad again, and I do the same.

"If you had truly loved him, Princess, would it have been such a hardship to live with him in Siyaad?"

She shook where she stood, everything inside her balling up into an unbearable knot in her stomach. Ayaan became a blurry form as he turned away.

She had been so angry with Faisal for not taking her away, so heartbroken that he would put her status in Siyaad, and all it entailed, before her.

I won't be the one who will steal you away from your fate, Zohra. Those had been Faisal's words.

She grabbed the wall behind her, knees shaking under her.

Can you not view it as anything but a sacrifice?

Her father's words pricked her. Was she, once again, clinging to her stubborn anger and letting life pass her by? Was she going to spend the rest of her life waiting for someone to save her, as Ayaan had done just now, instead of saving herself?

CHAPTER SEVEN

AYAAN LEANED AGAINST the hip-length wall on the roof terrace, letting the peace and quiet steal into him. But even with the rooftop lit up, the dark black of the night seeped into his blood, working its shadows on him. He hadn't seen Zohra after yesterday, not even at the dinner with her family just now.

He hadn't wanted to inquire after her in front of King Salim and upset his already frail health. But after seeing the pain she hid from her father, the utter loneliness he had spied in her gaze, he didn't want to leave for Dahaar without seeing her.

He should have kept quiet about the man she had loved. But he had told her the bitter truth. Because the alternative had been to let her believe that she hadn't been loved. And he just couldn't do that.

A wave of possessiveness, selfish and unyielding, hit him hard. Did she still love that man? Was she even now bemoaning his loss somewhere in the palace?

His unwilling wife had left an indelible mark on the palace in just a few days, and more importantly, on his life.

In such a short space of time, Zohra had seen the truth, while his mother and he had struggled, danced around the issue, caused each other immense pain because they had each thought they were doing the best for the other.

Ayaan had endured the torment of seeing his brother's things, the medals from his military service, his degrees, the sword he had been presented, he even lived in the wing that had been specifically designed for Azeez when he had been crowned.

Because he hadn't wanted to hurt his mother.

But he couldn't bear it anymore, not when being near them stifled the breath out of him. So he had finally told her last night.

Ayaan had stood stiffly at the entrance to the day lounge she used, like one of the old iron-armored soldiers that adorned the palace, unable to move, unable to look into her eyes, terrified that she would touch him or even worse embrace him.

She had come to stand by him, and stopped suddenly as though realizing what her nearness did to him. "I will arrange a different wing for Zohra and you, away from the old ones. I only...want you to be happy, Ayaan."

To which he had nodded, incapable of answering, and walked away without a backward glance. Even though, for once, he hadn't felt like a pale shadow of his brother, hadn't felt the ball of guilt around his neck.

There were still things unsaid between them; her grief and his isolation were indefensible walls. But in that moment for the first time in eight months, the tight band around his chest had eased a little.

And he owed it to Zohra.

Every time he saw her, a little bit of his hold on himself loosened, forever vanished in the face of his escalating need to touch her. The need to feel like he could connect with at least one person in the world, to feel like he wasn't one man standing in the midst of a desert, alone. It was a dangerously seductive need.

Which was why he was standing here, waiting for his errant wife instead of on his way back to Dahaar.

He looked up as she appeared on the other side of the roof. A long-sleeved white shirt hugged her upper body, tucked into cream-colored jodhpurs. The outline of her torso, the long line of her thighs made his mouth dry up.

There was a strain on her features which fractured the mask of strength she donned so easily. She had left for Siyaad without a word to him, exactly as they had agreed. But her sudden disappearance had rankled more than he liked.

She stayed there, her gaze widening gradually.

He looked around, noticing what she saw. The rooftop glittered with hundreds of tiny, artistic lanterns lighting up the vast expanse, throwing orange packets of light everywhere.

A small table stood at the center of it, a traditional one of low height. A myriad of desserts sat atop it on silver plates, a silver jug with intricate patterns next to it. Two divans with plump cushions were placed either side of the table.

It looked incredibly romantic. A setting he himself would have orchestrated in another life. And he hadn't noticed it until Zohra had joined him, as if she was the only one who could awaken things in him that were not for mere survival.

He reached her side and leaned against the wall, smiling at the stiff way she held herself.

Finally, she met his gaze, extreme wariness in hers. "What is all this?"

"I asked Saira to summon you here to meet me. And that we were not to be disturbed." He looked around himself. "Apparently, Saira has a very active imagination."

"And I have no idea how to wake her up to reality," she said, shaking her head.

"Is it so unbelievable that for Saira, this life, this reality might not be so bad, Princess? Amira's wedding had been arranged, too. And I know that she was extremely happy. If you love Saira, you have to accept her reality, too."

She nodded without argument, her expression thoughtful.

"How long are you staying in Siyaad?" He hadn't realized he even wanted to know until the words left his mouth.

She frowned. "I checked with your assistant *and* mine before I left. There were no state functions or ceremonies that needed my—"

He cut her short, irritated with himself. "It was a casual question."

"Oh." Her frown didn't ease. "I thought you were flying back to Dahaara before…nightfall."

Her unspoken concern lingered between them. She knew what new surroundings did to him at night. "I will leave early morning tomorrow."

"Another night you will just forego sleep then?"

So she was aware that he had taken to skipping sleep for days together. He stayed silent, refusing to be baited into an argument.

The silence stretched between them.

"Was there a reason you *summoned* me here, Prince Ayaan? More interrogation about—"

He grabbed her arm and turned her toward him. "I never want him mentioned again, Princess, *ever*," he said, enunciating his words through gritted teeth. "Is that clear?"

She nodded, surprising him again. She was definitely acting strangely tonight and he didn't have to think too much to figure out why. "Why do you do that?" he said, fighting the flare of anger at her actions.

"Do what?"

"Call me *Prince Ayaan*? Address me as if we were…"

She quirked an eyebrow, the stubborn jut of her chin more pronounced.

"As if you were a stranger who hasn't seen me at my worst, as if you are not the one person who sees past the prince to the co—" She halted his words with her finger on his mouth, shaking her head. He pulled it away, accepting the very fact he had been fighting for three weeks. "As if you were a lowly servant instead of my wife, my equal."

Her eyes went wide, her mouth trembled. And his curiosity about her multiplied. *Why did she look so surprised?* "And I didn't realize I needed a reason to see my own wife," he said, uneasy with her uncharacteristic silence.

His gaze fell on her hair, and instantly the long, silky length of it draped over his pillow flashed in his mind. It was an image that teased him constantly. "Do I need one to tell her that she looks striking?"

She blinked, color seeping under her skin. She didn't smile though and he wanted to be the one who put it there. For one evening, he wanted to pretend that there was nothing wrong in his life.

He picked up the thin envelope he had left on the table and handed it to her.

She looked at his hand as if he had sprouted claws.

"My mother reminded me of another custom I didn't keep. The groom's gift to the bride."

She looked up at him, her gaze softening. "You spoke to her?"

He cleared the knot of emotion from his throat and nodded. "Mostly she did. But I said a few words, too."

A quiet joy lit up her eyes, her mouth curving into a wide smile. "That's…wonderful. She must have been ecstatic."

She grasped his hands with hers, and a longing of the

most intense kind swirled into life inside him. His gaze stayed on their hands, his throat dry.

She looked down at their hands and stilled. The tension around them could have detonated with the smallest spark. She slowly pulled her hands back as though afraid of just that, but he felt the tremor that went through her.

He leaned back against the wall, and after a second's pause, she did the same at his side. "You like her," he said, surprised. "Even with all the rituals she makes you go through."

She stretched her arms across the wall, a thoughtful expression on her face. The movement stretched the white shirt tight across her breasts and he looked away guiltily. "It's hard not to like her. She is so…strong. She bears so many responsibilities, she has been through so much and yet, through it all…" She cleared her throat. "She's your father's strength too, isn't she? She doesn't let him rule over her. With her by his side, I'm not surprised he was able to weather everything he has with such dignity."

Ayaan had always thought of his father as the strong one. Not that he thought his mother weak. To Ayaan, she was a woman, a mother and nothing more. And yet no one would have been able to stay standing after what had happened five years ago, but his father had kept going.

Because he'd had his wife. And he had taken on immense pain by lying to her. Zohra might not understand it but Ayaan understood why his father had done it.

When you had something or someone so precious, you had to protect her from any pain. In a different reality, he…

He quashed the thought before it could take form. *This night, these stolen moments with her, this was his reality.*

Even this was wrong. But for one night, he didn't want to be honorable.

He wanted to be just Ayaan. Not the son of grieving parents, not a shadow left behind of a beloved brother, not the wrong man to have survived, not the crown prince who was choking under the joy of his people.

He pulled up her hand and placed the envelope in her palm. "This is more of a thank-you than a ritualistic gift."

She took it with trembling hands, the envelope slipping from her grip. He held her fingers in a steadying grip and heard the slight catch in her breath. His own breathing balled up in his throat. She turned it over and over in her hands.

"After a few unsuccessful ideas, I called Saira," he said, to puncture the seductive allure of the silence, to fight the intimacy the evening weaved upon them. "Luckily, she informed me you had no love for jewelry before I settled on a behemoth rock."

Whatever lingered on her lips never found a voice. She opened the seal and the small slip of paper fluttered in her hands. She scanned it quickly, a frown knotting her brows. "What is this?"

"Your itinerary. Saira told me how much you'd always wanted to see Monaco."

Shock widened her beautiful eyes. "My father refused to let me go and I didn't have enough money to go on my own."

"Maybe he was worried you wouldn't come back." Suddenly, he couldn't imagine this world, *his world,* without her. Unease skittered up his spine.

"I turned eighteen six years ago and I have American citizenship. I have a little money to my name and an uncle who lives in Boston. If I had truly wanted to leave, I think I would have left by now." She frowned, as if realizing the import of her own words.

"So...." she swallowed visibly, "this is a trip to Monaco?"

A thread of hope whispered in those words. Utter satisfaction swept through him.

"In ten days, I am heading into the desert for the annual tribal conference." He spoke the words almost without choking. That in itself was a victory. "You can leave for Monaco that same day in a private jet. A family friend will greet you there and take you to the resort we own. My parents have been informed. You will have a security detail. You have a week to yourself, Princess. Without obligations, duties or anything royalty related. The only condition—"

"I won't bring shame upon Dahaar," she whispered.

He turned her around, something in her tone tugging at him. She didn't sound happy, or surprised. She sounded utterly crushed. "I know that it's not exactly the lifetime of freedom that you want, but—"

She moved closer to him, and placed her finger on his mouth. The simple touch pinged along his nerve endings, making him aware of every inch of his own skin. "It's the most thoughtful gift anyone's ever given me."

Her gaze shone with unshed tears, more beautiful than the precious gems he had perused last week. He clasped her face with his hands. "They why do you have tears in your eyes, Princess?"

She clasped his wrists, and smiled through the tears. It was filled with such bleakness, such heart-wrenching desolation that his heart constricted. He waited for an answer that never came.

He could handle the Zohra that was all fire and attitude but this…this hurting, vulnerable Zohra, this he couldn't handle. He couldn't bear to be near because he couldn't *not* touch, *not* comfort. And the comfort he wanted to offer took only one form.

It shook him from within, this need to taste her mouth, to crush her against him.

He backed up against the wall just as she turned toward him, testing his will to the last frayed edge. Before he could blink, she was standing close, too close. He could see himself in her eyes, could see the blue shadows under them and worst of all, he could see the ache in her eyes. Her hands found purchase in his. Her body tilted forward and he was incapable of moving away.

He swallowed, assaulted by an avalanche of sensations and desires. The scent of her bound him to her effortlessly, the whisper of her body's heat sparking an inferno in his. He closed his eyes, willing himself to do the right thing.

She rose up on tiptoes, curled her hands on his chest and kissed him on his cheek.

The touch of her soft lips, the accompanying murmur of *thank you*, the brush of her body against his, and he became unraveled. It was a moment he wouldn't forget in ten lifetimes; a sensation that seeped into his very cells.

The hunger he had been denying himself roared into life with a vengeance. He gripped her nape with his fingers, dragged her against his body and found her mouth with his.

Sparks of pleasure ignited inside him.

Her mouth was so soft, her shocked gasp lost in the friction between their lips. He licked her lower lip and it went straight to his groin. His blood roared in his ears.

He deepened the kiss, forcing her to open up to him and she did. Her surprise lasted maybe two seconds and then she was kissing him back with the same frayed edge of need.

She tasted like everything he had imagined, like sunshine and light, like an oasis in the desert. He worshipped her mouth with his own, his hunger for more burning through him like a wildfire. The graze of her breasts against his chest shredded the last edge of his control.

Grasping her by the waist, he tugged her up until not even a whisper of air could come between their bodies, until every inch of him was trembling, feverish with the need to possess, to consume, to...

He filed away every little sound she made, filed away the feel of her body trembling with pleasure, filed the erotic hunger that swept through him as he stroked her tongue. This taste of her, this feel of her, it had to be enough to root his sanity in ten days.

Zohra felt dizzy with the powerful sensations flooding through her. It was a scorching heat that threatened to turn her inside out, an aching need that began pulsing between her legs.

The taste of Ayaan exploded in her mouth, her whole world reduced to him.

The ground felt like it had been stolen from under her. Her hands laced together around his neck, and she realized she was off the ground.

The assault of his mouth was relentless, stealing her breath and infusing it with his own. Pleasure and pain fused together, rippled out of her in a guttural sound as he tugged her lower lip with his teeth.

His hands around her waist loosened, moved up and down over her back. A string of Arabic fell from his mouth and she realized he wanted to soothe her.

Except she didn't want to be soothed. She wanted to be ravaged, she wanted to forget her own mind, she wanted to...she burned with escalating need everywhere he touched her.

In return, she sank her fingers into his hair, and pressed herself closer, angling her mouth, giving him everything he wanted and more.

One hand at her back pressed her hard against him, one at her nape so that she didn't move, every hard muscle, every ridge and hollow of his body imprinted itself over her, branding her. The hard ridge of his erection rubbed against her belly and a lick of sinful heat bloomed low within her.

His groan surrounded them when she moved restlessly.

His lips learned every inch of her, deep, languorous strokes on one breath, biting and sucking the next. Reverent one minute, passionate and possessive the next. Just when she thought she would expire from the sinful heat his kiss evoked, his mouth left hers and moved toward her jaw.

His hands traveled feverishly over her waist, her back, her name falling from his lips.

She shivered uncontrollably. Her heart pounded, every beat of it a whispered warning.

She wanted to let him fill the hole she had found in her life yesterday. She had already been feeling vulnerable after what Karim had said, and what Ayaan had made her face about Faisal.

But it was Ayaan's gift that crystallized everything for her. This was what her future was going to be—dream holidays with no one by her side.

This loneliness, it was going to be there forever, shriveling her from the inside out. Her future stretched out endlessly with no lasting attachments, no purpose.

The need to find comfort in his arms, to lose herself in his touch, it scraped her raw. She was no more real to him than she was to anyone in her life. But she didn't want to care. She wanted to use him just as he was using her.

She kissed him back with every pent-up longing inside her. Tugging her mouth away from his, she ran her hands over his chest, feeling the solid, hard muscles tighten painfully at her touch.

His mouth found the pulse at the base of her neck. She threw her head back and groaned when he nipped the skin with his teeth. He traced the spot with his thumb, licked it with his tongue.

His fingers moved over her neck, to the slight opening of her shirt. His tongue laved at her lower lip again, and his hand covered her breast, the tips of his fingers splayed against the shape.

She jerked, a pang of delicious need shooting down between her legs.

He didn't move his hand farther, his harsh breaths the only sounds around them. His lips caressed her neck, breathing words into her very cells. "You are turning me inside out, Zohra."

Her name on his mouth, the ragged edge of need in it was an intimate caress, a crack in the fortress around him.

She clasped her fingers around his wrist, and held his palm over her breast, needing the pleasure only he could give. She pushed herself into his touch, shuddering as the tip of his finger grazed her taut nipple. Need knotted there.

His hand tightened over her breast and she moaned.

Before she could draw a much-needed breath, she felt the air around her turn chilly, felt the sharp sting of his retreat.

His cheekbones were flushed with color under the olive skin, his eyes hazy with desire. His chest rose and fell with each breath. His fingers held her with a hard grip. The first sign that not every aspect of him was under control.

Except, he released her and stepped back. Her gut tensed.

She moved closer to him again, every sense alive, as though waking from a long slumber. "Don't call it a mistake."

He didn't. The bleakness in his gaze, the tension simmering around him said it all. "I should not have stayed back or asked to see you." He ran a hand through his hair, palpable rage vibrating beneath his jerky movements. "It will not happen again."

"I have never met another man who detested himself more for what he is, for possessing the smallest weakness. Despite your best efforts, you are a man, not God. There is a limit to how much you can rise above a man's needs and desires."

"*God*...Zohra? I am barely even a man."

"*By whose standards?* Will you forever measure yourself against your brother?"

A muscle tightened in his jaw, his gaze flashing absolute fury. "Don't. You. Dare. Mention. Him."

Zohra backed down. She couldn't bear to see the anguish in his expression. She took his fist in her hands, unclenching his long fingers one by one.

Ayaan closed his eyes, unable to think with her hand in his. Her skin was soft against his, her fingers trembling. He shivered, every cell in him hungering for her, to touch and shape every rise and dip of her body, to give in to what both of them wanted. Would she be that soft everywhere? Would she welcome his touch everywhere as eagerly as she had enjoyed his kiss? Would she be shocked at all the ways he thought of having her?

"You like being near me, you like touching me," she said, the boldness she sought not hiding the little shiver spewing into her words. "That's why you are here. You made a conscious decision, didn't you, Ayaan?"

He drew a ragged breath in, realized why she had never uttered his name. His name on her lips sounded like an intimate caress that crossed an invisible boundary that neither of them had wanted to breach.

"Tonight you decided to indulge yourself. But tomorrow you will despise yourself for taking this moment. You can't even bear to look at me."

He snatched his hand back, shock robbing him of speech. Every word she said could have been plucked out of his mind. Almost as though she had a direct line to his thoughts.

Self-loathing pounded through him in waves, but not enough to hide the sharp pulse of fear beneath. He had thought to enjoy an hour in her company. But the truth of his hunger for her was far more lethal.

She had somehow become his only way out of a crushing isolation, the one person he sought out instead of running away from, the one person who made him crave normal things even as she brought his darkest fears to the surface.

"If you are saying I came here planning to kiss you—"

"You didn't but it happened. You find comfort near me." She shrugged, reducing his earth-shattering need for her into something inconsequential. "I don't even care that it has nothing to do with me."

How could she be so alluring and frustrating at the same time, so damn perceptive and thickheaded that he wanted to shake her? He fisted his hands at his sides. He would not touch her again. He had done enough harm. "You think the fact that I am drawn to you has nothing to do with you?"

"I'm beginning to see what a clever, cunning man my father is, beginning to understand what Karim meant," she said, shaking her head. "If you were a different man, one not plagued by the atrocities you had to endure, you wouldn't have looked at me, much less married me. But like you said, reality is better if one accepts it. I am beginning to see how miserable I have made myself by not doing that.

"I have been alone for eleven years. I have no friends,

no one to lean on, no one to tell me that I am ruining my own happiness."

She was thinking of the man she had loved and there was nothing he could do to stop it. She moved toward him again and he braced himself. As if she were a knife that could tear into his flesh, a bullet that could lodge under his muscle.

When had this slip of a woman gained so much power over him? How?

She met his gaze, a quiet strength emanating from the very way she held herself. "I have no strength left anymore to be alone, to beat my head against things I cannot change."

He felt spine-tingling cold. There was no other word for the chill that suddenly permeated him inside out. "Zohra... don't."

"I can't go back to Siyaad as a cast-off wife. I can't spend the rest of my life among those people…not even for Wasim and Saira. Neither can I turn my back on them. Which means…this life with you is the only option left to me. And I am not going to fight it anymore."

"You have chosen a hell of a time to stop fighting your fate. Except nothing has changed here," he said, jabbing his temple.

Her gaze was unrelentingly stubborn. The knot in his gut tightened another notch. "I have seen what you think is your weakness and I have not run away. You do not see me as someone tainted. Isn't that enough of a start?"

Anger roiled through him, turning his very blood into bitter poison. "You want to be my wife and play happy family? You want to lie down next to me at night when I devolve into nothing but an animal scared of its own shadow? You want to bear the children of a man who is a disgrace on the very name of his ancestors?"

He hated her at that moment, hated that she was not a traditional kind of woman who wouldn't have dared question his actions, hated that she was a constant reminder of everything he couldn't have, hated that she dared to call him out on his weakness.

"Do you want to strip the last thread of dignity from me?" he shouted, his throat hoarse.

She pushed at his chest, her lithe form shaking from head to toe. Even in her studied indifference toward their relationship, she had been temptation personified. Now she felt like a powerful sandstorm that could bury him beneath the weight of his own needs and desires.

"Is your dignity more precious than living your life? I'm not talking about love and rainbows, Ayaan. In this life, I know that there is no place for anything but duty. And I'm making my peace with that. You came to my rescue, you promised to ruin Karim for what he said to me today. Why can't I—"

His blood still boiled with remembered rage. "You are my wife. Your honor is my honor. I will ruin any man who looks at you wrong, who dares to insult you."

"Can't you see how unique that very statement is in my life? No one has ever looked at me the way you do, as someone worthy of honor, of respect. You are entitled to all that and I'm not? If I can be of help to you, if I can—"

"You think you can save me? That all it takes is for me to open myself to you, to lose myself in your body and I will magically be a whole man?"

"You are a ticking bomb. You barely sleep, you are killing yourself with that physical regimen, you work hours that no sane man does. If you find a minute's comfort in being with me, in…touching me, I am…"

"You will let me into your bed knowing that I'm just using you?" he asked, making his words as insulting and mocking as he could, falling lower than the scum who had insulted her, "Knowing that you won't mean anything more than a willing body to me, knowing that I will never love you?"

She met his gaze unflinchingly, the resolve in her eyes unbroken. "I don't care. I want to have a purpose to my life. I want to…belong in Dahaar."

He shivered where he stood, ice-cold fingers clamped around his spine. "Forgive me, Princess. But I am not one of the projects you take up to fix."

"Then don't touch me ever again. I mean it, Ayaan. No rituals, no gifts, no gestures for the sake of the damned public, I don't even want to breathe the same air as you."

He moved closer to her and she stilled, as if she was gathering herself into a tight ball so that not even his shadow touched her.

Desire was a deafening drumbeat in his very veins.

Had she any idea how much she had worsened his torment by making that offer, how much he wanted to let go of the little honor he had and possess her? How every cell in him wanted a taste of the escape she offered, how much he wanted to steal a moment's pleasure, seek a moment's peace with her?

Because that's what her presence gave him. An irresistible combination of pleasure and peace, except it came with a very high price.

"All or nothing, Zohra? And if I don't agree? If I continue to touch you and kiss you whenever I want without agreeing to your ridiculous proposal?" And he wanted to. He wanted to take the little he needed without guilt cloying him, without regret scouring him. "We both know all it takes is for us to lay eyes on each other to feel it."

"But you won't, will you? You're furious that I dared change the rules on you." A lone tear trailed down one cheek and she wiped it away roughly. "I might know nothing about traditions and customs. But I know a little about honorable men, about men bound by duty, men like my father and you." Bitterness poured out of every word she uttered. "You would rather see the people around you suffer than violate your esteemed principles. You will no more let yourself touch me again than you will realize that you are so much more than the memory of a man long gone."

CHAPTER EIGHT

AYAAN STARTLED, WIDE-AWAKE, sweat beading on his fore-head, the bed sheets tangled around his legs. He pulled on his sweatpants and walked to the veranda of his new suite.

The sky was gray, with dawn's first light still a little while away. But he could see the hubbub of activity that had begun near the helipad in the grounds behind the palace. The cold air chafed his bare chest and face, settling deep into his pores. But he couldn't move.

Ground lights illuminated the path, while the lights of buggies used to transport luggage lit the path to the helipad.

One week, all he had to do was to spend one week in the clutches of the desert, in the very place where they had been attacked, where he had seen his brother and sister fall.

Fear fisted his stomach with cold, hard fingers, choking his breath. He gripped the metal balustrade with tight knuckles, reminding himself to breathe through it. It was just his mind playing tricks on him.

But nothing helped. Instead of fighting it, he gave in to the shivers quaking through him and slid to the ground.

He was the crown prince of Dahaar, second son of King Malik Aslam Al-Sharif, a descendant of the Al-Sharifs who had ruled over Dahaar and the desert for ten centuries. Their history was rich, violent, immersed with stories of men who had conquered the desert in all its harsh glory, who had found a way to survive in its unforgiving climate and created a livelihood for their families and tribes.

And he, Ayaan bin Riyaaz Al-Sharif quaked with fear at the thought of a journey into the desert. Shame pounded through his blood.

The conference hadn't happened in six years. One more year would not matter, his father had said, concern softening his shrewd eyes.

And Ayaan had indulged the idea, had felt relief at the temporary reprieve. Until he had seen the one woman whose very presence reminded him of every weakness he couldn't defeat, taunted him with the offer he couldn't accept.

Zohra.

Neither could he wipe the memory of how she tasted. She was a madness in his blood, rivaling the one in his mind.

How many things would he put off, how many duties would he postpone because he feared he was not enough, because he was afraid of what might push him that last step into the darkness waiting for him? He couldn't stand it anymore. He had to know, he had to try, even if he fell over the cliff. He had lost everything in the desert, he had lost himself, but he couldn't let it take any more from him. When he looked at Zohra next, he wanted to have the knowledge of at least having tried, even if he failed.

Or history might as well erase his name from the majestic Al-Sharif dynasty.

Zohra hugged herself tight, shifting from one foot to the other. Her long-sleeved tunic and leggings underneath would be too warm in the desert sun, but even with the pashmina she had wrapped around herself, it was not enough for the early morning chill.

She blinked as the wind buffeted her from both sides. The idea of spending a week in the desert, amid strangers with only Ayaan for company was enough to turn her inside out.

But she couldn't just wait around, wondering if she would ever be able to break from this life, wondering if she would ever have something reaching normal. So she had contacted her old organization and taken on a new project. Meeting the tribal chiefs of Dahaar was an opportunity she couldn't pass up. Not even for Monaco.

"What are you doing here?"

She steeled her spine and turned. The guards and the maids waiting behind them watched Ayaan and her with a hungry curiosity that was becoming the norm.

His face a study in cold fury, Ayaan stood a few feet from her. The frost in his eyes could cut through her skin given half the chance.

"I'm waiting," she said, aware of the tremor in her voice. "Just as you are, for the captain to say that it's okay to board."

His hand clamped over her arm, his scowl fierce. She could feel every ridge, every groove of his fingers, heard the fracture in his harsh breathing. Her belly dipped and dived, the memory of how his mouth had devoured hers seared through her.

"Into the tent. Now, Zohra," he said, flicking his head at a small tent nearby.

Zohra followed him, glad that one of them was keeping an eye on propriety.

All of Dahaar was greedy for every little detail about him. His country loved him but it was also waiting with bated breath, wondering if he would lose it, wondering if their prince would descend into that pit of darkness from which he had risen.

Because even with the strictest confidentiality enforced in the palace, it was clear that their prince was spiraling, toward what no one knew. He worked at a ruthless pace that left normal, healthy people dropping in exhaustion, he was extremely rude to anyone who dared defy him, his relationship with his parents was strained.

He was like a wounded animal that was raring to maim and hurt anyone who dared come close.

Not that anyone could question his sanity or his decisions regarding Dahaar. Not after the past ten days where he had spent countless hours in negotiation with the Sheikh of Zuran building a strategy to counter the terrorist groups that were a threat to all three nations of Dahaar, Zuran and Siyaad. The same groups that had tortured him, that had killed his brother and sister. Not after two terrorist cells had been taken down in one month under his strategic planning.

The media had declared that he was a better statesman than his father was and speculated about the leaps of progress that Dahaar would make under his rule.

If he survived the year...

And standing on the sidelines, watching him push himself without interfering, Zohra had never felt more powerless, more useless.

The moment she entered the tent, he reached her. After ten days of keeping her distance, Zohra was starved for the sight of him.

"Believe me when I say this, Zohra. I have zero patience today. Now, why are you not on your way to Monaco?"

Zohra frowned. Tension radiated from him, the skin tugged tight over his lean features. "I decided to holiday later. Right now, I'm coming with you to the desert for the tribal conference."

"I know how much you have embraced your duty, Princess," he said, sarcasm dripping from his tone, "but let me tell you the truth. No one truly cares whether you are present or not."

His words cut to the weakest part of her. "True, but without me who will dare to tell you that the veneer of civilization is slipping, Your Arrogant Highness?"

"This is the first conference with our tribes in six years." His tone gentled, his gaze lingering over her in an almost pacifying way, the intense hunger in it belying his casual words. "If you are there, your safety will weigh on me."

She had never felt so aware of another person, so clued in to every nuance in a word they said, every gesture they made. She wanted to shake him and comfort him at the same time. "I'm not a stranger to desert life. I used to run a project in Siyaad that—"

"I know about your Awareness Projects, Zohra. You travel to the desert in teams and educate the tribes about basics—hygiene, disease, education, women's health."

"Then are you going back on your word and forbidding me from continuing my work, my life as before?"

He leaned close and her skin snapped to life. The faint scar on the top of his left eyebrow should have made him look flawed. Even just a little would have been fair. Instead, it only added to his powerful personality. "You would like that, wouldn't you? I think nothing would make you happier than if I became that arrogant bastard you envisaged that first night in Siyaad."

She swallowed past the knot in her throat. "If you turned into an arrogant jerk, and by the way you are halfway there, I wouldn't have to worry about you killing yourself.

I would be the merriest widow in the world, wouldn't I? All the freedom and none of the duties."

His mouth touched the corner of hers, and her knees wobbled. Molten heat prickled along her skin even as she cursed her betraying body. "Is Faisal going to be there, Zohra?" He whispered the words into her skin—an assault on her senses and a cutting insult all wrapped in one. "Is that why you are so eager to return to work?"

She pushed his hand from her, tears gathering in her eyes. "You think I proposed starting a life with you ten days ago and now am panting to see Faisal again? I guess you really are no different when it comes to what you think about me, are you, Ayaan?"

She turned away from him, hating the fact that he could wound her so easily. His opinions were beginning to matter too much, and yet she had no way to stop it.

Before she could take another step, he pulled her back to him. He held her loosely this time, his thumb catching the tears that threatened to fall. "*Ya Allah*, I'm not worthy of your tears, Zohra." The frost in his gaze thawed, his mouth lost the tightness. He ran a hand through his hair, looked around, as though searching for the right words. His gaze found her again, hungry, intense. "I spoke without thinking. That remark…it has nothing to do with you and everything to do with me. Please accept my apology."

The air left her lungs in a loud whoosh. "Then accept that I'm coming with you, Ayaan. I did nothing to violate our agreement in the past ten days. I stayed far away from you and believe me, it was a miracle in—"

"You exist, Zohra. That is torment enough for me."

Her heart skidded to a halt. His words spoken through gritted teeth were soft, and yet rang with a depth of emotion. The hungry intensity of his gaze was etched into her mind, the naked want in it inched its way around her heart.

He turned around and walked out.

Hugging herself hard, Zohra stared at his back. Familiar resentment flared at his dismissal. She should turn around, she had never ventured where she was not welcome before.

But she had also spent eleven years doing everything she could to prove that she cared nothing for Siyaad. Perversely, her every action had been shaped by the very thing she refused to be dictated by.

Nothing she had done had been because she'd wanted to do it. She had thought she had loved Faisal, that she hadn't fought back against her father's family because she'd never wanted a place among them, now…now she was not sure of anything.

But when it came to the man who had married her… she wanted to stand by him. Not because it was her duty, not because of what it would mean for her future. But because she wanted to.

It was a crystal clear sign in a sea of murky actions motivated by her anger toward her father, by years of hurt that she had nursed into bitterness.

She had no name for what drove her to it, she didn't even understand it.

But whatever demons haunted Ayaan, she would stand by his side while he battled them. For however long she could.

CHAPTER NINE

SITTING AROUND QUIETLY while Ayaan discussed important matters with the sheikhs of eight different tribes, dressed in an elaborate silk gown that weighed a ton, Zohra wondered what she had gotten herself into.

It was her own fault for talking herself into this trip at the last minute and jumping in without learning anything. She didn't wish she hadn't come, just that she had come armed with knowledge. Like why she was sitting on the biggest divan in the tent with her face hidden by a veil, being studiously ignored by everyone in the room.

The four times she had traveled to the desert encampments in Siyaad, she had been one of three women who had worked there. And no one, including Faisal, had known who she was in the beginning.

Which meant the tribal leaders had barely tolerated her and the other women, and only because their project had been authorized and funded by her father.

Everything had been completely different since Ayaan and she had arrived this morning. The fact that the future queen of Dahaar had graced them with her presence, something they had not been expecting, had thrown the tribal leaders into a hubbub of activity. And before she blinked again, the men had disappeared.

A velvet path had been laid out for her to walk on, and

smiling girls dressed in traditional Bedouin clothes had thrown rose petals on it. Her trembling hand in Ayaan's, Zohra had faltered. She had thought she would feel like a fake and yet, for the first time in her life, she was more excited than disinterested. Maybe because beneath all the fanfare, she was still going to do what she had always enjoyed or maybe because of the man standing next to her.

She had thought his anger over her presence would thaw. But instead, it felt as if she was sitting next to a volcano. Any minute, he was going to implode and she had no idea what would rip the shred of control that was holding him together.

From the cursory glance she had taken around her when they had arrived, she knew the tents were on scales of luxury she hadn't seen when she had traveled before. The campsite was designed around an oasis of native ghaf trees. About four Bedouin-style tents made of richly patterned lambs' wool were scattered around.

They had been immediately provided refreshments while women had arrived from the different tribes to welcome her. Within minutes, Ayaan disappeared leaving her under their care. When they had politely inquired if she was ready to listen to their requests, she had been shocked, even though it was what she had come for.

And so she had spent the afternoon, familiarizing herself with the different tribes, making notes herself, which had surprised the women again, given she hadn't delegated the task.

She had barely rested in her tent when she'd been woken up to be readied for the night's feast. Fortunately, her stylist had packed the emerald silk caftan the queen had had custom-designed for Zohra.

She'd let her maid dress her in the traditional way. Her hands and feet were once again decorated with henna, of the temporary kind this time. Her hair was brushed back and decorated with an exquisite gold comb with diamonds in between. Over it came the veil, woven with pure gold that fell to her upper lip.

When she had turned to the tribeswomen to refuse, one of them had smiled shyly, and burst into an Arabic dialect. Loath to remove that smile, Zohra had kept quiet.

Now, around fifteen men and women sat on smaller divans interspersed around them, all turned just a little bit toward the one she was sitting on. Ayaan was walking around greeting them one by one, accepting their gifts and passing them on to the guard standing back.

An elaborate feast was laid out in the center on a low table, the aromas wafting over and tickling Zohra's nostrils.

Then came that musky scent with something else underneath it that meant Ayaan was moving close. Her breath hitched in her throat. Her vision limited, every other sense came alive at his nearness.

Her hands, tucked in her lap, trembled as he came near.

She could pinpoint the exact moment his gaze fell on her, in the way the very air around them charged with tension.

One of the women burst into Arabic just as he neared her, something between a song and a poem, a beautiful melody that filled the space. Her heart hammering in her chest, Zohra fought to stay still as he tugged the edges of the veil and lifted them up to reveal her face.

His face a mask of tension, he lifted her chin, turned toward the room and said, "My bride and your future queen, Crown Princess Zohra Katherine Naasar Al-Sharif."

His voice glided over her skin. She fought against the shiver that threatened to root itself into her very bones. Congratulations, spoken in Arabic, overflowed around them.

She struggled to stay still as he sat down next to her,

the solid musculature of his thigh flushed tight against hers. Keeping a smile in place, she unlocked her hands and turned. "Shouldn't it be me who is furious, Ayaan? After all, you unveiled me like I was a gift."

His mouth was a study in his fight to calm himself. "On the contrary, it is respect that they offer you. The tribal leaders won't look upon your face unless I grant them permission. Just as I wouldn't presume to speak to a sheikh's wife without proper introduction."

"Like we were your prized possessions."

He held a silver tumbler to her mouth, and she realized the whole room was watching them, their own tumblers raised in mirroring actions. "Drink, Zohra."

His command brooked no argument. Zohra took a sip clumsily. Heat spiraling to life between them, the intimacy of the simple action stole her breath. A drop of it lingered at the corner of her mouth. Ayaan swiped at it with a long brown finger. Desire flew hotly in her blood as though he had lit a spark on her skin with that contact. The cool sweet liquid did nothing to dim the heat blossoming inside her veins.

His gaze staying on her, Ayaan took a sip from the same tumbler and a cheer went up around the room.

"At one point in time the tribes were barbaric people, fighting with each other, among themselves for their very survival. In the last century, civilization has taken root but only a little. In this world, women still need protection—whether from other members of the tribe or other tribes or even royalty themselves. It is a mark of respect, of reverence, something that is taken very seriously. And my duty, whether I agree with their principles or even their form of life, is to respect and protect it."

He turned toward her, and Zohra felt the force of his gaze right down to her toes. Triumph glittered in his eyes, turning them into an indescribable golden hue. "Have you had enough of playing at duty, *ya habibati*? Are you ready to admit that this world is not for you?"

A month ago, or even a day ago, she would have agreed with him, would have been intensely frustrated at the very least. She still was, if she was honest with herself. Sitting there like a package to be unwrapped went against every grain of belief she had fought hard to retain in this world.

But she had also seen and heard firsthand what an important role women played in the tribe's hierarchy from her discussion with the women this afternoon. It was not a life she could see herself living, but she understood it.

Maybe it was the man who took the effort to explain it, or maybe she was seeing the same world, the same traditions and customs without prejudiced lenses.

She shook her head, and had the satisfaction of seeing the mockery in his face relent.

"No, I didn't like being unveiled as if I were something incapable of independent thinking, nor do I like being thought of as your possession, even if it is the most respected one. But neither am I ready to run."

"Why agree to it at all?" His gaze rested on her, curious. "The veil, this ceremony, everything. And don't tell me they forced you. You have no reason to indulge these people. I have seen you in action, Zohra. You are every inch the princess when you wish to be. I am surprised you didn't turn up here in jeans and T-shirt just to thumb your nose at it."

"So little faith in your wife, Ayaan? However shall we get through the next half century in each other's company?"

His mouth tightened again. "Do not challenge me. Your actions in the past decade speak for you."

"I did resent it. But then I thought of you…" A blaze of

heat sparked in his eyes immediately, and she hastened to add, "of your mother and father, of everything your family has lost to protect the tribes' way of living, their independence. And I realized, whether or not I added to your family's name and glory, whether or not I ended up as a minor deviation in your family tree, I wanted to do nothing to lessen it. So I gave in. And I am also realizing that it hasn't made my own beliefs any less."

He stared at her without blinking, and she felt a hot flare of satisfaction that she had surprised him. But it didn't last long, because a truth far more chilling than that suddenly clicked into place in her mind.

"That was why your lives had been sacrificed, wasn't it?" she said, her words loaded with a shiver, with pain she couldn't expel.

His answer was to turn into a block of ice next to her.

She clutched his hand and just as she had guessed, it was ice-cold, rigid. "I read about the history of your tribes but until now, I didn't realize. That's why the terrorists captured you and your brother and your sister.

"They wanted control over the tribes, didn't they? They took you from this very place five years ago and held you hostage? That's why you—"

"Yes," came his gritted answer and even now, she was sure it was only to stop her from probing further.

A knot clawed up her throat, and tears stung her eyes. And this time, she couldn't stem them. She didn't even try. "And your father refused?" She posed it as a question but she already knew. In her heart of hearts, she knew what this life was, she thought she had made peace with it ten days ago, accepted it as her reality.

But the truth about Ayaan's capture hit her like an invisible blow. Her chest was so tight it hurt to breathe.

Her father had walked away from her mother and her.

Ayaan's father had gone an extra step in the name of duty. He had refused to negotiate with a terrorist group, instead he had chosen to forfeit his sons' and daughter's lives.

Two had been killed, and one tortured to madness. But he hadn't bent.

She shivered uncontrollably, and Ayaan's hands wrapped around her shoulders, the heat from his embrace almost, but not quite, enough to thaw the chill in her blood.

"My father did his duty, Zohra. And if the same circumstances came to pass again and it was our child, the very same child who would be the product of the life you are so eager for, that was held hostage, I would be forced to do the same, too. I would probably go mad, take that final leap into darkness while doing it, but I would still do it."

His arm pressed into her shoulders, the heat of his body a deceptively safe haven around her. But nothing could have tempered the chill in his eyes, or the cruel smile that played on his lips. "Are you still eager to belong in Dahaar, Princess, to be my wife in every way that matters?"

Ayaan laughed as he stood at the entrance to the abandoned stables about half a mile from the encampment. Five years of neglect showed in the decrepit structure.

From the moment he had stepped onto the desert floor, the structure had mocked him, jeered him, called to him with its very presence. To resist that call, to pretend that it didn't exist, to pretend it wasn't the cause for the very cold that pervaded his bones, filled him with a white-hot fury.

He had not even indulged the idea of sleeping tonight. So he had ventured out and found himself lingering outside Zohra's tent. There was something to the acute disillusionment, the pain in her eyes that had tugged at him even as he had painted the cruelest picture of what life with him would hold for her.

He had wanted to go in, take her in his arms, do what he could to wipe it from her mind. He understood the loneliness that never left her eyes, understood how it leeched out the simplest of joys from one...

Apparently, his mind had more control than he had assumed because he had no idea when he had moved toward the stables.

He stepped over the threshold, the high dome-shaped ceiling giving it a cavernous feeling. It was a long, rectangular interior, giving a direct view of the empty stalls.

More than one lamp had gone out, the light from the remaining feeble ones just enough to prevent the whole area dissolving into utter darkness. He ran his fingers over his nape, feeling the chill in the air seep into his pores. Goose bumps instantly pebbled over his skin. The smell of the horses and the hay, the echoes of the soft whinnying of beasts long gone hit him with the force of a gale. Every hair on his body stood to attention, his core temperature quickly dropping.

Beware of your triggers. When you feel an episode coming, put yourself in a trigger-free zone.

The words of the trauma specialist reverberated through his skull.

He closed his eyes. Fear dug its claws into him, chipping away conscious thought.

He had loved horses and stables once, it had been his lifeblood. He had spent countless nights in the Dahaaran stables hiding from Azeez. That boy was, however, dead.

His legs struggling to keep him upright, he walked the perimeter of the stables.

He knew what was going to happen. And yet he couldn't walk away. If he was damned to have these episodes for the rest of his life, then he would bloody well have them when and as it suited him.

Distress fingered up his spine and knotted at the base of his neck. He curled his fists, focusing on the simple act of breathing in and out. The quiet took on a life of its own, becoming his worst nightmare. It hammered at him, inching its way past every rationale, every shred of sense he threw its way.

He was a twenty-six-year-old man who was skilled in three different martial arts.

But his psyche didn't understand reason, recycling and feeding itself on fears and terrors from five years ago. The unflinching quiet, the smells and sounds of the stable, all of them pushed under his conscious, inciting reactions that had no base in reality.

A frustrated growl escaped his mouth. He slid to his knees, an invisible rope tugging away at him. And then it came.

The sound that drowned his whole body into a mindless chill, that pierced holes in him. Nausea whirled at the base of his throat. He closed his eyes and gave in to the darkness.

He was sitting on the hard floor, his foot bent at an awkward angle. Winds from the desert howled outside.

A soft grunt reached his ears followed by a dragging movement across the floor of the stables.

Ayaan, can you hear me?

The scent of blood mixed with hay filled Ayaan's nostrils. His fingers gripped slender shoulders, his knuckles beginning to hurt from the tight grip. But he couldn't let go, he would never let go of her. He just needed a moment. His shoulder hurt like hell, and a bullet had grazed his head on the left. Blood dribbled thickly into his left eye.

His vision blurred with tears and his own blood, he felt woozy. That dragging sound came again, the sound rippling across his arms. It was a sound that filled him with the fiercest anger. A cold hand gripped his thigh, its grip strong despite the tremors in it.

Ayaan, you have to leave...

*No...*he roared.

That trembling hand tried to pry his grip off the body in his arms. Ayaan held on tighter. He couldn't let go, ever... he had already made a mistake when he had hesitated to fire, he couldn't make another. Bile filled his mouth. He retched to the side, wiped his mouth.

All he needed was a minute. Once his vision cleared, he would get her out of here...

That dragging sound came again, followed by stuttered breathing.

Ayaan, listen to me. It is too late for Amira and me. You have to leave...now.

Nooooooo....

Ayaan screamed again until his throat hurt, until his head felt as if it would burst from the inside, until pain and loathing was all he became. If only he hadn't frozen like that, if only he had moved faster, if only he had blocked the next shot with his body...so many if onlys....

Something landed on his shoulder, jarring his thoughts. With a scream that never left his throat, he surged to his knees and slammed the intruder against the door of a stall.

Adrenaline pounded through him, rage singing in his veins. This time, he would not hesitate.

One chance and he would drag them all to safety. That's all he needed, one chance.

A soft gasp broke through the mist pounding through his head. He reached out and realized the body of the intruder was slender, almost frail. In that second-long fracture in his focus a well-aimed kick landed on his shin.

The curious scent of roses teased at the edge of his mind. He stilled. That scent was wrong. There should only be blood, tears and the stench of his own fear. There shouldn't be...

He opened his eyes and jerked back so hard that he hit the wall with the back of his head. As his head throbbed, he stilled, his chest so painfully tight that he couldn't breathe.

Dressed in dark trousers and a white caftan, Zohra leaned against the wall, her long hair falling onto her chest over one shoulder.

Bile swam up his throat and Ayaan held it off by sheer will. He moved toward her, his movements shaky and slippery. Emotion balled up in his throat, and he had to breathe through it. Fear beat like a tribal drum in his blood as he tugged her gently.

She fell into his arms, and he thought he might be sick again. He traced the pulse at her throat with the pad of his thumb. And exhaled in painful relief.

Exquisite brown eyes slowly fluttered open.

"Zohra, can you hear me?"

"Yes," she said in a low whisper, "and now that you know that I wasn't about to attack you, can you please let go of me?"

With a curse, he loosened his fingers.

She pushed at his shoulders and he let himself fall back onto his haunches, his gut churning with a vicious force. Her fingers around her nape trembling, she leaned back against the wall and closed her eyes.

Her chest rose and fell with her slow, painful breathing.

He could have hurt her so easily... If he hadn't stopped when he had...

Terror pounded through his blood, a vise squeezing his chest. His hands shook, delayed shock pulsing through him from head to toe. "I could have killed you."

Fire erupted in that beautiful gaze. The fear was all gone now and she was pure, ferocious anger. Her small body bristled with the force of her emotion, her chest rising and falling with it.

She raised her hand and even realizing what she intended, Ayaan couldn't move, couldn't stop her. She slapped him hard, the sound of it ringing around them.

Her chin wobbled, tears falling onto her cheeks. "I am beginning to believe you are truly mad." Her voice was as sharp as the sting of the slap she had delivered. "Why else would anyone invite such pain upon themselves? You knew what might happen to you here. The desert, these stables, this is why you have been such…a monster this past week, why you kept everyone away…" She wiped her tears on her sleeve.

"You saw your brother and sister die here. Why walk in here?" She shoved him again, feeble as her energy was. "I want an answer."

In the face of her angry energy, he clasped her gently, a knot in his throat. "If I hid from it, if I pretended that it didn't exist during this trip, it would forever haunt me. I needed to come here, I needed to see what it could do to me." *When I looked at you next, I needed to know that I faced it instead of hiding.*

Shaking her head, she tugged his hand off her. "And if it had pushed you past that edge, if it had robbed—"

He pulled her to him and tucked his face in her hair. "That was a price I was willing to pay." He swallowed hard, the scent of her seeping into his cells. "My life, Zohra. How could you be so stupid as to follow me?"

She pushed him again, tears flowing freely across her face, trying to break free. "And you think you are not fit to be king, that you don't have what it takes? You are a ruthless bastard, Ayaan. You have all the arrogance that is required to rule your blasted country. Now, let go of me."

"No," he said loudly, crushing her with his arms, emotion robbing him of any sense.

She landed across his knees, the air knocked out of her. She fought him every inch of the way, but he didn't give a damn. He kept his grip on her gentle, but letting go of her was a concept he just couldn't grasp in that moment. She pounded her fists into his stomach. He held her shoulders in a tight grip and forced her head down.

As if sensing his intentions, she stilled. She felt soft and warm against his thighs. Combing his fingers through her hair, he checked for any swelling. There was none.

"There's no swelling, Ayaan," she said, wriggling under his hold.

He closed his eyes, fighting the wet heat of tears prickling at the back of his eyes.

With his hand under her shoulders, he dragged her toward him, nothing gentle left in him anymore.

"I told you there is no swelling, Ayaan. I was just disoriented for a few seconds, that's all. I—"

But he was past caring, past honor, past good sense. He moved to his knees, lifted her up and started walking out of the stables.

"Ayaan, put me down," she said squirming against him.

He tightened his hold on her, crushing her against him. *Did she have any idea how delicate she was? Did she not know what a mindless beast he became in the throes of a nightmare, what a chance she had taken with him?* "No."

"Ayaan, please, you are scaring me."

He had to laugh. *She was scared now?* The woman was scared now after putting him through that? "Again and again, I warned you to stay away from me. But you didn't listen. You made a choice, *ya habibati*. That choice has consequences."

He took the path toward his tent and a shudder went through her. "Where are you taking me?"

"To my tent."

"The maid will tend to me. I want a bath and I want to sleep."

"You can do all that in my tent."

"Why?"

"I could have seriously hurt you, Zohra. A few more seconds and I would have…" He pulled a deep breath in. The hard knot in his throat remained, his chest so stiflingly tight that it was a wonder he was able to breathe at all.

"But you didn't, Ayaan." Her fingers feathered over his jaw. "You stopped. Ayaan, please, it was my choice to follow you, mine. This is not your fault. You couldn't know who it was. You were drowning in that memory, you were not yourself. You can't hold yourself—"

"When you should have cowered from me, you didn't." He stepped over the threshold of his tent and dismissed the guards. "I close my eyes and I see you…against the wall. *Ya Allah*…if you…"

He threw her on the bed, shivering from rage. Her face was pale, her brown eyes glittering in the light of the lamps. "I could not let you go through that alone, Ayaan."

"That image will haunt me now, *ya habibati*." He knelt on the edge of the bed, the need to hold her close, the wanting to touch her, kiss her, blending into an unbearable ache. "Only one thing will banish that image."

She shivered again. "What?"

He shook from head to toe. He wanted to fill himself with the scent of her, with the feel of her. He wanted to hear her scream in mindless pleasure, he wanted to see her thrashing, crying as she came apart in his arms, he wanted to reassure himself that she was alive, again and again.

He swept off the bed, and walked to the entrance to

summon a maid for her. Stripping off his sweat-soaked shirt, he threw it. Utter masculine pride filled him as her gaze swept over his chest with a hunger she couldn't hide. "A new image of you, *habibati*, naked and writhing under me, begging me to be inside you, calling my name as you come undone." He smiled, the dark hunger he had held on to so tightly unleashing inside him. "I am going to make you mine tonight, Zohra. And you are going to wish you had never laid eyes on me."

CHAPTER TEN

ZOHRA WOKE SLOWLY, her eyes adjusting to the soft light of
the unfamiliar tent. Her limbs felt too heavy to move, as if
they were filled with molten honey. Blinking, she pushed
her hair out of her eyes and realized it was still damp from
the bath Ayaan had ordered for her.

Solar-powered lamps illuminated a tent that was just as
luxurious as hers but much larger. Frowning, she moved
to get off the high bed and gasped, feeling an echo of pain
in her shoulder. She rubbed it just as Ayaan materialized
on the side of the bed.

His hair was damp, and he wore nothing but sweatpants. With a sprinkling of chest hair, the lean muscles
of his torso beckoned her touch. She fisted her fingers in
the sheets.

Just the sight of him in touching distance, in the same
bed, weaved an intimacy that tugged at her. His words as
he threw her on his bed came pounding back and a tingle
swept down her body.

She remembered the maids coming in and pouring hot
water into the claw-foot tub. And undressing her and giving her a massage despite Zohra's objections.

The prince's orders, one of them had whispered with
a smile.

"Please tell me I did not faint," she said, inwardly cursing herself. She wanted to add nothing more to the burden of guilt he already carried.

"I think you like falling asleep in bathtubs, *ya habibati*," he whispered and she breathed in relief.

He sat in front of her, his face close to hers. And Zohra had to remind herself to keep breathing. His fingers found the sore spot on her shoulder. "Here?"

She nodded, the rough texture of his tone a velvet caress. His fingers moved with long, lingering strokes, reducing her body to a mass of sensation. The tang of his skin burrowed into her blood. More than physical hunger uncoiling inside.

She touched his chest, felt the shift of hard muscles under her seeking fingers, pulled herself forward until she was surrounded by the fortress of his lean body. With a sigh, she wrapped her hands around him, everything in her bracing for his rejection.

Instead, his arms came around her and he held her tight. Her throat locked down, and Zohra squeezed her eyes shut. It lasted only an infinitesimal moment but his embrace encompassed everything he was.

His fingers crawled up her nape, into her hair. She felt the press of his mouth at her temple, the whoosh of his breath over her skin. Swallowing her moan, she hid her face in his shoulder.

"You smell divine, *latifa*."

She had no control over the next thing she did. She opened her mouth and licked his skin. Warmth billowed in her lower belly and pooled between her legs. He tasted of sweat and salt, like a hunger she had never known before.

A tremor racked his lean frame, the race of his heart a loud boom in her ears. "I want to be inside you so much that it is a physical ache..." The naked want in his tone rolled over her skin. She tilted forward and laced her fingers at his nape. "But, *Ya Allah*, Zohra, after everything you have seen, you still want this?" He buried his head in the crook of her shoulder. His mouth was hot and wet against her skin, branding her, his touch possessive, even as he struggled with himself, with honor that was his very blood. "Because if I touch you, I have no will left anymore to stop."

Her stomach dived even at the thought that he might leave.

The image of him with his head in his hands, his features wreathed in pure anguish—it should have sent her running. Instead, for the first time, she felt the weight of the duty he shouldered with pride and grace, understood the honor he found in giving it his all, the struggle he took on every day without a complaint.

Because this was what he was born to do, this was his reality. She ached to be a part of his reality.

She wanted to give him pleasure, she wanted to be the escape he sought, she wanted to be with him because for the first time in as far as she could remember, Zohra felt no struggle, no confusion, but the rightness of this.

"Ayaan…" she sighed, wondering why her heart always had to choose the hardest path, "I am here not because this is something I have been warned not to do, not because it pushes the boundaries, not because I want to lash out at someone. I want this, I need this, *for me.*"

She whispered his name again and again over his skin, the beat of his racing heart the only sound she could hear, his lean, hard body the only thing she could touch. She ran her hands all over his chest, loving the ripple and shift of the hard muscles at her lightest touch.

Another curse ripped from his mouth, another shudder racked his powerful body. With his hands in her hair, he tugged her up. His gaze lit with the blaze of a thousand suns, his desire, his demons, his struggle—everything was laid out for her to see.

He stole her breath in that moment and she had no idea how to hold on to it, how to stop from losing herself in him.

He groaned, the sound weighed down with so much regret. "I have asked for it but I have no contraception, Zohra. And I cannot take a risk—"

"I have been on the pill for a long time," she said, a niggling concern rising to the surface.

His gaze glittered with something unsaid, and Zohra wondered if the perfection of the moment was already fractured. "Ayaan, I know what—"

"Shh…" he said, clasping her face in his hands. "You want me as I am, do you not, Zohra?" She nodded, her heart crawling into her throat, the tightrope she was walking between want and something far stronger blurring at the beauty of the man holding her, both inside and out. "And I want you just the way you are."

He pulled her up until their mouths were inches apart. Anticipation coiled in her stomach, her muscles molten. His mouth was warm, soft against hers, his control a strung out live wire around them. His hands were on her hips, as he licked her lower lip.

Sharp coils of pleasure arrowed lower when he nipped it and licked it again. Demanding, owning, possessive, and this time without an ounce of control. He bit her, licked her and stroked her and did it again. And again. Until their breaths mingled, until their mouths fused, until the rasp of his skin was etched into hers.

Breathing was something he granted her every other moment, and Zohra let herself be taken over.

An erotic swipe of his tongue, a quick sweep of his palms down her body, a whisper of sinful promise at her ear in Arabic. Lost in a sea of sensation, Zohra sank her fingers into his hair and tugged. Pushed her body against his and ran her hands feverishly over his back. "Please, Ayaan…" Her voice broke on a needy sob.

His hands moved to her shoulder, over her arms, his gaze hungry and intense. "I have no memory of another woman's body, Zohra, no memory of feeling this kind of hunger, this kind of need to possess." He licked the pulse at her neck, his breath fanning the flames of her own desire higher. "Do you know how much I have wanted to taste your skin, *ya habibati,* how much I have thought about you like this, how I would stand outside your door and try to remember all the reasons I couldn't come inside and take what I wanted?" He sucked the same spot and she melted into his body. "I threw you out of my bedroom but the scent of your skin remained." He brought her hands to his erection and she jolted at the feel of it. The pull between her thighs intensified at the thought of that velvet hardness entering her, moving inside her. "I have been without relief for a month because I couldn't bear to touch myself. Because what I wanted was your hands on me, your mouth on me." Wetness pooled between her thighs at the shocking eroticism of his very thoughts. She palmed his arousal and he jerked out of her grasp, his fingers clamping hers in a tight grip. "No, Zohra." His fingers traced the neckline of her gown, and her skin snapped into life. "You cannot touch me until my ears are echoing with the sound of your moans, until I have kissed every inch of you, until I have licked you between your thighs…"

Her breath balled up in her throat. His mouth moved along her neckline, trailing wet heat along her skin, kissing and tasting, winding her tighter and higher. The ache between her thighs flared stronger and hotter.

She was so lost in what his mouth did, how it hovered over the curve of her breast, how his very breath seeped into her skin that she had no idea when his fingers had tugged the hem of her gown upward and over her head in one smooth movement. A cool breeze greeted her skin, and instinctively, Zohra lifted her hands.

But his gaze remained lower and she followed it. Molten heat spread across every cell, every inch of her. Her panties were of the sheerest cream-colored silk, cut so deep that they barely covered her mound. And they had tiny white stones at the hem that caught the light of the lanterns hanging from the top and glittered.

"I..." Zohra swallowed as he ran a knuckle over the hemline, a fierce rush of wetness drenching her. "My stylist packed my bags," she finished lamely. He laid his palm, big and warm, fingers down, against her mound and Zohra jerked, and arched into his touch. The bundle of nerves at her sex cried for more. His mouth against her temple, he applied the tiniest of pressure with his fingers. And she sobbed, dug her teeth into his shoulder.

"I told them to ready you for me." He swiped his tongue along the seam of her ear. And she shivered. "Also, remind to me thank your stylist."

The roguishness in his tone was just as arousing as his fingers, and Zohra pushed into his touch.

His hands clasping hers, he bared her torso to his sight.

His eyes, darkened like a desert sky at dusk, roved over her breasts. Her nipples tightened into aching buds.

She squeezed her eyes shut. The sound of his breath, harsh and uneven, pinged over her nerves and she felt a hot rush of satisfaction. "My imagination could not do you justice, Zohra. Do you know how many times I have imagined this?"

She felt his fingers on the curve of her breast and moaned, the relentless dull, ache between her thighs turning into a sharp pull. Felt his abrasive fingers cup the weight of her breasts and jerked. Felt the tip of his fingers circle the tight, painful bud and shivered. Felt the wet heat of his mouth at the valley between, heard him draw in a deep breath, almost reverent. And she shook all over, her legs folding under her. But of course he held her up.

His hair-roughened arms wrapped around her waist, keeping her exactly where he wanted her. Her breasts turned heavy and aching, her throat dried, her breath stilted, but he didn't touch the tautened tips, didn't give her what she wanted, teasing, taunting, until a sob crawled up her throat.

She clutched his hand, ready to push herself into his touch. But he gripped her wrist. His breath fanned over her mouth just before he laved her lips again. "Open your eyes, Zohra."

She looked down and saw the blunt square tips of his dark fingers tweak one aching nipple. Jerking at the pleasure that arrowed right to her core, she moaned. "Look at what I am doing to you," he said in a roughened voice that was pure eroticism.

The sight was so compelling that Zohra couldn't close her eyes even if he asked her to.

He pinched the nipple, and her knees came off the bed. His arm around her waist locked her in place as he bent and sucked the nipple into his mouth.

His name was a cry on her lips that reverberated around the tent, probably in the desert itself. Sinking her hands into his thick hair, she held him in place—a shameless request, a raw command, all rolled into one.

And he suckled deeper, longer, until all she could feel, could see, could hear was the raw strokes of his tongue over the hard tip. Pleasure drenched every cell, every thought on him, every inch of skin quivering with need.

He pushed her back onto the bed with his weight and

Zohra folded, as if her limbs were nothing but sensation. He kissed her navel and downward, and she came off the bed. With a silky, golden-hued scarf, he gently tied her wrists before she could understand his intent. With a kiss on her mouth, he put some pillows under her head. "So that you can see what I am doing to you," he whispered.

Heat unlike anything she had known scoured through her as he trailed wet, hot kisses over the hem of her thong. Then he pressed his mouth against her mound, drew a shuddering breath in. The sheer fabric was no barrier to the sensations that grew within her.

And then he was tugging them off her unresisting legs, spreading them wide, and leaning over her. "Look at me, Zohra," he said, in a voice so heavy with desire, so laden with pleasure that it echoed through her.

Zohra met his gaze and forgot to breathe. She fought against the ties at her wrists, the need to touch him, the need to return the pleasure a dark craving inside her. His fingers were featherlight on her inner thighs, his gaze lust-soaked, primitive, that of a conquering warrior.

And then she felt his breath on the most sensitive part of her and he swiped at the throbbing flesh of her clitoris with his tongue.

Zohra bucked off the bed, shaking, the pleasure that spread through her so acute, so addictive that her hips moved on their own. She cried aloud when he took another long, leisurely lick. A kiss came next, the image of his lush mouth against that quivering bundle shockingly intimate in her mind. He did it again and again and tight coils of sensation gripped her lower belly.

She made sounds—sometimes a sob, sometimes a moan, sometimes his name, begging, whimpering, her head thrashing against the bed, her throat dry. Spiraling need pulled at her, pushed her out of her skin, building when he was there, fragmenting in the infinitesimal moments his touch retreated.

And then he sucked at her core.

Her orgasm rocked through her with the force of a sandstorm. She gasped for breath, the sound spilling from her mouth was erotic to her own ears. Waves of pleasure—acute, breath-robbing—drenched her inside and out. And yet he didn't stop. His hands locking her hips, he continued stroking her with his tongue until he wrung every ounce of pleasure from her body, until she was nothing but a mass of quivering sensations.

The aftershocks of her climax still tumbling through her body, she fell back against the bed. A shiver climbed up from the base of her spine and this time it arose from something inside her, something that wouldn't settle down, something that asked questions she couldn't answer. Keeping her tied hands above her, she moved to her side, a strange shyness coming over her.

His face a dark shadow in front of hers, Ayaan pushed the damp hair from her forehead and kissed her temple. His palm moved over the curve of her hip, over her shaking legs, over her back. The way he cocooned her soothed something inside her that shouldn't have needed soothing. "Zohra?"

Her name on his tongue nestling deep into her, Zohra heard the unasked question and gave an answering nod.

Unwilling to look into the strange feeling, she pushed her bound wrists toward him.

He shook his head, pure masculine arrogance brimming in the golden brown depths. "I have never seen anything so erotic as you coming." His fingers traced the curve of her butt, drew maddening lines up and down her spine. "I think I might get addicted to it."

When he touched his mouth to hers, she moved her

head, although not before the taste of him seeped into her lips. "I think the entire encampment heard me, Ayaan," she said, her lust-soaked body catching up to the niggling warning from her mind. "Is it—"

"Nowhere near enough, *ya habibati*," he said, grasping her question without being asked. Pushing her back into the bed, his body settled on top of hers. The hair on his legs rasped against her, the angular contours of his hips an intimate caress. He felt heavenly on top of her, the heavy weight of him a pleasure that rendered her mute.

"Ayaan?"

His face buried in her nape, he smiled. "Hmm...?"

"I..." the words she wanted to say rose to her lips and fell away. Fear was a tight knot in her throat. This moment with every inch of him flush against her, the ever-present shadows in his eyes at least held back for now, she didn't want to fracture its fragility, she didn't want to risk another's name entering it.

She arched as he sucked at her neck, and then licked it. "I want something from you."

His grip on her hips tightened an infinitesimal bit. "Tonight, anything you want, *ya habibati*."

"I have dreamed of touching your scar, of kissing it, of tracing it with my tongue."

She felt the rush of his exhale between her breasts. In the next second, her wrists were unbound. And he fell back against the bed.

She took in the sight of him, her breathing, raspy, shallow.

His hair falling onto his forehead, his arms resting above his head, the contours of his chest narrowing to his waist, the hard, tight abdomen, lean hips covered by the sweatpants, olive-colored skin gleaming with a sheen of sweat—it was an intimate sight she hugged to herself, a sensual feast that would forever be etched onto her mind.

Staying on her side, she ran tentative fingers over the winding scar, felt the puckered tissue. Tears rose in her throat and she swallowed them down. No, there was no place for sorrow in this moment either. "How did you get it?" she breathed the question into his skin, hiding her face.

The tangy scent of him held her in place, the gentle stroke of his fingers in her hair rooting her to that moment.

"They bound me with a metal rope that had several knots in it."

A matter-of-fact reply.

She caught the sound of horror before it left her mouth. Sliding close, which rubbed her breasts against his side, she pressed her lips to the scar. His hands tightened in her hair, his abdomen bunched so tight that it took her a moment to understand.

He liked it.

Pulling herself up on an elbow, she ran her tongue slowly over the length of it, peppering it with kisses. "Turn around," she said.

And to her delight, he did. With his darkly hungry gaze trained away from her, she was bolder. Sliding to her knees, she kissed it all the way across his torso. Her nipples grazed him again and this time, they both groaned.

"And again," she whispered, and he lay on his chest.

She bent forward to reach the other side, and her hand fluttered over his chest, down to his navel and farther below.

Until her fingers grazed his erection. A hoarse grunt fell from his mouth, his hips thrusting upward into her hand. She palmed it, the rigid, pulsing length of it sending a rush of wetness to her core.

And then, before she could blink, he was on top of her, deliciously heavy.

His gaze collided with hers. Naked desire burned bright with dark shadows that always lingered but something else shimmered in his eyes, something that burrowed into her heart, wound itself around her. "You didn't ask me permission to do that."

A glimmer of contentment, that was what it was.

It was a gift, it burst through her like an explosion, a sight she gripped tight.

He pressed a hard kiss to her mouth, and Zohra felt the tempo of his kiss change. His hands moved over her body, thorough and erotic but now, there was an urgency that shattered that iron-fisted control. When he settled between her thighs and probed her entrance with the head of his erection, every thought disappeared from her head. And Zohra was lost again.

Would it ever be enough?

The unrelenting question pounded through Ayaan, mingling with the desire coursing through his blood, reverberating in every cell.

It had to be, he threw an arrogant answer at himself.

Because this was sex, after all.

Zohra might be nothing like the women he had known, but his body was reveling in the pleasure, in the simple act of touching, of kissing.

Ayaan ran his mouth over the pulse at Zohra's neck, the taste of her tightening the need drumming through him. Her thighs automatically fell away, making a place for him, cradling his erection, the rasp of her quivering thighs against him unraveling the last thread of his control.

She moved under him, a rasping sound from her throat.

Her breasts rubbed against his chest and his arousal tightened into steel.

He licked one taut nipple, and she arched like a bow, her hands sinking into his hair. He pulled it into his mouth and she screamed his name.

It was a needy, throaty sound that ripped through him. "Please Ayaan..." she whispered at his ear, before flicking at his earlobe with her tongue. "I want to touch you, I need to..."

Shaking his head, he ran a finger over the swollen flesh between her legs. She dug her teeth into his shoulder. He plunged a finger into her sex and she bit him, hard.

Ya Allah, she was wet and ready for him. He wanted to pleasure her again, bring her to climax, suffuse himself with the taste and scent of her but the sight of her pink flesh, wet and ready for him, and his own hunger—selfish and relentless, rode him hard.

Pushing her legs wide, he rubbed at the entrance with his penis. Sweat beaded on his forehead, every inch of his body throbbing for possession.

"Spread your legs for me, Zohra," he said, in a voice that was far from his own.

When her boneless legs moved farther apart, he kept his hands on her hips and entered her in one hard thrust.

Stars exploding in his eyes, she clenched him tightly. Heat poured through his muscles, pushing for friction, the walls of her sex stretching around his erection. He was about to pull out and ram back into her when the stillness of her body filtered through to his lust-soaked mind.

He looked into her eyes, and saw the truth reflected there. Shock poured through him. "Of all the things to be lying about, Zohra?" he said, followed by a vicious curse he hadn't ever uttered before.

Regret punctured the pleasure, but only a little. His

thighs quaked at having to stay still. He pulled back, inch by excruciating inch, his shoulders feeling like steel rods at the pressure he put on them to be slow, to be gentle, when she moved the tiniest inch beneath him.

He bent down and nipped her lips, not hard but not gentle either. "Stay still, Zohra," he said through gritted teeth, his skin sweaty, his hair drenched, and his body sliding out of its skin with the need to move.

But of course his willful wife paid no heed. "It doesn't hurt, Ayaan, not anymore. It just feels…" Her hands gripping his shoulders, a thoughtful look on her face, she wiggled her hips upward again. "Ahhh…it feels full and achy and so good…Please, please move…"

Heat spiraled down his spine. With a curse that reverberated around them, he pushed back into her. Her throaty moan scraped along his skin, the experimental thrust of her hips blinding him to anything but sensation.

Pleasure soaked into his skin, rammed through his nerves until there was nothing but the wet heat of Zohra, of his wife. Giving in to his body's natural rhythm, he moved again. There was no finesse to his thrusts, no filter on the words that left his lips. Her thrusts met his in perfect rhythm, the sounds she made became needier, faster. He willed his body to wait for her pleasure by the skin of his teeth.

On the next move, he rubbed the swollen flesh with his fingers and she fell apart like a thunderstorm. Her muscles contracting against the sensitive flesh of his arousal, pulling every inch of pleasure from him, he thrust again and orgasmed in an explosion of heat that touched every nerve, rocked through every inch of him.

Pleasure receded, the first wave of need blunted for now, and questions pounded back into him. He reversed their positions, still joined intimately.

Her arms instantly rose to cover her breasts. She looked down at their bodies still joined and a fierce blush claimed her cheeks.

"You were a virgin."

Her gaze flew to his. "Yes."

He pulled her hands from her breasts, fresh need rippling through him at the sight of those pale pink nipples. She held herself stiff, and the savage that he was, it turned him on. "You said—"

"Let go of my hands, Ayaan."

"No," he said and pulled her up until she was astride him in his lap. His erection thickened, lengthened inside her.

Her brown gaze flared wide. "Oh….you are—"

"Yes, *ya habibi*. It's a long way down from the edge."

The most masculine, arrogant, savage satisfaction gripped him now that the initial anger at her lie faded. He frowned, even as he relished the feral feeling.

Fierce emotions—either passion or fury or even love, he had never been capable of them. And yet in that moment, he couldn't stem the savagery of his emotions.

Questions hurtled through him but he fought the urge. He would not bring another man's name into this bed with her. Not tonight, not ever.

He was the only man to have possessed her, the only one who had known her in the most intimate of ways.

Her hands resting on his shoulders, she tried to wiggle out of his lap. The erotic friction of their joined bodies intensified a thousandfold.

Their mingled groans, the scent of sex—it was an irresistible aphrodisiac.

"You lied to me."

"I said and did whatever I thought I needed to, to get out of the wedding," she said. "But Faisal never asked for what I would have offered. I used to tease him for being so bound to traditions and customs that were laid down ages ago. But I think I understand now. And I…"

He clasped her chin, forcing her to look at him. "Finish your thought, Zohra. Because this is the last time I will tolerate his name on your lips, the thought of him on your mind."

She looked at him, unblinking, the depth of emotion in it a reminder of what a force this woman was. "I am glad he never asked, Ayaan."

He closed his eyes and breathed through the cloud of need that had his hips leaning upward into her. She had been a virgin, he reminded himself with the utmost effort. He needed to be gentle, even if it was a little late, he needed to let her body get used to him. "What does it make me that I am glad that he didn't take it, Zohra? That your body has known only me, that…"

She lifted her hands, sunk them into her hair and tugged it back. It was such an unconsciously sensual movement that he lost that tenuous hold on himself. "Like I felt when you said that you don't remember another woman's body, when you said you never felt pleasure like this before?" He couldn't help himself. He cupped her breasts and rubbed the tight nipples with the heel of his palm. "Whatever you think it makes you, I am one, too. So be kind to yourself," she said, and arched into his touch with a sigh.

He bent his head and licked one nipple. She jerked, moving up and down, and it was his turn to groan. "Your breasts…I am never going to have enough. And you go up in flames when I touch them."

"Yes," she whispered, her spine so straight that he wondered if he would break her. Her lips were swollen from his kisses, the marks from the stubble of his jaw outlined on her neck and breasts. What in the name of God had she unleashed in him? She leaned her forehead against his and the trust in her action branded him. "I…it feels like I will combust…" She arched her body again, as if asking him for more, "…if you stop."

Just once more, he promised himself. He would taste her just once more and then stop. Let her body breathe, let her rest. He pulled the nipple into his mouth and suckled. And she sobbed, his name falling in a guttural request from her lips. He heard his name on her mouth, the whimper of pleasure she made, that shredded his composure.

They were sounds he would never have enough of.

Burying his mouth at her neck, he fought for control. With her hands locked around his nape, she pushed closer to him until her breasts dragged deliciously against his chest. And kissed him on the mouth.

He gripped her hips when she moved, heat he had no strength to check built up inside him again. "You will be sore tomorrow, *ya habibati*."

Her tongue traced the seam of his lips, her eyes twinkling. His grip loosened on her, his body moving of its own mind. She sucked on his tongue next and he lost the fight.

He thrust upward and she moved down. He pumped his hips faster, and she matched his rhythm. He cursed and she laughed. Leaving her to set the rhythm, he took her nipple in his mouth.

And she shattered with a guttural sigh. His own climax followed, rippling through him, breaking him apart and putting him back together and changing him.

Taking her with him, he fell back to the bed, and held her tight against him.

His memory wasn't that corrupted to think his body had once known this kind of pleasure, his mind not so broken to think what had occurred was normal, to believe that it was anything short of spectacular.

Six years ago, he would have reveled in the discovery, taken it for granted as another of life's gifts, shouted it out from the rooftops. The man he was today couldn't stop the cold ripple of fear that churned in his gut, couldn't shake the feeling that anything this good couldn't last.

CHAPTER ELEVEN

MEET ME AT the stables.

Ayaan looked at the note a little girl had fluttered in his hand. Frowning, he looked up and realized he had missed half of what Imran, his security chief, had said.

Motioning him to repeat, he walked toward the stables. And promptly stopped on the path when Imran was done. "So this information comes from the same source who provided us information last time on where the terrorist group will convene next?"

Imran shook his head. "No."

Intelligence about a terrorist gathering in Dahaara the next month... It was the third time this information was coming his way. Information that had been accurate the first two times but was beginning to sound too good to be true. And this time, it was coming from a different source.

Something niggled at Ayaan, even though he couldn't exactly place it. "See if you can trace it back to the source," he said, taking another step in the direction of the stables.

"Are we not—"

"We are not acting on this until we figure out if there is a connection," he said, dismissing him and covering the distance to the stables.

Imran had requested this meeting two days ago, and Ayaan, unable to focus on anything, had forgotten.

Like a teenager riding the first waves of infatuation, his mind, and his body, refused to focus on anything but on the image of Zohra underneath him, her beautiful brown eyes bewitching with raw need, sparkling with trust, the tight heat of her body, the heady moans from her mouth.

At some point past midnight, when he had exhausted them both, they had finally fallen sleep. Dreamless sleep, Ayaan had realized with a shock the next morning.

It had been two days since, two days where she had occupied his every thought, during which, interestingly, she had avoided him just as he had, where he had had more than enough time to berate himself for what he had done, to find numerous reasons why he could not do it again.

Even if his body, forever in a state of painful arousal, didn't understand the fact.

He made his way to the stables, curiosity for once trumping the distinct unease he felt anywhere near it.

He stood inside, the echo of everything he had gone through in there rumbling through him. He understood the spine-tingling fear that had driven him to take Zohra, the need to keep her close, the need to lose himself in her body, but in the cold light of the day, the evidence of the instability of his mind skewered through him.

The scent of her carried to him through the light breeze, his body thrumming to life as though a switch had been turned on. He turned around to face her and frowned. Dusk was still a few hours away yet she had wrapped a thin shawl over her torso with white leggings under it. Her hair was covered with a scarf of the same color, and she looked the very picture of vitality, of life, an embodiment of everything he was not.

"Ayaan," she said, as if she needed to force him to acknowledge her presence, as if the memory of how she tasted, how her body clenched him tight wasn't etched into his very cells.

"You have been avoiding me," he said. Tugging the scarf from her neck, she dropped it to the floor. Sunlight glinted in her hair, turning it into strands of coppery gold. "Are you regretting what happened?"

"No. And I'm not the one who's doing the avoiding. I just didn't hound you like I usually do." She ventured farther in and tugged the huge door closed. Then her fingers pulled the shawl she had wrapped around her torso. Inch by inch, she unwound the fabric until it fell to the ground with a soft whisper.

She wore a sleeveless top, in the sheerest see-through silk in gold. With the light from the high windows behind her, every inch of her body was outlined under the thin fabric. He swallowed, the shadow of her lacy bra, the indent of her navel instantly drowning him in images and sensations of how she had felt beneath him.

Walking around the stables, she came to a halt near him. "I have ordered for it to be demolished."

He raised a brow even as he enjoyed the raw command in her tone.

Sinking her hands under the top, she slowly peeled off her leggings. The sight of her long, bare, sun-kissed thighs set need coursing through him, rattling his self-control. "It serves no purpose other than to remind you of what you had to endure."

"It's not the only thing that reminds me of everything I have gone through and everything I am not," he said, studying her with a hunger that was becoming all too familiar. The sight of the thin strings of her panties dried up his throat. "And demolishing it won't fix me, Zohra."

Shaking her head, she reached him, a resigned smile on her lips. "Maybe I don't think you need fixing, Ayaan.

There is one thing I wish to do here before it goes down, though."

She was upset and she was battling it with her fierce strength. He didn't question why or how he knew. He just did. And in this mood, she was a force to be reckoned with.

He covered the last step between them before he realized he was moving. Being near her and not touching her was akin to not breathing. Their gazes held, speaking to each other, assessing each other, and he immediately felt surrounded by her warmth.

Warmth that had a different source from the desire that flew hotly in his veins. This time, he willingly lost the fight, surrendered his will to her.

His fingers trembling, he touched her forehead. She exhaled on a whoosh. "Are you all right?" Burying his nose in her hair, he took a deep breath, until she was all he knew, all he felt, all he was. "Everywhere?"

Her chin tilted up, she held his gaze even as pink scoured her cheekbones. "I am not going to break so easily." Her words were a challenge, a gauntlet thrown down. And yet, he could be the one who could break her, who could crush that indomitable spirit.

She ran her fingers over his jaw, and he closed his eyes. Her touch feathered over him, fanning the flames of desire that always simmered. It had taken him an incredible amount of control to not go looking for her in the past two days.

The indescribable pleasure he had found with her was addictive, but he could still do without it. But the warmth of her smile, the quiet contentment he found near her, he was afraid they would be his downfall.

The pads of her thumbs brushed over his forehead, his nose, his lips. When he would have stopped her, she pushed his hands away. "You will not deny me this."

"Giving orders, Princess?"

Her hands moved lower, lingered over his neck. "No, simply exercising my rights as your wife."

She kissed his cheek, tugged at his earlobe with her teeth, scraped them over the pulse in his neck. Her nimble fingers began unbuttoning his cotton shirt. Need gripped his belly, his arousal instantaneous, powerful and relentless.

She pushed him against the wall and he let her, enjoying the daring in her gaze, more than content to see how far she would go.

Pushing his shirt off his shoulders, she kissed his pectoral. "You are like steel covered in velvet. My fingers itch to touch you, to scrape you, to mark you as you did me."

His breath balled up in his throat. "Do it," he said, wondering how easily she enslaved him.

She raked a fingernail over one nipple and he fisted his hands at his sides.

Her hands clasping his on either side, she bent and scraped her teeth over the other nipple. A hiss of breath left him as his skin felt too hot, too tight to hold him. Her pink tongue darting out, she licked him, and his erection twitched.

Like a cat licking up cream, she rained soft, wet kisses over his chest, his abdomen, around his navel. His muscles knotted so tight that it almost hurt, but he resisted the urge to sink his hands in her hair.

She licked a path next to the line of hair disappearing into his jeans, and he bucked off the wall. He closed his eyes, fighting for control. Instead the image of her mouth around his arousal burned in his brain. He felt her fingers undo the button, tug the zipper down.

Heat billowed in his blood, curled in his muscles, threatening to shove him out of his own skin.

He uncurled his fingers and plunged them into her hair. "Stop, Zohra," he said, uncaring that his tone was begging for something even as he spoke the words that said the opposite.

She sank to her knees at his feet, full of fluid grace. She looked up, her eyelids droopy with lust. "Remember how you gave me a gift, Ayaan?"

He nodded, his throat hoarse.

"Apparently, the bride is supposed to give one to the groom, too. The next time you think of this place, I want you to see me like this—on my knees, with my mouth around you."

An unbearable longing churned through him. "You don't have to do this, Zohra."

"I want to. Just as you wanted to learn and taste every inch of me."

With a smile that he would never forget curving those lushly erotic lips, she tugged his jeans and boxers down. And his erection sprang free.

Clamping his jaw tight, he closed his eyes. He heard the harsh rasp of her breathing, just before she wrapped her hand around his hard length, her fingers tightening as they moved up and down.

He instantly jerked his hips forward, coils of pleasure shooting down his groin.

Until he felt the tentative flicker of her tongue over the head. Heat blasted through him.

"Oh…" she said, her breath feathering over the wet tip.

He sucked in a breath, tried to get his vocal glands to work. "What?" It was all he could say.

"I see why you liked doing it so much." Her pink tongue flicked out again and stroked him in a leisurely lick that tugged tight over every nerve ending. "Every time I do that, I feel this ache…." She shifted restlessly on her knees, before licking him again.

He banged his head against the wall, a low growl ripping from this throat when she closed her soft mouth over the head.

"Where?" he rasped again, his brain only capable of single words.

He heard her soft groan in the moment that she caught her breath. "Between my thighs. Every time I taste you, I feel it there," she said, before sucking him into her luscious mouth again. His shoulders trembled, his knees quaked, a fine sheen of sweat covered his entire body.

She continued pleasuring him with her tongue and her mouth until he shook with the sensation of it, until curse upon curse fell from his mouth, until he could feel the intense rush of his climax building, a roaring fire inside him.

Holding on to the last vestige of control, reining the animal part of him that wanted only to find release, he tugged her up.

Her skin was flushed, her gaze soaked with lust. With movements that lacked both finesse and gentleness, he tugged her panties down and lifted her up against the wall. Her legs wound around his hips just as he thrust into her in long, smooth motion.

Pleasure, so acute that it bordered on pain, rode through him.

This time, he didn't stop or think. He gave in to the need pounding upon him, the musky scent of her arousal telling him everything he wanted to know.

His orgasm was a breath away, but he didn't want to ride the wave, not without this amazing woman he had married falling headlong into it with him.

He wanted her to splinter, he wanted to hear his name on her lips, here—in this place of all places—where something inside him had been forever lost, in the one place that stood for everything he was not and that she deserved.

With a voracious need that he now knew would never be satisfied, he pushed her top up until he found bare skin. He tugged the lace of her bra down and found a taut, aching nipple.

He pinched it between his fingers and she came undone. He kissed her mouth, loving his name on it as he pounded into her, their mingled groans and grunts rippling through the air.

Her hands in his hair, her teeth dug into his shoulder, just as he came in a fierce rush of pleasure. She whispered his name just as he wanted and it stole over all the cracked, broken places inside him.

Nothing would fix him, he knew that now, but in the moments when he was with her, Ayaan could almost believe that he was a better man, a man worthy of the amazing woman. Stealing a kiss from her, he righted their clothes and crumpled to the ground.

Leaning against the wall, he pulled her close until she was cradled between his thighs. Wrapping his arms around her, he kissed her shoulder, clutched her to him tight.

The most amazing kind of contentment ballooned up in his chest that he wondered if he would burst from it. "Thank you, Zohra," he whispered, his heart beating loudly, loath to fracture the fragility of the moment.

She nodded. He had no idea how long they sat like that. But as minutes passed, Ayaan felt the tight fist of fear this place held in his core relent. Running his hands over her shoulders, he wrapped his arms around her waist.

"Zohra?"

"He has had another heart attack."

Her words were so soft that he didn't catch them until

he felt her shiver. "I will arrange for your transport within the hour."

"I don't want to go."

She turned suddenly and hugged him hard. Her arms clamped around his neck, her face buried in his chest, Ayaan felt a fierce rush of tenderness swamp him. She was hurting and he understood the feral urge inside of him that wanted to fix everything for her.

"I am scared, Ayaan," she said, breathing the words into his neck.

He frowned at the shiver that spewed into her words. It spoke of a Zohra he had never seen or heard. "You afraid, Zohra? Of what?"

"Of truth, of seeing him, of learning of things that I never let my father say. But I have to ask him this time."

He held her as she steadied herself, as she found her own strength again. "Remember what you said about truth, Princess? That even in its bitterest form, it is better than the sweetest lies. You have evaded it for thirteen years now, have let the very idea of it have power over you. He could have let you go to your uncle, he could have let you go through your entire life thinking he was dead, he could have easily shrugged off your responsibility, he could have placed so many restrictions on how you led your life. But he didn't. It is time to face the truth, Zohra, time to see if it can really break you as much as you fear."

"It didn't break you, Ayaan. Being in this place, living through it, you are still standing."

The very contentment he had felt a moment ago slid off him.

Still standing, that was what he was, that was what every small step he took amounted to in the end. Not that he gained control over his fears, not that he had made a small amount of progress, no.

His victory would always be that he hadn't fallen back into the madness.

Even after he had realized the truth of what had happened to him, he hadn't resented his life, he had accepted his reality without complaints, shrugged on the mantle of duty to the best of his ability.

But the moment he was near her, this crippling need flared inside him—to be more than what he was for her, this emaciating, perverse anger over circumstances he could not change, it gnawed at him.

Wasn't that why he had risked this journey to the desert, risked his lucidity and everything it meant to his parents and Dahaar? Because he wanted to be a better man for her? Wasn't he compromising the one thing he still had, his sense of duty, his honor, in her name?

Zohra burrowed into Ayaan's embrace, even as she felt his cold retreat. Two days—she had held herself back, checked every impulse to go to him before she lost the little headway she had made with him.

The need to bear his pain for him, to help him through it, festered inside her. She couldn't. Instead, she had wanted to dilute it, loosen its hold on him. And she was glad she had tried, she was ecstatic that he had let her, that she had held power over him in that moment, in making the powerful, honorable man that he was sway with need for her.

But that pleasure, she realized now, would always come at the price of losing whatever small connection she found with him.

Because until he realized everything he already was, Ayaan would loathe any pleasure he let himself feel, reject any happiness he found with her.

It was what she found with him, too. Even in his grief, his nightmares, being with him was what made Zohra the most alive. As if she had woken up from under a heavy blanket of resentment, of misplaced anger, of fear.

Even in the short time she had known him, seeing his struggle to rise above what he was, his honor in always doing the right thing, Zohra was finally awake. In a way she had never been until now.

She turned around in the cocoon of his arms, clasped his jaw, took a greedy kiss from him. As if she could bind him to her will by touching him. Because whatever she had from him, it was never enough. And today, she wanted another piece of him, she wanted something he had never given anyone else, she wanted his pain, his suffering. "Will you tell me what happened here?"

She thought he would refuse, shut her out, walk away. His tight grip on her fingers was the only sign that he had even heard her. "I have never spoken of it, to anyone." A smile curved his mouth, bitterness etched into every strong line of his face. "Is this the final test, Zohra? Because if I speak of it, it will forever change how you see me. You will see what I see when I look in the mirror."

"You can't imagine what I see when I see you. Please, Ayaan."

"It was going to be the last time our entire family attended the conference because Amira was to be married in a couple of months. Our parents had already left with most of the guard thinking we were accompanying them. But Amira and I learned that Azeez was staying back and decided to confront him."

"Confront him?"

His breath fanned over her nape, his hold on her tighter. "The three of us, we had always been close. But something had been eating at him for almost a year. He became a different person, not the brother we knew. It hadn't escaped our parents' notice either. His coronation was only months away, and he had been avoiding both Amira and me. So we thought it was the best chance.

"And before I knew it, we were surrounded on all sides by armed men. But the strange thing was that Azeez had been prepared, he surprised them by instantly going on attack. He was something to watch, the way he fought. And we had a good chance of getting out of there, too. I caught the gun that he threw at me, but then a bullet hit Amira and I...I just froze."

If she hadn't felt his chest rise and fall, Zohra would have thought he had turned into ice right in front of her eyes. He raised his hand and looked at it as though he still held the gun. His face puzzled, his mouth held the bitterest of contempt.

And she found no words to say to him that could break through the dark cloud of self-loathing that poured out of his every word.

"I could not raise my hand and shoot. I just couldn't. To this day, I ask myself why not. When he needed me, when my sister needed me, I failed.

"I didn't shoot or even move to cover him. He got shot in the hip, and a bullet grazed my head...but even then, I just stood there, staring at him, useless.

"When I woke up next, Amira's body was next to me while Azeez...he couldn't move."

Zohra wiped her own tears, the deep chasm of grief beneath his monotonous tone ringing through her. She forced herself to ask the next question, even as she never wanted to hear it again. "Did he die in front of you?"

With a smoothness that startled her, he stood up. She saw the tremble in his hands as he pushed his hair back. He paced like a caged tiger, the fury rattling from him a tangible thing in the air. "No. They bound me but not him, because his leg was already useless. Blood...there was so much of his blood everywhere. He kept telling me to try to leave…until suddenly he just lay still and they dragged him out of there. They needed us for negotiation. I remember thinking he would get medical aid, thinking…

"I didn't see him again, have no idea what they put him through.

"I remember every moment of that cursed day until then. I have no idea how long they held me, how I escaped, no idea where they buried him. It's the question I see in my mother's eyes when she looks at me and I don't have an answer. I have racked through my mind, but I…"

"Shhh…" Zohra whispered, hugging him, her own tears beating a path down her cheeks. She was not sorry she had asked. Because this grief was a part of him and she wanted all of him. She only wished she could bear its weight for him, even if for an infinitesimal second.

"Every time I hear the word courage associated with me, I cringe, I fall deeper into the pit of my own shame. Are you disgusted by me now, Zohra?" His words whipped through the air around them, polluting everything they had shared just minutes ago.

She held his face in a tight grip, a lump lodging in her throat.

Her chest was so tight that it was a wonder she could breathe. It hurt to see him hurt, it hurt that she couldn't help him, it hurt that he would never embrace the little happiness he found with her. It hurt so much that her stomach lurched, her breath halted in her throat as an image of her life, forever waiting for him, within reach but far away, stretched in front of her.

He would do his duty by her, stand by her, maybe even create a child with her—because this pull between them was stronger than either of them, but he would never look at her with happiness, never accept her love, never return it.

Fear like she had never known before filled her veins.

How had she fallen in love with a man who was the very epitome of everything that had gone wrong in her life, a man who would give her his name, his honor, his life in the name of duty but not his heart?

And this time, Zohra understood what love meant. She understood that it was not a battle of wills, of individual needs and desires, that it demanded sacrifice, that it demanded everything one had. It flew through her, strengthening her and weakening her, glorifying her and damning her, freeing her and yet forever binding her to him.

She sucked a deep breath in, striving to hide the biggest truth of her life. If he realized even a flicker of what she felt for him, she knew he would banish her from his life. She would lose even the little she had.

"You were twenty-one years old, Ayaan. After all these years, can you not forgive yourself even a little?" she asked, her own sorrow bleeding into her words, "Can you not permit yourself to pursue your own happiness?"

His refusal was impenetrable, sealing her fate right along with his. "Not when it cost them their lives." The darkest of smiles curved his mouth, a cold chill dawning in his gaze. "I think you know me better than I know myself. You knew what you were going to get and you still wanted it, Princess." His mouth found hers in a punishing kiss, every stroke of his tongue a brand of possession, every caress calculated to master. He licked the seam of her ear, and Zohra clutched him swaying on her feet. "Do you want an out now, Zohra?"

She met his gaze, her heart in her throat. "Will you give it to me if I wanted it?"

He lifted her up and carried her out of the stables. "No. I have cast off what little honor I possessed, Zohra. Now you are bound to me forever, damned to this life right along with me."

Lacing her hands around his nape, Zohra hid her face in his chest, an intense sadness weighing her down. Just as he had said, she had entered this relationship knowing what she was getting herself into. And yet suddenly, she realized with a sinking feeling, that it was not going to be enough.

Her heart wanted everything.

CHAPTER TWELVE

AYAAN WALKED INTO the suite assigned to him in the Si-yaadi palace and stared at Zohra's sleeping form in his bed. Familiar desire and something else—a fierce long-ing—wound through him at the sight of her.

He should have known he would find her here wait-ing for him, refusing to let him avoid her, refusing to let him hide.

But then, he still couldn't get used to the fact that she shared her body, her mind, her life with him willingly.

Restlessness that was becoming second skin scoured through him. He paced the perimeter of the bed, his gaze constantly straying toward her.

He had been fighting the cloud of awareness that had been coming at him for the week he had spent here in Si-yaad. But this time, he was not enough to stop it, he could not hide from what he became, what he was changing into because of Zohra.

Because of the woman who deserved the best any man could give.

He had understood, been fascinated by, Zohra's strength from the moment she had stormed into his suite and stood by him through his nightmare. But this past week she had become something truly magnificent, she had become a princess. And she hadn't needed anything from him.

She had been a lioness when defending her brother and sister from the manipulative clutches of her extended family, a clever, quick study in her understanding of the immediate state affairs that needed to be organized, a formidable opponent to anyone who had dared question her role in King Salim's affairs.

She had been a sight to behold when she had addressed the nation of Siyaad after her father's funeral.

Ayaan had finally understood why King Salim had pushed for this marriage. He had thought marriage to the crown prince of Dahaar would achieve for Zohra her rightful place in the world, remove the stigma of her birth.

And yet, in just a week, Zohra had proved how wrong her father had been. She had needed neither the weight of the Dahaaran crown behind her nor Ayaan's support—either as her husband, or even as a man who could validate her place in Siyaad, in the way their archaic culture dictated.

But the primitive instinct in him that had somehow been nurtured by his madness of five years had risen to the forefront again. Why else would he feel things an educated man, a man supposed to lead his nation on a path of progress should be ashamed to even think?

Her strength in the week following her father's death, her confidence in taking on any number of challenges without quaking, the conviction of her own beliefs—Ayaan had been alternately amazed and weighed down by it, the worst of his fears crystallizing into undeniable truth.

Resentment was an acrid taste in his mouth, followed by utter shame at the level he could sink to.

He was a worse man than he had ever thought that he had indulged, even if for a few seconds, the idea of Zohra being a weak woman, of Zohra needing his help, of Zohra leaning on him for strength.

Even growing up with archaic customs that elevated a man while downplaying a woman's role, he still had never looked down on a woman. How could he when he had grown up surrounded by his mother's quiet strength, Amira's cutting wit and incredible confidence?

And yet Zohra's strength had only brought out his inadequacy, the bone-deep chill that said she deserved so much more than he gave her.

After knowing the resentment and sheer indifference Zohra had faced for so long, after hearing the echo of that pain still reverberating in her words, this conflicting whiplash of his own emotions, the wave of his intense desire and the crest of his self-condemnations, this was what he had to give her?

Caught up in his own personal pain, he had retreated from her, instead of standing by her. Of course, he had been by her side for all the public ceremonies and state functions. But he had not once inquired after her as a husband, had not offered a moment's comfort as a lover, had not even extended the minimum courtesy of meeting her eyes.

Because he had been terrified that she would see the truth in his eyes.

And still she came to his bed, she still sought him out, she still wanted to share his nightmares.

She would forever try to save him while he would damn her.

Even that realization was not enough to keep him from her. The greed inside him to be near her, to touch her, to feel her hunger for him, had no bounds or rules.

Pulling the long tunic he wore over his head, he climbed onto the bed. He turned on the bedside lamp, and lay on his side, content to watch her. He pushed strands of her silky hair back from her face.

Leaning on his elbow, he rubbed the pads of his thumb over her mouth, the familiar ache in him building with the velocity of an approaching storm. He sucked in a deep breath.

He had accepted long ago that it was always going to be like this with her. Nothing had changed. The pleasure he found with her was intense, binding him to her. He rode the wave at night, until nothing but self-loathing remained during the cold light of the day.

This fierce princess had become his salvation and his purgatory.

Zohra came awake the instant she felt Ayaan's hard body thrashing next to her. Sleep melted away as his soft whimper traveled over her skin. She turned the bedside lamp on just as his arm shot out. She held it hard between her hands, the chill of his skin a shock to her. Hot tears rose to her eyes. Turning to face him, she held his shoulders, the drumbeat of her heart thudding in her ears.

Sweat beaded on his forehead, the tendons in his neck stretched out tight.

Just as she had done that night so many weeks ago, she whispered to him, ran her hand over his forehead and tried to calm him. She had no idea how much time had passed before the tremors that racked through him stilled, the shadows of pain on his face retreated. She brought his palm to her cheek, forcing back her tears. She kissed every ridge and mound on his palm, breathing his name into it, feeling every inch of his pain as if it was her own.

His gaze fell open and landed on her.

And she braced herself for his wrath. He looked at her, his expression inscrutable, his mouth a straight line that gave no hint of what he was thinking.

But he didn't speak. Instead he pulled her down to him,

his breathing still uneven from the physical energy he spent during the nightmare. When he pulled her into the embrace of his body, Zohra melted into it, joy bursting out from her heart. It was more than enough for her that he understood that she wanted to be here, that he didn't question her right.

She tucked herself in as close as she could get to him. His arm was a heavy weight over her waist, their breaths slowly finding a matching rhythm. Her bones felt like they were molten, a strange mixture of lethargy and well-being turning her blood sluggish.

His hand moved over her arm, over the indent at her waist, up and down, again and again. His face was buried in her hair, his breath fanned over her nape. Just the fact that he was holding on to her, drawing comfort and strength from her presence filled her with an incredible, quiet joy. It was an intimacy that tugged at the deepest part of her, that burrowed itself into her skin.

She needed no words from him, she wanted no declaration of love. She only wanted to be by his side for the rest of their lives, to be there whether or not he needed her, to learn from him what honor and duty truly meant, to help her brother become an honorable, strong man like him.

She pulled the hand that rested under her torso and buried her face in it, tried to choke back the tears that somehow had gained a foothold in her tonight.

She had no idea how long they stayed like that and she didn't care. His breathing evened out, his touch offering comfort to her. She was scared to even breathe for the fear of fracturing the moment, for the fear of reality intruding on it.

Until suddenly his touch changed, his breathing raced.

His palm still moved over her bare arm, over the dip of her waist covered by her silk pajamas. But now his fingers pressed into her, demanded her skin react to his touch, re-member every line and ridge of his palm. His other hand became seeking as it stole under her arm. The moment his long fingers covered her breast, Zohra moaned and shame-lessly arched into it.

She had no idea how he disposed of her pajamas, or when he pulled her top over her head. Except suddenly, his body was a furnace of desire behind her. His chest rasped against her back, his erection a delicious, heavy weight against her buttocks. His leg covered hers, moved over hers creating a delicious friction that she wanted to feel everywhere.

His fingers pulled at her nipple, and she sank deeper into the mindless pleasure he incited. His erection length-ened and hardened against her. The image of the rigid length tucked against her bottom sent sparks of pleasure exploding over her skin. As sweat beaded her forehead, a relentless ache built in her groin and she moaned.

"Zohra?"

A whisper, a question, a command—her name on his lips reverberated around her.

Did he doubt her compliance? Did he not realize yet that her mind, her body, her soul—they were all his to command?

"Ayaan," she replied simply, knowing that he would understand.

Languorous heat uncurled inside her at the friction of his palm over her inner thighs.

The other hand continued playing havoc with her nip-ple, pulling, tugging, bursts of sensation arrowed down straight to her sex.

She moved restlessly, needing his touch at her core, her skin too frayed to contain her. He instantly understood. His fingers delved through her curls, opened her for his touch and stroked the quivering bundle of nerves. And then he thrust two fingers inside her.

Her release was so close that Zohra closed her eyes, clasped his wrist tight as if afraid he would stop. He kissed her temple as though understanding her need, whispered scandalous words that drove her another inch closer. Her entire body was poised over the edge, desperate to soar, when he rubbed his thumb over her clitoris.

Again and again, with a sure rhythm that toppled her over the edge. Her orgasm exploded inside her, turning her body into a million sparkling lights.

Her muscles were still quaking with the force of her release, her lungs struggling to catch a breath when he said, "Lift your leg, Princess."

His tone was nothing but raw command. Not that Zohra wouldn't have done anything he asked of her. She lifted her leg and he entered her.

This time, there was nothing but carnal intent, nothing but desperate desire in the way he thrust inside her.

The force of his passion, the wild abandon with which he took her, did not scare her. She followed where he went, trusted him with her body, splintered again when he wrenched another orgasm from her oversensitized body but underneath his desperate caresses, underneath his uncontrollable hunger, Zohra could sense a black cloud building.

His body convulsed behind her, his climax going on and on but even his hard kiss on her mouth couldn't shake her fear that something was terribly wrong.

Her muscles were weightless, her skin clammy with sweat. She made no sound as he picked her up and walked to the attached bath. Something was coming, she knew it in her bones, something wrong. But this time, she had no courage to face it head-on, no energy to fight. So she stayed silent, let him wash her in the huge sunken tub.

When he tugged her to him in the tub, she went willingly. When he pulled her onto him until she was straddling him, she hid her face in his shoulder. When he kissed her softly, slowly, as though she was the most precious thing in the world, she melted. When he suckled at her breast in deep, long pulls, she thought she would burst out of her skin. When he ran his hands all over her body, masterful, exacting, inciting, she gave in to the pleasure riding her again. When he buried his face in her neck and thrust upward into her, she let the tears fall.

He didn't ask her why there were tears and she didn't tell him. She didn't ask him what drove him tonight and he didn't tell her.

His hunger for her was insatiable, his every touch, stroke and kiss increasingly desperate and less controlled. And Zohra's need for him was no less powerful. Every caress, every sensuous assault of his mouth, of his fingers, she took everything with a relish and returned it back.

At some point, *when* she knew not, her mind simply shut down and Zohra sighed in bliss. She only wanted to feel right then. He carried her back to the bed. She thought he would find his own bed. But he didn't leave her.

He pulled the quilt to cover them both, kissed her temple and Zohra gave into sleep.

This time when Zohra woke, she was instantly aware of the exquisite soreness between her thighs. Every muscle quaked, her blood ran sluggish in her veins. She looked toward the huge windows and realized dawn was almost there. At some point during the night, she had lost count of how many times she had woken up to Ayaan kissing her, stroking her, tasting her, loving her, as if he couldn't talk himself off the ledge, as if his thirst for her knew no beginning, no end.

And every time, she had been right there with him, shocked at how much pleasure her body was capable of feeling, of how addictive and exhilarating it could be every single time.

Realizing that the bed was empty, she stood on shaking legs. Even tugging her thick hair back and binding it into a ponytail taxed her arms.

She slowly pulled on her pajamas and a silk robe, sensing his presence close.

She found him in the sitting area. His hands on his thighs, his upper body slanted forward, his very posture radiated tension.

For a few minutes, Zohra hung back by the sheer curtains that fluttered in the predawn breeze.

It had been two weeks since she had left him in the desert encampment for Siyaad, two weeks in which she had mourned her father's death, helped Saira and Wasim deal with their own grief, and somehow also found the strength to step in front of her family and face them down. Even though Ayaan had arrived only a few days after her, and had been present at all the important events.

He had not, however, said even a word to her since his arrival.

Lost in her own grief, she hadn't minded. His silent presence had been enough for her. She had borrowed strength from it, knowing that he would catch her if she fell, even if he didn't put it in so many words.

She had been so grateful for his presence that she hadn't realized when something began to fester between them, something she couldn't identify even as she racked her brain. She could feel the connection they had found slipping from her fingers like sand, could feel him retreating but had no way to stop him.

So she had come to his bed, despite the fact that he had

forbidden her to be near him at night. And just hours ago, she had been ecstatic that he had slept next to her, hadn't asked her to leave.

But now, the same silence stretched taut around them, deepening the chasm between them, dragging him further and further away from her. She must have made a sound because he looked up. And sprang to his feet as if she were an explosive that could detonate any second.

Even in the meager light of the table lamp, she could see the dark color that rode those sharp cheekbones. "Zohra, you are…I…I lost all control."

Heat pumped to her own cheeks now. She struggled to hide the questions that shot at her from all sides. "I am fine." She shoved the fear that was clawing at her and smiled. "Everything you did, I wanted, Ayaan. Was I not vocal enough?"

His gaze burned brighter, hotter, the sharp angles of his face reflecting the tightly reined in emotion within him. "*Ya Allah,* I behaved like an animal. I…"

She covered the distance between them and practically fell into his arms. She couldn't bear it if he became a stranger again. "I am definitely sore, though."

His curse should have turned the air blue. His hands stayed on her shoulders, his entire body stilling in that way of his.

She kept her arms around his waist, and found comfort in the fact that he hadn't pushed her away.

"I am sorry you didn't get a chance to speak to him, Zohra," he said, piercing the heavy silence, his embrace a safe haven of warmth.

The storm of regrets and grief she had kept at bay while shouldering her responsibilities for the first time in her life broke through at the tender concern in his words. He held her as she cried softly, for her, for her father and for her mother, for everything she had lost through sheer pig-headedness.

She met his gaze, and smiled through the tears. "He left me a sheaf of letters that told me everything I wanted to know."

"Letters?"

She nodded. The truth had hurt, but it had also freed something inside her. "Letters from my mother to him, even after he had left us for Siyaad. With pictures of me. Letters she wrote him until the day she died."

Ayaan frowned. "Are you saying she knew?"

Zohra nodded again, seeing the same confusion she had felt mirrored in his gaze. "She knew everything about him. She knew that there might come a day when he would have to leave her for Siyaad, to do his duty. And he did, just as they had known he would have to. He left us but they kept in touch. They argued, even in the letters. He asked to see me, and she refused, again and again. Said she didn't want me to pay the price for the happiness she found with him, didn't want me to be caught between them. I guess I was never supposed to know that he was alive. Except something happened that neither of them foresaw. She died. And...."

Her throat seized as Zohra realized once again what it must have cost her father to learn of her mother's death and to bring her to Siyaad.

"I can't believe King Salim could have been so selfish, so reckless," Ayaan said, pulling her out of the pit of regrets.

Zohra frowned at the anger that simmered in his words. "I was angry when I read those letters, angry that neither of them told me the truth. Even after I was old enough to understand. But not anymore.

"They took a chance on love, Ayaan, they grabbed their

happiness while they could, decided whatever short time they had was still worth it. Knowing that they had loved each other, knowing that my father had never deceived her, knowing that he loved me enough to bring me here—" Tears ran over her cheeks again. "—it fills me with joy. How can I hold the fact that they loved each other so much that they risked such unhappiness for the rest of their lives against them?"

Her body stilled as Zohra waited for his answer. Her heart pounded as his silence gave the answer his lips didn't, and one she didn't want to hear at that.

She ran her fingers over his jaw, over his cheekbones, traced the scar above his eye, as fear held a visceral grip inside her chest.

"You told me your mother never really smiled again after he was gone, that she wouldn't even look at another man. That to the day she died, something in her was forever broken while he…he moved on with his life. Had a wife and started a family."

Looking up at him, Zohra braced herself, knowing that the very ground that she was standing on was going to be pulled out from under her. "Weren't you the one who understood the need to sacrifice your own child in the name of duty? My father did his duty but he also let himself love. He took a chance and found happiness even if it was for a limited time."

"He damned the rest of her life in the name of love. He made you pay the price."

"They both paid the price, Ayaan. It was a decision they made together." She straightened herself, striving to fight the cold chill that was seeping into her. Every word felt like an effort. "You don't agree with me?"

"No. But what I think does not matter, does it, Zohra? What matters is what you think." His voice roughened in texture, as though he had to catch a breath to continue. His fingers caressed her face, desperate, fierce. "What matters is, apparently, you are exactly like your mother. You have the brightest spirit, the biggest heart I have ever seen."

His words should have elevated her to a higher place, should have filled her with happiness, but they didn't. The hard edge to his words only heightened her sense of something being very wrong.

"But I am not like King Salim. I will not damn you to a life filled with unhappiness."

His words knocked the breath out of her, tilted the very axis of her life. And Zohra forced herself to ask the question that was quietly gouging a hole inside her. "What are you saying?"

Ayaan fisted his hands behind him.

She took another step in. "Answer my question."

"You deserve a better man, Zohra. You need a man who will love you, who will cherish you, not use you at night and then expose you to his insecurities the next day." It was the hardest words he had ever spoken. "I do nothing but take from you, I have nothing to give you."

Her anger pulsed between them, just as sharp as the desire that suffused the very air around them. "Why do you not see what you have already given me? Honor, respect. You are my strength, Ayaan. I wasted thirteen years of a good life, lived it as if in a cloud, lived it with so much anger and hurt inside. I see you and I am ashamed of myself. I see your strength, your sense of duty, your honor, and I think this is what I want to be. You have not complained once at what you suffered. You push yourself every day to rise above yourself, physically and mentally.

"I do not care that you froze in a fight when you were barely a man. You have proven yourself to the world a thousand times over. Do these not count toward something?"

"It is not my strength or my lucidity that I doubt anymore, Zohra," he said, once again struck aghast by how perceptive she was. He had pushed himself in so many ways with a raging need to prove his worth to himself. He had pushed himself to the breaking point, to the last frayed edge of his mental and physical strength.

And he had emerged the victor but the hollowness in his gut had not faded. In the face of Zohra's strength, in the face of his own guilt and recriminations, they counted to nothing. "It is what I cannot give you, *ya habibati*."

"You have no right to call me that."

"The sounds you make when you come are still ringing inside my ears. I will call you whatever I please."

She shook from head to toe, her fury a palpable thing. Her mouth curved into a sneer even as tears shone in her eyes. "Not if you break the vows you made to me, not if you banish me from your life. You will not touch me, you will not even utter my name on your lips, Ayaan. Are you ready for that?"

He could not bear to see her like this—hurting, breaking. "I do this for you, Zohra."

"Don't you dare tell yourself that. You do this for yourself, to satisfy the guilt beneath which you have decided to live. So what happens now?"

"You will stay in Siyaad for an indefinite time. Your family needs you, Siyaad needs you. No one will wonder at your absence in Dahaar. And when the right time comes, I will let it be known that we have separated, that it is I who is lacking as a husband."

Her tears drew paths over her cheeks, bitter anger turning those beautiful brown eyes into molten rocks. "And the power to make that decision lies solely with you?"

"Something inside me is broken, Zohra. All I want to do is to lose myself in you, hear my name fall from your lips, again and again, but…" He gripped his nape, struggling to find the right words. "It will always be followed by this emptiness inside, by this self-loathing that I cannot fight. Before long, you will be stuck in that vicious cycle too and I will corrupt everything that is good and beautiful about you."

Her arms around her waist, she swayed where she stood, the pain in her eyes shredding him. But he had to hold fast for her sake.

"You have conquered so many obstacles, overcome so much for so long to become the man you are today, to become the prince that Dahaar needs. Can you not fight this last demon, Ayaan, for the woman who loves you with every breath in her body, with every—"

Ayaan placed a finger across her lips, but not before her words blasted through him with the force of an explosion. His stomach tightened, his throat seized up. Time seemed to have frozen at that minute. Looking into her beautiful, giving eyes, he wondered how he could have been so blind.

The love and acceptance there knuckled him in the gut.

She pulled his hand off her mouth, her slender shoulders trembling. "Truth, remember? The truth doesn't change because we don't want to hear it. I am in love with you. And whatever you face, we will fight—"

"I cannot fight it, Zohra. It is stronger than me."

She pummeled his chest, her slender shoulders shaking with the force of her anger. "It is not that you cannot fight it, Ayaan. It is that you don't want to fight it."

"You think I want to forever be a man haunted by his past—"

"Yes, you do." Her words echoed around them, bounced

off the walls, ringing with her belief. "You have judged yourself, found yourself guilty and you accepted this as your punishment. Not once in the time I have known you have you railed against it, not once have you resented it. You resent the fact that you cannot beat it but not the why of it. You cannot take a chance on us because God forbid you find happiness while your siblings are dead, right?

"And if you cannot see that, if you want to live the rest of your life stifled under that guilt, then you *are* right. You are not capable of loving me, nor do you deserve my love."

Ayaan stood there, unmoving, unblinking as Zohra wiped her tears and left his suite, left his life. The same way as she had entered it—shifting the very foundation of everything he stood on.

She was in love with him.

That incredibly amazing, wonderfully strong woman loved him. Even with his heart splintering inside him, Ayaan felt the high of her words in a dizzying whirl.

Of everything she had said, he knew one thing was for sure.

He was already in love with Zohra.

He was not surprised by the realization, or shocked. He simply, irrevocably, undeniably was. Maybe if he hadn't fallen in love with her, they could have had a life together. A life free of any emotional complications, a life free of passion, a life dictated by duty and mutual respect.

But it was the life-altering, heartbreaking love that flowed in his veins for her that made him question everything he was and he was not, that wished he was a better man for her.

He sank to the sofa behind him, his shaking knees refusing to hold him up. The scent of her was etched into him, it surrounded him, intensifying the hollow ache in his gut. He had thought he had known the worst in his life. But he had been wrong.

Nothing could be worse than the aching void in his gut. He would never look into Zohra's eyes, never see her laugh, never feel her touch again.

CHAPTER THIRTEEN

THE DEAFENING QUIET of the desert snarled inside Ayaan's mind, scratching its fingers up and down his spine. He forced himself to picture Zohra, laughing at him, challenging him, loving him. The fear didn't recede but the thought of Zohra diluted it enough for him to not fall back into its pit.

He could have left this matter to his security team but something he couldn't shake had lodged in his mind. Something about this man niggled at him.

It had taken Imran a month to unearth all the hidden sources of the recent terrorist intelligence and of course, it had been traced back to the same man who had fed them information the first two times.

Which meant he had intentionally covered his tracks. And Ayaan had instantly known something was wrong. It had taken his team another two weeks to find his whereabouts, two weeks of hell, in which Ayaan missed Zohra with an ache that had become a constant companion.

The whisper of harsh breathing, the sounds of footsteps, which he wouldn't have heard on the gravel road except for the fact that the man's stride was out of step, fell on his ears and Ayaan leaped from his crouching position behind the tent.

He couldn't have taken a breath before a blow came at

him, grazing his jaw. Shaking off the jolt of pain up his jaw, Ayaan returned a blow, and pushed the man to the ground. The man's leg shot out from under him, and Ayaan tackled him to the ground, his heart leaping into his throat.

Moonlight flickered over features that were as familiar as his own. A deathly chill fell over Ayaan as he collapsed to the desert floor, his muscles quivering with shock.

His throat choked with tears, his chest so tight that he thought he would explode. Shock waves paralyzed his mental processes as he stared at the man he had worshipped his entire life, the man he had held in higher regard than his father, the man who had taught Ayaan everything he knew.

The man who had fallen in front of him five years ago while Ayaan had froze, had stood there like a coward.

The desert wind howled around them as his heart pumped again. Surprise abated and a joy, unlike he had ever known flooded Ayaan.

His brother, the true prince of Dahaar, was alive.

Ayaan dismissed the security outside his office in the main palace wing, closed the door behind him and ran a hand over his eyes. His head pounded as if someone had hammered away at it relentlessly. He had been awake for forty-eight hours straight, and sometime yesterday, right when his mother had started crying as though her heart was breaking—again, a twitch had begun behind his left eye.

He knew that this was only the beginning of the hardest time of his life. And the fact that he had turned his back on the one woman who would have brought him solace, who would have understood his pain, who was the one shining point of his life, was an acrid taste on his tongue.

Since he had returned to Dahaar two days ago, the hours had seemed endless, each blending into the next, the things he had to take care of unending, until he thought he would break under the weight of it all.

He had kept Zohra's face at the forefront of his mind through it all, drew strength from the image of her warm smile, rooted himself in her belief that he could beat anything.

He had bent but he had not broken.

Now he was exhausted, both physically and mentally, and he ached to see her, to hold her, to share this fresh grief with her.

Ya Allah, he would give anything in that moment to hold her.

Pushing away from the door, he walked past the sitting area into his office beyond.

And as though he had conjured her out of his very imagination with sheer desperate craving, there was his wife, pacing the floor. Emotion knotted his throat, rooting him to the spot.

He must have said her name aloud because she was hurtling toward him before he could blink. She hugged him tight, then stepped back, her gaze hungrily sweeping over him.

"I heard the news. Is it…Is he…" She frowned. "How are you taking it? You look…exhausted."

Ayaan blinked, a host of emotions vying within him— the need to hold her tight against him was the strongest. He sucked in a deep breath, greedy for the scent of her.

Until she had spoken, he hadn't realized how good it was to be asked, to know that his state of mind mattered. Of course, it mattered to his parents too, but right now, they needed him more than he needed them.

She was dressed in stylishly cut gray trousers and a light blue silk blouse. The delicate arch of her neck, the strong pulse thudding there, the stubborn jut of her chin, the flare of her arrogant nose—he was starving for the sight of her. Shaking his head, he tried to focus on what had bothered him about her statement. "Only four people know that he is alive."

"Khaleef told me," she said, the concern in her voice fading back. "And before you bring down your wrath on him, remember this, Ayaan." Her voice broke on his name, but she continued, her chin tilted high. Pure steel filled her words. "I care about Dahaar, about the king and the queen. I have every right to this information."

Despite the journey to hell and back in the past two days, Ayaan smiled. And in that very moment, he saw what he had been too blind to realize until now. This beautiful, amazing woman was a gift he had been given and due to his cowardice he hadn't been able to accept it. "Are you done, *ya habibati?*"

"No. And you can't send me back to Siyaad either." Her words reverberated with a confidence that brooked no argument, but her tight fists at her sides gave her away. "I refuse to hide, refuse to lick my wounds in private as I have done for so long, refuse to let someone other than me decide my fate, decide what I deserve and what I don't.

"Whether you want me or not, I am your wife. I have a right to live in Dahaara, a right to learn everything I need to be the Dahaaran queen, a right to your parents' love. I have earned my place, Ayaan. And if you can't bear the sight of me, then it is on your head. But you try to send me back and I will show you what a Siyaadi princess is truly made of."

It was the most magnificent sight he had ever beheld. His heart pounded in his chest. He moved closer and ran his fingers over the pulse beating frantically at her neck. "Adding to my nightmares, Zohra?"

The resolve in her brown eyes melted, giving way to the

cutting pain she hid. It punched him in the gut. "If that is how you see me, then so be it. But I have never wanted to be the cause for your—"

"Shh…I meant it would be a torture to be near you and to not touch you, to not hold you." He breathed into her hair. Tugging her toward him, he held her at her waist, loosely, striving for control over himself. "All I feel is joy when you are near, pure, freeing, like I have never felt before. How can you think you bring pain?"

"I will kill you myself if you leave me again, Ayaan." Fighting words, but Ayaan heard the pain in them.

"Shh…." he said, and ran his palm over her back, up and down, more to soothe himself than her. She was so fragile in his grip, and yet inside where it mattered this woman he had had the good fortune to marry, this woman he had had the temerity to fall in love with, had a core of steel and a heart as big as the desert.

And he would spend the rest of his life loving her as she deserved to be loved.

He touched his forehead to hers, his heart lodged in his throat. "You brought light into my life. If not for you…" He shook as the grief he'd held at bay since the minute he had laid eyes on his brother burst through him. Tears he couldn't stem, tears that needed to be shed, wet his cheeks.

Her slender arms tightened around him, her body a cocoon of warmth. And everything she gave him was a precious gift. "Ayaan?"

"I have seen what it means to be truly broken, Zohra."

Her heart crawling into her throat, Zohra clasped Ayaan's chin and tugged it up. Fear beat a tattoo beneath her skin. Even in the most painful moments, even when he had been drowning in his nightmares, she had never heard such stark desolation in his words. "Whatever it is, Ayaan, we will beat it together."

"You have already saved me, *ya habibati*. I was just too stubborn, too blind to see it. But he…there is nothing inside him, Zohra."

A ghost of a shiver passed over her at his words. "Your brother?"

"If eyes were windows to the soul, then there is no soul left in him." He tugged her hard against him, his arms steel vises that could snap her in two. Rising on tiptoes, Zohra held on, letting him take what he wanted from her.

"I was so afraid, Ayaan. Khaleef said he was in bad shape. And my heart sank. I thought seeing him like that would mean—"

"That guilt would claw through me once again? It does. It hurts so much to see him like this. But the worst is knowing that for God knows how long he has been aware of his identity and he has been in hiding. If I hadn't followed up on that hunch, we would have never known he was alive. He doesn't want to be here. And even in the state he is in, it took both Khaleef and me to force him to come with us. And my mother, *Ya Allah*—"

"How is she?"

Ayaan smiled and kissed her again, intense sadness still clouding his eyes. "He refuses to see her or my father, said he will put a bullet through his head if I bring her to him."

Shock waving through her, Zohra frowned. "You think he would?"

"Whether he is bluffing or not, he knows I won't risk calling him on it. He said he wants to be free of this family, he wants nothing to do with any of us. If I became mad, he…he has devolved into pure emptiness. Maybe my madness protected me from the worst."

Anger fired those words and Zohra stared at Ayaan. His family, his duty, his country—they had always come first with him.

"For the first time in my life, I wish I could walk away from all this, steal you away, give you a life free of my demons, a life free of duty… All I want is to prove my love to you but all I see is more pain, more sorrow ahead. If you leave me…if you walk away, that is what I will become, too. And I don't want to, Zohra.

"I want to live with you, I want to laugh with you, I want to snatch any happiness I find with you. If you don't leave tonight, there is no turning back, *ya habibati*. I will never ever let you go again, not even if you beg me."

He clasped her cheeks, his long fingers greedy in the way they moved over her. His gaze shone with everything Zohra wanted to see in it when he looked at her—his pain, his honor and his love. It was all she ever wanted. "I am in love with you, Zohra. You were right. I let guilt pollute everything I felt for you, everything I found with you. But no more, *ya habibati*. You and I and our happiness together, I will allow nothing to mar it. Will you still have me, Zohra, knowing what lies ahead for us?"

Zohra kissed him, melting into his embrace, joy flooding every inch of her. His hunger matched hers, as his mouth moved over her lips as if he would never get enough. "There was no turning back for me from the moment you kissed me, the moment you came to my defense, the moment you said my honor was your honor. I will always love you, Ayaan."

She tucked her face into his shoulder, she clutched his shirt in her fingers, striving to fight the depth of emotion that overpowered her. The love she felt for him had already been fierce, but now that he had accepted it, now that he had admitted what she and their happiness meant to him, it flew through her with an incredible force.

She would allow no one to add to his burden, not even

the brother who meant everything to Ayaan. She would allow no one to steal even an ounce of happiness from him.

"You can't give up on him, can you? I am sure he knows that, too. And whatever you have to do for him, for Dahaar, I will be right by your side."

His fingers moved over her cheeks, his gaze glittered with a happiness that stole her breath. "I am never going to stop loving you, Zohra, will never forget what you brought into my life."

"And what you brought into mine, Ayaan. Never forget that either."

He nodded, kissed her again and picked her up. "There is one problem, *ya habibati*. I still don't think you should be sleeping beside me at night. I don't want to ever wake up and learn that I hurt you even a little. I couldn't bear it."

Breathing through the happiness that constricted her chest, Zohra nuzzled into his neck. "I have the best idea about how to take care of that, Ayaan."

Gold fire lit up his eyes.

"How about we cuff you every night before you sleep? That way, I won't get hurt and you are…"

Ayaan laughed, the naughty glint in his wife's eyes sending a thrill running through him. The guilt, the pain, they would all forever be a part of him, but as long as he had Zohra by his side, he would tackle them. Because he also had a taste of utter joy. "Your wish is my command, Princess."

* * * * *